THE PROTECTOR

A MEDIEVAL ROMANCE

BY KATHRYN LE VEQUE

THE BLACKCHURCH GUILD:
SHADOW KNIGHTS SERIES

KATHRYN LE VEQUE
NOVELS

ARE YOU SIGNED UP FOR KATHRYN'S BLOG?

You'll get the latest news and information on exclusive giveaways, exclusive excerpts, coming releases, sales, free books, cover reveals and more.

Kathryn's blog followers get it all first. No spam, no junk.

Get the latest info from the reigning Queen of English Medieval Romance!

Sign Up Here

kathrynleveque.com

England's most elite training guild.
Knights of the highest order.
Numquam dedite. Never surrender.

The History of the Blackchurch Guild

St. Giles de Bottreaux was a knight who had been disgraced for using unconventional tactics. Having served the Duke of Normandy, he was present at the Battle of Hastings. Unfortunately, he caught wind of a Norman lord who was about to betray the duke, and he tortured the lord to gain valuable information about the Saxon resistance.

He was vilified for it.

St. Giles was released from the duke's service because the rebel Norman was both a rich man and a distant cousin of the duke's. With no means of income, St. Giles and his brother, St. Lyon, wandered England, unable to find a suitable position. In desperation, they were forced to become part of a Saxon pirate group out of Watermouth, Devon.

Realizing that piracy was lucrative and putting their knightly skills to good use, the brothers quickly rose in the ranks and ended up commanding their own ships. St. Giles eventually formed his own pirate crew with the help of his brother, men known as Triton's Hellions. Their ships were the *Argos*, the *Mt. Pelion*, the *Pagasa*, and the *Athena*. St. Giles' specialty was in recruiting disgraced knights and giving them a new and rich career. Those knights began training other knights for a life of piracy at an abandoned church on the shores of Lake Cocytus in the Exmoor forest. The place was called "Blackchurch" because it was a black, burned-out shell of a former sanctuary.

But such a place, hidden from the world, was a perfect staging ground for a warriors' guild.

More trained men meant more ships and more wealth. The pirate ships sailed the known world, bringing back men as well as treasure. As the years passed, those same ships brought diverse warriors from all over the world to the shores of Devon. While St. Giles settled in to manage their growing empire in the Exmoor forest, St. Lyon assumed the pirate enterprise. All of the trained warriors he brought to Blackchurch combined with other elite trainers to create the most complex and comprehensive battle training system in the world.

England, who had always dismissed Blackchurch as a pirate training ground, gradually became aware of the quality of those who had completed the course. They were the best-educated warriors in the world. The Earl of Wessex was the first to come to St. Giles and ask him for some of the fine men he'd trained. Soon, fully trained knights with good reputations began asking for admission to the training grounds to learn the "Blackchurch way" of life and warfare. It became lucrative and prestigious. St. Giles' grandson, St. Andrew de Bottreaux, was granted the title Earl of Exmoor by Henry I because St. Andrew gifted the king with an elite group of specialized knights who saved the king on more than one occasion. Soon, the Crown got behind this extraordinary training ground.

Blackchurch's reputation was cemented.

These days, Blackchurch is far less about piracy and far more about training the most coveted and skilled warriors the world has ever seen. Men and women are accepted as long as they are qualified and can pass the entrance test. Every trainer has a specialty—new classes of recruits are formed monthly from qualified applicants from all over the world, and each group of recruits spends at least six months with every trainer. To pay for their training, they either pay the fee once they pass the entrance test or they pledge a portion of their salary once they graduate and find a position. Training is harsh and intense. It is expected that even out of the vetted recruits, most will fail. Those few who succeed become forever known as Shadow Knights, a coveted title denoting their superior status.

As graduates say, you don't simply survive Blackchurch.

You *become* Blackchurch.

THE FAMILY TREE OF DE BOTTREAUX AND THE TRAINERS OF BLACKCHURCH

De Bottreaux tree (Lords of Exmoor, who run Blackchurch):

St. Giles b. 1040 – was part of the conquest of 1066, died 1100. Brother, St. Lyon, served with him as a pirate, and it is St. Lyon's descendants who continue to run the pirate conglomerate known as Triton's Hellions. Now run by St. Abelard de Bottreaux.

St. Simon b. 1070 – d. 1135

St. Andrew b. 1094 – d. 1160

St. Paul b. 1119 – d. 1195

St. Denis b. 1147

St. Denis has two sons—St. Gerard (died 1212) and St. Sebastian, a.k.a. "Sebo," b. 1171 and 1173 respectively. Both trained at Kenilworth and Warwick Castle. Veterans of the Third Crusade.

Current list of trainers (moniker is listed after ancestry):

Tay Munro (Scottish/Greek) – the Leviathan – teaches endurance, physical fitness, structure, and discipline. He's the boot camp, the gateway to the rest of the training.

Sinclair "Sin" de Reyne (Norman) – the Swordsman – sword training, warfare, military history, how to command an army, etc.

Fox de Merest (Norman/Saxon) – the Protector – teaches men how to defend and kill using daggers and other weapons. He's the "MacGyver" of Blackchurch. His class is about defense and thinking outside of the box.

Payne Matheson (Scottish) – the Tempest – Teaches offense. Instructs men on how to size up enemies and figure out their weaknesses. How to fight battles from the ground up.

Kristian Heldane (Dane) – the Viking – He is sea-bound. Everything he does is on water—fighting on water, instruction on boats, etc.

Creston de Royans (Norman) – the Avenger – Interrogation, treatment of the enemy, anything underhanded. How to handle torture and difficult conditions. (Sometimes works in tandem with the Conquistador)

Aamir ibn Rashid (Egyptian) – the North Star – Military history (global) and tactics from other armies. Understanding different cultures and how that dictates their fighting techniques.

Cruz Mediana de Aragón (Spanish) – the Conquistador – Conquest and diplomacy, politics, and art of negotiation. Bribes, coercion, and leverage. (Sometimes works in tandem with the Avenger)

Ming Tang – (Chinese) – former Shaolin monk. Name means "bright water" – the Dragon – fighting kung fu, using hands and feet only. Fighting with the mind and not a weapon.

Meditation for a warrior to calm the mind and the spirit.

Bowen de Bermingham (Norman/Irish) – the Titan – Warrior etiquette and responsibilities, discipline, hand-to-hand combat, using the landscape/land to one's advantage, living off the land, concealment, stealth. Sometimes works in tandem with the Leviathan and the Tempest.

Location Map for The Blackchurch Guild
Exmoor Forest, Devon, England

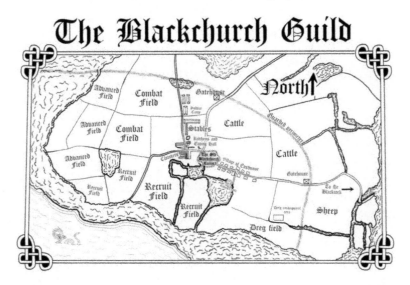

They call him the Protector.

But once upon a time, he was a knight who had failed in his greatest duty.

It has been said that the Plantagenet royal family is full of vipers. No one knows that so well as Sir Fox de Merest, a knight of the highest order once given the ultimate assignment—to protect a royal bastard from the rage of Eleanor of Aquitaine. It was a task he failed miserably at—he fell in love with the woman he was supposed to protect. That failure resulted in her being committed to a nunnery.

As the Blackchurch trainer known as "the Protector" at the most elite warrior training school in England, Fox has carved out a niche for himself training new recruits and distancing himself from the crushing failure of being unable to protect his love from a furious dowager queen. No one knows of his past, but ten years after his abject failure, the subject rears its ugly head again.

Fox's lady love was Gisele of Hampshire, royal offspring of Henry the Young King, and now her uncle, the current king, is brokering a treaty that would see her plucked from the convent where she has taken her vows and thrusting her into the limelight of a strategic marriage. Fox is now tasked with saving her from a marriage that would certainly cause her death and taking her to safety—again. He must take a leave from Blackchurch to try to finish what he started those years ago.

Can he complete his task, as ordered, without running away with her for good this time? Or will he deliver her to another convent in secret and simply walk away? Love, it seems, has no reason—and no boundaries, royal or holy.

For Fox and Gisele, it may be the ultimate sacrifice.

AUTHOR'S NOTE

Here we are with another Blackchurch tale!

I've really fallen in love with this series and the men and women involved. There's something very powerful about trainers of men, guiding and molding an entire generation of warriors, only in the case of the Blackchurch Guild, it's generation after generation.

Fox and Gisele's story is really different—the way it's framed and the way it's ultimately told. I don't think I've ever written a story "this way" before, so you're in for something different and something, I think, that is well told. I hope so, anyway. In the first Blackchurch story, we didn't get a sense of just how tortured Fox de Merest was. It was hinted that he had a secret, but we didn't know, exactly, what it was.

Now, we do.

Just a reminder about this series, in particular. One thing that's different is that it really doesn't involve heavy ties to other series. We have new families and new main characters, including a Shaolin monk and the son of an Egyptian lord. I love bringing in these new and diverse characters, into a guild that is more worldly than anything in England. That's what makes a series like this so interesting. To refresh your memory about this series, here's some of the description from Book 1 of the series (for reference):

One of the things that is different about this new series is the diversity. The thirteenth century was when men started really exploring the world. Especially with the advent of the

Third Crusade, travel was more "normal" than ever. The Silk Road from China, which had started as trade routes back in the fifth century, was introduced to the Europeans around this time. Men and material came along that route, so piracy at that point was becoming more lucrative. People from China, India, Afghanistan, and many other regions and countries were now coming to Europe. Immigration was happening. It's very exciting to have some of those worldly travelers show up at the Blackchurch Guild.

In some of the notes prior to the start of the story, I've outlined the basis of the Blackchurch Guild and given you a scorecard of sorts so you know who the players are. You'll meet them, of course, but sometimes it's good to have some reference material when a lot of people are being introduced. Mentions have been made about the Blackchurch Guild in the Executioner Knights series because a couple of their own have trained there, so it's time to clarify why even the Executioner Knights have a healthy respect for the Blackchurch Guild. Once you "graduate" from their training course, you're known as a Shadow Knight. That's like being called a general or doctor or lawyer—it's a title earned, and it means something.

Blackchurch is intended to be one of the "worldliest" places in England at this time in history, meaning it's very diverse when it comes to its trainers. Lord Exmoor spared no expense in gathering the greatest military teachers he could find, including a former Shaolin monk. Shaolin kung fu and Chan Buddhism began about one hundred years after the fall of the Roman Empire, well in advance of the High Middle Ages, when this book is set. Therefore, we have a Shaolin monk whose religion, at that point, had been around for about seven hundred years. Was it possible that such a man would make it all the way to England? Of course. The Silk Road, the legendary trading route, had been in existence for hundreds of years before the year in which this story is set. It is more than feasible that men from the far east of England would make their way along that road, traveling west until they couldn't travel any further. This is also just after the Third Crusade, in which hundreds of men from countries in the Levant and points even further east and south made their way into Europe. This was a time of migration and of cultures learning of other cultures, so our former Shaolin monk isn't only possible—it's probable.

Now, on to this book specifically. It's structured very differently from any other book I've written because with Fox and Gisele, the bulk of their romance happened before Fox's time at Blackchurch. In fact, he is at Blackchurch because he fell he love with a woman who was meant to be his duty and they were separated, so it was important for you, as the reader, to catch a glimpse of their romance before the actual Blackchurch Guild story takes place. The Protector's story is a blend of Fox and Gisele's story before—and during—the Blackchurch Guild. You'll see what I mean once you start reading.

Of note, a location called Canonsleigh Abbey has a central role in this story. Canonsleigh really is an abbey in Devon and it has an interesting history, but I'm making it a nunnery about fifty years before it really was turned into a nunnery (it was simply an abbey with priests before then).

Lastly, you're going to see a cameo by one of my old-timey heroes, Keller de Poyer. Keller was in *The Whispering Night* and then had his own tale in *Netherworld*. He was an Executioner Knight before there really was such a thing, though he doesn't appear in any subsequent EK novels. But he's in this novel and he has a pivotal appearance. If you haven't read *Netherworld* yet, do so. He's a great hero. In fact, this book involves characters from three series—the Executioner Knights, the de Nerra family, and, of course, Blackchurch. All lovely tie-ins!

With all that out of the way, the usual pronunciation guide

and things to note:

- All of the de Bottreaux men (Lords of Exmoor) have first names that start with "St." (Saint). When speaking informally or referring to each other, they drop the "St." You will see this in dialogue, and it is not a mistake—that's how they are traditionally addressed.
- De Bottreaux—duh buh-TROW
- Very minor, but the heroine's name is Gisele—and she goes by Gigi at times. The "G" is a soft "G" sound. At one point, the hero talks about calling her Giggie to irritate her—hard "G" on "Giggie." Like giggle. No wonder she was mad, eh?

And with that, I sincerely hope you enjoy Book Two in a brand-new series that I'm absolutely thrilled to write. Hold on and enjoy the ride—it's a wild one!

Hugs and happy reading!

PROLOGUE

Year of Our Lord 1214
The Blackchurch Guild
Exmoor, Devon

H E'D HAD THAT dream again.

It wasn't exactly the same, as dreams rarely followed an identical pattern, but the theme was the same. The feeling was the same. In the dream, she was so close that he could almost reach out and touch her. That maddening moment when he could feel the warmth radiating from her body as if she were somehow real and alive. In dreams past, he tried to grasp her flesh, but his fingers never quite came into contact with her.

This was one of those times.

So close, yet so far.

He supposed he should have been grateful to dream like this, a dream in which he could see the woman he missed so desperately and loved down to his very bones. Seeing her was like a salve to his soul, but on the other hand, it was like ripping a scab off a wound that refused to heal. In truth, it probably never would.

Sitting on the bed, he put his feet on the ground and his

elbows on his knees, putting his face in his hands as if trying to wipe away the intense feelings that the dream seemed to bring about. Every time he had a dream that involved her, he felt as if someone had taken a shovel and scooped out his insides. He was left with a hollow shell, feeling emotions that were stronger than anything he'd ever known and unable to do a damn thing about them.

They consumed everything.

In years past, he had taken to drinking when these dreams would come about, but it took him quite some time to realize that the alcohol wouldn't numb what so desperately needed to be numbed. It wouldn't soothe what so desperately needed to be soothed. That being the case, he had given up drinking heavily, although that didn't mean he didn't think about it. Even now, as he sat in the cold and dark silence of his bedchamber, he was thinking of the warmth and comfort a drinking binge would bring him. He'd had these feelings before, and it was difficult not to fall back into that trap, but he'd become more adept at avoiding it as the years went on. He had worked too hard to fail at the post he currently held, and since he'd already failed at one post, long ago, he knew what it meant to regain something that he had lost.

He wasn't willing to risk his position as a Blackchurch trainer.

Oh, he had been trusted before. He had been a well-trained, elite knight, and he'd earned a solid reputation at a young age. He had been very proud of that and very proud of the fact that he'd gone to serve one of the most important men in England, the Earl of Hampshire, Val de Nerra. Through that position, he had also come into contact with England's greatest knight, William Marshal, and there had been times when his liege had allowed him to complete a task or fulfill a purpose for the Marshal. He had been extremely proud of that until the last mission he undertook for the man also known as the Earl of Pembroke.

That had been his greatest failure.

And his greatest joy.

The end of the mission had been the most difficult thing he'd ever had to face. It wasn't as if he'd failed the Marshal, or even Hampshire, in the fighting sense. His failure had been in the emotional sense. When his mission had concluded at Canonsleigh Abbey in Devon, he knew he couldn't return to what most men would consider a normal life. Back to Selborne Castle, seat of the Earl of Hampshire, to resume his normal duties and pretend his entire life wasn't in upheaval. Nor could he return to the service of Pembroke. That association had ended. When he had been at his wit's end, standing in the ruins of everything he'd worked for, it had been a dear friend who had seen his desolation and sent him on his current path.

He had sent him to the Blackchurch Guild.

Slowly, he stood up, making his way to the table against the wall that held a basin of cold water. He splashed himself in the face and on the neck as if trying to wash away the remnants of a dream that never fully left him. Whenever he had these dreams, his hollowed-out gut filled with the same emotion he felt the day he'd had to leave her behind, and it took him days to shake it. Over the years, however, he'd noticed the dreams weren't as frequent as they used to be. He wasn't sure if he felt better or worse about that—better because he was being awoken less frequently by those chaotic memories or worse because the pain seemed to be fading. He swore that pain would be with him, as fresh as the day he'd first experienced it, every day for the rest of his life. But it did, indeed, seem to be fading.

Did that mean memories of her were fading, too?

He simply didn't know.

He found a towel in the darkness and dried off his face and neck. He was wearing linen breeches, which he always did when he slept because he'd learned long ago never to sleep naked like most men did. One couldn't be prepared for an emergency if one did not have on at least one article of clothing that preserved one's modesty. But he pulled a tunic over his head, covering his broad chest and partially covering those linen breeches. After pulling on his boots, he lumbered out of his bedchamber and down the stairs.

A starry night was calling him.

He had to admit that he spent a good deal of time looking up at the sky. He'd always been fascinated by those pinpricks of light and how they moved. When he was young, the priests used to tell him that they were the souls of the good men who had died before him, and when he grew older, his trainers told him they were the souls of dead knights. Clearly, the belief was that there were millions of dead men in the skies above, but they glittered so beautifully that he really didn't care if the eyes of the dead were upon him. He gazed back, fascinated by them.

But there were times when he hoped they might give him comfort.

It was a cold night with a cold wind blowing in from the northwest. The moon was mostly full, illuminating the land of the Blackchurch Guild around him. A place that had become his home over the years, a place with fellow trainers such as himself, men he looked upon as brothers. He had a brother, an older one, a rather selfish bastard he wasn't much fond of, so he considered Blackchurch his family.

He was grateful for that.

In front of him, he could see the waters of Lake Cocytus glistening in the moonlight. The massive lake was part of the Blackchurch lands. The Blackchurch Guild itself covered several miles of prime Devon lands, property that had been in the de Bottreaux family for generations. St. Denis de Bottreaux was the most recent heir to Blackchurch in a long line of men who had built Blackchurch into the prestigious and powerful institution it was today, a training ground for the most elite warriors the world had ever seen. St. Denis had taken a chance on an emotionally crippled knight who showed an almost supernatural fighting ability.

And he'd been here ever since.

There were rocks, big and small, scattered along the shore of Lake Cocytus, and he took a seat on one of the larger boulders, watching the water ripple beneath the moonlight. There was something soothing about it, easing him from the horrors of his dream, reminding him that he'd landed in a good place. He'd never known the camaraderie he'd come to know at Blackchurch, and it was something he was grateful for. With the gentle lapping of the lake and the moon above, he could feel himself relax.

Until he heard footsteps approach from behind him.

He didn't panic for two very good reasons—it wasn't in his nature to panic and also because anyone trying to sneak up behind him would have used stealth. Not that anyone could make it inside Blackchurch's perimeter, so the thought of an unknown threat was ridiculous, but he reckoned whoever it was wanted him to hear them. They were being quite deliberate in their footsteps.

So, he waited.

"I thought it was you," a voice said behind him. "I saw you leave the village and head in this direction. What in the world are you doing, Fox?"

Sir Fox de Merest turned to see one of his closest friends, Tay Munro. Known as the Leviathan, one of the premier trainers at the Blackchurch Guild, Tay was big and bad-tempered. He was the trainer of new recruits, known as dregs, the very first trainer they ever experienced at Blackchurch. With his brutal manner and no-nonsense attitude, Tay weeded out the unworthy.

"What are you doing awake at this hour?" Fox countered. "Shouldn't you be tucked away with a couple of babies sleeping between you and your wife?"

Tay shook his head. "The youngest one is teething," he said. "Brendon is screaming at the top of his lungs and has been for hours, it seems. I've been walking the floor with the lad so my wife can get some sleep, but she finally gave up and took him from me. Now, she is walking the floor with him."

Fox grinned. "Athdara will not be pleased that you have abandoned ship and come out here to sit with me," he said. "You'd better return, or she might take a stick to the both of us."

Tay snorted. "She would have to catch me first, and she cannot run very fast because she is pregnant," he said with some confidence. "Therefore, I thought I'd come out here with you for a few moments. I love my children, but I can only take so much of them before I must have an adult to converse with. I am not accustomed to having children about all of the time."

Fox laughed softly. "You had better get used to it," he said. "You have two sons and your wife is pregnant with what I am sure is a third. If you did not want so many all at once, mayhap you should have slept in separate beds."

It was Tay's turn to laugh. "Are you mad?" he said. "You've seen my wife."

"I have, in fact."

"She is magnificent."

"She is."

"And I am supposed to restrain myself with her?"

Fox shrugged. "The result of your lack of restraint are those tiny little men you seem to so easily breed," he said. "That is your punishment."

"Or my reward."

Fox looked at him with a dubious expression, but they both broke down into soft laughter. Overhead, a nightbird soared through the sky, catching their attention as the humor between them faded. But the mood was still warm as two friends sat in comfortable silence. Behind them, they could hear the distinct sounds of footsteps, but neither one of them seemed too concerned. A man with dark hair, dark eyes, and a manner of dress that did not originate in England came up behind them.

"It is the middle of the night," he said in words that bore a slight accent. "I thought I was seeing phantoms out by the lake, but I realized it was the two of you."

Fox turned to see another dear friend, Ming Tang, as he stood there looking up at the stars. He was shorter than most of the larger trainers at Blackchurch, but that smaller stature did not mean smaller strength. His body was solid muscle. Sinewy and powerful, Ming Tang was not only an anomaly in England, but he was an anomaly anywhere in the Western world. There were few like him, this man who had made his way from the Far East by way of land and sea, finding his way to Blackchurch, where he taught skills that put their recruits above any warrior on any field of battle. Mysterious arts where a man used his hands and feet to fight, using technique over sheer strength to subdue a man.

Ming Tang was a legend.

"What are you doing up?" Fox asked. "It is not like you to prowl the night."

Ming Tang headed over to a rock next to Tay and planted himself on it. "And it is not like the two of you to have a conclave in the middle of the night," he said. "Is something amiss?"

Tay looked at Fox, who didn't say anything for a moment. When he did, it was barely above a whisper.

"I had that dream again," he muttered.

Tay glanced at Ming Tang before replying. "I thought so," he said quietly. "There is not much that will get you out of a warm bed, but those nightmares have been known to. I've seen you go without sleep for days, afraid the night terrors will return."

Fox's gaze moved over the moonlit waters. "It has never affected my duties."

"Nay, never," Tay agreed. "Mayhap Ming Tang and I can keep you company whilst you clear your mind enough to go back to sleep."

Fox sighed faintly, thinking of the men he worked with and how well they knew him. Or how well they *thought* they knew him.

Perhaps that was the point.

Tearing his gaze off the lake, he looked between Tay and Ming Tang. *His brothers.* Perhaps it was time they knew more than what Fox had been willing to allow.

"You are good friends," he said after a moment. "And I

must apologize."

"For what?" Tay asked.

"For not telling you everything."

"About what?"

"Her."

Tay lifted his eyebrows. "Her? Who *her*?" Then it occurred to him, and he nodded in understanding. "Ah… that 'her.' The 'her' of your nightmares. You told me about that, once."

"I know," Fox said. "Ming Tang knows, too. But I did not tell either one of you all of it."

Ming Tang answered softly, "I assumed you would when you were ready. I am certain that I speak for Tay also when I say that it is your choice to speak of it or not. But if it would help settle your mind, we will listen."

"It has been almost ten years," Fox said, glancing at Ming Tang with some irony. "When did you think I would be ready?"

Ming Tang shrugged. "In a day, a month, or twenty years," he said. "It is not for us to demand an explanation of your past. You will tell us when, and if, you want to."

Fox took a long, deep breath. "I want to," he said. "At least, I feel that I need to."

"Finally?" Ming Tang said. "That is a big decision for you."

"I know."

"Speak, then. We will listen."

Fox studied his face for a moment. "Just like that?" he said. "Is it so easy for you to say that?"

"What do you mean?"

"Haven't you ever been the least bit curious all these years?"

"Every man has a past," Tay said before Ming Tang could reply. "As I said, if you want us to know, you will tell us."

"But in all the time we've known each other, I've never

spoken a word."

"If you intend to do so now, we're listening."

Fox turned back for the lake, gathering his thoughts. Odd how he felt like speaking of something he'd kept buried for ten long years, something he'd pushed down and down again until he was buried so deeply he wasn't sure if he could ever resurrect it again. But the most recent dream had him reconsidering that, for the things a man kept buried often emerged in other ways—in emotions, actions, or, in his case, dreams.

Perhaps if he spoke of it, he wouldn't be so haunted.

"I'm not even sure how or where to start," he muttered. "What do you know about me? About my past, I mean. What do you really know?"

Tay shrugged. "I know that you are the son of the Earl of Keddington," he said. "I know that you have served in the king's guard in years past and that you have Saxon blood. I think we all know that."

He was looking at Ming Tang, who nodded in agreement. Fox looked at the pair of them appearing ghostly beneath the moonlight.

"That's it?" he said.

"What more do I need to know?" Fox said. "You are a man of good character. That is all that concerns me."

Fox snorted softly. "As it should," he said. "But the truth is that my father was, indeed, the Earl of Keddington and my mother was the daughter of the Earl of Morton. She was a Douglas, as Scots as they come. I was born to privilege, so I have always had the best of everything—training, education, everything."

"Well done, lad."

Fox grinned. "It wasn't my doing," he said. "It was generations of de Merest men. My ancestors came to this land with the Duke of Normandy. Unfortunately, I have a worthless older brother who inherited the earldom, so as the second son, I must make my own way, and that is exactly what I've been doing all these years."

Tay pondered that. "I am sorry about your brother," he said quietly. "As you know, I also have a brother, but he is not worthless. Merely… simple. A grown man with the mind of a child."

"I know," Fox said. "I have always admired the way you have spoken of him. You love your brother, and that is clear. But I do not love mine. He's suspicious and greedy, which means once he became the earl, I knew that I would never return home. Knowing him, he would lock me in the vault and throw away the key."

Tay frowned. "Then I agree that you have stayed away from your home," he said. "It is sad, nonetheless, but I understand."

Fox simply nodded, trying not to linger on the brother who hated him when he'd never given the man reason to, other than the fact he was simply a better man and a better knight than his brother could ever hope to be. Jealousy was an ugly motivator.

"I trained at Kenilworth Castle and Prudhoe Castle," he continued softly. "When I was a knight, I went into royal service until the Earl of Hampshire requested my fealty from the king. The request was granted, and I went to Selborne Castle in Hampshire, the earl's seat."

Tay was listening intently. "Val de Nerra is the Earl of Hampshire," he said. "He used to be the itinerant justice of Hampshire, as I recall. That was long ago. I also seem to remember that he was involved in the murder of Thomas Becket."

Fox shook his head. "He wasn't directly involved," he said. "He tried to stop them but was somehow implicated in the plot, for which he was entirely innocent. Henry understood even if the church did not. In any case, I went to serve him, but as it turned out, it was at the order of William Marshal for a specific purpose."

"What was it?"

Fox hesitated a moment before answering. "I will preface this by saying what I tell you must not leave your lips," he said, looking at both men. "Not even to your wife or anyone else at Blackchurch. Denis knows because he is close to the man who recommended me to Blackchurch, but no one else does, or should, know."

"You have our word," Tay said as Ming Tang nodded.

Fox turned to the men who were about to know his darkest secret. "I was assigned the task of guarding a royal bastard who had been sent to live with de Nerra and his wife," he said. "The girl was the daughter of Margaret of France, the wife of Henry the Young King, and William Marshal. When the child was born, she was moved to de Nerra and made a ward for safe-keeping. I was brought over from the king's household to protect her."

Tay was engrossed in what was inarguably a rather serious royal scandal. "God's Bones," he muttered. "So the Marshal fathered a bastard with Margaret? I'd heard rumor, but rumors are like snowflakes. They fall and then fade away and no one ever really knows if they ever really existed in the first place. But you're saying this rumor happened to be the truth?"

Fox nodded. "It is."

"But why you? Why were you given the assignment?"

"Because I had served with the Marshal under Henry," Fox

said. "I was very young, of course, but made a sufficient enough impression that the Marshal asked for me by name."

"So you went to Selborne," Tay said. "How long were you there?"

Fox thought back to the days when he had been a young knight, exuberant and full of wonder at the world. "Twelve years," he said slowly. Then he snorted softly. "I was so honored that Pembroke asked for my service that I did not even realize what I'd gotten myself into until it was too late. That's when I met her."

Tay's eyebrows lifted when he realized whom he meant. "And the mysterious 'her' enters the situation," he said. "Who was she? A daughter of de Nerra?"

"The bastard."

That drew a reaction from Tay. "The Marshal's daughter with Margaret?"

Fox nodded. "She was my duty," he said. "That is why I was hand-selected by Pembroke. He wanted me to watch over his daughter. Of course, she was quite young when we first met. She had seen ten years and I had seen twenty-two. I was knighted at seventeen years of age, fully fledged, and I served Henry the last few years of his life. I was considered an elite knight even back then, so Pembroke and Hampshire and other great warlords who served Henry knew me by name. Being selected to protect Lady Gisele was quite an honor, at least to them. They thought they were honoring me. But they were really condemning me."

"Condemning you to what?"

"A life of despair."

Had Tay not had a wife he was madly in love with, he might not have understood that statement. But he did understand it.

He understood it a great deal, and he sympathized.

"What happened?" he asked somewhat gently.

Fox cleared his throat as he thought on his reply. "Gisele and I were like oil and water at first," he said. "She was very young, and I was so full of arrogance that I was unbearable. I took it upon myself to teach her, curb her, and, if necessary, discipline her, which she did not accept well. Believe me when I tell you that even from a young age, she was a spitfire. She was twice as intelligent as I was and better educated even at ten years of age—but more than that, she was simply brilliant. I could see it in her even as a child. Our relationship, at first, was purely professional. I was her protector and nothing more."

"Did she know why?" Tay asked.

Fox nodded. "She did," he said. "Truly, she was so bright, she would have figured it out at some point, and de Nerra made the decision to tell her for her own safety. But being told she was the daughter of a queen turned her into a tyrant. Christ, Tay, you have no idea what a tyrant she became, and that lasted a couple of years. There were times when I wanted to beat her with a switch and too many times when I had to bite my tongue because of an imperious command she gave me. Lady de Nerra could see how Gigi treated me, and she finally gave me permission to spank her one day, because she'd become an absolute nightmare and it was decided that only I could stand up to her. So, I spanked her."

Tay fought off a grin. "Did she settle down?"

Fox didn't hold back the smile when he saw Tay struggling. "She did," he said. "From that point on, all I had to do was lift an open palm to her and she would behave. She knew better than to push me."

"The relationship must have improved because you called

her Gigi."

Fox grinned. "For those two years of hell, I called her Gig," he said. "Lady Giggie sometimes. She hated every minute of it, so I'm sure, in my own way, I did push her into behaving so poorly. You have to remember that I was quite young myself and not beyond a taunt or two. But after she settled down, she was Lady Gisele, and our relationship became more companionable. I was more of an uncle or a brother, and the more mature she became, the more we could speak at length without antagonizing each other. She told me her hopes, her dreams. We finally became friends. She spoke of her future and of the young men she had her eye on."

"Oh?" Tay said curiously. "And how did you react to that, given the fact you had feelings for her?"

Fox shook his head. "Not back then," he said. "She was quite fond of boys and young men when she had seen thirteen, fourteen, and even fifteen years. But when she turned sixteen, something… happened."

"What?"

Fox lifted his big shoulders. "I do not know," he said. "Suddenly, Lady Gisele de Salisbury became a woman, but not just any woman—a woman of exquisite and ethereal beauty."

"De Salisbury? That is the name she bore?"

"It was the Marshal's mother's family name," Fox explained. "It was meant to give her some obscurity, and it did—for a time, anyway. Shall I describe her to you?"

"Please."

Fox took on a distant expression as he remembered a woman he'd not seen in ten long and agonizing years. In fact, he closed his eyes so he could envision her better.

"She has eyes the color of the sea," he said softly, reverently.

"Big, expressive eyes with long, silky lashes. They turned down slightly at the ends, which gave her a natural expression as if she was always dreaming. Very dreamy-eyed. Her skin is like alabaster, perfect in every way, and her lips are shaped like a rosebud. When she smiles, it's a smile unlike anything you've ever seen. It lights up everything around her. She's surreal, my Gigi. As if a door to heaven opened up and she stepped through."

Tay was smiling by the time Fox finished. "I can hear it in your voice," he muttered. "I can hear the love you have for her. I thought I was the only one who felt love like that, but you... you feel it, too."

Fox nodded, his smile fading. "I do," he said. "Now imagine being separated from your love for ten years."

Tay was no longer smiling either. "I cannot," he said. "I do not know how you survive each day, Fox. I would have been a madman years ago."

Fox sighed heavily. "I *am* mad," he murmured. "Those dreams I have are the madness. I cannot be with Gigi, so I dream about her, and it's excruciating every single time."

Tay couldn't have felt worse for his friend. He looked to Ming Tang, who had remained largely silent throughout the conversation, and the two exchanged sympathetic glances. Reaching out, Tay put his hand on Fox's shoulder.

"Then why not figure out some way to be with her?" he asked. "Is it truly impossible? Or are you simply following orders to stay away from her?"

"I am following orders."

"Where is she now?"

"At Canonsleigh Abbey."

Tay's dark brows lifted in surprise. "Canonsleigh?" he repeated. "That's not far from here."

"Fifteen miles and a million years away," Fox said softly.

"And you have not seen her in all that time?" Tay asked, incredulous. "Even though she is so close?"

"Even though she is so close."

"But why?"

Fox looked at him then, and Tay swore he saw tears glistening in the man's eyes. Tears of pain, of longing. Given that he was seeing those tears in the eyes of the most composed man he knew, the realization was shocking. But it also underscored the pain Fox lived with, every day of his life.

Pain that neither Tay nor Ming Tang had never fully understood until now.

"Do you truly wish to know?" Fox asked. "It will take all of my strength to tell you."

"Please. Tell me."

Fox did.

PART ONE

CHAPTER ONE

Year of Our Lord 1204
Selborne Castle, Hampshire

"HE DID IT!" came the scream. "Theo did it! I'm going to tell Papa!"

It was chaos in the kitchen yard of Selborne Castle. Beneath a bright blue sky that had just cleared of a few summer rain clouds, the type that blew in and blew out quickly, the ground was wet and slippery, too slippery to outrun an angry rooster that had been dropped into the kitchen yard to terrorize the young women who were stealing cheese from the buttery.

The children of Val and Vesper de Nerra were at it again.

"Run!" A young woman with hair the color of glistening honey was moving faster than her companion. "Charlotte, *run*! He'll catch you and scratch you to pieces!"

Even the servants were running as the furious rooster chased anything that moved. It would have been hilarious had the rooster not had spurs that were quite sharp and capable of doing damage, but Charlotte's younger brother hadn't considered that. He was on the roof of the stable adjacent to the kitchen yard, watching the girls scatter and having a howling good time at their expense.

Charlotte could see her gloating brother as she ran for the gate, which he had locked when he dropped the rooster into the yard.

"Theo!" she screamed, now running toward the postern gate. "I'm telling Papa!"

Theodore de Nerra was laughing so hard that he could barely breathe. He didn't actually think the rooster could catch his sister, but part of him hoped it did. Perhaps the little ninny would think twice before again putting some sort of purgative she'd stolen from the physic, who had been visiting the castle to help cure his mother's allergic rash, into his food. God only knew what poison Charlotte had put in his stew, but it had been enough to keep him up all night with fluids coming uncontrollably out of both ends of his body. He knew it was her because she'd been the one to serve him the night before. It was one more volley in a long line of volleys between them, the ongoing war between brother and sister.

But he had planned his revenge well.

His mother had a large chicken coop that she was quite proud of, and Theo had annoyed one of the roosters until it was bristling with anger. Then he'd carried the feathered tornado over to the kitchen yard when he knew his sister was there. True, she was there with a ward of the family, and it was unfortunate that Gisele de Salisbury was caught in the mayhem.

Collateral damage in the ongoing war between Theodore and Charlotte.

"Theo? What are you doing up there?"

Theo stopped laughing long enough to look down at the man who had asked the question. He was a seasoned knight, someone Theodore looked up to. In fact, the man was like a brother to him, as Theo had known him more than half his life. He pointed to the kitchen yard.

"Lottie is getting her comeuppance," he said. "She put something in my food last night that had me up until dawn, so I put the rooster in the kitchen yard with her and locked the gate. She cannot get out."

The man gazing up at him from the stable yard cocked a disapproving eyebrow. "That is a big rooster," he pointed out. "If it spurs her, your father will have your hide."

Theodore knew that, but he was still defiant. Mostly defiant, anyway. At his age, as he had seen sixteen summers, his defiance could be more foolish than fact-based. "It cannot catch her," he said confidently. "You worry too much, Fox. Both Lottie and Gigi run too fast. It cannot catch either of them."

Fox de Merest's face went slack when he realized what was going on. He immediately turned for the kitchen yard.

"You *idiot*," he said to Theodore. "Gigi is in there with her?"

Theodore frowned as he swung himself over the side of the roof, which was quite low to the ground because the stable itself was built into a slight indent in the earth. "Why so concerned?" he said. "Gigi runs faster than Lottie does."

Fox would have slugged Theodore in the face if he'd had the time, but there was no time to waste. The women were in danger. He reached the gate leading into the kitchen yard and, seeing that it was locked from the outside, unhinged the bolt and threw it back. Yanking open the gate, he could see the rooster prancing around, searching for victims, and two young ladies huddled on top of the buttery roof. He headed straight over to the structure, holding his arms up to Gisele.

"Come down from there," he said. "Come down before you fall down."

Gisele wasn't apt to climb down with the rooster still on the prowl. "Not until the rooster is caught," she said fearfully. "He is trying to stab us!"

Fox sighed sharply, looking to Theodore, who had just come in through the kitchen gate. "Catch that damnable rooster before it hurts someone," he said. "Put it back where it belongs and leave it there."

Theodore didn't like the fact that Fox broke up his fun. Big, powerful, serious Fox. A wooden plank had better humor than he did. As Theodore begrudgingly went after the rooster, Fox went to Gisele and grabbed hold of an ankle.

"Come on," he said, gently pulling. "Come down."

But Gisele resisted. "The rooster is still running loose."

Fox simply shook his head, coaxing her to at least lower herself into his arms. He ended up carrying her across the kitchen yard as Theodore was being attacked by the rooster over near the fence. He was trying to grab the bird, but the feathered bully had no intention of being captured.

The fight was on.

"It serves you right," Fox shouted as he headed from the gate.

Theodore kicked the bird away as it tried to stab him. "A true friend would help me!"

"You do not deserve it."

Fox set Gisele on her feet before heading back into the yard to pull Charlotte off the roof also. With both women clear of the kitchen yard, where Theodore was now trying to use a shovel to stun the bird, Fox shut the kitchen gate and left Theodore to deal with his own mess. He faced Gisele and Charlotte, who were grinning up at him.

"You are a good and true man, Fox," Charlotte said. "Thank

you for saving us."

Fox dipped his head gallantly. "It was my pleasure," he said. "Do you require any further assistance?"

Charlotte giggled and shook her head, shooting Gisele a long look before dashing off toward the keep, undoubtedly to tell her mother what Theodore had done. Fox and Gisele watched her go before Fox spoke softly.

"I suppose she knew well enough to leave us alone," he said.

"She usually does."

Gisele turned to look at him. A man she'd known half her life, someone who was part of her as much as her lungs or her heart. She couldn't breathe without him, nor could she stand to be away from him for any length of time. When it came to Fox de Merest, Gisele had been hopelessly, and completely, in love with the man for six years.

Six long and agonizing years.

"Time alone is so rare," she murmured. "Shall we take advantage of it?"

His lips twitched with a smile. "God, I hope so."

"The usual place?"

His pale gaze moved around the stable yard, which was relatively empty at this time of day. The animals were fed, chores were done, and it was the quiet part of the afternoon when most people were either napping or off doing inconsequential things.

He cleared his throat softly.

"Aye," he agreed. "I will meet you there."

Gisele turned away without another word. She knew where their usual place was, but getting there without being seen was the trick. There was a barbican to the south of Selborne, covered stairs leading down to a small, fortified chamber that sat on the banks of a small river called the Well Head.

Selborne was a very old castle, a Saxon fortress built well before the Duke of Normandy came to the shores of England, and there had been a time when the Well Head was a river that connected with larger rivers that traveled to the sea. Supplies could be brought to the barbican via the waterways, but those days were long gone. At some point, the wooden walls had been replaced by stone, as had the rest of the castle, and the small moat around the fortress had been widened. Drawbridges and gatehouses were now the main point of entry, and the big chamber on the banks of the small river was old and dusty and abandoned.

It was their safe haven.

Gisele was very casual in her path to the barbican. It wasn't normally guarded, but the gate was secured, an old iron and oak gate that opened to the protected stairs. It was near the keep, in an area where they stored the wagons, and Gisele kept a sharp eye out as she made her way into the corral of wagons. Ducking low, she was able to get to the gate, open it, and slip through.

Quickly, she made it down the dusty, steep steps.

The room at the bottom was another dusty space, forgotten by time, but she and Fox had managed to build it up as a chamber for only the two of them, a place where they could be alone in a world that very much wanted to keep them apart. The fortified chamber she found herself in had an even smaller chamber inside of it, one that had once stored things and could be locked from the outside. That was the chamber that she and Fox used for their very own, with a rope bed and stolen furnishings like a fine coverlet and hides on the floor. There, they could pretend there was nothing standing between them. Where they could make-believe that theirs was a normal relationship and that, ultimately, they would be together. It was a forgotten chamber of dreams. Gisele was so afraid that it was all they would ever have.

So afraid that, in the end, all they would have were memories.

It seemed that was all they had even now.

Gisele had known Fox a long time. They met shortly after her tenth birthday when he'd come to Selborne from Winchester Castle, where he'd been in service to the king. Exceedingly tall, with broad shoulders, a big neck, and muscular arms, he presented the perfect image of a powerful knight simply at first glance. But when one looked a little closer, they could see his dark hair, chiseled features, and the pale blue eyes of a handsome, and young, warrior. Those comely looks had the maidens of Selborne whispering and sighing when he walked by, but he was full of youthful arrogance and had no interest in any woman other than Gisele, because he'd come to Selborne for a specific purpose.

And Gisele knew what it was.

She'd known of her parentage for quite some time, mostly because William Marshal, the Earl of Pembroke, was a frequent guest at Selborne, and she and Charlotte and Juliana, Charlotte's older sister, had once overheard a conversation between the Marshal and Val de Nerra, the lord of Selborne Castle and Charlotte and Juliana's father. The girls, who eavesdropped on a regular basis because they were nosier than cats, got an earful when they heard the Marshal allude to the fact that he was pleased with his daughter's education and thanked Val for guiding Gisele. More pieces of the puzzle fell into place the more the conversation progressed, and when the Marshal had departed Selborne, Gisele confronted Val with what she'd heard. He'd threatened to spank her for listening in on a private conversation, but eventually relented and told her everything.

Fox had arrived shortly thereafter.

They'd spent years antagonizing one another, something she giggled at now, but something that wasn't entirely humorous at the time. She swore there were moments when Fox was going to take her over his knee, but he never did. The young, prideful knight had shown an extreme amount of patience with her, and Gisele knew it, so she supposed that was when she started realizing Fox de Merest was something special.

It was a spark that grew.

Six years later, it was a roaring inferno.

"Christ," Fox hissed as he came in through the door and shut and bolted it behind him. "Theo caught sight of me and I had to outsmart him."

Gisele looked at him with concern. "Do you think he'll follow you?"

Fox shook his head, moving to the old table he'd brought down here and striking the flint and stone against the cold taper. As the wick came to life with a small flame, he turned to Gisele.

"He's no fool," he said, removing the gloves he was wearing. "He knows about this chamber. About us. But he will not come down here, and he'll discourage anyone else from doing the same."

Gisele collected the gloves he'd tossed on the table and stacked them neatly before moving to an earthenware pitcher and some cups.

"They all know," she said softly, pouring him a measure of wine that she'd brought down a couple of days ago. "All of the de Nerra siblings. No matter how petulant they are to each other, they haven't spilled our secret in all of these years."

"True."

"I heard a rumor that you were taking men to Ramsbury Castle," she said, handing him the cup. "Any truth to that?"

He took a sip of the somewhat stale wine. "There is," he said. "The Duke of Savernake is holding a gathering of local warlords."

"Why?"

He set his cup down and began unfastening the belt and scabbard around his waist. "Because John has the backing of some French mercenaries," he said. "We've heard tell that they are heading for our shores, and, more than likely, they'll be close by Selborne because they'll probably come into Portsmouth. If that is the case, we must be prepared."

Gisele watched him lay the scabbard on the table and work on removing his tunic. "John," she murmured. "My uncle, the king. Well… my mother's husband's brother, in any case. I am related to a man no one can stand."

He pulled the tunic over his head. "You are *not* related to him," he said. "You do not carry his blood."

"That is not what everyone else thinks," she said, sitting down on one of the two chairs in the chamber. "Everyone thinks I am Henry the Young King's offspring and that is why I've been protected all these years. You think that I do not know that, but I do. William Marshal does not acknowledge me because he is trying to protect my mother's memory. What would the world think if they knew Margaret of France bore a bastard out of wedlock?"

Fox eyed her. This wasn't an infrequent conversation, at least the fact that she was the Marshal's bastard, but bringing up Henry the Young King was something new.

"Why do you speak of Henry the Young King?" he asked. "Where did that come from?"

Gisele shrugged, lowering her gaze and looking at her hands. "I don't know," she said. "It just came to mind. I suppose it is my frustration talking."

"What frustration?"

She gestured to the room with a soft white hand. "With this," she said. "With everything. With the fact that we must always meet in secret. I wish with all my heart that we could live and love like a normal couple."

"You used to say that as long as we could be together, it did not matter."

She sighed faintly and looked at her lap. "Mayhap it did not at one point," she said. "But it matters now."

"Why?"

"Because I want more now," she said. Her gaze came up again, meeting his imploringly. "I have loved you for six long years, yet you cannot marry me. I cannot marry you. You have asked for permission only to be denied. I am growing weary of meeting you in a dark and dingy room because it is the only way we can express our love."

More of the same conversation they've been having as of late. Her frustration, and his, wasn't anything new, but they were in a very difficult position, and he sensed that she was becoming impatient with it.

"It could be worse," he said. "There could be no secret meetings at all."

"I realize that."

"Then you should be grateful for the time we have together, such as it is."

"I am," she said, but quickly corrected herself. "I am *not*.

Fox, I want to be your wife. Can we simply not run away to France and be married? You are a fine knight. Any lord would be thrilled to have your fealty, and we could live in the open, as man and wife."

He pulled off the linen undertunic he was wearing, exposing his broad, beautifully muscular chest. "We have been over this, my love," he said patiently. "Nay, we cannot run away."

"Why not?"

"Because we would run away from everything we know," he said. "The people, the places… everything."

Her cheeks were starting to redden. "Everything that keeps us apart."

"Everything we've worked for."

Her eyes flashed. "Everything *you've* worked for, you mean," she snapped. "I am quite willing to leave everything behind because there is nothing for me here, but you… you are not willing to leave the reputation you've built nor the position you've achieved. That's why you won't leave with me, Fox."

"That is not true."

"It is never more obvious than when you try to deny it."

He cocked a dark eyebrow at her. "What do you want me to do?" he said, trying not to become irritated with her. "What do you want me to say?"

"I want you to be honest with me," she said. "It is clear that your position and profession is more important to you than I am. At least be honest and tell me so I know where I stand."

"Is that what you want?" he said. "What then? How do you feel when I tell you that I love my career more than I love you? Does that make you happy?"

She scowled, but he could see that tears were close to the surface. "Then it is true," she said. "You do love your knighthood more than you love me."

Fox looked at her. That beautiful, fiery woman he couldn't live without. She had hair the color of sunlight through honey, dark blonde and glistening, as it tumbled to her buttocks. Her eyes were incredibly unique as well as stunning, a sort of pale blue-green color, large and tilted slightly downward. Her lashes, long and dusky, were part of that magnificent picture. Fox could have stared at her all day, and, truth be told, there were times when he had. But above the beauty and the emotions he'd long felt for her, he had to admit there was some truth in what she said. He loved her, but he didn't want to leave everything behind.

He was still trying to work that all out.

"You are a woman with royal blood," he finally said. "Your mother is a queen, Gigi. Your father is England's greatest knight. Your pedigree is astonishing. Of course I love you more than my knighthood, but it isn't as easy as that. Women like you do not simply run away from everything, and most certainly, they do not run away with a simple knight. Is that all you feel that you are worth? Running away from a situation rather than facing it head-on? Is that the extent of your bravery?"

The tears began to glisten in those big eyes. "You know it is not," she said. "But I want to be your wife. I want us to live openly and love openly, not hide our love as if we are ashamed of it."

He held up a hand to silence her. "Listen to me," he said. "Listen to me again so I will tell you what I have told you before. The Marshal denied permission for our marriage because he does not feel that I am worthy of you. That is true—I am not, not yet. He was kind about it, but I still have a great deal to accomplish before I am worthy in his eyes. Do you not have the patience for me to attain that?"

Her brow furrowed. "I do have patience," she said. "But I am not getting any younger, you know. Most women my age are already married."

"Most women your age do not have men willing to wait for them, no matter how old they become," he said. "Whether you are sixteen or twenty-two or forty, I will still be here to marry you, Gigi. I will not give up until I do. But you must let me work for it so that the Marshal will give his permission without reserve. Can you at least understand that?"

Gisele had heard those words before. It was true that she was very impatient, but Fox had a way of putting things so she could comprehend and see the logic. With a heavy sigh, she closed her eyes briefly and hung her head again. "I understand," she murmured. "I do not like it, but I understand."

He went to her, kissing her on the top of the head. "I know," he said. "I do not like it either, but I know it is better this way for the both of us. I love you, and I do not want to be on the run with you. That would be no life for us, constantly afraid of being followed or discovered. Do we not deserve the dignity of a proper marriage?"

He was right and she knew it, but her impatience and frustration had the better of her. Tilting her head back, she gazed up at him.

"And you will not leave me for someone with whom a marriage would be a simple thing?" she asked.

He shrugged. "Probably," he said. "If she was rich enough. But not today."

"How mercenary!"

He fought off a grin. "I know," he said as if completely unconcerned. "If you do not realize I have a mercenary heart by now, that is your misfortune."

With a smirk, she slapped him on the buttocks, and he laughed low in his throat. Reaching down, he pulled her up against him, gazing down into that face he loved so well.

"You are a petulant, ridiculous child, and I do not know why I put up with you," he said. "But you are *my* petulant, ridiculous child, and I love you very much. There is no one else, Gigi. There never will be. Only you."

With that, he slanted his mouth over hers, hungrily, and Gisele responded immediately, latching on to him, her hands in his hair as she pulled him down to her. Lips fused, Fox picked her up and carried her over to the bed, where they both ended up falling onto the straw mattress. Fox was on top of her, his arms going around her as he kissed her fiercely. She was sweet, delectable, and warm. Everything he expected of her and everything he craved.

His passion flamed.

Fox began to remove her from her gown. Fortunately, it wasn't restrictive, and when the ties were loosened, she easily slid out of it. He pulled it off her feet and threw it onto the ground, pulling off his leather breeches in nearly the same motion. Nude, he reclaimed his place on top of her, his mouth descending upon a taut nipple.

Gisele groaned as he suckled her, his heated mouth sending bolts of pleasure through her body. He took his time with her, as he usually did, for he was a thoughtful lover. He had been for nearly six years, ever since he took her innocence in a most tender and beautiful way. She knew his body, his moves, the way he touched and liked to be touched, and her hands moved down his body, caressing his buttocks as he nursed upon her.

In the midst of his mouth to her breasts and belly, Fox's fingers probed the dark curls between her legs. Welcoming his intimate touch, Gisele opened her legs to him, letting his big body settle between them. This was how their lovemaking usually went, with Fox kissing and suckling and touching every part of her while she lay there and let him. He inserted a couple of big fingers into her body, and she drew her legs up, groaning. She was already hot and slick, her body prepared itself for his entry, but when he tried to mount her, she squirmed out from underneath him, pushed him onto his back, and put her mouth on his manhood.

Now, Fox was the one groaning.

He didn't usually like her to focus on his manhood prior to joining his body with hers because he was always so eager to get to the heart of the situation. To feel himself within her was a greater pleasure than anything she could do to him otherwise. But he'd taught her how to pleasure him with her mouth, something she had very much wanted to learn when he'd first introduced her to the art of lovemaking, and he had to admit that he was a good teacher. She did a damn fine job of it. She plunged her mouth on him again and again, suckling as she went, and in little time, he'd had enough. Any more of it and he'd erupt, something he didn't want to do.

Yet.

Pulling her up by her hair, he rolled her onto her back again, pushed himself between her legs, and thrust his long, hard length into her warm and quivering folds. Gisele sighed with pleasure, bringing her legs up, wrapping them around his thighs as he thrust into her. Her hands moved over his body, feeling the texture of his skin as her nostrils drew in the scent of his musk. Her hand moved between them, touching their bodies where they joined, and she fondled him as he made love to her. She savored every thrust, every movement, with the greatest of enjoyment. She bit him gently, on the chest, and he growled with pleasure.

When the moment of her release came, Gisele was catapulted into a blinding climax, nearly screaming with ecstasy until Fox covered her mouth with his own to silence her. Even though they were off in their own little world, he still didn't want anyone hearing them. But her release set off his own climax, and he quickly pulled back to remove himself from her body, as he always did when they made love. He didn't want to fill her with his seed and risk a pregnancy, but as he moved to withdraw, she locked her legs behind his buttocks and forced him to remain inside of her. Doing exactly what he didn't want to do but unable to stop himself, he spilled deep into her body, deeper still when he felt her climax again around him, less forcefully than before.

It was sheer heaven.

For the longest time he simply lay there, embedded in her, feeling her hands roving over his body, caressing him. She was holding him, cradling him, refusing to let him pull out even when he tried to do it again. She just held him there, feeling him in her, taking delight in their mating.

Fox finally lifted his head.

"If you do that again, I will never bed you again," he muttered, his voice low. "If you think to force a marriage by conceiving a child, then that is a stupid and reckless thing to do."

Gisele stared at him for a moment before unwrapping her arms and legs from him and pushing him off her. Without a word, she hunted down her shift and surcoat, which he had removed in one piece, and brushed off the dust from the floor where it had laid. Silently, she put on the shift, then the surcoat, as Fox sat up in bed and watched her. After pulling on her leather slippers, she smoothed her hair before going to the door, opening it, and leaving the chamber.

She hadn't said a word the entire time.

Fox sat alone on the bed, thinking of the volatile lady he was so in love with. Of course he hadn't meant what he'd said about not bedding her ever again, but he did think her actions were stupid. She wasn't stupid by nature, but she was bold and impatient at times. He wondered if she knew what would happen to them both if she became pregnant. She thought she was forcing him to do what she wanted, but the truth was that she would be creating a worse situation than they were already in.

But he knew he'd hurt her feelings.

With a heavy sigh, he stood up and went in search of his clothing, dressing quietly and efficiently, his thoughts lingering on Gisele. He knew she wouldn't apologize to him—she was too stubborn for that. He'd known her more than half her life and had never known her to apologize for anything, so they would be angry with each other for a few days before they started speaking again and then go on as if nothing had ever happened. That was what they usually did, although sometimes they would talk about it again and reason through it. That only happened over the past couple of years, as she matured—and, frankly, as he matured. She was growing up, becoming a reasonable and astute woman, but in moments like this, he could still see the young girl who simply wanted her way. That was something they were still wrestling with.

But that didn't mean he was content for her to be angry

with him.

By the time he strapped on his scabbard, he knew he was going to go out into the bailey and find her, probably try to soothe her. Men in love did stupid things, too.

But he didn't much care.

CHAPTER TWO

"SHE IS HERE? And we are certain?"

Three men stood at the mouth of the gatehouse of Selborne Castle, gazing up at the enormous, red-stoned fortress with a hint of trepidation in their expressions. They were dressed in the style of the French court, with leather and silk and pointy shoes, and had a small wagon that carried their instruments and baggage. They were minstrels, or so they told everyone, but the truth was much different.

Much darker.

Music was simply the perfect cover.

"She is here," a man replied. He had bushy eyebrows and a scruffy look about him. "The *comte* has paid men well for the information, and this is where they said she is. She is a ward of the Earl of Hampshire."

"Her name?"

"Gisele of England," the man replied. "At least, that was what she was called at birth. But Henry's death saw her go to loyalists of her father, presumably to keep her away from his enemies. Mayhap they meant to keep her birth a secret, once, but that was long ago. It seems that many know of her these days, at least according to Angoulême, so locating her was not difficult."

A large man with receding blond hair and a dour expression turned away from the sight of the castle and reached into the wagon to pull forth a jug of something. His face was red from the mild heat of the day and the fact that they had traveled a great distance. He took several long drinks of the contents of the jug.

"Then let us get this over with," he muttered, wiping his mouth with the back of his hand. "I find the entire situation disgusting."

The man with the bushy eyebrows turned to him. "Why?" he said. "You are being well paid for your skill, Bernard. Why does it matter what you must do to earn it?"

Bernard glared at him. "It matters, Corbeau," he snapped, beating on his chest. "I am a musician. I have always been a musician. But ever since you entered into that unholy alliance with the Comte de Angoulême strictly for the money, we have been doing things we should not be doing. I do not know why I let you talk me into this."

Corbeau smiled lazily and turned back to the sight of the imposing castle while the man next to him spoke up.

"You've been able to send money back to your wife and daughters, Bernard," the man reminded him. "It is money they need."

Bernard rolled his eyes. "Shut your lips, Edouard," he hissed. "It is blood money. Now with a young girl we must... we must..."

He couldn't finish. All he could do was shake his head and move toward the sturdy pony that had been pulling their wagon all across England. They'd purchased the little beast when they arrived in London, and now they found themselves in southern England, at a place called Selborne Castle, where they were to complete a task they'd already been paid handsomely for.

But Corbeau knew of his friend's reservations. Bernard was a complainer, but they needed his strength. He was also quite cunning, a problem solver. Leaving Edouard, Corbeau moved to Bernard's side as the man checked the harness on the fat, little pony.

"You cannot look at it as blood money," he told his friend quietly. "As minstrels, we were making no money at all. Our families were begging in the streets to eat. Angoulême has allowed us to buy food and pay for homes with our earnings. And we are providing a necessary service."

Bernard looked at him sharply. "Service, you say?"

Corbeau nodded firmly. "Indeed," he said. "We are doing Angoulême and his daughter a favor. That puts us in the man's good graces... and in hers."

Bernard snorted. "The woman is the bloody Queen of England," he said. "She has knights and soldiers at her disposal. Why us? Why must it be us?"

Corbeau put a hand on Bernard's shoulder because he was becoming animated. And loud. It would not do for a soldier at the gatehouse to hear this conversation. If they did, all would be lost.

"Because no one will suspect the minstrels," he said softly. "If she sent her knights, then they would know she was behind the girl's death. Bernard, the situation is this—we have a young queen who is trying to please her husband, and she has asked her father for help."

"By killing a young woman?"

"Gisele is a threat," Corbeau said. "She is a threat to the

throne because her father was Henry the Young King. John does not have an heir at the moment, and if something happens to him, this girl holds enough claim that John's enemies could marry her to a foreign prince, and together, they would rule England. John is worried about this, so his wife, wishing to please him, has asked her father to rid John of this girl. She threatens everything, Bernard. If John dies, Isabella is no longer queen and this girl assumes her place. The Comte de Angoulême wishes to avoid this. Can you not understand?"

Bernard sighed heavily. "So Angoulême sends his spies to England to locate this young woman," he said with disapproval. "He must have paid handsomely for someone to have discovered she is living with the Earl of Hampshire."

Corbeau nodded. "As I said, it was not a well-kept secret," he said. "If you ask the right people, they will tell you. Angoulême knows enough of the nobility in England to find out what he wishes to find out, and even the most loyal knight might tell you what you wish to know for the right price. The girl is living with the Earl of Hampshire—a man, you will recall, who was involved in the death of Thomas de Becket those years ago. He is, therefore, dangerous. But we can get close to the girl and no one will suspect."

"And how are we supposed to do this?"

Corbeau's gaze turned to the fortress again. "Tonight, we play for the evening meal," he said. "It will be our way of paying for shelter for the night. Undoubtedly, the girl will be at the feast. It will simply be a matter of getting her away from the others, and what we do, we do quickly. We will find some place to hide her body, and we will be gone before they discover her."

Bernard thought on that, coming to grips with it, before taking a deep breath and turning toward the fortress. "Then whatever we do will need to be towards the morning," he said. "The gates will be locked all night, I am certain, only to be opened in the morning. We will do what needs to be done when the gates open so we may quickly depart."

Corbeau smiled, clapping him on the back in a show of camaraderie. "Of course," he said. "We shall be very quick about it."

"And once we flee, where do we go?"

Corbeau threw a thumb over his shoulder. "Portsmouth is not far," he said. "We can find passage to Cherbourg. We will go home. Even if they suspect it was us, they will never catch us. We will be well into France."

Bernard still wasn't thrilled about their task, but it couldn't be helped now. They'd been paid a good deal of money to eliminate yet another Plantagenet threat—in this case, the daughter of one of the king's brothers. In the annals of the Plantagenet family, murder and betrayal was nothing new, only this time, it was coming from a very young queen who was desperate to please a husband that had not been kind to her. At least, that was the rumor. As the Comte de Angoulême had explained, it was Isabella's hope that John would see her devotion to him if she eliminated a threat to his throne.

And that was why the minstrels were here.

They had a princess to kill.

CHAPTER THREE

"Gigi?"

A woman in fine clothing called up the stairwell to the third floor where the girls in the family had their bedchambers. She could hear voices up there, so she called up again.

"*Gisele?*"

A face appeared at the top of the steps as Gisele peered down the stairwell. "Aye, my lady?"

Vesper, Lady Hampshire, pointed in the general direction of the great hall. "Dearest, we have visitors tonight, and I want you to make them welcome, please," she said. "I've just received word that a traveling band of minstrels will be seeking shelter for the night. Will you find them beds? And I want them to play tonight. It has been a long time since we've had music in the hall."

Gisele, who had just changed into the fine silk garment she would be wearing for the evening meal, nodded firmly. "Aye, my lady," she said. "Right away."

"Good lass," Vesper said. "And take Sophie with you, please. She can help you. But make sure she dresses *properly.*"

Gisele knew what she meant. Sophie de Nerra was the

youngest de Nerra child, a twin to her brother, Theodore. She was several years younger than Gisele, but a good lass and a hard worker. However, she had a terrible habit of refusing to wear shoes, something her mother was desperately trying to break her of, so young Sophie was dressed in a lovely blue garment, but shoeless like a pauper. When Gisele took her back to the wardrobe to find shoes for her, Sophie pitched a fit until Charlotte had to sit on her. Gisele was able to get the shoes on her dirty little feet, but they were tied on quite tightly so she wouldn't kick them off.

That made for a miserable Sophie.

Dragging the pouting young woman behind her, Gisele quit the chamber and headed down the stairs. The keep of Selborne Castle was an enormous, square-shaped structure with six floors—five of them above ground and one of them below ground. Whereas some keeps could be rather small, with perhaps one or two chambers to each floor, Selborne's keep had at least four or more chambers to each floor, except for the third floor, where Lord and Lady Hampshire had their master chamber. It took up most of the floor, with only a smaller chamber across from them that was used as a nursery when the children were quite small. Now, the girls had their own floor and the boys had their own floor, and the keep was always filled with the laughter of family and children.

It was one of the things Gisele loved about the place.

There had always been so much joy.

In truth, Selborne was the only home that she had ever known. It didn't matter that she wasn't a natural-born daughter of the earl and his wife because they'd never made her feel any differently from the rest of their brood. Even when she knew who her parents were, that never mattered to her. Perhaps she had been born of the body of Margaret of France, and the blood of William Marshal flowed through her veins, but the people who had raised her were her true family.

And that meant their children were her siblings, including Sophie, who was grossly unhappy by the time they reached the keep entry. Her feet were killing her, she declared, and she was going to be crippled for life if Gisele didn't allow her to remove her shoes. Gisele listened to the whining all the way across the bailey, ignoring most of it, dragging the girl behind her like a barge. Once they hit the great hall, however, the situation changed and Gisele let go of her prisoner. The cavernous chamber was empty for the most part, smelling of smoke and piss and of the dogs that roamed the hall. They were over by the hearth now, with the minstrels that she'd been told of, so she turned to Sophie.

"Now," she said quietly. "We have been asked by your mother to make our visitors comfortable. We will go over and introduce ourselves, and while I see to some food, you will see if you can find a warm bed for them. The servants sleep in the chamber next to the kitchen and there's an alcove near the kitchen door, so mayhap they can sleep there. See to it, will you?"

Sophie nodded in resignation. "Aye," she said impatiently. "And then I'm going to tell my mother that you were cruel to me."

"Good," Gisele said. "Tell her anything you wish."

"She will punish you."

"Not before she punishes you for lying about me and the entire situation," Gisele said, lifting an arched eyebrow. "Well? Are we going to argue, or are you going to do what you've been told?"

Seeing she wasn't getting anywhere with Gisele had Sophie stomping off in the direction of the minstrels. Gisele caught up to her, noting the men had caught sight of them. There were three of them, surprisingly well dressed for traveling musicians, who tended to be poor. Coming to within a few feet of the group, Gisele came to a halt and faced them.

"My name is Lady Gisele, and this is Lady Sophie," she said, indicating the unhappy young woman beside her. "We have been sent to see to your comfort. Lady de Nerra said that you have agreed to play during the feast?"

A man with bushy eyebrows nodded. "Indeed, my lady," he said, his French accent heavy. "I am called Corbeau, and my companions are Bernard and Edouard. We are very happy to play for the beautiful daughters of Lord and Lady Hampshire."

"*I'm* a daughter," Sophie said, angry at Gisele enough to distance herself. "Lady Gisele is only a ward, but she thinks she is in command."

Gisele smiled thinly as she casually took a step sideways and ended up nearly crushing Sophie's left foot. As Sophie bit off a cry, Gisele continued to smile.

"In this case, I *am* in command," she said evenly. "You will remain in the hall until you are told otherwise. I will have food sent to you. Do you require anything further?"

Corbeau seemed to be looking at her intensely. His gaze lingered on her for a moment before he answered. "Nay, my lady, thank you," he finally said. "I… I do hope you and the other ladies will enjoy the music. It is always nice to see young women enjoying themselves with a dance. Is there any music you like in particular?"

Gisele shrugged. "I am not sure," she said. "Do you sing?"

"Very much, my lady."

"What do you like to sing?"

Corbeau looked at Bernard, gesturing for the man to pick up his citole. As the big man with the faded blond hair began to strum, Corbeau picked up the tune and began to sing.

The moon is beautiful, bright and deep,
And she has many secrets she likes to keep.
After wine and lots of sleep,
Sweet dreams come to her, with stars to reap.

He had a lovely voice, and the song was gentle and pretty. Gisele brightened. "I like that," she said. "Will you sing more tonight?"

Corbeau dipped his head gallantly. "I will, my lady," he said. "I will sing anything you wish. Mayhap you should like to hear songs from your homeland?"

"I was born in England," Gisele said. "Any song you sing of England is acceptable."

"Then mayhap you should like to hear songs of your family or the town you are from?" Corbeau said. "I know many. Different towns have different songs."

Again, Gisele shrugged. "I was born at Winchester," she said. "It is not far from here. Do you have any songs about Winchester?"

Corbeau thought a moment before shaking his head. "I do not," he said. "But I shall think of some to sing for you. It would be my honor."

With a smile of thanks, Gisele turned away from the trio, pulling Sophie, who finally broke away and rushed toward the servants' alcove on her way to the kitchens. As she moved, she made sure to show Gisele that she was removing her shoes. As she bolted from the servants' exit, shoes in hand, Gisele sighed in resignation. Sophie was lovely, naughty, and spoiled, but she was also quite charming, which made it difficult for anyone to discipline her. She was about to follow the girl's path, as she, too, was heading for the kitchens, when a shadow in her periphery caught her eye.

Fox was standing in the hall entry.

Gisele's first reaction was the same reaction she always had when she saw him—she smiled. But when she remembered their last exchange, her smile disappeared unnaturally fast and she quickly turned for the servants' alcove.

"Wait," Fox said, his voice low and firm. "Do not go. Who was singing?"

Gisele paused, gesturing to the minstrels near the darkened hearth. "Over there," she said. "They will be entertaining us tonight."

"And one of them decided to sing to you?"

"He was demonstrating a song."

"To you?"

"To me."

Fox stepped into the hall, his eyes glittering as he beheld the minstrels. "Which one?"

Gisele could immediately sense his mood. He tended to become jealous when it came to her, so this wasn't anything unusual. Realizing he was feeling fits of jealousy again, she faced him, arms folded across her chest.

"I am not going to tell you," she said frankly. "But know that other men do find me attractive. You are not the only one."

Fox looked at her. "Tell me or I'll slay all three of them."

She snorted. "I'd like to see you explain that to Lady Hampshire."

"I will tell her that they attacked you. She will applaud me."

"And I will tell her that you are lying."

"Who will they believe? A sworn knight or a lady who lets strange men sing to her?"

At this point, Gisele was trying to keep a straight face. He wasn't entirely serious, but serious enough. He could be quite petulant when the mood struck him. Turning her nose up, she looked away.

"I would rather be sung to than called stupid," she said quietly.

He knew that would come up. Inhaling deeply, he shook his head. "I said your behavior was stupid," he said softly. "I did not say *you* were stupid."

"You ruined a beautiful moment, Fox. That was cruel."

He cast her a long look. "If I hurt your feelings, I apologize," he said. "But you frighten me sometimes. I do not like being frightened."

"How on earth did I do that?"

His brow furrowed. "Think about it," he whispered. "Do you have any idea what would happen to me if you became pregnant? You would be sent to a convent at the very worst, but I… I would face judgment. I would have everything stripped from me, and you would never see me again. Is that what you want?"

Remorse rippled across her face. "You would not be sent away," she said. "But you would be forced to marry me."

He shook his head even before she finished. "You are mad if you think so," he said. "I do not wish to find out which one of us is correct. Either way, it would be a very bad thing. Is that truly how you wish to be married, Gigi? In disgrace? You would be shamed, at the very least. How can I make you understand that being patient is our only hope of a respectable marriage? If you try to force this, it will not end well for either of us."

By the time he was finished, she was tearing up. "You make it sound so terrible."

"It *will* be terrible if you do not stop being foolish and trust me," he said. "It is bad enough that I have taken your innocence before it rightfully belonged to me, but if they find out that we have been carrying on as we have… it would be a disaster."

She blinked and the tears streamed down her cheeks, tears she quickly wiped away. "I am sorry," she whispered. "It is only that I love you and I want to be with you."

He softened. "And I love you," he murmured. "But I want to do this the right way, Gigi. I want to honor you. You deserve nothing less."

"Will you not ask the Marshal again for permission to marry?" she asked. "He may have changed his mind."

Fox sighed. "The last time I asked him was two years ago," he said. "I do not think he has changed his mind."

"But you can ask," she insisted softly. "Would it help if I asked?"

"It would *not*," he said flatly. But he paused, unable to stomach her sad face. "I will think about it. Mayhap… mayhap I can think of an argument he cannot refuse. If I can think of something logical and persuasive, I will ask him again. Will that satisfy you?"

"It will."

"No more… foolishness?"

Sniffling, she shook her head and wiped at her eyes just as Sophie returned through the servants' alcove. Barefoot, with her shoes nowhere to be seen, she bound over to Gisele as the woman tried to compose herself.

"Cook says there is no room in the keep for them," Sophie said. "She says they must sleep in the hall."

Gisele nodded. "Thank you," she said. "Will you now return and ask the cook to send food to them?"

Sophie frowned. "I thought you were going to ask?"

"I stopped her," Fox said. Then he gestured toward the servants' alcove. "Please go and ask the cook. I still have business with Gigi."

Sophie rolled her eyes and turned back for the door. She had a bit of a soft spot for Fox even if he only had eyes for Gisele, so she would obey his requests above anyone else's, her parents' included. Fox watched her go before speaking again.

"If I hear that minstrel singing to you again tonight, I will cut his tongue out," he said quietly, though there was a glimmer of mirth in his eye. "See that you do not encourage him."

"I might," Gisele said, dabbing the last of her tears away. "If you do not properly worship me, I'll find someone who will."

"That is something a man would say."

She broke down into soft giggles. "I learned it from you."

Fox chuckled, giving her a sweet wink before casting a long, and unhappy, glance at the minstrels on his way out. Gisele watched him go, her heart full and light, as it usually was when she saw him. After six years, the thrill of his voice, of any interaction they had, was still there. It had grown better with time.

With a smile on her lips, she went about her duties.

CHAPTER FOUR

"**I**T *IS* HER," Bernard muttered, his mouth full of bread. "It is a stroke of fortune that we have seen her and spoken to her. Now what?"

They were sitting in a corner of the hall, which had servants moving about it in preparation for the evening's feast. They had bread, cheese, and some kind of stew between them, and they were quickly eating so they could begin playing. But the revelation of their very target had them thinking ahead to what must be done.

The real reason they were at Selborne.

Corbeau shoveled bread soaked in the stew into his mouth. "She has informed us that we will sleep in the hall," he said, chewing. "That is unfortunate, but given our profession, I did not expect better. Undoubtedly, however, she will be in the keep, so we must find a way inside. Bernard, the servants are coming in and out through that small door on the other end of the hall. Mayhap you should see what is on the other side. It could be a way in."

Bernard was still eating, but he turned to watch the busy servants as they came in through the door that was opening on a regular basis. The hall was dim, the door small, but he suspected what Corbeau suspected—it was a way into the keep.

"I would wager to say the kitchen is on the other side," he said, returning to his bread. "It is possible the kitchen is separate from the keep, you know."

"That is what you will find out."

Bernard nodded, falling silent as he finished what was left of his hearty meal. He still wasn't entirely comfortable with what they had to do, and he was trying to convince himself that this was a task, like any other. It was a young woman who meant nothing to him. But the problem was that he had two daughters himself, slightly younger than the young women they were supposed to kill.

Murder.

No, he still wasn't comfortable with it, but it wasn't as if he could refuse. The money he earned for things like this had given his daughters a chance at a decent life, and his wife finally had things she deserved. But it was at a price.

He was paying a very high price.

And there was nothing he could do about it.

CHAPTER FIVE

I T HAD BEEN a long time since Gisele had experienced such
frivolity.

The minstrels who had sought shelter for the night were
surprisingly good. They'd had musicians in the past, traveling
groups that seemed to go from castle to town to castle, looking
for shelter and food and perhaps a few coins for their performances, and sometimes those performances weren't worth the
food or the coinage. Sometimes, they could be quite terrible, but
not in this case. The three French minstrels were actually quite
good.

The night was chilly and the moon was full, casting its sil-
very glow over the landscape. Torches were lit up on the
battlements of the castle, staving off the night as the sentries
went about their duties. Inside the hall, it was smoky and smelly
and cloyingly warm as the minstrels played tune after tune,
much to the delight of the men who were crammed into the
hall. The only women in the hall were the lord's wife and
daughters, and the soldiers wouldn't dare ask those women to
dance, so they ended up dancing with each other in front of the
hearth.

It made for a loud party.

The more the evening wore on and the drunker they got, the more hilarious the dancing. Sometimes they would dance in couples, but more often than not they would simply dance in a circle or by themselves, gaily twirling about and generally making a spectacle of themselves. Gisele sat on the dais with her family, watching the dancing and enjoying a meal of boiled beef and carrots. The fare was quite good, as it usually was, because they had an excellent cook, but tonight's meal had the added attraction of the festivities and gangs of drunken soldiers.

Gisele sat between Charlotte and Sophie, watching the men dance and have a good time, while Fox and the eldest de Nerra son, Gavin, sat on the other side of Val. Theodore sat across from his father, but he was being punished after the escapade with the rooster earlier in the day. His father was permitting him to eat with the family, but he couldn't linger. When he was finished eating, he had to return to his chamber and go to bed. That being the case, Theodore was dragging out his meal to the very last drop.

"I want to dance," Sophie said wistfully. "Look at the men— they're having such a good time. I want to have a good time, too!"

She was leaning on Gisele as she said it, the woman who, only hours earlier, had been her worst enemy. Gisele's gaze lingered on the soldiers dancing to a lively tune, all of them quite drunk. She, too, would have liked to dance, but not with that lot. Worse still, Fox wasn't much of a dancer. She would have to be content to watch.

"Ask Theo to dance," she said. "Mayhap he will dance with you."

Sophie sat up, making a face. "I will *not* dance with my

brother," she said distastefully. Her focus moved down the table. "I wonder if Fox will dance with me."

"You can ask him."

Sophie was on her feet, moving down the table and interrupting the conversation between her father and her brother and Fox. They were in mid-sentence when she confronted Fox, very nearly demanding he dance with her. Before Fox could answer, Val told his daughter that it would not be proper for her to dance in a group of drunken soldiers.

After that, the battle began.

Sophie was very much like her father—stubborn and determined—but in this case, Val was the one in charge, and Sophie didn't like that. She wanted what *she* wanted. When her father denied her again and told her to sit down, she did the opposite. She ran to the area in front of the hearth where the soldiers were dancing and yelled at them, telling them all to clear away. Puzzled, the soldiers did as they were told by the fiery young de Nerra daughter, and once the area was clear of any men, Sophie began dancing by herself.

That brought her father.

Val went to his stubborn daughter and politely asked her to stop dancing and return to the table. Sophie refused, telling the minstrels that she wanted them to play something quite cheery, but the trio looked to Val for permission. Val wouldn't give it, holding up a hand to silence them, before once again asking his daughter to come away with him and sit back down. Sophie predictably refused and became quite irate at the minstrels for refusing to play. With a heavy sigh, Val went to his daughter and grabbed her by the arm, pulling her away from the minstrels as she howled. He pulled her all the way out of the hall, leaving the soldiers laughing at the antics of the youngest de Nerra, but they quickly resumed their dancing.

"I'd better go and make sure Sophie does not try to jump from the window," Vesper said, watching her husband tow their unhappy daughter from the hall. "Val tries to reason with her, but it is impossible. She needs a firm hand, and he simply will not do it."

Gisele fought off a grin as Vesper left the dais, following the path her husband and daughter had taken. She was about to comment on it to Charlotte when a hand suddenly appeared in her face.

"Come along," Gavin said. "Let us show these fools how to dance."

Gisele was reluctant, mostly because Fox had viewed Gavin as competition from time to time, even though she had only ever looked at the man like a brother. He was big and dark and handsome, and had no shortage of female company, but she'd grown up with the man. There was nothing romantic about it.

"Must I?" she said.

"You must."

"But I'll be the only woman out there."

Gavin snapped his fingers at Fox, beckoning the man's attention and pointing to Charlotte. "Dance with my sister," he ordered Fox. "Look at her—she's dying to hop about."

Fox rolled his eyes. "No offense to Charlotte, but I'd rather slit my wrists."

Gavin frowned. "What is wrong with the two of you?" he said, meaning both Fox and Gisele. Reaching out, he grasped Gisele by the wrist and pulled her to her feet. "Come along, my fine lass. Let's show them how it's done."

Gisele had no choice. As Charlotte went over to Fox to coerce him into a dance, Gavin dragged Gisele to the dancing area in front of the hearth and cleared out a wide space where they could twirl. Commanding the minstrels to play something lively, a jaunty tune filled the air and Gavin began to move.

Unfortunately, Gisele did not.

She wasn't sure what dance he was engaging in, as there were many she'd been taught, but the truth was that she'd never been any good at them. Aye, she loved to dance, just like most young women, but she didn't have a good deal of grace when it came to the movements. Gavin was a few steps into the dance when he realized she wasn't following him, and, frustrated, he positioned both of her arms correctly and began coaching her on which direction to go in, which foot to place first, and so forth.

For Gisele, it was as painful as pulling teeth.

In fact, she would have preferred that.

But her embarrassment wasn't for long. When Fox and Charlotte appeared, Charlotte had to do the exact same thing for Fox. He was quite coordinated, even graceful at times, but he simply hated to dance, and, more particularly, he didn't want to do it with Charlotte. He and Gisele kept glancing at each other as they twirled around with different partners, and at one point in the dance, all four of them joined hands and danced in a circle. When they'd finished taking a couple of turns around the circle, they broke off into couples again, but Fox immediately went for Gisele, leaving Charlotte and Gavin to pair up.

When she realized her handsome partner had left her for someone else, Charlotte stamped her foot angrily and rushed off in a huff, leaving Gavin standing alone. With his sister having a tantrum, Gavin looked at Fox and Gisele, who now had their arms intertwined, and shook his head in resignation. He knew it would do no good to try to get his partner back.

With a lift of the shoulders, he headed back to the dais.

Fox simply grinned.

"You do not have to continue dancing if you do not wish to," he told Gisele. "I know this is not your favorite activity."

Gisele smiled slyly. "Why would we stop?" she said. "I can touch you in front of everyone, and it is perfectly proper. I should not wish to pass up this chance."

Fox watched her, his eyes glimmering. "Agreed," he said softly. "I should not wish to pass up this chance, either."

"Then you will continue to dance?"

"As long as you wish, my love."

Gisele's smile broadened as she twirled around and, at one point, crossed in front of Fox and tripped on her own feet. Fox had to grasp her quickly to steady her, which he did with pleasure. Any chance to touch her. Just as he was pulling her in for another twirl, the music came to a halt, and they were forced to separate. As Gisele curtsied to him, smiling sweetly, Fox didn't think his heart could be any fuller.

He began to think of their earlier conversation.

Perhaps she was right. Perhaps he did love his career more than they loved her, because, at the moment, he couldn't really remember why he refused to run away with her. He was starting to think that perhaps he *was* putting his own ambitions over what was important in life—the love of a good woman. He knew that if he searched his entire life, he would never find someone like Gisele. She was a once-in-a-lifetime woman, a rarity in a world that was harsh and cruel, and where love often didn't matter in the long run when it came to a marriage.

But for some, it did.

Fox had seen plenty of miserable marriages in his lifetime. In fact, other than the Earl of Hampshire and his wife, he couldn't really think of a marriage he knew of that was a happy one. They were so rare. He knew that he and Gisele shared something very special, and as he looked at her and the lovely dress, with her hair flowing and beautiful, he knew that he simply couldn't give up on what they had. He had told her he would wait for her, and it didn't matter how old she was, but the truth was that it mattered to her. She wanted to marry him now.

God, was he really putting his own selfish wants over her?

As Fox debated that very question, the minstrels began to play again, and the same man who had sung to Gisele earlier in the day was now singing again. Fox turned to see a man with bushy eyebrows and bright eyes singing a ballad as he gazed quite intently at Gisele. Feeling his jealousy rise, Fox turned to see how Gisele was reacting to the attention, and he was immediately inflamed by the expression on her face. She was smiling at the singer in a way that she should only be smiling at him. When she gave the minstrel a little wave, the mood was set.

And it wasn't good.

Fox had never been very good at controlling his jealousy when it came to Gisele. In the early years of their association, he simply attributed it to his protective nature. That was what he told everyone, and that was what everyone believed, but as he grew older, he knew that it wasn't simply protectiveness. It wasn't the fact that guarding her was his task. It was the fact that he felt something for her, so the feelings of jealousy were not new.

Infuriated, he simply turned and walked away.

Gisele was well aware that Fox had stormed off. She had to admit that she was rather cruel when it came to playing on his jealousies because the truth was that, in a way, she needed that reinforcement that he felt something for her and truly did love her, and in her immature mind, watching his fits of jealousy proved that he really did. It was a stupid game they'd played for years. Therefore, she let him walk away, thinking he'd gone back to the dais to stew. When she glanced over her shoulder to see where he was sitting, she was surprised to see that he hadn't returned to the table at all. A glance around the great hall showed that it was empty of Fox, so she left the minstrel singing his sweet ballad and rushed from the hall and out into the darkened bailey beyond.

Fox was halfway across the bailey when Gisele spied him, and it looked as if he might be heading for the knights' quarters, so she trotted after him.

"Fox!" she called. "Wait!"

He didn't slow down. He kept walking at a clipped pace, and she had to run in order to catch up with him. By the time she reached him, he was nearly to the old door of the knights' quarters. In fact, he put his hand on the latch, but Gisele practically threw herself against the door to stop him.

"Wait!" she said again, putting herself between Fox and the panel. "Where on earth are you going?"

His jaw flexed as he looked at her. "To bed," he said. "Clearly, there is no reason for me to remain in the great hall."

Gisele could see how upset he was, and she fought off a grin, leaning back against the door so he couldn't open it. "I am in the great hall," she said softly. "Am I not reason enough?"

"You do not need me there."

"I will always need you, Fox."

He grunted and yanked the door open so that she stumbled away. After stepping through, he slammed it behind him. When

Gisele rushed over to open it up, she found that it was locked. He'd bolted it from the inside. Rattling the latch, she banged on the door.

"Fox!" she shouted. "Open the door this instant!"

"Why?" he called from the other side. "So you can test me and tease me? I do not deserve that, Gigi."

She sighed heavily. "I was not testing you, nor was I teasing you," she said. "The minstrel is an old man, Fox. Do you really think he is a serious threat to you?"

"Threat or not, you have behaved in such ways before to make me jealous," he said. "It does not matter who it is—a squire or an old man, or any male of convenience. You do it to hurt me. If you do not like my reaction, then mayhap you should not do it."

She stopped rattling the door, looking at the panel as if to see him on the other side. "We go through this too much," she said after a moment. "You grow jealous even when I've done nothing wrong. Is it a lack of trust that makes you this way? Have I ever run after another man? Have I ever even pretended to? Of course I have not. But you think the worst of me. You must not trust me at all."

The door was yanked open and he stood there, glaring at her. "I trust you," he said. "It is everyone else I do not trust. Need I remind you that I was sent to protect you from harm? It is my duty not to trust anyone else, yet in moments like this, you taunt me and tease me because you are trying to draw a reaction from me to make you feel special. As if you have all of the power and can control me to your whim. That is not a fair way to treat me, and you know it."

She was trying not to get defensive. "You take this far too seriously."

"How would you feel if I did the same thing to you?" he snapped back. "You know there are many young women who would not treat me the way you do. What if I were to flirt with them and then tell you that you were foolish to react to it?"

By this time, Gisele was starting to pout. "That is not fair."

"Of course it's not fair," he said. Then he pointed a finger in her face. "You are a grown woman, Gisele. It is time you started to act like one. If you love me, act like it. But if you are not sure, then you had better tell me now."

Her pout had turned into anger. "I have been telling you for six years that I love you," she said. "It is *you* who does not love me enough to marry me, so do not turn this around on me as if I am the one with the problem."

"And you know why I cannot marry you."

She took a step back, being lured into an argument that was becoming increasingly tense between them. "Because you are a coward," she said. "Your words of love to me are empty, Fox. You tell me you love me, you bed me regularly, but there is no action behind your declaration of love. Is that all I have become to you? A convenience? Something to toy with? As long as you tell me you love me, you are telling me what I want to hear, and I give you want you want. I give you all of me. But that is as far as it goes, because when it comes to true action and proving that love for me, you will not do it."

He was grossly displeased with her by the time she was finished. "Now I must prove my love to you, and the only way to do that is marriage?"

"Actions speak louder than words."

His eyebrows lifted. "If that is true, your words speak quite loudly," he said. "You do not get what you want, so you throw a tantrum. Honor and patience mean nothing to you, Gigi. If you do not get what you want immediately, then I am a coward and my words are meaningless. Am I understanding you correctly?"

"You are."

"I just wanted to make sure," he said, but something in his eyes cooled. "Now I know what you truly think of me, so I will bid you a good evening, Lady Gisele. Sleep well."

The door shut in her face. Infuriated and deeply saddened that he'd ended their conversation on such a sour note, Gisele turned away as the tears began to flow. Was he right? Was she throwing a tantrum and tossing out insults because she wasn't getting her way in all things? Or did her desperation stem from a desire to marry the man she loved and bear his children, to have a home of her own and live a life that all normal young women wanted to live?

Gisele had to take a hard look at herself.

So much of her life was beyond her control. It always had been. Fox was the one constant, and she'd loved him from an early age, but perhaps that was the problem—she was singularly focused on him. He'd always been with her and, God willing, always would be, but they were in a quagmire of stagnation when it came to their relationship. Trying not to openly sob, she furiously wiped the tears away as she headed toward the keep. If Fox wasn't going to ask William Marshal again for her hand in marriage, then perhaps she would. Fox had told her not to, but she wasn't going to listen to him. If she didn't take the initiative, she'd be an old maid by the time they were permitted to marry—*if* they were permitted to marry.

Perhaps her real father needed to know her wants and feelings.

Perhaps it was time for the Marshal to be put on notice.

CHAPTER SIX

I T WAS VERY late.

The fire in the hearth of the great hall was burning low at this hour, but the hall was surprisingly cozy. Corbeau and Bernard were sleeping next to the warm bricks, feeling the heat radiating through their bedrolls. Everything was dark and quiet around them, with a few soldiers sleeping in the hall in different corners, but Corbeau and Bernard were quite alone. In fact, it was just the two of them.

Edouard was inside the keep.

That was something they'd worked out as soon as their target had left the hall, following the path of the enormous knight she had been dancing with. While Corbeau continued singing and Bernard continued playing his lute, Edouard had slipped out toward the servants' alcove, blending in with the servants going in and out of the kitchens, which were in the sublevel of the keep along with the storage. He'd managed to get inside and hide so that when the keep was locked up for the night, he remained.

They needed someone to unlock the door for them.

It was all very clever.

Corbeau had been feigning sleep, but the truth was that he had been awake, watching the servants come and go and then, finally, the soldiers settling down for the night. When the last soldier settled down, the candles were extinguished, and the snoring began, he waited a nominal amount of time before elbowing Bernard.

"It is time," he whispered. "We must go."

Bernard yawned but he was up, taking two daggers with him as he and Corbeau snuck across the hall, staying low so they were almost level with the tabletops. Their movement would be less noticeable if anyone happened to be awake. They headed for the servants' alcove, the door of which was bolted from the inside, so they moved the squeaky bolt and prayed that no one would hear them. Every pull on the bolt resulted in a new squeak, and there were four pulls until the bolt finally came free and they were able to open the door.

They were over the first hurdle.

It was dark and cold outside, with a brilliant moon overhead, as they moved swiftly for the keep. They had to pass through some open space near the stables before coming to the gate to the kitchen yard, and they had to dodge their way over to it because of the sentries on the wall. Not wanting to be seen, they stayed to the shadows until they made it to the yard gate. When a pair of nearby sentries headed in the other direction, they quickly opened the gate and slipped through. Once inside the yard, they were able to make it over to the kitchen door without being seen.

Then the wait began.

It was at least two hours before the door finally rattled. Bernard had been sleeping against the wall of the keep while Corbeau kept watch. He was edgy and nervous, and furious that

Edouard had taken so long. But when the door finally creaked open, Corbeau and Bernard slipped in quickly, into the dark kitchens, where they found a place to hide.

Hiding under a table, they struggled to find their bearings in the blackness of the kitchen.

"We cannot stay here too long," Bernard whispered. "The kitchen servants will be up before dawn to bake bread, and they will find us here. We must move quickly."

Corbeau knew that. The smell of smoke and wood and yeast and myriad other food smells filled his nostrils—comforting smells, but he was there for a purpose. His target was somewhere in this keep, and he was going to find her, but the trick would be finding her and avoiding the enormous Earl of Hampshire, who was also probably in the keep. That was an obstacle they'd realized fairly early in the evening when they were introduced to Hampshire.

Corbeau didn't want to face that man in a fight.

But duty and money compelled him forward. He'd been partially paid for this task already, and a king's ransom awaited him and his friends once the job was completed. Money that would see him buy a home for his eldest son, a simpleton of a man who could hardly dress himself. With the money, he could buy the lad a home and pay for someone to help take care of him. Perhaps his son could even learn to be useful with a small garden to tend. Or perhaps he could learn a trade. In any case, Corbeau was determined to see his mission through.

He had to make it to the upper floors.

Silently, he motioned to Bernard and Edouard, slinking out of his hiding place and into the darkness, finding the small, narrow stairs that led up into the levels above. The three of them were able to make it into the keep entry, dark and barren at that hour, but they could see the mural stairs that led into the living areas above. That was where they'd find their target. Bernard had his daggers in both hands as they began to make their way up the steps.

One dark, dusty stone at a time.

ᛤ

HE COULDN'T SLEEP.

Fox had tried, but all he'd managed to do was toss and turn. He could not stop thinking about his last words with Gisele. It was true that over the past couple of years they'd had similar conversations that ended similarly, but this one was different. He'd never shut a door in her face before. He didn't like that she had called him a coward, probably because that was the very thing he had been wrestling with himself. He'd been wondering if his actions had been selfish and cowardly, only she had been brave enough, or perhaps bold enough, to actually put it into words.

Putting his selfishness in the words.

In that instance, she wasn't wrong. At least, he was coming to think she wasn't wrong. Normally, after these discussions, he simply went about his duties and forgot about it. It was something that usually blew over. He wasn't sure why this conversation was different, except for the fact that a look in her eyes when she called him a coward had been so... cold. There had been something cold in her eyes, and it had, in turn, caused him to be cold as well. It simply didn't seem natural for him to be cold where it pertained to her, and after tossing and fidgeting for several hours in his bed, he decided to do something about it.

He was going to seek her out.

But it was more than that.

Fox hated to admit that he'd always had a strange intuition where Gisele was concerned. That had started years ago, and he'd always believed it was the result of the fact that he had been assigned to protect her, so his intuition when it came to her was always overreactive. When he had first been assigned to guard her, he worried about her constantly. He worried that when he was sleeping, the entire criminal population of England was on her doorstep, plotting to abduct her. Perhaps it was an overactive imagination, or perhaps not. He'd never quite been able to figure that one out, but as he pulled on his breeches and yanked the tunic over his head, he was feeling increasingly pulled toward her.

He had to see her immediately.

Unfortunately, he knew where she was, and that was in the locked keep. It wasn't as if he hadn't broken into the keep before to get to her, because there were times when he simply couldn't stand being away from her, not even for a night. Usually, the lock on the kitchen door was easily manipulated, and he'd been able to get in that way many times. As he headed out of the knights' quarters, he was resigned to the fact that he would once again be picking the lock on the kitchen door to get to the woman he loved.

He'd become quite good at it over the years.

It was a brilliant night, if a little cold, with a bright moon in the sky that was beginning to set. He could see the sentries on the wall, their torches blazing against the darkness. He crossed the bailey and made his way to the area between the hall and the stables and the kitchen yard. The very same yard where he had saved Gisele and Charlotte from the raging rooster. Passing through the gate into the yard, he went straight for the kitchen door.

There was a lock, usually set at night, but in times of trouble there was also an enormous iron bolt on the inside that secured the door regardless of whether or not the lock was engaged. He'd brought a small dagger with him because he needed that to pick the lock, and after a few tries, and a little bit of jiggling, the lock popped open. Opening the panel, he slid inside.

Now, it was simply a matter of making it up the stairs to Gisele's chamber without being seen or heard. That had happened once or twice in the past, and he'd been forced to hide in the shadows until the earl or his wife went back to bed after inspecting the bedchambers for the source of the mysterious sounds. He swore one time that Val saw him, or at least the outline of him, but the earl never called him out on it. If he saw him, he'd simply ignored it, but considering Fox's entire purpose for being at Selborne Castle was to guard Gisele, perhaps the man had merely resigned himself to the fact that the lady's guard was always present, in any circumstance.

Truth be told, however, Fox didn't think Val was that stupid.

He suspected the man knew what was going on.

As he entered the dark and vacant foyer, a smile creased his lips as he thought of the earl and the position the man found himself in. Val and his wife had raised Gisele, essentially, so he was for all intents and purposes her father, only he wasn't. In this case, he was simply making sure she was safe and sheltered and protected, but the man had never really disciplined her. It wasn't unusual, because Val didn't seem to discipline any of his daughters, so the women at Selborne Castle tended to have free rein of the place, Gisele included. That bold, determined woman that he loved so much was used to having her way, and

Val de Nerra was to blame for it.

Damn the man.

But Fox didn't blame him.

Fox, too, was willing to let her have her way in all things. He knew it and she knew it, and no matter what they'd said to one another earlier, he felt bad about their fight and simply had to apologize before another hour passed. He further realized that he had to speak to William Marshal again. He was coming to think that Gisele had, indeed, been correct. He *was* a selfish coward. But thoughts of an apology and of the joy in forgiveness were his last calm thoughts before screaming filled the air.

After that, there was only chaos.

CHAPTER SEVEN

G ISELE WAS IN a dead sleep when someone put a hand over her mouth and dragged her onto the floor. Disoriented and terrified, she tried to scream, but hands were around her throat. That sent her into a panic, and she began to kick and fight, catching whoever had her off guard. A well-placed hand to the throat of her attacker was enough to cause him to loosen his grip on her throat and on her mouth. She knew it was a man because he was big and he was strong, but when the hand came away from her mouth, she screamed as loud as she could.

She wasn't sure she would get another chance.

Across the chamber, Charlotte awoke to a struggle. There were people in the chamber, she could see in the darkness, and when they saw that she was awake, one of them rushed toward her. Frightened out of her wits, she screamed loud enough to be heard in Scotland, which roused the entire keep. As the figure running toward her tried to grab her by falling on the bed, she leapt out of his way and raced to the door, which was already open. Charlotte's piercing scream brought her father barreling down the stairs with his broadsword in hand, while racing up the stairs came another figure. Both Charlotte and Val caught a glimpse of Fox before Val charged into the chamber, only to be met by a man with a sword.

With that, the fight was on.

Gisele was in a bad way. She'd managed to roll underneath her bed, but two of the three attackers in the room were trying to get at her. One of the men had daggers, but Fox was on the man in an instant. Val quickly dispatched the man who had challenged him, shouting at Fox as he raced to protect Gisele.

"Fox!" he boomed. "Take it!"

Fox turned just as Val tossed his broadsword, the hilt end of it sailing toward Fox, who deftly caught it. The weapon was quite weighty on the pommel, which was fortunate, considering Val was throwing a razor-sharp blade at him. But Fox managed to grab it, turning it on a man who had two daggers in his hand. Unfortunately, in the moment Fox took to catch Val's weapon, one of those daggers sliced him on the arm. But Fox hardly felt it—all he was concerned with was dispatching the men who had broken into the keep and were trying to kill the women.

Kill Gisele.

That realization brought blind rage. Fox's sword arced wickedly in the faint light of the hearth as he sliced off one of the man's hands. The hand, still holding the dagger, fell to the ground as the man screamed in pain. Another arc of the blade saw the man's head separated from his body. The body collapsed at his feet and the head landed somewhere over near Val, who leapt over it as it rolled on the floor. He was heading for the bed, where an attacker had Gisele by an ankle, but that ended abruptly when Fox bounded over the bedframe, cutting the man's arm in two. From the elbow down, his left arm still held Gisele's ankle but quickly fell away when she kicked it. Meanwhile, Val had the man by the hair, yanking him away from the bed and from Gisele. Fox descended on him, the tip of the bloodied sword pointed right at the man's neck.

At that point, the fight was over.

"Who in the hell are you?" Val demanded, pulling the man's head up by the hair. The light was still weak, but there was enough to see the features, and Val's eyes widened. "Damnation... the minstrel!"

The man, with bushy eyebrows and bulging eyes, was holding his left arm aloft, pain rippling across his pale face.

"I am better at singing, my lord," he said, grunting in agony. "But now, it seems, I shall never play my citole again."

He laughed with irony, and Fox jabbed him in the neck with the tip of the sword. "Shut your lips," he growled. "Who are you? Who has sent you?"

The man looked at him, his eyes reflecting the misery of his defeat. "I am Corbeau," he said. "My friends were Bernard and Edouard. We have been together for many years."

"As assassins?" Fox said, dropping the sword and jerking the man into a sitting position. It was clear he could no longer do any damage. "Tell me the truth and I will end your life painlessly. Refuse and I will cut each finger from your hand, followed by the hand itself, and pieces of your arms, until you have nothing left. I will carve you like a Christmas goose, so it is in your best interest to tell me everything."

"Why?" Corbeau said, trying not to look at his severed arm. "It does not matter what I tell you. All you should know is that they will not stop."

"Who will not stop?"

"Those who want the princess dead. Anyone standing in the way will be killed, too."

Fox was about to point the broadsword at the man's neck

again, but Val put up a hand, silently telling him to cease. As he was the former itinerant justice of Hampshire and one of the leading men for law in the country, a situation like this was better suited to his particular talents. He knew what he had to do.

He looked Corbeau in the eye.

"I want you to understand something clearly," he said calmly. "I have the power to find out who you are and where you came from. It may take some time, but I will do it. Then I will find out if you have any family. If you do, I will send men to kill them. Your sons will be murdered, your daughters cut into pieces for the dogs, and your wife... Let us say that your wife will watch it all before we finally make sure she joins your children in hell. Do you understand what I have told you so far?"

By the time he was finished, Corbeau was pasty with regret and horror. He had his arm elevated, so he wasn't dead yet, but he knew he would be shortly. He knew they would not tend his arm, so it was only a matter of time before the blood drained out of him. With Bernard and Edouard dead, his entire mission was at an end.

Everything was gone.

He felt a stab of regret at that, but he also knew something like this had always been a possibility. He was a pragmatic man. Now, it would be a matter of saving those he left behind, because there was no reason for him to remain silent if it would keep the English dogs away from his family. He didn't doubt the older warrior's threat for a moment. Not one damn moment. But he also knew he had a bargaining chip—he knew something they wanted to know, and there was a price for that knowledge.

The tables were about to turn.

"If I tell you, will you send men to protect them?" he asked, his lips quivering.

Val was looking at him seriously. "From whom?"

"Angoulême."

Val was momentarily puzzled. "Angoulême," he repeated. "The queen, you mean?"

Corbeau shook his head. "Her father," he said. "We have come at the command of her father."

Val's puzzlement grew. "Why in the hell would Ademar send someone to my home?" he said, scowling. "I do not personally know the man. We have no quarrel."

He referred to the comte by his given name rather than his title. Corbeau shook his head, but he was growing weak. "Not you," he said, his gaze fixing on someone behind them. "*Her.*"

Both Fox and Val turned to see who the man was looking at, and they weren't surprised to see Gisele standing several feet away, in the arms of Charlotte and Vesper. Val's gaze lingered on Gisele a moment before he returned his attention to Corbeau. He had a very bad feeling in the pit of his stomach.

"The woman you were trying to grab under the bed?" he asked.

Corbeau nodded. "Aye."

Val didn't dare look at Fox, fearful he'd see a surge of rage in the man's eyes. "Why her?" he asked quietly. "Why does the Comte de Angoulême want her dead?"

Corbeau had to take a deep breath because he was starting to feel faint. "He does not," he said. "But his daughter does. It was Isabella who asked her father to send us. She wants the girl dead because she is a threat to her husband's rule. As she is the daughter of the Young King, there are those who could seek to supplant John with her. You know this, my lord, do you not? Surely you know the identity of the woman in your home."

Val's jaw twitched as he finally looked to Fox, who was riveted to Corbeau. He looked coiled enough to snap.

"Does John know about this?" Val asked after a moment.

Corbeau was beginning to fade. The arteries in his arm were pumping bright red blood all down his arm, his torso, and onto the floor. It was only a matter of time before the heart would pump no more.

"Nay," he said, his eyes drooping. "Isabella is the dangerous one. For her husband's sake, she will not stop until Gisele of England is dead. And I... I must have your word, my lord. My family... Will you... you..."

He never finished his sentence. His eyes closed and his head tilted to one side as he took his last breath. Fox let go of him, letting the man fall to the floor as he stood up, gazing down upon him and realizing what had happened this night. His worst nightmare had come to life, and had he not been in the keep already, it would have had devastating consequences. Three assassins, all of them trying to kill Gisele, and that strange intuition he had when it came to her safety had put him in the right place at the right time. This time, anyway, because based on what Corbeau had told them, this wasn't some random attack. The order for Gisele's death had come from the highest level.

Fox was still trying to come to grips with the news.

"Papa!"

Gavin was suddenly in the doorway with several soldiers, all of them armed to the teeth. When he saw all of the blood and carnage, his eyes widened.

"Jesus," he said. "What has happened here?"

Wearily, Val stood up from his crouched position. "Get these... these bodies out of here," he commanded quietly, motioning to the dead in the chamber. Then he looked to his wife, who was standing several feet away with Gisele and Charlotte in her arms. "Get them out of here, love. Take the children upstairs and put them to bed, all of them."

"Wait," Fox said, looking to Gisele. "Did they injure you?"

Gisele was verging on terrified tears, but she shook her head quickly. "Nay," she whispered tightly. "I am unharmed."

That was good enough for Fox to let her go with Vesper. The countess pulled Charlotte and Gisele out of the chamber, running in to Sophie and Theodore out on the landing. The two youngest de Nerra children were terrified, and Vesper took them to the floor above with her, taking all of them into her vast chamber. With the children being tended to, Gavin's men moved into the room and began hauling out the bodies—and the pieces of them. As the soldiers were moving out, Gavin went over to Fox and his father.

"What in the hell happened?" he demanded, confused by the entire happenstance. "Who were those men, and how did they get in here?"

Val watched one of the soldiers pull Corbeau out of the chamber by his ankles. "Those were the minstrels who sang in the hall tonight," he told his son. "But they were not minstrels as much as they were assassins, sent by Queen Isabella's father, Ademar."

Gavin was completely lost. "Ademar?" he repeated. "But why? Assassins for whom?"

"Gisele."

Now, Gavin understood a little more. He, too, knew who Gisele's true parents were, so he wasn't surprised. But he was concerned. He stood aside as one of the soldiers picked up Corbeau's severed arm from the floor and carried it out.

"So we have assassins again," he muttered, eyeing his father. "Years ago, we had the pair that tried to enlist as Hampshire soldiers."

"I remember."

"They did not make it this far."

"Nay, they did not, thanks to Fox."

"And when Gigi was first brought here as a child, there was that nurse who tried to abduct her."

"I remember."

This wasn't the first time an attempt was made on Gisele. But that was something they never spoke of. They tried to pretend everything was fine, always, and they were one big, happy family, safe and unfettered.

But that wasn't the case.

The old nurse who had been loyal to Queen Margaret, Gisele's mother, had wanted to abduct the infant and return her to the queen, but she'd been stopped and disposed of by Val himself. Then there had been two assassins who posed as soldiers to get into the same fortress as eleven-year-old Gisele. No one was ever sure where they'd come from because Fox had killed them before they could be interrogated, but suspicions were that they'd come from enemies of Young Henry. And now, Queen Isabella was in the mix of enemies wanting to see an innocent young girl dead.

It wouldn't be the last time, they knew.

It was something they could no longer ignore.

"Papa," Gavin said hesitantly. "This is the third time."

"I am well aware, Gavin."

But that wasn't good enough for Gavin. He glanced at Fox,

whose gaze was fixed on the floor, before returning his focus to his father. "But this time, they made it inside," he pointed out, as if his father didn't already know it. "They could have killed her, or Lottie, or Mama. They could have killed any of the women who got in their way."

Val couldn't maintain eye contact. He ended up looking at the blood on the floor. "I realize that," he said. Then he snorted wearily. "I had hoped that John had forgotten about the woman he believes to be his brother's child, but it seems that is not the case. This time, Isabella is after her."

Gavin shook his head. "And she will send others, since these assassins failed."

"That is what one of the assassins said."

"Then it is true," Gavin said firmly before returning his focus to Fox. "I know you have been sent to protect Gisele, but we must be realistic. Gisele's mere presence is putting my entire family at risk."

Val threw up a hand to stop his son's tirade. "Hold," he commanded softly. "Gisele did not cause this."

Gavin wasn't having any of it. "What do you mean she did not cause this?" he said, pointing at all of the blood around the chamber. "These men would not be here were it not for her. Of course she caused this."

"You cannot blame her."

"Would you say that if Lottie was lying dead on the floor right now?" Gavin said, becoming angry. "Or what if Mama took a broadsword to the chest trying to protect Lottie and Gisele? Would you be so calm about the situation then?"

Val didn't say anything. He turned away from his son and away from Fox, who had so far remained silent through Gavin's tirade, and wandered over to Charlotte's messy bed. He was a man lost in thought, because something critical had happened this night, something that could quite possibly change the situation at Selborne. Perhaps, in the back of his mind, he had always known the situation with Gisele would come to a head, but he was honestly hoping those who might view her as an enemy would simply fade away. There were always political enemies and targets, but they tended to change with the seasons.

But not this time.

Everyone believed Gisele to be the child of Henry the Young King. The *only* child. That was where the problem lay. No one knew she was, in fact, the offspring of William Marshal, though Val knew there had been rumor to that effect when she was first born. Val and William Marshal were old friends, and that was why he'd agreed to take the girl and raise her. He loved her like a daughter, but the truth was that she wasn't *his* daughter. More than that, Gavin was right—Charlotte could have been collateral damage, and in that case, he would have never forgiven himself for putting her in such danger.

Had what he'd tried to ignore finally come to pass?

Val was a fair and just man. He'd built a reputation on that. But when it came to the women he loved—and a woman he considered his daughter—he was having a difficult time separating the pragmatic lord from the protective father. His gut told him what he needed to do, but his heart was standing in the way.

After several long moments, he turned to the knights be-hind him.

"Have the servants clean up this blood quickly," he told Gavin. "Fox, come with me."

Leaving a frustrated Gavin to order the servants around,

Val headed to the floor above with Fox on his heels. It was quiet on this level, not even a whisper, so he silently told Fox to stand by the master chamber door while he continued inside.

Vesper was sitting near the hearth with Sophie in her arms, rocking her sleeping daughter even though the child was well beyond rocking age. Curious, Val peered over at the enormous bed he shared with his wife only to see Charlotte, Gisele, and Theodore sleeping in it. All of the children who remained living under his roof, except for Gavin, were in that chamber, safe and sleeping. Silently, Val bent over Vesper and gently scooped Sophie from her arms, before going over to the bed and carefully laying her next to her brother. He smiled when he realized how unhappy that would make her when she awoke and found herself sleeping next to Theodore, because the pair were like oil and water, but they looked rather sweet tucked in together.

His children.

He had to protect his children.

The smile faded from his face as he turned to Vesper, who was looking at him rather anxiously. He went to her, taking her by the hand and pulling her over to the door, which was cracked open. She didn't know Fox was on the other side of it, and that was his intention. He wanted Fox to hear what he, and Vesper, had to say, but he didn't want his wife to know. He was afraid she wouldn't give her honest opinion if she knew Fox was listening.

"Are Gigi and Lottie well?" he whispered. "They did not suffer any injury?"

Vesper shook her head. "None," she said. "Although Gigi has a scratch on her ankle where she was grabbed, it is nothing serious."

Val sighed with relief. "That is good."

Vesper reached out, grasping his hand. "Who were those men?" she said, finally allowing him to see the fear in her eyes. "How did they get in?"

Val lifted her hand to his lips for a gentle kiss. "Assassins sent by Queen Isabella," he murmured. "Evidently, she is trying to eliminate any threat to John's throne, though I am surprised to know it is her. She never seemed to take much interest in her husband or England in general."

Vesper pondered the news before speaking. "I've heard he is very cruel toward her," she muttered. "She is a young wife, and he does not pay her much attention. But imagine what attention he would pay to her if he knew she would kill for him."

"You think she is trying to gain his favor?"

"Why else?"

Val grunted softly, shaking his head to the idea of a young queen and her quest to prove her loyalty to an apathetic husband. "If that is true, then Gigi is in great danger," he whispered. "Gavin is afraid that the assassins will come back, and then come back again, and Lottie or even you or Sophie might be in danger. Because Gigi is in danger, you are all in danger."

Vesper's gaze moved to the bed where Gisele and Charlotte were sleeping soundly, but Theodore had evidently kicked Sophie, and she was half-asleep as she kicked him back. Her features rippled with sadness, with concern, and perhaps even indecision. As attached as Val was to his children, including the woman he'd raised from infancy, Vesper was even more attached.

It wasn't an easy situation for any of them.

"The moment Gigi was placed in my arms as an infant, I

knew I loved her," Vesper whispered. "She was such a beautiful baby. Remember?"

Val nodded. He, too, was looking over at the bed. "I do," he murmured. "All of our children to that point had been so strange looking as infants that I remember thinking Gisele was perfect."

Vesper looked at her husband, frowning though she was on the verge of laughter. "What a terrible thing to say," she said.

"It was true."

"They all looked like *you*."

Val snorted, trying to keep quiet as Sophie and Theodore finally settled down. When the bed was still again, he looked at his wife.

"I love Gigi," he said. "If this was my decision, I would keep her with us forever and protect her to the death. But it is not up to me."

Vesper looked at him. "Why do you say that?"

Val put his big arm around her shoulders, pulling her against his torso. "Because I have committed a terrible sin," he said. "I have fallen in love with her. She is my child and I love her like a daughter. But the truth is that she isn't—and our real children are potentially in danger because of her. *You* are potentially in danger because of her. I need your clear head, love. I need your counsel. Does she stay? Or does she go?"

Vesper's gaze was still lingering on the bed. Charlotte, on the end, had begun to snore. "If one of the children born of my body were in danger, would you send him or her away?"

"Nay," he said. "But she was not born of your body. When she came here, we knew there might be trouble. We've been fortunate that our own children have not been injured in the attempt to get to Gigi, but I fear that luck may not hold forever."

Vesper looked at him. "What do you want to do?"

"I could not live with myself if something happened to my family."

"But where would you send her?" Vesper asked, deeply concerned. "Where would she go?"

Val sighed faintly. "The Marshal gave me explicit instructions on what to do should her presence at Selborne become impossible to maintain," he said. "He has made arrangements with Canonsleigh Abbey in Devon to take her in. She will become a postulate and, eventually, a nun. He wanted me to send her there when she came of age, but I could not bring myself to do it. Another failure of mine."

Vesper was surprised. "And you did not tell me this?"

He shook his head. "There was no need to," he said. "But now it may be her only hope of safety."

Vesper was stricken with the news. "That is why Pembroke would not allow her to marry."

"Exactly."

"Does Fox know this?"

Knowing Fox was on the other side of the door, Val felt rather bad that the man was hearing such information for the first time. "He has not been told before this moment," he said. It was the truth. "But the Marshal never intended his daughter to marry. I received the impression from him that because she was a bastard, he felt the best place for her would be in a nunnery. Mayhap God will not judge her so harshly for her sinful birth were she to devote her life to him."

Vesper's mouth had popped open in shock. She again looked to the bed, where Charlotte was snoring loudly, and shook her head with sorrow.

"Poor Gigi," she whispered. "She wants to marry Fox."

"I know."

"She has wanted that for a very long time."

"There is nothing I can do about it," Val said. "I am not trying to sound cruel, but this decision came from the Marshal. I must follow his directive. Mayhap it is best to move her to Canonsleigh now so that she will be safe... and so will our children."

Vesper pulled away from him, taking a few steps toward the bed as she wrung her hands. It was clear that she was torn, as only a mother could be, but it was also clear that she was thinking on what Val had told her.

Mayhap it is best...

As a mother, she was protective, even of a child she had not borne. But for the sake of her children by blood, she knew there was only one decision she could make.

And her heart was breaking.

"We must protect our children, Val," she finally muttered, tears glistening in her eyes. "Send Gigi to Canonsleigh and make it known that Gisele of Hampshire no longer lives at Selborne. That should deter her enemies well enough. Even if they discover where she is, they will be unable to get to her. She will be safe, and so will we. But if she remains here... I fear that it will be bad for all of us."

"Aye, it will."

"We must send her away so she will be safe because, clearly, we cannot protect her."

The decision had been made. As difficult as it was, as heart-wrenching as it was, it was the only decision that *could* be made. Val simply nodded, leaning in to kiss Vesper gently before leaving the chamber and shutting the door softly behind him. In the dimness of the landing, he could see Fox standing over near the stairwell. Knowing the man had just heard some devastating information, he made his way over slowly.

"You already knew," Fox said before Val could speak. "You already knew that there was no chance for me to marry Gigi, yet you did not tell me."

Val wasn't surprised that was the first thing out of Fox's mouth. He knew the pair were in love—everyone at Selborne knew. He'd tried to discourage it in the beginning, but in spite of his admonitions, the love between Fox and Gisele could not be cooled. It grew, and he finally gave up trying to prevent it because it was stronger than he was. When Fox approached the Marshal for Gisele's hand, Val had known what the answer would be, but he didn't try to stop him. Better Fox be deterred by the Marshal himself.

But now...

"I could not tell you," he said. "Fox, Gigi is not my daughter. Pembroke already has her life preordained."

"You should have told me."

"Pembroke is the only one who can tell you something like that," Val said, growing stern. "It is not my place. But now you know, and, on the morrow, you will escort Gigi to Canonsleigh Abbey in Devon. She must go tomorrow, Fox."

Fox's composure fractured. "Tomorrow? But... why? Why so soon? If Isabella sends more assassins, it will be months from now. Why must she leave tomorrow?"

Val could hear the pain in Fox's voice. "Would you prefer to draw this out?" he said, somewhat harshly. "How will you feel watching her day after day, knowing that in a month or two, she will be taken to a nunnery? Would it make you feel better? Or would it tear you apart, knowing every day with her was borrowed time?"

"It is better than no time at all."

"Enough, Fox," Val snapped softly. "This is not your decision."

Fox realized he wasn't behaving professionally, but where Gisele was concerned, he simply couldn't separate the protector from the lover. But he knew he was verging on behaving like a fool. "Forgive me," he said after a moment. "It's simply that... it's so soon. That is all I meant. It will be hard on her."

Val shook his head. "Do not demean yourself, Fox," he said. "It will be hard on *you*. Admit it. But while you are giving in to unproductive emotion, remember that you are a sworn knight. Not just any knight, but one who has served both the king and William Marshal. You are one of the best I have ever seen, and I have seen many. Do not shame yourself and your reputation by giving in to emotion. Gisele is your duty. She should have only, and always, been your duty, but a few years ago, you crossed the line. You fell in love with a woman you could never have, and that is a failure on your part. Telling me that it will be hard on Gigi to move her swiftly to Canonsleigh is beneath you."

Fox was stiff by the time Val finished. Nothing he said was untrue, but the man would have done less damage had he slapped Fox across the face. It was harsh hearing the reality of Fox's behavior coming from Val's lips, but in those words, Fox could hear direction. Val was giving him direction. He was telling him what he needed to do, as a knight and as an honorable man. They were at a crossroads, and Fox had to choose the right path.

As difficult as that choice might be.

"I never meant to fail you, my lord," he finally said, his voice quiet. "I never meant to allow my feelings to show."

Val backed down a little. "I know," he said. "But you have

put yourself in a very precarious position. You have fallen for a woman who is meant for the cloister, and you have been carrying on with her for years. Do you think I do not know about your little love nest in the barbican? Of course I know. I know everything that goes on at Selborne. My failure was in letting it go on and not sending you away when I discovered what had happened. It was my wife who convinced me otherwise, so you can thank her. But do not fail me on this last and most important order where it pertains to Gigi, or I swear by all that is holy that I will tell the Marshal everything, and you will find yourself cleaning garderobes at the Tower of London. Am I making myself clear, de Merest?"

Fox was horrified and ashamed, but trying desperately not to show it. "You are, my lord."

"Then I will tell Gigi in the morning that you are escorting her to Canonsleigh," Val said. "Be ready to depart by noon. Do you know how to get there?"

Fox shook his head, feeling sick and defeated. "I know how to get to Devon, but not Canonsleigh," he said. "I can stop in Taunton and ask for directions."

"Indeed," Val said. "Prepare a small palfrey for Gigi. She can ride on her own."

God, it sounded so final. So final and swift. Fox wanted to protest again, to demand Val find another way so Gisele would not have to be sent from Selborne, but he knew it would be futile. He'd look foolish and weak if he were to beg, and, at the moment, he was already in danger of damaging his reputation in Val's eyes. So much had become clear this night, and Fox realized that although he was willing to do anything for Gisele, he wasn't willing to disgrace himself and ruin everything he'd worked for.

It was that selfishness in him again.

The selfishness was taking over.

"How big of an escort would you have me form, my lord?" he asked, sounding dull and defeated.

Val paused. He could see the stress and pain on Fox's face, even in the darkness. The man was going to do his duty, but it was going to eat him alive. The fact that he could never marry the woman he loved was a blow he was reeling from, and Val felt a good deal of pity for him. That kind of loss could topple even the strongest man, but a young knight like Fox...

He was sure the man's heart was in a million pieces.

"No escort," he murmured. "You alone will escort Gigi to Canonsleigh. That is my gift to you both, Fox. You can spend those last days together, just the two of you, to make memories to last you a lifetime. But do not take it as an opportunity to flee with her. If you violate my trust, I will track you down no matter where you are, and I will punish you. Is this in any way unclear?"

"It is clear, my lord."

"Good," Val said, his gaze lingering on a man who seemed to be on the verge of cracking. "Once you have safely delivered her to Canonsleigh, you will ride to Pembroke Castle and tell William Marshal what has happened. He is usually in residence at Pembroke at this time of year."

"Aye, my lord."

With that, Val walked away, heading down the stairs and leaving Fox standing in the darkness, digesting what he'd been told. What the next few days and weeks would bring for him, and after that... after that, there would only be darkness. No Gisele, no life, and no love.

Sinking back against the wall and sliding down to the ground, Fox wept.

CHAPTER EIGHT

S HE HADN'T SPOKEN to him in four days.

Four long, excruciating days of travel from Selborne Castle to Canonsleigh Abbey in Devon, a wild and mysterious land and the gateway to Cornwall, where magic ruled. Four days of just the two of them, riding alongside one another on roads that were not well traveled but in good condition. Four days of forests and fields, of sunlight and clouds. Four days of deer in the distance and hawks riding the drafts overhead, and of plodding along, listening to the birds sing.

But there were no voices.

Gisele couldn't speak.

She was too devastated.

True to his word, Val had informed her of her destiny the moment she woke the morning after the assassins had attacked. He had taken her into his solar and informed her alone. Fox had been standing underneath the windows of the solar that faced onto the bailey, so he could hear every word. He heard Gisele's disbelief, her resistance, her denial, and finally her tears when she realized that Val was serious. He even heard her beg.

He would have begged, too, had he thought it would do any

good.

But begging was futile.

Fox hadn't slept at all the night before. There was no motivation to sleep, only a sense of impending doom. That morning, he had seen Gavin, but he couldn't manage to speak to the man, knowing it was Gavin who had ultimately started the discussion of sending Gisele away. Fox's logical mind knew that Gavin was only doing what he felt best to protect his mother and sisters, but there was something inside of Fox that would never forgive him for making Gisele the sacrifice for that freedom.

Nay, he could never forgive Gavin for that.

Even as he stood beneath the solar windows, he could see Gavin near the gatehouse. He was trying very hard not to focus his animosity on a man he'd known for many years, a man he considered perhaps his closest friend. All he could hear was Gavin's condemnation of Gisele, the woman he loved, and he wasn't sure there was any going back from that. In fact, once he took Gisele to the nunnery, he wasn't sure there was any coming back to Selborne Castle in general.

He suspected the memories would be too difficult to effectively serve.

When Val summoned his wife to come to the solar to comfort Gisele, Fox had heard enough. He left his post beneath the windows and went to pack his possessions and prepare his horse. He had been asked to do that the previous night, but he'd failed to do it because he was so upset about the situation at large.

Therefore, it was at the dawn of a new day that he returned to the knights' quarters to pack everything he owned into two large saddlebags. He then proceeded to the stable, and there he had the stable servants prepare his trusty steed, a horse that was perhaps as old as he was. The animal's name was Merlin, and Fox had received him many years ago from his father when he was a squire. Merlin had been a seasoned warhorse even back then, and Fox swore that Merlin had taught him a thing or two. That young, arrogant squire had learned a few things from an old horse who wouldn't take any foolishness.

He loved that horse like a brother.

There was some comfort in spending time with Merlin that morning, realizing how much his life was going to change. It was good to have some continuity, even if it was with a grumpy old horse. The stable servants prepared Gisele's favorite palfrey, a pretty bay mare with a big white blaze down the front of her face.

With the horses ready and waiting, Fox had gone to the kitchens to prepare provisions for their journey. The cook, an old woman who had been at the castle since the days of Val's mother, was sad to hear that Gisele was leaving. Sniffling and wiping her nose, the old woman packed a good amount of food into a large sack, food that would travel well. When that was finished, she broke down and wept, sobbing all over Fox and hugging him as if he was one of her own children leaving forever.

It was probably the truth.

With the horses prepared, Fox went to the bailey to wait for Gisele to make an appearance. He suspected it was going to take some time, as she had to say farewell to the only people she'd ever known as her family. He was going to have the next few days with her, but for them, this was it. This was the moment. Therefore, he remained patient. He left that time to the de Nerra family as they bade farewell to a woman they had raised. Given that they were a loving family, Fox knew it was an emotional parting.

Near the nooning hour, Val and Vesper brought Gisele out of the keep. Val was carrying her satchel, a big one that was nearly stuffed to overflowing, and he handed it over to Fox, who strapped it on to the back of her saddle. Meanwhile, Val and Vesper hugged Gisele and bade her farewell as Gisele wept deeply. As Fox pretended to tighten the straps that held her satchel, he could hear Gisele apologizing for causing such trouble and begging to be permitted to remain. It was Val who held her tightly and told her that her destiny lay elsewhere but that he would always consider her his daughter. It was incredibly distressing and incredibly unfair, for all of them.

It made a sad parting even sadder.

Val finally brought Gisele over to her palfrey and lifted her up as she continued to weep. He made sure her saddle was secure and kissed her farewell. By this time, Vesper had lost her composure, and she was standing a few feet away, telling Gisele that she loved her and that she would write to her. Stoically, Fox mounted Merlin, gave a little kick to the rear of Gisele's palfrey, and moved her out toward the gatehouse. The last he saw of Val and Vesper, they were weeping in each other's arms.

That had been four days ago.

Now, they found themselves in Taunton, a larger city in Devon. It was heavily populated for a town on the fringes of England, with dirty streets that weren't particularly well kept and at least two dozen taverns, inns, and hostels. There was a great deal to choose from, but Fox remained on the outskirts of the town, assuming anything on the edges wouldn't be as crowded as those toward the town center. He found an inn called The Dog and the Rabbit, a neatly kept place with a livery adjacent to it. He reined Merlin toward the mouth of the livery and turned to Gisele, who was sitting silent and pale upon her palfrey. He gazed upon her face for the first time all day before speaking.

"We are in Devon," he said quietly. "Tomorrow, I am certain we will reach your destination of Canonsleigh Abbey, so are you going to let our last few hours be wasted with silence? If that is your intention, let me know now, and I will not speak another word. You can enter the nunnery with the knowledge that you'll never have to see me or speak with me again. Is that your wish, my lady?"

Gisele had been staring straight ahead, almost in a daze. But his words had her eyes moving in his direction, even if her head wasn't. She was clad in the same clothing she'd worn since the day they departed Selborne, a pale brown dress and a cloak to match. It was a traveling ensemble, designed so that any dirt from the road would not be noticed. She had the hood of her cloak pulled over her head, shielding her pale face from the sun and elements. Her eyes, moving slowly, finally found him.

"I do not know," she said, her voice hoarse from sheer unuse.

"That is not an answer."

"It is the only answer I have."

That only seemed to inflame Fox. Grabbing his saddlebags, he motioned for her to dismount her horse.

"Very well," he said. "Get off the animal and come inside. I will find you a room, and you will stay there until morning. You can spend it alone, and I will find a room at another establishment because, clearly, you want nothing to do with me. I can easily grant that wish, my lady."

Gisele did as she was told and slid off the animal before untying her satchel and taking it off the saddle. But she didn't move beyond that. She just stood there even as he moved toward the inn. He was to the door when he realized she wasn't following, so he waved his arm at her.

"I will not carry you," he said. "If you want a roof over your head tonight, you must move your feet."

Gisele remained still. After a few tense moments, she spoke. "You are letting them do this to me," she said. "Tell me why I should not hate you for it."

That was the most she'd said to him in four days, and Fox was having a difficult time with his temper. "I do not care if you hate me," he said. "After tomorrow, it does not matter what you think or what I think. You will go to the abbey, and I will go along my way, and we will never see one another again, so if you feel you must hate me, that is your affair. I do not care in the least."

Her pale face was starting to flush. "The fact that you do not care is obvious," she said. "You did not fight for me at all."

"How do you know?"

"Because you never said a word the entire time Lord and Lady de Nerra were saying their farewells," she said. "You did not try to talk them out of it."

"Is that what you think?"

"You did not fight for me!"

She was raising her voice, and he retraced his steps over to her, throwing his saddlebags at her feet in a fit of anger.

"You do not know what I did," he snarled. "You do not know that I argued with Lord de Nerra until he threatened me. You do not know that I had no idea the Marshal had always intended for you to be given over to Canonsleigh and never had the decency to tell me when I asked for your hand. You do not know that I was given as much false hope as you were, and mayhap more, hope that I could make a name for myself and thereby be worthy of you in the eyes of the Marshal. You do not know that I feel cheated and deceived and humiliated and that my love for you wasn't taken seriously by William Marshal or Val de Nerra or, worst of all, you. So, nay, I do not care what you think of me, because this entire experience has ruined me. I have a hole inside of me where my heart used to be, and all you can do is ignore me and berate me. Therefore, I do not care what you think. Tomorrow, I'll be well rid of you."

Tears were streaming down Gisele's face by the time he was finished. She blinked, and they spattered. "Fox..." she whispered. "I..."

"Cease," he commanded sharply, reaching down to pick up his saddlebags. "I do not want to hear your apologies. They are meaningless."

He slung the bags over one shoulder as she let out a sob, covering her mouth with her hand. "I am sorry," she whispered through her fingers. "I am sorry you feel so hurt. But I have just lost the only family I have ever known. I am losing everything, too."

He put up a hand. "Spare me," he said. "Men and women lose precious things all of the time. You are not the first and you will not be the last. But the fact that you blame me for your woes is so very telling, Gisele. You have accused me of being selfish, but the truth is that you are far more selfish than I could ever be. You seek to blame others for your problems, and to point your finger at me is shocking. Shocking and unfair."

She sobbed again, into her hand. "I said I was sorry," she said. "Men have attempted to kill me, I have lost my family, and now I will be unable to marry the man I love. I will live a celibate life with no family, no future. And I am not supposed to be upset?"

"Be upset all you want," he said. "But do not direct it at me. I am not your enemy, Gisele. You would do well to remember that."

With that, he turned for the tavern and marched over to the door, pausing to turn and look at her expectantly. Gisele knew what was required of her, so she trudged over to him, satchel in hand, as Fox opened the door. She stepped inside, and he went in after her.

The inn was small, low-ceilinged, and smelled of rushes. They took a few steps into the common room and were suddenly hit with a wall of smoke from a fire that was blazing happily in the wide-mouth hearth. Fox grasped her by the arm and pulled her with him until he found the innkeeper, whereupon he asked the man for two rooms for the night. The man only had one, his largest, and Fox took it, following the man to a big chamber that overlooked the street. It was cold and dark, but the innkeeper quickly went about lighting a couple of tapers.

"I'll have coals brought in for the brazier," he said. "Will you want food?"

Fox looked around the chamber, which was large enough to sleep five or six adults comfortably. "Aye," he said. "What do you have tonight?"

"Capon pie and omelets," the innkeeper said. "I just took some bread out of the oven."

"Bring it," Fox said. "Bring a lot of it. We are very hungry."

As the man ran off, Gisele made her way over to the bed and set her satchel upon it. "Do you think I could have a bath?" she asked, her voice weak. "I have no idea if the nunnery will even allow such a thing, so I may as well have one while I can."

Fox set his saddlebags against the wall. "You are not going to prison, you know," he said. "I am sure the nunnery is civilized. I am sure they have things like baths."

"Do you know for certain?"

"I've not been there to see for myself, if that's what you mean."

"*May* I have a bath, please?"

He grunted wearily and nodded his head as he crouched down and opened up his saddlebags. There was a brief knock on the door before a serving wench barged in, bearing a tray with cups and wine. As the woman set the items upon the only table in the room, Gisele opened up her satchel and began to carefully pull forth her things. She was hunting for her soap and a clean shift. After the serving wench scurried out, Gisele cast a long glance at the knight crouched on the floor.

"Fox?" she asked softly.

"What is it?" He didn't look up from his saddlebags.

"Are you planning on sleeping in this chamber with me?"

"Aye."

"In the same bed?"

"Aye."

Gisele stopped rummaging through her satchel and looked at him. "Am I really not going to ever see you again?"

His movements slowed, but he still didn't look up at her. "I do not know," he said honestly. "You are going to a nunnery, Gigi. It is not a place for men."

"Won't you even try?"

"Not if it is not appropriate."

She didn't say anything for a moment. She watched him rummage through his saddlebags, looking for… something. She didn't even know what he was looking for, but he seemed to be spending an inordinate amount of time looking for it. Perhaps he really wasn't looking for anything.

Perhaps he simply needed to keep his hands busy.

As she watched him fumble with the contents of his saddle-bags, it began to occur to her that she had brought them to this point. The attack of the assassins had been shocking enough, but the news that she was to leave Selborne Castle and travel to an abbey she'd never even heard of, a place that would be her permanent residence for the rest of her life, had been over-whelming. At first, she wondered what she had done to warrant such a punishment. Surely the two people who had raised her, people she considered her parents, couldn't just send her away so carelessly.

But she had been wrong.

Val had tried to explain it to her. Her true father, he had said, had given him explicit instructions many years ago of what to do when his bastard daughter came of age. Gisele had never been aware of any plans for her life, but according to Val, there were indeed instructions. She was to grow up amongst the de Nerra children, and then she was to be tucked away in a nunnery far from civilization.

Hidden.

She was to have a life, and then she was to have it taken away.

Perhaps the past four days hadn't been punishment for Fox as much as it had been Gisele reconciling herself to the course her life had taken. To the future she most definitely did not want. A future that did not include marriage or Fox, or any of the hopes and dreams she had grown up expecting. She was to become a nun and live a life of service, something that horrified her. It was the furthest from what she wanted. She knew that

Fox believed her days of silence had somehow been aimed at him, and perhaps in a way they were, but not entirely. Her statement to him—*tell me why I should not hate you*—had been one of fear and grief. She knew he wouldn't fight for her. He wouldn't risk everything for her. He had a career he was protective of, something he had worked hard for, and there was a large part of her that actually understood that. He wouldn't save her.

Perhaps she had to save herself.

I must control my own destiny!

She could run, but he'd only catch her. Catch her and take her to that miserable place where she was to live out the remainder of her life, alone. Perhaps, in the end, she didn't deserve someone as wonderful as Fox, and she was all too aware. She was young and immature at times, and he was seasoned and strong. She loved him with all her heart and soul, every fiber of her being, ever star in the heavens.

But she couldn't have him.

She couldn't have anyone.

Worse still was that while she couldn't marry him, he was perfectly free to marry whomever he wanted. Of course she wanted him to be happy—that was perhaps the one mature wish she had for him. She wanted him to be happy in his life, even if that life didn't include her. But she'd never thought, until this moment, that she wouldn't be part of it.

He was to go on without her.

As that thought sank in, Gisele was coming to wish that the assassins had been successful. Perhaps if she'd known how this would have ended, she would have welcomed death.

Perhaps she would still welcome it.

It didn't seem that there was much for her to live for now.

Desolate, Gisele fell silent. She stopped looking for soap and a comb and simply sat on the stool that was near the bed and hung her head. She was tired, overwhelmed, and depressed. When Fox finally stood up from his saddlebags and left the chamber to order a bath, she got up and went to his possessions, hunting around for something to take away her pain. It had reached that point, in her mind, and she was singularly focused.

Nothing left to live for.

She'd rather be dead than without Fox.

Gisele found an assortment of sheaths for daggers that were undoubtedly on Fox, still, as they had been traveling and he would not travel in anything less than a combat-ready form. But there was one rather long dirk tucked away in the bottom of one saddlebag, and she pulled it forth, going over to the bed and sitting down on the floor on the opposite side, against the wall. Fox would come in, think she was simply pouting, and more than likely not speak with her. He wouldn't come to see why she was sitting on the floor. They'd spent four days ignoring one another, and she just needed another few minutes of his apathy. It would only take a few minutes for her to bleed to death.

As she sat on the floor between the bed and the wall, facing away from the door, she began to weep. Desperation clutched at her, thoughts of a bleak future consuming her until she could think of nothing else. There was relief in death, wasn't there? No more pain, no more fear. No more life without Fox by her side, and, in truth, perhaps he would be better off without her. The more her exhausted, brittle mind played tricks on her, the more she began to believe that was the answer.

Death was the answer.

I'm so sorry, Fox.

Taking the razor-sharp dirk, she cut into her left wrist, gasping at the terrible pain, before doing the same thing on her right wrist. The agony was terrific. Setting the dirk onto the floor, she kept her arms down so the blood could drain out on the floor, and lowered her head.

Forgive me, please. Oh, God, forgive me.

Forgive me...

☙

FOX DIDN'T WANT to spend their last evening together fighting.

Six years of what had been some of the most significant moments of his life threatened to go up in smoke because Gisele was upset and bewildered, and rather than try to help her through it, he'd become belligerent. She tended to be emotionally immature at times, and he'd weathered those moments with her because the overwhelming majority of their time together had been filled with love and laughter. She was joyful—so very joyful—and he couldn't even count the times when her laughter had made him feel so genuinely happy. Her happiness gave him happiness.

He didn't want those moments to be buried with a bad parting.

He'd come out to the common room to find the innkeeper and order Gisele a bath, and as he waited for the innkeeper to come in from the livery yard, he thought more and more about the future he and Gisele were facing. Certainly, the initial shock of William Marshal's directive for Gisele's destiny had been a harsh one. Fox had felt he had to honor that, which was why he was on the road now. He was honoring the Marshal's wishes by taking Gisele to Canonsleigh Abbey. But he was coming to think that there was no reason for him to change his intentions when it came to Gisele.

Perhaps this didn't have to be the end.

When the Marshal had made the arrangements for Gisele, she had been an infant. That was twenty-two years ago. He had no way of knowing she would fall in love with a man and love him for six years. He had no way of knowing that she would become the center of that man's universe. Although Fox still didn't know why the Marshal hadn't told him of Gisele's destiny when he asked for her hand, perhaps it was because Pembroke didn't think Fox was serious. Perhaps he thought Fox would simply accept the denial and get on with his life.

But that certainly wasn't the case.

He was going to have to prove to the Marshal that he would not forget Gisele.

As Fox pondered that thought, he began to feel hope. Hope that had been stripped from him for four long days. Val had ordered him to Pembroke Castle after leaving Gisele at Canonsleigh, and Fox decided to use that opportunity to plead for Gisele's hand. He was going to beg and bargain any way he could, and if the Marshal still denied him, then perhaps he'd do what he'd told Gisele he wouldn't do... He would take her and run off to Normandy or another part of France and marry her. Perhaps he'd be a disgraced knight, but he'd have Gisele, and that was all that mattered.

... wasn't it?

Fox was starting to think it was.

He wasn't going to be selfish any longer.

The innkeeper came back inside, and one of the serving wenches explained what Fox wanted. The innkeeper, a man of considerable girth and a ruddy face, agreed to send a tub and hot water to the rented chamber. He also agreed to send a serving girl to help the lady bathe, which satisfied Fox. While he was standing in the kitchen, he grabbed a hunk of bread and began to eat it as he directed the kitchen servants to pile everything they could on a tray so he could take it back to Gisele. With a renewed sense of hope and even joy, because he knew Gisele would be thrilled with his decision, he headed back to the room with two serving women behind him bearing trays of food and more drink. Opening the door, he could see Gisele sitting on the floor on the other side of the bed.

He could just see her head, lowered. Knowing she was still brooding, perhaps even weeping, he silently indicated for the servants to set the food on the nearest table. Once the wenches deposited the trays and cleared the chamber, he closed the door behind them. His focus turned to Gisele, who still hadn't moved a muscle.

Softly, he cleared his throat.

"Would you like to eat?" he asked. "I've ordered a bath. It should be brought shortly."

She didn't answer. She simply sat there, head lowered. He could really only see the back of her head from where he was, so he moved away from the table, toward the bed, struggling not to become irritated with her. That never solved anything. He thought to tell her about his ideas and, ultimately, his decision, thinking that should bring her out of her mood and they could discuss things rationally. She was still shocked and bewildered by the entire circumstance, and he realized that rather than butt heads with her, he needed to help her feel the hope that he was feeling. As he'd thought before, he didn't want their last hours to be ones of animosity. He wanted her to know that he was determined to ensure they had a clear path for the future.

"Gigi, I've come to a decision," he said, moving slowly toward the bed. "Although I will still take you to Canonsleigh on the morrow, I've decided to seek William Marshal and plead for your hand. I will not allow him to deny us yet again. I have been thinking... He made the decision for Canonsleigh when you were born, before you had a life. He made the best decision he could at the time, I'm sure, but he did not take into consideration that you would love and be loved. I can offer you a much better life than anything Canonsleigh can offer you."

Gisele didn't respond. She didn't even move. Fighting down his frustration, he came closer.

"Did you hear me?" he said. "I am going to ask for your hand. And if he does not give his permission for a marriage, then... then I will take you and we will flee to Normandy. My mother has family there. I am certain I can find a position in France, somewhere, and we will be married. It's what you wanted, Gigi. Are you not pleased?"

Still no reply. Annoyance bloomed, and Fox came around the side of the bed, prepared to snap at her—and saw puddles of blood on the ground.

Terror tore through him.

"Christ," he hissed, falling to his knees and grabbing her. She was only semiconscious, and she flopped against him as he grabbed her arms, seeing all of the blood. "God, no. *Oh... God!*"

He nearly bellowed the last word, slipping his big arms under her and heaving her onto the bed. He wasn't sure where the blood was coming from because it seemed to be all over her. Her neck was clear, as was her chest, but when he got a good look at her hands and wrists, he realized what she'd done.

His heart sank.

"Oh... Gigi," he whispered painfully, looking at her pale face. "Why, my love? Why would you do such a thing?"

He knew the answer. God help him, he knew. Desperation had controlled the dagger that had done the deed. But he couldn't give in to his grief. If he did, all was lost.

She was lost.

Forcing himself to think logically, he knew he needed to bind her wrists and do it quickly. In a flash, he grabbed the hem of her garment, which was a durable broadcloth, and ripped a section of it off the bottom. It was a strong fabric, however, and didn't tear well, so he pulled a dagger from his belt and slashed at it, carving it into strips. Rapidly, he bound her right wrist, as tightly as he could, before moving to her left wrist and doing the same thing. He was positive that he was cutting off the circulation to her hands, but that couldn't be helped at the moment.

With her wrists tightly bound, Fox used the other strips of cloth to tie her arms over her head and lash them to the wooden bedframe. He was just finishing the ties when the door opened again and the innkeeper appeared with two men behind him, lugging the bathtub. One look at the bloodied woman on the bed, being tied up, and the innkeeper stumbled back, knocking the bathtub to the ground. But Fox caught sight of the man and leapt off the bed.

"I need a physic," he commanded breathlessly. "My lady has greatly injured herself, so send for a physic immediately. I also need rags—clean rags. Bring all you can. And hot water, too. *Hurry!*"

The man fled, taking the two servants and the tub with him. Meanwhile, Fox leaned over Gisele, who was pasty and unconscious. He pulled an eyelid up, watching her eyes sluggishly respond. Her breathing was shallow. Quickly, he inspected her legs and feet to make sure there were no more injuries before returning to her face.

"Gigi?" he whispered, his voice trembling. He patted her lightly on the cheeks. "Gigi, can you hear me?"

She didn't respond. Growing despondent, Fox went to the table where wine sat in an earthenware pitcher along with two cups. His shaking hand poured wine into a cup, and he went back to the bed, trying to force a little down her throat.

"Gigi?" he said again, trying not to break down. "Can you hear me, love? Open your eyes for me, please."

Gisele coughed as he tried to force her to drink some wine, but it was only a reflex. Realizing she wasn't going to respond to him, Fox was genuinely at a loss. Distressed beyond reason, he stood up and set the cup back on the table, watching her for a moment as he ran a nervous hand through his dark hair. He had no idea what more to do. He had no idea if he'd even been in time. He'd been gone from the room for several minutes, clearly long enough for her to take a dirk and slit her wrists.

It was then that he began to understand the depths of her despair.

Despair he hadn't really listened to.

Oh, God… He'd said terrible things to her.

"I didn't mean it," he said hoarsely, going back over to the bed and sitting beside her. "I did not mean it when I said I did not care what you thought. Of course I care what you think. I always have. I'm so sorry, love. Please forgive me."

Tears swam in his eyes. Reaching up, he stroked her face before feeling for a pulse just to make sure she was still alive. When he could feel her pulse, weak and rapid, he closed his eyes, and the tears streamed down his cheeks.

"The physic is coming," he whispered. "He will heal you and you will never do this again, do you hear? This was my fault. I was not understanding enough. I should have listened to you. I should have been calm, and then you would have been calm. I feel as if I am to blame for this, and I am so terribly sorry, love."

Gisele didn't stir. Not that he expected her to, but he had to say what he felt. Guilt threatened to consume him as he watched her shallow breathing, noting that the blood had seeped through the bandages he'd tied so tightly around her wrists. He couldn't even hold her hand in her hour of need. Leaning forward, he kissed her on the chin, his hand on her head, trying to give her some comfort, perhaps trying to give himself some comfort as well.

He'd never felt so helpless in his entire life.

Fox wasn't sure how long he sat there, his forehead against her chin, his hand on her face, her arm, feeling her warmth beneath his fingers and convincing himself that there was still life in her. He didn't know where she got the dagger to do the deed, but he suspected it was one of his. He had a couple in his saddlebags, and she must have found one. He was losing all sense of time when the door suddenly swung open and the innkeeper returned with a big, sweaty man in tow. The man was tall, bald, and carrying a basket with him. Fox quickly stood up, weaving unsteadily as the man set his basket down and turned his frowning features in Gisele's direction.

"What happened here?" he demanded. "Was there a fight?"

Fox shook his head. "Nay," he said, confused by the question but wondering if the man meant he had fought with Gisele and he'd somehow wounded her. "There was no fight. Are you the physic?"

The man nodded and sat down on the bed, heavily enough to jolt Gisele. He peered in her eyes before putting an ear against her mouth, listening to her breath.

"My name is Johann," he said. "Who are you? The husband?"

Fox blinked at the question that caught him off guard. "Aye," he said after a moment, knowing that the innkeeper was listening, and he didn't want the man to know they were not married, since he'd rented one chamber for the two of them. "I am her husband. My… my wife has been upset, and she seems to have cut her wrists in her sorrow."

Johann immediately began to untie the bindings on her hands that fastened them to the bedframe, and they dropped down as he began to unwind the bandages to get a look at the damage. He peered at both of her wrists, though they looked like a bloody mess from where Fox was standing.

Johann grunted.

"They're not cut too deeply," he said. "But I'll need to sew them. How long did she bleed?"

Fox shook his head. "Not long," he said. "I can only guess it was several minutes. I was gone when she did it and came back to find her on the floor."

He gestured to the opposite side of the bed, which caused the physic to get up and look at the blood on the floor that he was indicating. He grunted again.

"It could be worse," he said.

"Then she will live?"

"Probably," Johann said. "But keep her away from the daggers, for the love of Mary. If she's so fickle and foolish, keep her away from anything sharp."

Fox didn't like the man summarizing Gisele's character in such a demeaning manner. Even if it *was* true, at least in this instance. But he was so relieved that he didn't say anything to the man, who brought his basket over to the bed and began to rummage around. He pulled out a needle and boiled catgut, but not before cleaning the wound and blood from around the cuts with some of the wine that Fox had tried to force her to drink. With speed and with skill, he put small stitches in each wrist where she had cut herself.

Now that the frenzy of saving her life was over, at least for now, Fox sat next to the food, which had grown cold, and watched the physic tend Gisele. For all of the man's brusque and sweaty nature, he seemed to be competent. Once he'd sewn the wounds, he washed them again with wine and bound them up in clean, boiled linen. It was past midnight by that point, and as Fox watched anxiously, Johann finally stood up from the bed.

"She will sleep," he said, looking at Fox. "It could have been much worse. Had she cut deeper, it would have been. Let her sleep, and when she awakens, give her warm milk and beef broth. She must regain her strength."

Fox nodded wearily, rising to his feet. "When can she travel?"

Johann shook his head. "Not for a couple of days, at least," he said. "She must be kept in bed, and she must be kept quiet. Whatever upset her enough to drive her to this, forget about it. Do not fight with her. She must rest. Do you understand?"

Fox nodded. "I do."

Johann's gaze lingered on him for a moment before he looked away, bending over to pick up his basket. "I will come back in the morning," he said.

He moved past Fox, opening the door to find the innkeeper standing on the other side. He waved the man aside and continued on as Fox went to the door and caught the innkeeper's attention.

"We will need the room for at least two more days," he said. "I will pay you well."

The innkeeper nodded. "Very good, m'lord."

"And the physic says she will need warm milk and beef broth."

"She shall have it," the innkeeper said. "And he's not our usual physic."

Fox frowned. "He's not?" he said, feeling his outrage rise. "Then why did you send him to me?"

"Because he is the only one on this end of the town who tends the ill, m'lord," he said. "He used to be a priest. A Hospitaller."

Fox's eyebrows rose. That bit of information meant something to him. "He's a Hospitaller knight?"

"Aye, m'lord."

"But he is not the town's physic?"

The innkeeper shook his head. "Nay, m'lord," he said. "He tends the dead and tends the graveyard at St. John's church. Truth be told, he's most often found lying in the street with an empty wine bottle in his hand. We were fortunate tonight. He's not been drinking."

Fox understood a little in that statement. That big, sweaty physic had once been a Hospitaller knight, one of the most prestigious ranks of knights in the world. They were healers and fighters and political players. One simply didn't leave the ranks, at least by choice. That made Fox the least bit curious about the man who had introduced himself as Johann, but he couldn't give him further thought than that. His attention, as it should, returned to Gisele.

There was nothing left now to do but wait.

God help him...

CHAPTER NINE

S OMEONE WAS SNORING.

Gisele wasn't sure who it was, but as she gradually became lucid, she began to realize that someone was snoring like an old bull.

It was difficult to open her eyes. Her eyelids felt as if they were stuck together, but gradually, she was able to peep them open and see that she was in a chamber she didn't recognize. There was a wall in front of her, of rough plaster, and a window set into it that had an uneven wooden frame. Shifting slightly, she could see that she was in a bed, though whose bed, she had no idea. She didn't know where she was. When she lifted a hand to push her hair out of her face, she could see that her wrists were bandaged.

Bewildered, she stared at the bandage, having no idea how or why that had happened. She couldn't remember. In fact, she couldn't remember anything at the moment, so she stiffly rolled onto her back to get a look at the room as a whole.

Off to her right, she could see the source of the snoring, which was still going on at an epic volume. Fox was sitting in a chair, his head back against the wall behind him and his eyes closed as he slept the sleep of the dead. In all the years she had known him, she hadn't actually slept in the same room with him, so the snoring was something new. It was incredibly loud and, in her opinion, rather humorous. A faint smile creased her lips as she watched him suck all of the air in the room into his lungs and then blow it out again. It made her chuckle.

"Fox?" she said weakly.

There was no response. He couldn't hear her over his own snoring, so she tried again when the sound died down.

"Fox?

The second time, she was a little louder, and he heard her. His eyes flew open, staring into space for a moment before he quickly oriented himself. He came away from the wall, sitting up in the chair, his gaze moving to the bed where Gisele was on her back and grinning faintly at him. When he realized her eyes were open, he very nearly vaulted off the chair toward the bed.

"Gigi?" he said incredulously. "You're awake!"

She wasn't sure why he was so amazed. "And how am I to sleep through your snoring?" she said. "You're going to bring the walls down one day."

He was clearly surprised, chuckling because she was awake. In fact, his joy knew no limits as he realized she was conscious and oriented. "Thank God," he said reverently, sitting on the bed next to her. "How do you feel?"

She shrugged. "Well. Tired, I suppose. Why?" She brought a hand up to rub her eyes, but the bandages caught her attention again, and she held them up to get a better look at them. "Why are my arms wrapped like this?"

Fox watched her, quickly realizing that something was off by the way she was asking questions she should already know the answer to. "Do you not remember what happened when we came to the inn?" he asked.

Her right hand was still up in front of her face, but she looked around the chamber. "Is that where we are?" she said. "What inn?"

Another puzzled answer. It seemed to Fox that she was having some difficulty recalling the events leading up to this moment. She seemed to have no recollection of the inn, or why her wrists were wrapped. It was possible she didn't have any recollection of even why they'd come. Given that she'd been unconscious for a couple of days, clearly, her body was reacting to great trauma. Not wanting to upset her all over again, but still feeling obligated to remind her, he proceeded carefully.

"What is the last thing you remember, love?" he asked.

Gisele rubbed her eyes. "I remember Selborne and the feast," she said. "We danced."

"We did. What else?"

She stopped rubbing her eyes. "The minstrels," she said. Then horror overtook her expression as her memory started to return. "The minstrels! They tried to kill me!"

Fox put his hands on her upper arms, trying to soothe her. "They did," he said. "But we saved you. Lord de Nerra and me. What else do you recall?"

She was still clearly frightened at the memory of killer minstrels, but she thought on his question. "I remember... I remember being told I had to leave my home," she said. Then she closed her eyes for a moment, sighing heavily. "We are on our way to Canonsleigh, aren't we?"

"We are."

"How close are we?"

"Within a day's ride."

She opened her eyes, looking at him as the tears began to

pool. "And we will go tomorrow?"

He stroked her arm. "We will go when you are feeling better."

"But what happened to my wrists?"

Some memory was coming back, but she didn't seem to remember that part, and he wasn't sure he wanted to tell her. It seemed to him that she seemed much more alert than she had been since they departed Selborne, so perhaps something in her overworked mind had briefly snapped. Slicing her wrists was not something the Gisele he knew would do, which was why the action had shocked him so. But she'd been driven to the brink of collapse, and her mind, overworked and in shock, had somehow faltered. Temporary madness had claimed her. If two days of sleep had healed whatever had cracked, he didn't want to stir the pot again.

"You hurt yourself," he said. "It is of no matter now. All that matters is that you are feeling better, and I cannot tell you how glad I am. If you feel well enough, we have something to discuss."

She nodded, but she was looking at him closely. "What is wrong with you?" she asked. "You look so weary."

He knew he did. He'd been up, sitting vigil over her, since the moment he discovered that she'd tried to kill herself until just a short time ago. She caught him snoring when he hadn't slept for days. Weakly, he smiled.

"I've had things to attend to whilst you've been sleeping the hours away," he said, trying to make light of it. "Of course I look weary. Am I no longer handsome in your eyes?"

She smiled, lifting a bandaged hand and laying it on his stubbled cheek. "You will always be handsome in my eyes," she said, but her smile soon faded. "Please tell me this will not be the last time I tell you that, Fox. Please tell me that even after I go to Canonsleigh, we will be in contact with one another. This is not the end."

It was a subject they'd covered when they arrived at the tavern, when harsh words had been spoken. Thankfully, she must not have remembered. He had a chance to correct those bitter words he deeply regretted. He put his hand over hers as she laid it upon his cheek.

"Nay," he said softly. "This is not the end of our story. How could it be? A love like ours does not happen every day. It would be a crime to see it come to an end. That is what I wanted to speak with you about."

"What?"

He kissed the palm against his cheek before continuing. "I am taking you to Canonsleigh when you feel strong enough, that is true," he said. "I am doing it because I have been ordered to, not because I want to. I know you understand that. But once I leave you off, I am going straight to Pembroke Castle to demand the Marshal allow us to marry. I will not be put off again."

Her eyes widened. "You are?"

He nodded firmly. "I am," he said. "Furthermore, if I am denied, even after I tear the place apart with my demands, I will return to Canonsleigh for you, and we shall go to Normandy, where my mother still has family. We will be married and live as man and wife, the way we were meant to be."

A smile crept over her lips, one of joy and disbelief. "Truly?"

"Truly."

"And we will be together?"

He nodded, taking her hand away from his face and kissing

it again. "We will," he said. "You were right to call me selfish. I was. My career meant a great deal to me, and it still does, but you mean more. I am sorry I put you through so much misery whilst I realized that. But the truth is that I knew it all along."

She was smiling broadly, but tears were beginning to trickle down her cheeks. "Oh, Fox," she murmured. "You do not know how long I have waited to hear that."

"I do know," he said. "And I will always be sorry for it. I love you, Gigi. I love you more than anything in this world, my career included. Without you, I am nothing."

She lifted her arms to him, wanting to hug him, but being too weak to lift herself. Fox gathered her up against him, holding her tightly and thanking God they'd had the opportunity for this conversation. The Lord had been merciful by allowing him to right the situation. Perhaps they had to hit the very bottom before he could see the top, and now, they'd risen above it.

One way or the other, they would be together.

"How long do you think it will take?" Gisele asked, pulling back to look at him. "Days? Weeks?"

He grunted. "Possibly longer than that," he said. "I do not know how long it is going to take. I am going to try to gain the man's agreement, but that could take time."

"A long time?"

He nodded reluctantly. "It could," he said softly. "Wouldn't you rather have this done the right way than flee like cowards at the slightest show of resistance?"

She thought on that. "Aye," she said after a moment. "But he denied you once before."

"He did," he said. "And my guess is that he will deny me this time. But I will not give up."

Gisele forced a smile. "I believe you," she said. "And I will wait. It would be nice not to have to flee, I agree, but we will if we must."

"As a last resort, we will," Fox said. "But take heart, my love. I will not leave you at Canonsleigh forever. Mayhap you will be there weeks or months or even a year, but I will not leave you there forever, I swear it."

She lay back against the pillows, feeling weak and tired, but she also felt hope that she hadn't felt in a very long time. "I would rather wait a thousand years for a chance to be your wife for one day than never have that opportunity at all," she said quietly. "Whatever it takes, however long it takes, I will wait for you."

Fox was so very pleased that she was behaving like the calm creature he knew she could be. The frazzled woman since leaving Selborne was not usual for her. It was true that she could be emotional, and immature at times, but it was something she had been outgrowing. He'd seen it over the last several months. The woman before him was more like the woman she was coming to be.

And that reminded him of something.

Standing up, he went over to his saddlebags and began digging through them. He had all of his worldly possessions in those bags, everything he'd taken from Selborne. He soon found what he had been looking for and came over to her bearing a small leather pouch in his hand.

"I have something for you," he said. "I was going to give this to you when we married, but I will give it to you now. I want you to have it, something to remind you of me. It is something that is very important."

Gisele watched curiously as he pulled something out of the

pouch. It looked like a pendant, or so she thought, but when he held it up, she could see that it was a brooch attached to a pin by a short silver chain. Fox held the brooch closer to her, and she fingered it, seeing that it was a silver dragon's head with a garnet for the eye. Around the dragon's head, etched into the silver, were a few words written in Latin. Peering closely, she read them aloud.

"*Tenera et vera*," she said softly.

Fox smiled as he put it in her hand. "It means tender and true," he said. "This is a piece given to my mother from her own father, who was the Earl of Morton. He was part of the Douglas clan."

She looked at him in surprise. "Scottish?"

He nodded. "Verily," he said. "When she married my father, my grandfather gave her this brooch. *Tender and true* is the family motto, but when I look at you, it takes on an entirely new meaning, because I will forever be tender with you and I will forever be true. Those words belong to us, Gigi. I want you to have this as a reminder of my love for you."

Gisele was deeply touched. She took the lovely brooch, inspecting it in detail, before looking to him with a smile. "It is beautiful," she murmured. "And I can think of no better words to describe you, Fox. You are, for certain, tender and true."

He leaned over and kissed her on the forehead as her gaze returned to the brooch. She seemed quite taken with it, and that pleased him. But it also brought up something else he'd been thinking on.

"Since I do not know how long I will be with the Marshal, you will be obligated to live as a nun does," he said. "I do not think they will take everything from you, but if they try to take this, bury it. Do not let them have it. And if you ever need me before I can return to you, if is a dire emergency, then find a messenger or a servant and have them bring this brooch to Pembroke Castle, because I do not intend to leave there until I have the Marshal's blessing. That is where I'll be. If you send this, I will fly to your side, no matter what. This brooch will be the magic that will bring me to you. Do you understand?"

She nodded, clasping the brooch against her breast. "I feel much better now that I have it," she said. "Fox… I know that I have been hard on you at times. Cruel, even. I called you a coward, and I am very sorry I said that."

He chuckled. "You are sorry now that you have what you want."

He was teasing her a little, but she was serious. "That is not true," she insisted weakly. "I was sorry when I said it. But I was hurt. I should not have lashed out at you as I did."

He kissed her on the forehead again. "You were right," he said. "I *was* a coward. Whatever insults you have ever dealt me, Gigi, you were not wrong. In this case, you forced me to take a close look at my priorities. I have always been my first priority, but no longer. Now, it is you. Even though I will leave you off at the abbey, I will go on to seek your hand, and I will not stop until I have permission. If I cannot gain permission, then I will have a solid plan to flee to Normandy. Although you will be forced to dress like a postulate and pray twenty times a day, take solace in the fact that I *will* come for you. Canonsleigh is only temporary."

"I will, I promise," she said. But the warmth in her eyes soon faded. "But what if you never come back, Fox? What if… what if you are killed or sent away? What if you never come?"

"I will come," he said with quiet sincerity. "It may not be tomorrow, or in a month, or even in a year. As I said, I do not know how long it will take. But I *will* come, Gigi."

"But if you do not. How long shall I wait?"

He stroked her cheek. "Until your last breath," he murmured. "Expect that I shall arrive every hour of every day. Watch the road for my return. But if I do not return to you in this lifetime, know that it was beyond my control. Nothing but death could keep me from you, and if that is the case, then I will be the first face you see when you have breathed your last. In life or in death, I will be there for you. Have no doubt."

Gisele clearly took a great deal of comfort in that. "I do not."

"Good," he said, kissing her hand one last time before rising. "Now, I have been instructed to feed you warm milk and beef broth, so I will return shortly."

She wrinkled her nose. "Milk and beef broth?" she said. "Can I at least have some bread and butter?"

He shrugged. "I do not know," he said. "But the physic said milk and broth. You'll be a good girl and eat it."

"But—"

"*Eat* it."

Gisele broke down into giggles, blowing him a kiss as he headed out of the chamber. Once he was gone, she returned her focus to the brooch, the dragon with the garnet eye. It was the first tangible thing he'd ever given her that was a promise of their future together, and she treasured it.

Tenera et vera.

Tender and true, indeed.

Forever.

CHAPTER TEN

Canonsleigh Abbey
Devon

B URIED IN THE countryside of Devon and about a mile from
a main road that passed from Taunton to Tiverton and on
into Cornwall, Canonsleigh Abbey sat amongst the bucolic
fields and forests.

It was a surprisingly small abbey, but an important one. It
had once been a Saxon manor before the arrival of the Normans, who confiscated it and built onto it, creating a compact
but busy establishment right in the middle of the wilds. It was
set amongst the farms, so the abbey itself had fields of agricul-
ture, tended to by the nuns and the acolytes and others who
attended church at the abbey. There was a sense of community
when it came to Canonsleigh, including the priest who came in
from Wellington every week to say mass.

As Fox and Gisele rode up to the abbey walls, they could see
that the big wooden gates were open. Chickens wandered on
the grounds outside the walls, as did goats and a couple of
ponies. Out in the fields, they could see people tending the
crops. Entering the open gate, they noticed that the ground had

been paved with stone, unusual for such a remote abbey, and in the middle of the yard, an enormous oak spread its branches.

Truth be told, it looked quite idyllic.

Fox glanced at Gisele to see how she was taking their arrival, and she caught his eye, shrugging and smiling. She didn't seem too terribly distressed, thankfully. Fox's commitment to return for her seemed to have soothed everything, and with that knowledge, she could accept what temporarily had to happen. Off to her right, a fat orange cat had four white and orange kittens, and that caught her attention. She gasped with delight. Fox knew she had always been fond of cats, so he had a smile on his lips as he dismounted Merlin and made his way over to her, helping her dismount her palfrey.

"How are you feeling?" he asked. "Not too tired, are you?"

She shook her head. "Not at all," she said. "Did you see the kittens?"

He chuckled. "Aye," he said. "I know you are desperate to play with them, so why don't you keep the cats company whilst I find the mother abbess?"

She lifted her hand, shielding her eyes from the sun as she looked up at him. "You do not want me to come with you?"

Her still-wrapped wrists caught his attention. It had been a week since she awoke from her attempt to take her own life, but in that time, she'd recovered admirably. Better still, she didn't remember any of what led up to that moment, and Fox was grateful. She'd eaten well, slept well, and the wounds were healing quite well, so much so that Johann, the former Hospitaller, had been able to remove the catgut stitches. He still wanted her to cleanse the wounds with wine nightly, and he told her that in a few days, she could take the wraps off completely. Fox was relieved he didn't have to worry about her wounds, because there was quite a bit more he had to worry over these days.

Speaking to the mother abbess was one of them.

"Nay," he said after a moment. "Make friends with the cats and I will find the abbess. But do not stray from this spot. I will come for you once I've spoken to her."

Nodding, Gisele immediately headed over to the cat family, and Fox's gaze lingered on her for a moment as she knelt next to the cats and began petting the friendly mother. Satisfied she would be occupied for a time, and quite happily, he headed for the abbey.

The structure itself was single story, with a chapel that had a pitched roof and a small cloister that was walled off from the entry. The walls were made of pale stone, the kind that was mined in Devon and Cornwall, and he rang the old bell at the chapel entry, which was open, but he wouldn't go in. He didn't want to be perceived as a threat. He'd heard tales of nuns with swords and pikes gravely injuring men they considered a danger.

He waited.

Small women in heavy robes began gathering just inside the door, whispering. He could see them clustering in the shadows nervously. Fox kept his hands where they could see them so they would know he didn't have a ready weapon. There were a few children about, perhaps orphans or even servants, and one of them got too close to the door, so a nun reached out and grabbed him by the ear, yanking him away. Fox had to fight off a smile, hearing the poor child being dragged away for being curious.

"What does thee wish?"

A tall, thin woman in impeccable robes appeared. She was

covered from head to toe in fabric, with only her smooth, shiny face visible, and she was perhaps forty years of age. She was looking at him quite curiously as he bowed his head to her out of respect.

"Are you the mother abbess?" he asked.

The woman clasped her hands in front of her. "I am," she said. "What does thee wish?"

"My name is Fox de Merest," he said. "My father was the Earl of Keddington, and I serve William Marshal. May we speak in private, please? I come on business for the Earl of Pembroke."

That seemed to change the woman's curious features to an expression of surprise. There were still nuns hovering behind her, however, and she quickly turned to chase them away, save one—a small woman with dark eyes and dark hair on her cheeks and upper lip, who gazed at Fox with some fear. As the other nuns rushed off, the mother abbess emerged from the door, bringing the dark-haired nun with her.

"I am Mother Mary Cecilia," the mother abbess said. "This is Sister Mary Bernard. How may we assist you?"

Fox wasn't thrilled that another nun was present, but he didn't insist she leave. He faced the mother abbess.

"As I said, I come on behalf of William Marshal," he said. "Twenty-two years ago, he made arrangements with Canonsleigh to take one of his daughters as a postulate. I have brought the daughter to be delivered at the request of her father."

The mother abbess didn't reply right away. "The Earl of Pembroke, you say?" she finally said. "The man known as William Marshal?"

"Aye, your grace."

"I've not heard that name in some time. He is still alive?"

"He is, your grace," Fox answered. He eyed the woman a moment. "If you do not know of this arrangement, mayhap there is someone older who would know of it. I was told the arrangements were made some time ago."

The woman hesitated before turning to the nun at her side and whispering something to her. The dark-eyed nun turned quickly and disappeared through the entry. When she was gone, the mother abbess spoke quietly.

"I know of it," she said. "We do not transact much worldly business here, so I would recall a bargain struck in such a manner with a powerful lord, no matter how long ago."

"Then you *do* know."

The woman nodded. "You have brought the bastard."

Fox didn't know if he was comforted or disappointed that she actually *did* know of the arrangement. If she didn't know, and refused to take Gisele, his troubles would be over. He could use that as leverage in his marriage offer. But he was rather sorry to realize that was not to be. Perhaps some large part of him had been hoping for it.

"Aye," he said after a moment. "Were you told of it, then?"

She shook her head, as much as the restrictive wimple would allow. "I was here when the Earl of Pembroke sent men to make the bargain," she said. "I served the mother abbess at the time, Sister Mary Charity. I remember the men who came. I remember the story. I also remember that the Earl of Pembroke donated a sizable sum to our coffers. One does not forget that."

That was new information to Fox. *So the Marshal paid them well to take in his child*, he thought. He was starting to see just how much this move had been planned and felt betrayed, yet again, that he'd never been told. But he fought those emotions, as they were unproductive.

"Your grace," he said, lowering his voice. "His daughter, Lady Gisele, knew nothing of this arrangement until a few short days ago. There was an attempt on her life, and it was decided that she would be safer here at Canonsleigh. But we rode in through open gates. Nothing is secure. Is this how you always live?"

The mother abbess smiled. "We live a simple life," she said. "Thou only knows warfare, knight. We know God's love. It is everywhere, and we welcome anyone who wishes to serve Him."

Fox looked around, thinking that it would be far too easy for anyone to get to Gisele in this place. He wasn't sure that was what William Marshal had had in mind when he arranged for her to come. It was rather isolated, that was true, and the reality was that even if Isabella hired more assassins, they would probably never find out where Gisele had gone, but still... The open gates and lack of security disturbed him.

"I can see that you have much to give, your grace," he said. "But I am bringing you the bastard daughter of William Marshal and a woman of royal blood. That makes his daughter quite valuable, and there are those who will harm her if they can. Do you never close your gates?"

The mother abbess nodded. "In the evening," she said. "They are closed at night, and we lock our doors. But in the light of day, they are open. We are quite safe, I assure you."

"Does Pembroke know you keep your gates open?"

"The day he came, they were not locked."

Fox sighed heavily. It wasn't as if he could make the decision not to leave Gisele here. That decision had already been made. But he realized that he was looking for an excuse not to leave her here. *It's unsafe,* he would say. But the truth was that he couldn't very well take her with him to Pembroke and then explain he didn't like the fact that the abbey was wide open, and the mother abbess was living in a dreamland if she thought there was no violence in the world.

Nay, he couldn't do that at all.

He had to stop looking for excuses.

"Very well," he finally said, reluctantly. "I will bring Lady Gisele to you. She has found a cat to pet."

As he turned to go, the mother abbess called out to him. "Good knight," she said. "I assure you that the lady will be quite safe. You needn't worry."

Fox didn't believe that, but he didn't argue. He simply nodded and walked away, heading back around the corner of the chapel and seeing Gisele in the distance. She had at least two kittens in her arms, maybe more, and he headed in her direction, seeing the joy on her face as she cuddled the kittens. When she caught sight of him, she smiled brightly.

"Look at them," she said. "Are they not the sweetest creatures in the world?"

"The sweetest," he said, but he was distracted. "I have spoken to the mother abbess. She told me that the Marshal made a sizable donation years ago when he made the arrangements for you to come here. She is waiting for you."

Gisele's smile faded as she looked at him. "Now?"

"Now."

Her smile disappeared, and she put the kittens down gently before brushing her hands off and facing him. "I see," she said softly. "Has the moment you will leave me finally arrived?"

He didn't dare touch her in case the nuns happened to be watching. "We knew this moment would come, didn't we?" he said steadily. "We have said our farewells. I have told you that I will return for you, come what may. You know I love you madly and that your stay here is only temporary. Is there anything else I can tell you to make this transition easier for you?"

He was trying to be gentle with her, but the truth was that the moment was upon them. The moment they had both been dreading but the moment they knew would come. They'd spent the past week of her recovery in a surprisingly domestic situation at the inn, living in the same room, eating together every meal, and sleeping in the same bed every night. But there had been nothing sexual until last night, when Fox had gently bedded her one last time. When it came time for him to find his release, he hadn't withdrawn as he usually did. He remained in her even though she hadn't forced him like she did the last time. He simply held her tightly, absorbing their last moments together, committing it to memory for the days and weeks to come.

And she had done the same.

Now, Gisele wasn't sure she could keep her resolve to be brave. Everything they had needed to say to one another had already been said. They'd loved and touched and wept together. At least, she had wept while he held her. But the promise for the future was there. The hope was there. The brooch he gave her was pinned to her shift, under her traveling clothes, where no one could see it and no one could take it. Fox had even given her a pouch containing coin so she had it if she needed it. She had everything she needed.

Except him.

The time had come.

"There is nothing more to say," she finally said, her voice trembling but a smile on her lips. "We have indeed said everything we needed to say to one another. As I look at you, I am memorizing the lines of your face and the shape of your eyes. I am memorizing the sound of your voice so I can hear it every night in my dreams. The journey here... It was such a gift, Fox. It was some of the best time I have ever spent with you. Will you do something for me now?"

"Anything, my love."

"Will you please gather your horse and ride from here?" she said. "I will go to the mother abbess myself. I do not need you to take me."

He sighed faintly, seeing that she was trying very hard to be brave. Truthfully, so was he. "Are you certain?"

"I am," she murmured, her lips now quivering even though she was still smiling. "Go, now. Ride for Pembroke. I will be here when you are ready to return to me."

He wished with all his might that he could have taken her in his arms at that moment, but it was impossible. Instead, he smiled proudly. Sadly, but proudly.

"And I *will* return," he said. "Meanwhile... make friends with the kittens. Be useful. Learn a skill if they are willing to teach you."

She laughed softly. "What skill could they possibly teach me?"

He shrugged. "They have fields," he said. "Learn to plant a garden. I do not think Lady de Nerra taught you that."

"Nay, she did not."

"It might be useful if we are forced to flee and live in poverty because no one will hire a disgraced knight," he said, his eyes glimmering with mirth. "You can plant a garden and feed us."

She chuckled. "I will consider it," she said. "Go now, Fox. The longer you remain, the more difficult it will be to let you go. Please."

He knew that. His focus lingered on her, a thousand words of love and adoration coming to his lips, but he couldn't seem to speak them. Tears were stinging his eyes, but he fought them, struggling with his control. Instead, he forced a smile.

"I love you," he whispered. "And know that when I return, we are not taking any of those cats with us."

Gisele, who had been verging on tears, burst into laughter as he turned away, going to collect Merlin's reins. "That is what you think," she said. "I will have a dozen, and they are all coming with us."

He tossed the reins over the horse's neck. "If you do, I will have a dozen dogs with a taste for cat flesh."

"That is a terrible thing to say," she said as he swung his big body onto the horse. "Do not make me decide between you and my two dozen cats. You will not like it."

He snorted, indicating for her to pass him the reins of her palfrey. "Now it is two dozen?" he said, feigning outrage. "They are worthless beasts who will eat my food."

"And sleep in your bed."

He took the reins from her. "That is where I will take a stand," he said, wagging a gloved finger at her. "There will be no cats in our bed."

"Not even one?"

"Not even one."

Her eyes were glittering with humor as she gazed up at him. "Surely we can negotiate."

He shook his head. "Not on that, we cannot," he said. Quickly, his smile faded as he looked at her. "I am leaving now, my love. Gather your satchel and go to the mother abbess."

Her smile faded, as well. "I will," she said. "But I want to watch you ride away."

"Why?"

"Because I'll feel all the more joy when I see you return," she said wistfully. "Let me have my last look."

He smiled at her, patting a gloved hand to his chest in the same general area where she had the brooch pinned to her shift.

"Tender and true," he whispered.

Gisele smiled faintly, blowing him a kiss as he finally turned for the open gates. He never turned around to look at her again as he headed out to the road, but she stood there and watched him until he faded from view. Though her humor was gone, she didn't collapse in tears. Surprisingly, she felt strangely strong at his departure. Perhaps because it was a good parting, but also because she knew he would come back for her. Fox de Merest never made a promise he did not keep.

And she would be waiting for him.

Tender and true, indeed.

CHAPTER ELEVEN

Pembroke Castle
Wales

T HERE WAS NOTHING mightier or more imposing than the sight of Pembroke Castle.

It had taken Fox almost a week to reach the enormous, gray-stoned castle perched above the Pembroke River and surrounded by an enormous moat. William Marshal had received it by marriage about fifteen years earlier, and he had immediately begun replacing the old timbers with stone. He also built the enormous keep. It was a project that had taken many years, and even to this day, there were still parts of the place that were being reinforced with stone—but on the whole it was one of the more intimidating and powerful castles in England, if not in all of Wales.

The Marshal was quite proud of it.

William Marshal didn't spend all of his time at Pembroke Castle, but he was in residence seasonally. He would spend autumn and winter in London or at any number of his other properties, and usually he would spend spring or summer at Pembroke. The Welsh had never accepted an English lordship so deep in the heart of Wales, so William made it a habit of spending time in Pembroke with regularity simply as a show for the Welsh. For a man who had built his life on the politics of his country, he knew how important it was to establish good relationships with his neighbors, and he had done that. There was no real animosity, at least at this point in time.

Pembroke Castle was relatively peaceful.

As Fox came up the road, with a castle looming in front of him, he remembered that the last time he was there had been to ask for Gisele's hand in marriage. It didn't give him any warm and fond feelings to remember that moment in time when he'd been denied his wants. It was difficult not to let negative thoughts fill his brain as he approached the bastion, because he had come now to do essentially the same thing—ask for permission to marry.

He hoped that history would not repeat itself.

As he drew closer, the sentries began to notice his approach, and he could hear the cry go up. There was a town built up around the castle, and it went right up to the castle walls, which he could see soaring above the thatched rooftops. He was on the main street of the small city, and it was bustling at this hour. He knew that he was an enemy knight in enemy territory, although the town had become quite used to English knights going in and out of the castle. Children and the elderly scurried to get out of his way, but a few of the women paused and smiled at him rather alluringly. He didn't acknowledge them as he passed through and headed straight for the gatehouse. When the sentries demanded his name, he shouted back at them. In little time, the portcullis lifted.

"Fox?"

A big knight was coming underneath the portcullis, looking

at him with some delight. Fox grinned when he recognized his old friend, a man he'd not seen in many years. Dismounting Merlin, he went to greet him.

"Keller," he said with satisfaction. "My God, how long has it been? I thought they'd chased you up to some castle in the north?"

Sir Keller de Poyer cracked a smile, taking the hand that Fox offered and holding it firmly. "They did," he said. "Nether Castle is a beast of a castle that guards a very important pass."

"You're still stationed there?"

"I am, but I came here on business," he said, still holding Fox's hand and looking him over with delight. "It is good to see you again, my friend. Much has happened since we last met."

"No doubt," Fox said. "How long will you remain at Pembroke?"

"Not long," Keller said. "I must return home to my castle and my wife. I am anxious to see both."

Fox's eyebrows lifted. "You've *married*?" he said. "How did I not know this?"

Keller chuckled. "I have not seen you in years," he said. "It has been at least seven or eight years since we last spoke, right before I went to Nether. As I said, much has happened in that time."

"I can believe it."

"I have five children, too."

Fox's look of surprise was greatly exaggerated. "Five?" he said in shock. "Christ, Keller, must you outshine us all?"

Keller, in truth, was one of the most humble and deserving men Fox had ever known. He was an older knight, big and powerful and not overtly handsome, but he had a kind and generous heart. He would do anything for his friends and allies.

The fact that he'd had good fortune in marriage and family was something that did Fox's heart good, but Keller merely smiled at what sounded like a good-natured scolding.

"I have been fortunate," he said modestly, true to form. "I am much older than you, as you know. My time has come, and yours will, too. In fact, is there anything to report on that front?"

Fox tried not to let the question dampen his mood. His smile, once genuine, turned rather forced. "Nay," he said. "Nothing new."

"No special lady?"

Fox had known Keller for years. They'd served together before they had gone their separate ways, so he knew Keller was trustworthy. In truth, perhaps it would be good for him to confess his situation to someone who wasn't emotionally invested in it. Val had been, and the Marshal was. So was Fox, of course. But Keller wasn't. The man was older and wiser and would perhaps have something important to say about it, something that would be meaningful.

Or something that would cause Fox to rethink everything.

In either case, something in him needed to share his burden with this old and dear friend.

"That is a question with a very complicated answer," he said. "I realize we've not seen each other in years, but I have always considered you a friend. I hope you can claim the same about me."

Keller smiled. "Of course I can," he said. "I am honored to know you, Fox. What is it? Can I help?"

That question almost brought Fox to tears. Keller didn't know what he was asking, but it still felt good to have someone show concern.

"I wish you could," Fox said. "I truly wish you could, but perhaps you can only help in listening to my story. If you have the time…"

Keller answered quickly. "I have the time," he said. "For you, I will make time. Shall we go inside?"

"Is the Marshal in residence?"

"He is."

"Then I will tell you here, because it involves him."

Keller grew serious. "I see," he said. "Then tell me."

"You must take it to the grave."

"On my oath, I will."

Fox glanced up at the gatehouse, at the soldiers on the wall walk looking down at him and Keller. They were mostly alone, with people now and then walking in and out of the open portcullis, but no one was really paying attention to two knights in conversation. Fox removed his helm and ran a hand over his damp hair before speaking.

"This is not easy for me," he said. "It has been something that has affected my life for six years."

"Six years?" Keller repeated, deeply concerned. "Take your time, lad. Speak when you are ready."

Fox nodded, not wanting to take up too much of Keller's valuable time, as he considered how to begin the conversation. He realized there was only one way to start—from the beginning.

His tragic tale was about to unfold.

"About twelve years ago, I was sent to Selborne Castle," he said. "Do you remember that?"

Keller nodded. "I do," he said. "Val de Nerra's stronghold."

"I was sent there for a special purpose."

"And that was?"

"To protect William Marshal's bastard daughter."

That brought a reaction from Keller. "Oh?" he said, surprised. "I wasn't aware he had one."

Fox nodded. "He does," he said. "Her mother is Queen Margaret, wife of Henry the Young King. Surely you've heard the rumors of an affair between those two. That was gossip fodder long ago."

Keller tried to conceal his shock, but he wasn't doing a very good job. "I remember hearing something like that," he said. "It was very long ago, when I was newly knighted. Then the rumors of a child were true?"

Fox sighed faintly, thinking on the woman he loved with all his heart. "They had a daughter," he said. "A beautiful, smart, glorious daughter whom I have fallen madly in love with. I have protected her since she was a child, and, of course, there was simply a professional relationship until she came of age, but I have watched her grow. I have watched her become a woman. Six years ago, she told me that she loved me, and I realized I loved her in return."

Keller smiled. "That is a magnificent thing," he said. "Congratulations, my friend. But I sense everything is not as you hoped it would be?"

Fox shook his head. "Not at all," he said. "There are those who know of Gisele's heritage. She hasn't exactly been hidden, but more sent to be raised by de Nerra to allow her to blend in and live a normal life. But those who do know of her believe she is the daughter of the Young King—not William Marshal. Henry had his enemies. There have been three attempts on her life and safety, the most recent one coming last month. They very nearly killed her and one of de Nerra's daughters along with her."

Keller was listening intently. "I'm so sorry," he said. "But she is well? She was not wounded?"

"She was not wounded," Fox said. "But the heart of the issue is this—unbeknownst to me, the Marshal made arrangements for Gisele to be sent to Canonsleigh Abbey when she came of age. He has determined that she should take the veil and live her life there. I have already asked for her hand once, and he denied me without telling me anything about Canonsleigh, but de Nerra knew. After the last attempt against Gisele, which was orchestrated by none other than Queen Isabella, Val decided it was time to send her to Canonsleigh to protect her and to protect his own family. Not that I blame him, but I was charged with escorting her to Canonsleigh, and now I am here to ask the Marshal, once again, for her hand in marriage. I will not allow the Marshal to deny us again, but if he is unwavering, then I have decided to take Gisele and flee to France. I will not be kept from her, Keller. She is mine and I love her."

It was an impassioned speech. Keller was listening with great interest and great sorrow, seeing the man before him who was on the verge of exploding. He could see that in everything about Fox. Realizing Fox had come to Pembroke to essentially have a showdown with William Marshal over Gisele, he understood the seriousness of the situation even if Fox didn't. Not fully, anyway. Emotional men seldom considered the true implications. When Fox was finished speaking, he put a big hand on the man's shoulder.

"Of course you love her," he said. "Thank you for telling me, Fox. I am honored that you would take me into your confidence."

Fox had to admit that although he felt better about telling Keller, repeating the story had him riled up. "Everyone who knows about the situation has some emotional investment in it," he said. "Val does, I do, even the Marshal does. But you do not. I realize it is a great imposition to ask for your counsel, but I will ask just the same. I have nowhere else to turn."

Keller drew in a long, deep breath, clapping Fox on the shoulder again as he turned to look at the gatehouse. He was mulling over the question and his answer, understanding that this wasn't a simple situation in the least. The sensible side of him told him not to get involved, but the side that understood what it was to love a woman wasn't listening. This was a man's life, and he took Fox's confidence very seriously.

"You have certainly been busy since I last saw you," he quipped simply to lighten the mood. "Never let it be said that Fox de Merest is an uncomplicated man."

Fox smiled, though it was without humor. "That is my misfortune," he said. "But it is an unfortunate fact."

"It seems to be," Keller said, returning his attention to Fox. "And you are committed to asking the Marshal again for her hand today?"

"As surely as we are standing here."

Keller pondered that a moment. "If you truly wish for my counsel, I would advise you to put your emotion aside," he said. "If you go charging in to see the Marshal the way you are now, it will take very little for you to erupt. You look as if you are coiled, ready to strike."

"It is that obvious?"

"It is," Keller said. "And you will never get what you want if you do that. I know you understand that, Fox. Cooler heads must prevail, because any manner of anger is going to put Pembroke on the defensive, and he will never give you permission."

"Then what do you suggest?"

Keller removed his hand from Fox's shoulder and began rubbing his palms together, thinking. "If it were me," he said thoughtfully, "I would present the issue from more a matter of safety. If the lady has already been set upon, several times, and you are her assigned protector, would it not make it easier to protect her if you were her husband?"

"True," Fox said. "But she's at an abbey now, and the Marshal seems to think she is safer there."

"What is the abbey like?"

Fox rolled his eyes. "A gang of infants could rush in and overwhelm the place," he said. "There are no safety measures at all. The gates are wide open because they want to welcome everyone. The Marshal is putting his faith in the fact that anyone making an attempt against Gisele will think twice before violating the sanctity of an abbey, but you and I both know that when it comes to the deviant mind, the protection of God and the church will not make any difference."

Keller shook his head reluctantly. "Nay, it will not," he said. "You believe she would be safer with you?"

Fox nodded. "Very much so," he said. "But it is more than that. I love the woman and want to be with her. You are a married man—I assume you care for your wife?"

Keller nodded faintly. "I love her very much."

"What would you do if you could not be with her?"

"There is no such world where that is possible," Keller said. "I would make sure we were together, no matter what."

"And that is why I have come."

"I understand that this is about love," Keller said quietly. "It is not about her safety, but about love. However, I would not tell the Marshal that, because he will use it against you if he can.

I would use the matter of the lady's safety and see if you can convince him that she would be better off with a husband."

"And if I cannot?"

"Then you take her and you go to France," Keller said. "I know of another knight who has done that. Garren le Mon. Did you know him?"

Fox shook his head. "I have heard the name, but I did not know him."

"He was sent to spy on an enemy of the Marshal but fell in love with the man's daughter," he said. "He essentially faked his own death and fled with her to France. I would not repeat that if I were you. And do not use it as an example when you confront Pembroke. It will not go well for you if you do."

Fox nodded. "I will not speak of it," he said. "Then... then it is not unusual for a knight who has achieved much in life to flee if it means he can be with the woman he loves?"

Keller shook his head. "Of course not," he said. "But you must remember that if you do, you will leave everything behind. Everything you have worked for, the reputation you have built. It will be in ruins, and once it is gone, there will be no getting it back. Are you prepared for that?"

"I am."

"When do you intend to do this?"

"Now."

"You do not want time to think?"

"I do not need time to think. I've been thinking about this every day for six years."

"Does the lady know this?"

Fox nodded. "She knows," he said. "She agrees. She did not want to go to the abbey, but I convinced her that it was for the best, temporarily. However, I left her with my mother's brooch.

If she is in need of me before I can return for her, she is to send it to Pembroke Castle because I assumed I would be here for the foreseeable future. If she sends it, I will go to her. It is our signal if I am urgently needed."

"In case the assassins of Isabella find her?"

"Exactly."

Keller's gaze moved in the direction of the enormous bailey of Pembroke with the equally enormous, circular keep. He knew there would be no stopping Fox because the man's mind was set. He could see it in his face.

"I had come to Pembroke to discuss a particularly naughty Welsh lord," he said. "That was the business I had here. I was going to leave for home today, but I think I will stay for the night. It is too late to leave, anyway. The sun will be setting soon."

Fox looked to the sky. "The sun is directly overhead," he said. "The sun will not be setting for several hours, at least."

Keller wouldn't acknowledge that he was making flimsy excuses so he could remain while Fox spoke to the Marshal. "Come inside," he said, motioning to him. "Leave your horse at the livery and go to the great hall. I will summon the Marshal for you."

Fox began to follow the man, but he was eyeing him strangely. "You need not stay because of me," he said. "This is something I must do alone, Keller."

Keller kept walking. "I know."

Fox caught up to him. "If you remain to support me, though I greatly appreciate it, the Marshal may turn his anger on you," he said. "I did not tell you this so you could ride into battle with me. I do not want you to be needlessly put into his bad favor."

Keller glanced at him. "I have never been in Pembroke's bad favor in my life," he said. "He has few knights as loyal or as smart as I. Do not worry about me, Fox. If you do, you insult my honor."

Fox stared at the man for a moment before shaking his head, grinning as he looked away. "Please don't make me fight you about this."

"You would lose."

"I am younger and faster."

"I am older and more underhanded."

They looked at each other before breaking down into snorts of laughter. Fox knew when he was beaten.

"Very well," he said. "But if the Marshal punishes you because of me, do not say I didn't warn you."

They came to a pause as a stable servant came rushing out to take Merlin away. As Fox pulled his saddlebags off the animal and the servant led the beast away, Keller fixed on him.

"I won't blame you for anything," he said. "This is my choice. Do you not trust my wisdom?"

"Of course I do."

"Then know that I think it is important that there be a neutral party to mediate what will undoubtedly be a volatile conversation."

"You mean that you want to be present to keep me from doing anything foolish."

Keller simply lifted his eyebrows and resumed walking toward the keep, leaving Fox standing in the bailey, watching him go. He had to admit that the thought of Keller's calming and influential presence was comforting. He simply didn't want his friend to get into trouble for supporting him. If it came to that. But it might come to something else entirely. All Fox could do at that moment was wait until the prey was brought to the hunter, but the truth was that he wished he knew if he was really the hunter... or if he was the one about to be eaten.

He was about to find out.

 CƷ

IT SEEMED AS if the man had lived forever.

William Marshal, Earl of Pembroke, had been around for many years. He'd fought for three kings in his lifetime and, quite probably, would fight for more before his life came to an end. He'd been a simple knight who had worked his way up into a position of supreme power in England. His name was spoken with reverence amongst great warlords, but he also had his share of enemies. In this day and age, everyone did.

But the Marshal had learned to keep himself alive better than most.

Not only did he command a great army, but he was also an advisor to the king. He'd been an advisor to Richard the Lionheart and Henry II. He played the game of politics better than anyone alive because his mind was quick and he had the ability to think like his adversaries. But there was something else he was involved in, something that his allies knew about and something that his enemies only whispered about.

William Marshal was in charge of the greatest band of spies and assassins the world had ever seen.

They were known as the Executioner Knights. They were some of the most elite warriors who had ever carried a sword, men from a variety of backgrounds and with a variety of experiences, who helped William Marshal plot the course of England. In fact, Keller was an Executioner Knight, though his work had been in the periphery. Agents would accomplish a task and Keller was usually the one who cleaned it up or made sure the situation, or the location, was secure. He'd never actually been the lead agent on a mission or an assassination, but rather remained in the background to be called forward when he was needed. That was by his own choice. He wasn't as aggressive as some of the other agents, nor was he a cold-blooded killer as some were, but he was the most dependable man in the stable of William Marshal. In fact, the Marshal depended on Keller a great deal, and at one point, Keller had been the garrison commander of Pembroke Castle itself. Out of all the knights that William Marshal had at his disposal, Keller was one of the closest. The Marshal trusted Keller's opinions and his wisdom.

That was why Keller wanted to be present when Fox and the Marshal came together.

Fox knew nothing of Keller's position in the Executioner Knights. The members of the elite group were kept secret, even from allies like Fox or Val de Nerra. Of course, all fighting men had heard of the Executioner Knights, but those who hadn't confirmed the existence of the group spoke of ghosts and phantoms, rumors of these elite spies that probably didn't really exist.

But they did.

And the Marshal controlled them.

When William Marshal entered the great hall with Keller and spied Fox standing near the hearth, he knew something was amiss. There was no reason why Fox de Merest should be at Pembroke—a man he'd once considered recruiting for the Executioner Knights, but he'd ultimately decided Fox was needed more at Selborne protecting his daughter. Fox was excellent, and there was no doubt in his mind that he would make an excellent Executioner Knight, but Fox was simply needed elsewhere. When the Marshal made eye contact with Fox, he smiled weakly at the big, blue-eyed knight.

"Imagine my surprise when Keller told me that you had come to Pembroke," he said. "I nearly called him a liar, but then I remembered that he does not lie."

That was as close to a warm greeting as the Marshal was able to give. He was a man who had learned to control his emotions, whether it was joy or sorrow, a long time ago. No one could ever accuse him of being congenial.

Fox smiled weakly to the greeting. "He did not, my lord," he said. "It is agreeable to be at Pembroke again. I am impressed every time I come here."

"As is everyone else," the Marshal said. "Have you been fed yet?"

"A servant has gone to fetch me something to drink."

"Good," the Marshal said. "And why are we honored by your visit?"

Fox had been contemplating this moment for quite some time. William wasn't one for small talk, and he knew he would come right to the point of Fox's visit.

Fortunately, Fox was ready.

"De Nerra has sent me," he said. "There have been some developments with Lady Gisele."

That seemed to draw a mild reaction from the Marshal. "She is well, I hope?"

Fox gestured to the nearest table. "Shall we sit, my lord?" he said. "I do not mind if Keller remains. I have no secrets from him."

They were moving to the nearest table as the Marshal looked over his shoulder. "But I might," he muttered. When

Keller paused on his way to find a seat, William waved a hand at him. "Sit down. I was only jesting. Don't look so hurt."

Keller continued on to claim his chair as Fox and the Marshal sat across the table from one another. Keller was at the end of the table, like any good mediator, watching body language and wondering if he'd be restraining Fox before the day was through.

"You did not answer my question, Fox," the Marshal said. "Is Lady Gisele well?"

Fox nodded. "She is, my lord," he said. "But there has been an... incident."

"What incident?"

"Several days ago, at Selborne Castle, we had a band of traveling minstrels stop for the evening," Fox said, lowering his voice. "At least, we thought they were minstrels, but as it happened, they were not. They were assassins."

The Marshal's pleasant mood faded. "Their target?"

"Lady Gisele," Fox said. "Between de Nerra and I, we made short work of them, but before one of them died, he told us that he was sent by the Comte de Angoulême on behalf of Queen Isabella."

The Marshal's brow furrowed. "From Ademar?" he said. "Why?"

"Because the young queen is evidently trying to find favor with her husband," Fox said. "She knows, as many do, that Lady Gisele is the daughter of Henry the Young King. That puts her in line for the throne. Evidently, Isabella was attempting to eliminate the competition."

The news had the Marshal genuinely stunned. He wasn't terribly close to John these days, but he had been in the past. Like many advisors and counselors, he tended to fall in and out of favor at the whims of the king. But he knew enough to know that this was not an impulsive move by a young and clever queen. Anything Isabella did was well thought out.

"But Gisele suffered no harm?" he said.

Fox shook his head. "She did not, my lord."

The Marshal's focus lingered on Fox for a few moments before he averted his gaze as he deliberated the situation. After a moment, he shook his head.

"She wants to be her mother-in-law," he said. "Isabella admires Eleanor of Aquitaine greatly, but she does not have the intelligence that Eleanor has. However, she has the ruthlessness. And she has the means."

Fox could see both disgust and concern on the Marshal's face. "The assassin, before he died, told us that more assassins would come," he said. "He seemed to think she would not give up."

"And she probably will not until something else comes along that takes her attention," the Marshal said. "She will try to find another way to garner her husband's favor."

"Is it so necessary, my lord?" Fox said. "Why must she beg for his favor?"

The Marshal sat forward, resting his arms on the table. "Because John is not kind to her," he said. "He has ignored her since nearly the day they were married. She is very young, and he simply has no interest in her and, at times, is cruel. He takes other women to his bed along with his wife, and that is something Isabella cannot stomach. She is trying to prove her worth, and by eliminating the closest heir to the throne, she would do John a great favor."

Fox knew that, but he wasn't finished with his story yet. "There is something more you should know, my lord," he said.

"After this attempt on her life, de Nerra decided to send her to Canonsleigh. He told me that she had been pledged there as an infant."

The Marshal looked at him. "She has," he said steadily. "Is she already there?"

"I took her myself."

"Good," the Marshal said with some relief. "She will be safe there. Isabella will never find her, and even if she does, she will think twice about violating an abbey. Gisele is finally safe."

Fox's jaw twitched faintly. "My lord, I would never contradict you, but in this case, I must," he said. "She is *not* safe. Canonsleigh is a travesty of open gates and open arms when it comes to visitors. Gisele is in more danger there than she ever was at Selborne, but de Nerra insisted that I take her there, so I did. My lord, I have come to plead on Gisele's behalf. Canonsleigh is no place for her."

The Marshal fixed on him. The man had dark eyes, with the whites slightly yellowed with age, giving him a rather sinister glare in dim light. This was one of those times, because Fox could see that, behind that stare, the thoughts were churning. Something was building.

He braced himself.

"She could not be safer," the Marshal finally said. "She has been intended for Canonsleigh since the beginning."

There was a warning in that statement, but Fox didn't back down. They were on the very subject he'd come to discuss, and he wasn't going to let the moment get away from him. He faced the Marshal with as much intensity as he was receiving.

"If you saw it now, you would not agree," he said evenly. "The gates are wide open, the doors open, and people come and go as they please. Would it not make sense, my lord, to allow me to continue protecting her? I came to you before to ask for her hand, and I am asking you again. My feelings for her have not changed. I love her, and she loves me, and I believe I can protect her much more ably than a worn abbey and a group of passive nuns. Would you not agree?"

He'd done what Keller told him not to do—he'd admitted his love for Gisele without reserve. Not that the Marshal was stupid—the man had to know, even without Fox admitting it, that the knight was in love with Gisele. As Fox's plea settled, the Marshal seemed to harden.

"Fox, I appreciate your candor," he said. "I appreciate that you wish to marry her. But she is not meant for you, lad. I have told you that before."

"You did, my lord, but you did not tell me why."

"Because her destiny has already been chosen."

"But you decided that destiny for her when she was an infant," Fox said, trying not to become emotional about it. "You did not know she would have dreams and loves, but she does and she has. She is a woman of flesh and blood who wants a family and children. And I want those things with her. Am I not a reputable knight? I am the son of the Earl of Keddington. I will make a good husband to her, my lord, I swear it. I only want her happiness."

That plea only seemed to harden the Marshal further. "I have denied you, Fox," he said. "Please do not ask again."

He was effectively cutting him off, but Fox wouldn't have it. His composure began to slip. "Why would you not consider it?" he asked. "I do not understand. It is not as if you have any relationship with her. It is not as if you even know her. Do you know that she paints beautifully? Do you know that she loves cats? She loves to dance, but she isn't any good at it. Do you even know this woman that you hold power over? You have made these decisions for her without even knowing her, and I do not understand why you will not allow her to marry. Can you explain this to me so I can understand?"

The Marshal didn't like being questioned, nor did he like having it pointed out that he didn't know this woman, his daughter. He'd seen her many times when she was younger, a beautiful girl with big, dreamy eyes and dark blonde hair, but he began to realize that the older she grew, the more she looked like Margaret. That was something he tried very hard not to think about, but Fox's questions were pushing him into an area he didn't like to discuss.

"You need not understand," he said. "I have given you my answer. You will abide by it."

Fox was at a loss. He was struggling not to rage because he knew it wouldn't get him anywhere. Keller had pointed that out. In fact, he looked to Keller at the end of the table with an expression that suggested he was ready to tear the place apart. Keller lifted a hand, motioning Fox away from the table, and he took the command gratefully. He was afraid of what would happen if he remained there. As Fox walked away to cool his temper, Keller turned to the Marshal.

"I realize this is none of my business, my lord, but Fox told me of the love he has for your daughter," he said quietly.

William's head came up sharply. "*My* daughter?" he said. "You mean Henry's daughter."

"I am aware that she is your bastard with Margaret."

The Marshal was prepared to strongly contest that statement, but he simply couldn't do it. He and Keller were close— he was probably closer to Keller than almost anyone else, as a friend, so he couldn't lie to the man, not if he already knew the truth.

With a sigh, he looked away.

"Not many know that."

"I will take the information to my grave."

"That is not what I meant," the Marshal said. "I know you are trustworthy. I simply meant… When you said that, it reminded me of something I do not like to face."

"And that is why you are angry with Fox? Because he reminds you of an affair?"

The Marshal shook his head. "It isn't that."

"Then what? It is not like you to be unjust, my lord."

William peered at him. "And you think I am being unjust?"

Keller shrugged. "I do not know this situation, so I cannot say," he said. "But based on my observations, and what I know, you are being unfair to Fox. He is a good man, my lord. You know this. He is brave and true, and he would make a fine husband for Lady Gisele. It is not fair to him not to explain your reasons for denying his suit."

"He doesn't have to know everything."

"Doesn't he? Need I remind you what happened to Garren le Mon?"

That caused the Marshal to look at him—indeed, he remembered the best agent he'd ever had and lost because of politics. It was more complex than that, but the result was the same. William had lost a good man. After a moment, he shook his head with frustration.

"Men in love are foolish creatures," he muttered. "I know because I was one of them."

Keller suspected he knew why. "With Lady Gisele's mother?"

The Marshal's gaze grew distant as he remembered a pretty

young woman who had married into a messy political situation. "It wasn't simply an affair," he said after a moment. "I did love her. Henry wasn't kind to her at all, Keller, and somehow, I got involved. I was young and foolish, and when she became pregnant, Henry knew it was not his child. Of course, he could not tell anyone that, but he had not bedded his wife in a year. Margaret and I... It simply happened."

Keller wasn't unsympathetic to the extraordinary confession. "What happened when the child was born?"

William shrugged. "It was a complicated task to take her away immediately," he said. "I had to pay the midwives for their silence and complicity. Henry was told the baby died, but one of the midwives could not keep her lips shut, and she told someone—and the rumors began to spread. But Henry died soon after Gisele was born, and Margaret went on to marry the King of Hungary. Before I took the child away, however, I promised Margaret that she would be sent to a convent when she came of age so she could live a life of piety."

Now, the situation was starting to make some sense. "And that is why you will not let Fox marry her."

"Exactly. Her mother wanted her to take the veil."

"And because you loved her, you made her that promise."

"I did."

"Then you must tell Fox," Keller implored him. "Mayhap he will accept this much more than your simply denying him and giving him no reason for it."

The Marshal seemed to harden again. "I should not have to," he said. "He should simply take me at my word."

Keller shook his head. "You loved a woman you could not have," he said. "Now you condemn Fox to the same thing?"

"I will not be condemned to the same thing."

The words came from Fox, who suddenly appeared from the shadows behind Keller. When the Marshal and Keller turned to him, startled by his appearance when they thought he'd wandered outside, Fox addressed the Marshal directly.

"I apologize, my lord, but I did not leave," he said. "I thought you might confess your reasons to Keller were I not in the room, and my instincts were correct. You did. While I am wholly sympathetic with what happened with Queen Margaret, surely you realize you are punishing Gisele for your affair with her mother by condemning her to a life she does not want. She wants to be happy, my lord. Can you not understand that?"

The Marshal was grossly unhappy that Fox had eavesdropped on what should have been a private conversation. "I understand that you are pushing the limits of my patience," he said, standing up from the table. "I promised Gisele's mother that she would take the veil, and that is exactly what will happen. Now that you know, you will not ask me again for permission to marry her. I am sorry that must be my answer, Fox, truly, but it is the way of things. Gisele will become a nun, and I will find you a rich heiress to marry. It is the least I can do."

Fox was insulted by the mere suggestion. "I do not want an heiress," he said. "I love Gisele, and I promised her that, come what may, we would be together. My lord, if you will only go to Canonsleigh and speak with her, you will see that—"

"I am not going to the abbey," the Marshal said, throwing up his hands to silence Fox. "The decision has been made. Accept that and we shall all be happier for it."

"I cannot accept it, my lord. I *will* not."

There was defiance in that reply. The Marshal turned to Fox, who was standing several feet away, coiled like a viper. The man was ready to strike. What was it he had said to Keller? That men in love do foolish things? William could see that, above all else, Fox wasn't going to allow a denial to get in the way of what he wanted. He just knew, by looking at him, that Fox had already made alternative plans to this situation. Any prudent man would have.

William suspected what they were.

He had to make things clear.

"Fox, I want you to listen to me very carefully," he said, his tone a growl. "Are you listening?"

"I am, my lord."

"Good," he said. "Because I am going to be very clear with you. If you think to reject my denial and marry her, I will throw you in the vault and send men to Canonsleigh Abbey to take Gisele where you could never find her. By the time I release you from the vault, she will be long gone, and there will be no trace. You will never see her again, no matter what you do. Are you listening so far?"

Fox's jaw was twitching dangerously. "I am listening."

The Marshal took a few steps in his direction. "Then hear me," he said, as deadly serious as either Fox or Keller had ever seen him. "From this day forward, you will stay away from Gisele and Canonsleigh Abbey. I will know if you try to contact her because I will send people to watch the abbey from this point forward. I will tell the mother abbess to inform me if you try to send Gisele a message. If you do not want me to strip you of your knighthood and ensure that every warlord in England, Scotland, and Wales knows that you are a dishonorable knight and not to be trusted, you will obey everything that I tell you. Do you understand me?"

Fox had gone pale. He knew the Marshal had the power to

do just that. It was a shocking and terrible threat, indicative of the Marshal's resolve. It was the most horrible thing Fox had ever heard.

"I do," he whispered.

The Marshal moved closer to him. "Go back to Selborne," he muttered. "Go back and stay there."

Fox was so angry, so tense, that he started to quiver. The Marshal had upended his life, denying him the woman he loved, and now expected things to be as they always were. But they weren't.

Fox would never look at the man the same way again.

"Nay, my lord, I cannot," he said hoarsely. "If you are to deny me the only thing I have ever wanted in my life, the woman I love with my whole being, then I cannot return to Selborne, where her memory will be everywhere. I will serve anywhere else, but do not make me go back, I beg you."

"Then go back to the king," the Marshal said. "Or go back to your brother, the earl. Serve him for now. Find another liege, because I suspect the days of our association are over, Fox. I am sorry."

Overwhelmed, Fox simply turned away. He had to get out of there before he did something stupid, like wrap his hands around the Marshal's neck and squeeze. He was genuinely contemplating it. The man had just ripped his heart from his chest and stomped on it. He was struggling to breathe by the time he hit the entry to the great hall, hearing odd panting sounds and realizing they were coming from him.

I will take her away so that you will never see her again.

Truth be told, Fox knew the man had the power.

"Fox! Wait!"

Fox heard Keller behind him, calling to him, but he kept

walking. He wasn't sure where he was walking to, other than he simply had to get away. He made it another few steps before Keller was in front of him, putting his hands on his arms and bringing him to a halt.

"Fox, wait," Keller said with soft urgency. "Breathe, man, *breathe*. You must keep your wits about you."

"And how am I to do that?" Fox said, twitching with anger. "You heard what he said. He'll send her away if I contact her, and I'll never see her again. What kind of bastard does that?"

Keller tried to keep him calm. "He is upset," he said. "He loved Lady Gisele's mother, so discussion of the lady is a sensitive topic. As a man in love, you can understand that."

"So he punishes me?" Fox said, aghast. "He could not have Gigi's mother, so now he must keep me from Gigi?"

Keller gave him a shake. "Be calm," he said, more firmly. "His temper will cool. This can be discussed another day, but it must be done rationally."

Fox shook his head, feeling desolate as the reality of the conversation began to settle. "He will not want to speak with me," he said. "You heard him. He wants me to find another liege. He has released me from my oath."

Keller knew that. He'd heard it all. Truthfully, he really wasn't sure if this subject could be discussed on another day, given William's reaction and Fox's rage. Deep down, he thought that all might be lost, but he didn't want Fox to give up hope. Not when the man's life and love were in the balance. It was a true tragedy that a knight of Fox's caliber had been released from his oath. A man like Fox should be leading armies, not hunting for a new liege.

But that gave Keller an idea.

"I take it that returning to de Nerra is truly out of the question?" he asked.

Fox took a deep breath, trying to calm down. "I cannot go back there," he said. "The memories are too strong. I would see her everywhere I turned."

"And if you went to serve any of the Marshal's allies, you would be forced to see the Marshal again from time to time, and I suspect that would be… uncomfortable."

"That is true," Fox said. Then he snorted. "I am sure the Marshal would tell them that he released me from my oath and I would be passed on from warlord to warlord. I am already ruined, Keller."

There was such desperation in that statement. Perhaps the Marshal would become angry at him for helping Fox, but Keller thought that William had indeed been unjust. It had been a difficult situation to watch.

"Nay, you are not," he said. "You have skill and talent, and you are one of the better knights I have ever seen. You have something to give, Fox. And I think I know how."

Fox looked at him with disinterest. "How?"

"Have you ever heard of the Blackchurch Guild?"

Fox's brow furrowed at the introduction of a new subject. "Blackchurch?" he said. "I've heard of it. It is a training guild, isn't it? Unorthodox, from what I've been told, but I've also heard they train the best warriors in England. Why do you ask?"

Keller's eyes glimmered with something just short of hope. "They are located in Devon," he said. "Since you are seeking a new liege, would you consider going there to train men, mayhap? As I said, you have much to give, Fox. You are talented beyond measure. If none of the Marshal's allies will accept your fealty because the Marshal has cast you aside, then why not go where you can earn your living and train men to be the best warriors in the world?"

In spite of his emotional state, Fox's disinterest was quickly turning into interest. "Possibly," he said. "But I am certain I cannot simply walk in and demand they give me a position."

"You can if I send you with a letter of introduction."

Fox's eyebrows lifted. "Do you know them?"

"I fostered with St. Denis de Bottreaux, the man whose family owns the guild. We were good friends, long ago."

Suddenly, the hope that the Marshal had stolen from Fox was back in his expression again. "And you are willing to introduce me?"

"Without question."

"And if I am in Devon, I will be close to Gigi at Canonsleigh."

"Closer than you think," Keller said. "Blackchurch is near Exebridge, which is less than a day's ride from Tiverton."

"Canonsleigh is near Tiverton."

"Then it is a perfect location."

"You would do this for me?"

Keller could hear how badly Fox was hurting in those few short words. It wasn't rage anymore, but grief. Grief that he had been poorly treated. Grief that his devotion to Gisele had won the animosity of the most powerful man in England.

"I would do this for you," Keller confirmed quietly. "Give the Marshal time, Fox. Let him cool his rage. As you could see, this was a difficult subject for him, too. Go to Blackchurch and continue your life there. With your permission, I will talk to William when the time is right and see if I can smooth the situation. But for now... It is best that you go. You can accomplish nothing more here."

Fox moved his gaze over the structure of Pembroke, perhaps saying farewell to the life he'd known as a vassal of William Marshal. It had been a stunning achievement by a young knight, an achievement that was now in fragments. Somehow, he knew he hadn't handled the situation well. He'd done things Keller told him not to do. He'd been so consumed with achieving his wants that he'd made a mess of things, and now he found himself bereft. Along with the grief felt for Gisele, there was grief in the knowledge that what he'd worked hard for was also over.

"I told her I would be at Pembroke for as long as it took for me to gain the Marshal's permission," he finally muttered. "I told her this was where I would be if she needed me. What if she sends the brooch and I am not here?"

There was such sadness in his tone. Keller put a big hand on his shoulder. "The Marshal said you could not send her a missive, but he did not say that I couldn't," he said. "I will tell her you are going to Blackchurch. You will be very close should she ever have need of you."

Fox looked at him in surprise, tears in his eyes. "Christ," he murmured. "You would do that for me, as well?"

Keller gave his shoulder a squeeze. "I would," he said. "Better still... Mayhap I shall ride with you to Blackchurch and introduce you personally. Then I will go to Canonsleigh and tell the lady in person. She should know what has happened, don't you think?"

The tears in Fox's eyes made their way down his cheeks. "Tell her not to lose hope."

"I will tell her."

"This is not over, Keller."

"I know. And she will know that also."

Fox stared at Keller a moment before throwing his arms around the man and squeezing tightly. There was gratitude and joy in that embrace, but also sorrow. Sorrow that nothing had turned out the way Fox had wanted. But Keller was offering him hope. In his greatest darkness, there was a light. Perhaps not the light he'd hoped for, but light nonetheless. Even if he couldn't have Gisele, he could at least be near her.

From that day forward, Fox's life would change forever.

PART TWO

PART TWO

CHAPTER TWELVE

Blackchurch Guild

T HE SUN WAS just starting to light up the eastern horizon as Fox finished his tale.

As he'd predicted, it took everything out of him to relive those days that had been the catalyst for him to come to Blackchurch. He was pale and exhausted, hanging his head as Tay and Ming Tang watched him closely. They, too, had a sense of loss and devastation after such a horrific tale, and when they realized the story had come to a conclusion, they looked at one another in horror. When Fox had started his tale a few hours earlier, neither one of them could have guessed what would come out.

A forbidden bride.

The most powerful man in England.

A shattered heart.

It was too awful to believe.

"Did de Poyer do as he promised?" Tay finally asked, feeling as if he had no right to know but asking just the same. "If he has not, I will. I will ride to Canonsleigh this very day, Fox. I will tell Lady Gisele myself what happened."

Fox lifted his head, moving his weary gaze out over the lake that was covered in mist that had formed during the tale. "He went," he said. "He told Gigi that I was at Blackchurch and if she ever had need of me, to reach me here. But she never has. It has been ten years and she never has."

"Have you spoken to Keller since that time?"

"He sends me a missive about once a year."

"What does he say?"

"Unimportant things, really," Fox said quietly. "He speaks of Wales and his family. One time, about five years ago, he spoke of the Marshal to say that he has never quite gotten over our disagreement."

"Why?"

"I was his protégé," Fox replied. "He knighted me personally when I was seventeen. I think he looked at me as a son, and when things soured between us, it was... difficult."

"But not difficult enough that he would give you permission to marry."

Fox shook his head and looked away. "Nay."

Tay felt as bad as he possibly could. He looked to Ming Tang, a man of great wisdom, hoping he might have some words of comfort for Fox. The man had been hiding a giant of a secret that no one even suspected. It was little wonder he'd kept it all hidden. Taking the hint, Ming Tang rose from his rock and went to sit behind Fox, putting his hand on the man's shoulder.

"It sounds as if Keller de Poyer gave you good advice," he said. "He is your ally in this."

"He is," Fox agreed. "I do not know what I would have done had he not been at Pembroke when I arrived. Things could have been so much... worse."

Ming Tang thought carefully on his reply. "Have you ever heard of karma, Fox?"

Fox shook his head. "What is it?"

"It is the philosophy that every action has a reaction," Ming Tang said. "It is central to my religion and a few others. It means that men who do good will receive good. If they do evil, they will receive evil in return. I further believe that it means the universe is kind to those who need it, who earn it. When Keller was at Pembroke, it is because karma determined he should be there for you. He was what you needed, when you needed it. He turned a terrible situation into one that is settled, even if it is not ideal."

Fox thought on that for a moment. "I would accept that," he said. "But I have often wondered if the Marshal has gone to Canonsleigh himself and told Gigi that if she were to ever contact me, he would punish her. Or punish me. I have often wondered if he made that threat since he was determined to keep us apart."

"From everything I've heard about William Marshal, I would absolutely believe that," Tay said. "I served English warlords myself. I've heard what the Marshal is capable of."

Fox ran a weary hand through his dark hair. "Fear has kept me away from Canonsleigh all these years," he said. "The Marshal said he would put men there to watch for me, and he does not make idle threats."

"So you remain at Blackchurch, so close but yet so far," Ming Tang said softly. "Just to be near the woman you love."

Fox nodded faintly. "There were times when I thought I would simply ride to Canonsleigh, collect her, and take my chances running for Normandy," he said. "But I know the Marshal. He would not have let us go without a fight. It would have been a battle every day for the rest of our lives. But sometimes… sometimes I will admit that I do feel the urge to go to her. As if something is drawing me to her, something I cannot control. Those dreams I had last night are similar to dreams I've had before."

"Like what?" Tay asked.

Fox tried to remember the dreams, which seemed so intense and real at the time. "Dreams that have to do with the abbey," he said. "Sometimes, I'm at the gate and I cannot go in. Sometimes, I'm outside of the walls and I can hear her voice, but I cannot find the gate. Other times, I'm inside a room I do not recognize, but she is there, reaching for me. The dreams always end before I touch her."

"You mentioned you had a feeling like that when Isabella's assassins struck at Selborne," Tay said. "You said something compelled you to seek out Gisele, and by the time you got to her, she was in great danger. Had you not had that urge, she might not have been saved."

Fox sighed sadly. "I know."

"Do you think the dreams are prophetic?"

"I do not know," Fox said honestly. "I do not believe so. Surely she must be safe at the abbey."

"Are you sure of that?" Tay asked.

Fox wasn't, but he couldn't torture himself with that thought. "Are sure as I can be," he said. "Keller would have told me in one of his missives if something had happened. Mayhap I was wrong all along and it really is a place of serenity and safety. Gigi is living a peaceful life, even though it is without me. I can only pray she has found some happiness."

Tay watched the man as he spoke of Gisele, seeing the longing in his expression. It was on the surface, even ten years later.

"While I agree with your wish for her happiness, I will remind you that your life is not over yet," Tay said. "It has been ten years, but *only* ten years. You have many more to live, and so does your lady. William Marshal is an old man, and when he dies, his control dies. You can go to her then, no matter how old either of you are. Then you can be happy together, as you should be."

Fox looked at him. "I have thought of that," he said. "I have thought of paying for assassins to eliminate him, but the man is a professional spy. I do not think I would have much luck at it, and, frankly, he would discover it was me and my life would be forfeit. Nay, I cannot kill the man myself. I can only pray he dies before I do."

It was a solemn thought, to pray for a man's death so happiness could be achieved. The sky was growing lighter, and the assistants to the trainers were beginning to emerge from Blackchurch's village where all of the trainers and guild personnel lived, men who were out to prepare for the recruits for the coming day. It was the signal that Fox and Tay and Ming Tang needed to be on their way as the new day dawned.

But it was a night none of them would forget.

Least of all Fox.

He had relived everything over those hours when he told his story about Gisele. He felt as if he'd been through it all over again. Rising wearily from the rock, he stretched out his stiff body as Ming Tang and Tay also stood up from the cold, damp rocks they'd been seated upon.

"Thank you for telling us your story, Fox," Ming Tang said, but he was looking at him with concern. "Should I tell Axton to tend to your class today? Mayhap you should try to sleep for a few hours."

He was referring to Sir Axton Summerlin, a knight who had come to the Blackchurch Guild as a recruit but was already so skilled with a sword and in combat techniques that Fox had offered the man a position as his assistant. Roles like that were few and far between, very coveted by the recruits that came to Blackchurch, and Axton had proven to be more than up to the challenge. He was big and blond and menacing, so much so that the dregs had taken to calling him the Typhon, the king of all monsters. Whatever they called him, Fox considered him a tremendous asset.

"I appreciate your concern, but I am well enough to train this morning," he said as they began to head away from the lake. "Besides, I have enough trouble with Summerlin wanting to take my place on the roster of trainers, so I do not want to give him the opportunity to usurp me."

The three of them smiled weakly, knowing how ambitious Axton was. "If he tried to usurp you, know that I would defend you," Tay said. "He may be called the Typhon, but I am not called the Leviathan for nothing. I'm bigger and meaner than he is."

Fox chuckled. "That would be something to watch."

They were coming to the top of the ridge, away from the shores of Lake Cocytus, where the Blackchurch Guild was spread out before them. It was an enormous space, surrounded by a curtain wall on the east and the south, with the lake protecting the northern and western perimeter. From their vantage point, they could easily see the village in the middle of the property, a small village that had been absorbed into Blackchurch when it was formed generations ago. It was next to the burned-out hull of an old church, hence the Blackchurch name, and in the center of it all was Exford Castle, where the

Lords of Exmoor, the de Bottreaux family, had lived for centuries.

The Blackchurch Guild was a city unto itself.

A city that was coming alive as the sun began to appear in the eastern sky. To their right, toward the south, was where the dormitories for new, raw recruits was located. They were unofficially known as "dregs" and referred to as such by the trainers at Blackchurch. Trainees that had passed from the dregs and into actual training were known as recruits, so there was a difference in the hierarchy.

Dregs and recruits had different fields to work in. More advanced warriors had their own fields, too, at the top of the slopes, so they were much drier and on level ground. Every level of trainee was segregated, and every group of trainees spent at least six months to a year with any given trainer at Blackchurch, and there were several. One would teach tactics, one would teach archery, one would teach combat techniques, one would teach interrogation methods, and so on. Everyone had a purpose.

Fox's purpose was to train men on the art of defense. He'd been doing it for ten years now, and doing it perfectly. He trained men to defend themselves with weapons or without. He trained them to use their mind and not their brawn. When Keller had brought him to Blackchurch those years ago and introduced him to St. Denis de Bottreaux, the head of the de Bottreaux family and the man upon whose head all of Blackchurch rested, Fox had started off as an assistant to a trainer known as the Hawk. He was an older man who had served St. Denis' father, but he was getting too old for the physicality that training required. He had a disease of the joints that made it difficult to hold a sword. He saw brilliance in Fox, the quiet assistant with eyes that suggested he was perpetually in grief, but the Hawk, whose real name was Bat du Quay, knew there was a great man inside, somewhere, and he intended to bring him forth. Fox had worked with Bat for an entire year before the man dropped dead in front of him one afternoon.

After that, Fox became the trainer.

The Protector.

It was something he was proud of.

"I must get on, lads," Tay said, yawning, as they reached the top of the rise. "I've got a new class of dregs to punish this morning. Then I may go home and nap with my children. I'm an old man. I'm not used to being up all night."

Fox grinned. "You're an old man, anyway," he said, his smile fading. "But you're a great friend, Tay. For listening... Thank you."

Tay put his hand over his heart. "That you would trust me with your story means a great deal," he said. "I'm glad I know."

"So am I."

With that, Tay turned and headed toward his training field, an area near the southern portion of Lake Cocytus. It was full of rocks, and torn up, but that was how he wanted it. Tay was the very first trainer that any recruit came into contact with, as he was responsible for physical conditioning and endurance. He was the gateway to the rest of the recruits, a terrifying trainer known as the Leviathan who weeded out the unworthy.

Fox chuckled as he watched him go.

"He is always the happiest when he has new men to terrorize," he said to Ming Tang. "Sometimes I feel sorry for the dregs."

Ming Tang grinned. "He may terrorize them, but he is never unfair," he said. "Personally, if I saw a man like that as my first trainer, I would run in the opposite direction."

"I might also," Fox agreed. Then he drew in a deep breath of the crisp morning air, moving his gaze over to the field that belonged to him to see Summerlin and a couple of lesser men as they prepared the area for the day. "I, too, must start my day."

Ming Tang had his own class he had to attend to. "As must I," he said. "But I will again thank you for trusting us with the tale of your journey with Lady Gisele. But I must ask you again, Fox... Have you truly never tried to see her?"

Fox shook his head. "As I said, fear has kept me away," he said. "Keller told her what had happened, and I know she would not have left Canonsleigh. She is still there, still waiting."

"For you?"

Fox simply nodded. Ming Tang didn't ask any further questions, knowing that any thought of the lady must be excruciating for Fox, even ten years later, so he forced a smile and patted the man on the shoulder before continuing on to his own area, where he was to continue teaching more advanced recruits about the methods of Shaolin combat. It was one of the secrets to Blackchurch training, a valuable tool that warriors from the Western world were not taught.

But they were at Blackchurch.

Fox watched Ming Tang walk into the fading mist before continuing on to his area, where Summerlin and two lesser soldiers, men who helped with the class, were setting out weapons for the men to use. He was struggling to shake off the mood of the last several hours, thoughts of Gisele that clung to him like the mist that was struggling to lift. She was all around him on this morning, for speaking of her had brought her to life as surely as if she happened to be standing next to him. He could still see her face, those dreamy eyes gazing back at him as she threatened him with a dozen cats in their bed.

If only to have her with him, he would have taken the cats.

But he'd never tell her that.

Well... maybe.

"Good morn to you, my lord," Axton said, breaking into his train of thought. "Do you have instructions for us this morning?"

Fox looked at the big blond warrior and the two shorter, smaller men standing near him. They went by the names Brice and Cappy—competent soldiers, good fighters, but they'd never had the opportunity for education. That didn't matter much to Fox so long as a man was bright and willing, and the truth was that he'd much rather have men like them than a fully fledged knight like Summerlin, who coveted his position.

"Good morn, Axton," he said. "I will speak to the men this morning before we proceed because we are entering a new phase in their training. I want you to watch the group carefully today. It is the first time we've given them weapons, so I want you to make sure there are no decapitations or amputations. All we need is a careless fool in our midst."

Axton nodded firmly. "I will keep watch."

"Good," Fox said. "Let's see how this week progresses, and we may combine our training with what Sin is doing with his class. To see both perspectives, defense and offence, will be helpful."

"Shall I speak to Sir Sinclair, my lord?"

Fox shook his head. "I will," he said. "Let us see how our recruits do with a weapon in hand before I make my decision."

"As you wish, my lord."

The recruits were starting to arrive from their dormitory near Blackchurch's village, so Axton broke away from Fox to address the men and organize them into a group. It was the beginning of another day, in a long line of days that followed the same pattern, giving Fox a sense of comfort and normalcy. After the night he'd had, he welcomed it. Thoughts of Gisele began to fade, as they usually did, but they never faded away completely.

They were always close to the surface.

But he shook it off. He'd become good at shaking it off, focusing on what was now his life. He was a Blackchurch trainer, well paid, with fellow trainers that were like brothers to him. All of them. The kindness Keller de Poyer had shown him those years ago changed his life, introducing him to a new world where he was valued for his contribution, his skill, and his dedication. He didn't spend his days taking orders from de Nerra or wondering why the Marshal hadn't been honest with him about Gisele in the first place.

Those days were gone.

For ten years, he'd lived a new life with new people, with Gisele a half-day's ride from where he was living and serving. A half-day and a million miles away.

But that was what life had brought him.

Pushing all thoughts of Gisele from his mind, he faced a class of twenty-seven recruits who were ready to learn the more strategic details of defense and protection.

The Protector went to work.

CB

Later that night at The Black Cock Tavern
Exebridge, Devon

A MAN WITH a dagger in his hand went sailing across their table.

At The Black Cock, where only the brave and foolish dared to venture, a fight wasn't unusual. Two or three weren't unusual. Sometimes, two or three fights blended into one big fight and the entire common room of the seedy, smoky tavern went up like kindling. Those from Blackchurch had seen it too many times to count.

This seemed to be one of those times.

The tavern was full this night, stuffed with travelers and villagers and people who had found their way in to have a good time. Back in the kitchens, the smell of burned food mingled with the smell of unwashed bodies and stale alcohol. In the corner, a blind man played a wooden flute while his friend accompanied him on a drum.

All in all, it was a lively place.

Tucked back into a large alcove away from the bulk of the common room, several big men sat at a table. They had food and drink spread out all over the table surface and wooden bowls in front of them. Fox, Tay, and Ming Tang were three of the men at the table, along with their fellow Blackchurch trainer brethren. It wasn't unusual to find them in the tavern at night after a long day of teaching recruits. Even though Blackchurch had its own kitchens, and the food they provided was excellent, sometimes the trainers felt the need to leave the place where they lived and worked and find their way to The Black Cock simply to have a change of scenery.

Tonight was one of those nights.

The man that sailed across the table was thrown off by an enormous Scotsman named Payne Matheson. He easily tossed the man onto another table and crashed into their meal, breaking one of the legs of the table. As it smashed down onto the ground and all of the food with it, tables around it roared with laughter as Payne sat back down and resumed his drinking.

It was just another night at The Black Cock.

Whatever fight had started had quickly died down, and patrons were returning to their food and drink. The blind flute player struck up a lively tune, and the drummer beat quickly alongside him. Everyone at the table, all ten trainers from Blackchurch, were elbow-deep in their meal of boiled beef, venison pie, and other delights from the kitchens of The Black Cock. A couple of them were speaking about the food in Aragon, while a third was explaining that the best food came from Cairo. There was a disagreement, and stripped beef bones were produced and used as swords as they fought over their difference of opinion. It was quite hilarious to watch big knights with rib bones wielded like swords. Tay was bumped during the confrontation and roared his displeasure when his venison pie ended in his lap. Ming Tang patted his head to comfort him.

Tay tossed the pie onto the ground.

As the tavern dogs milled around their table, eating the pie, a pair of serving women approached the table with pitchers of wine. One woman had been at The Black Cock for many years, but the lass with her was new. She was plain and innocent looking, which, in a place like this, wouldn't last for long. The older serving wench, who went by the name of Beti, leaned against Payne.

"Do you have everything you need, my fine lads?" she asked cheerily. "If not, simply ask. I've got help tonight, and she can get you what you need."

The attention at the table turned to the new serving woman, who flushed madly when she realized everyone was looking at her. She forced a nervous smile.

"My name is Apple, my lords," she said. "Beti has been a kind teacher."

Beti laughed. "Is that so?" she said. "Then mayhap I can teach with these lads at Blackchurch. Do you know who they are, girl?"

Apple shook her head, looking around the table at the very large and, in most cases, very handsome men. "I am sorry, I do not," she said. "I am new here. But if you tell me your names, I will never forget, I swear it."

Payne spoke up. "Ye're in the presence of greatness, lass," he said in his heavy Scots accent. "Allow me tae introduce ye tae the men who forge the destiny of countries. We are the men of the Blackchurch Guild, and because we are so grand, we are given names that embody who we are and what we stand for. That big beast across from me is Tay Munro, called the Leviathan, a mythical creature of chaos and power. Tay's lineage comes from an ancient land. When we look at him, we see the myths that the world was built upon. That is why he is our Leviathan."

Apple looked to Tay, who looked so bored with the impressive introduction that he was on the verge of yawning. Payne continued.

"The man tae his right is Sir Sinclair de Reyne," he said, indicating a big, muscular knight with dark hair and piercing brown eyes. "He comes from one of the finest families in England. We call him the Swordsman for reasons that any enemy will tell you are abundantly clear. Next tae him is Sir Fox de Merest, whose father was the Earl of Keddington. He has served in His Majesty's ranks as a guard for the king, among others. That makes him more of a knight than most. We call him the Protector."

Apple was clearly impressed by two of the biggest men she'd ever seen, both of them exceedingly handsome and Norman-looking. They had that dark, well-seasoned, high-bred look about them. But they barely acknowledged her because they were eating, and Payne went to the next man.

"The lad seated next tae Fox is our Northman, Kristian Heldane," he said. "He is known as the Viking because that is his heritage. Kristian is a prince to his people, but he cannot return home, so he resides here and teaches our recruits the ways of the Northmen. And the man next tae him is from an excellent and warring family. He is our Avenger, Sir Creston de Royans, and a more brilliant military strategist ye will never find."

Apple studied both men with appreciation. The Viking, with his long blond hair and stunning blue eyes, was quite comely, and de Royans could have been mistaken for his brother with his fair and handsome looks. Truth be told, de Royans was quite lovely in a masculine sort of way. He dipped his head at her politely, something none of the others had done, as Payne turned to the remaining men.

"And these men are the most interesting," he said. He indicated a tall, dark-haired man at the end of the table who was lean and well built. "That is Cruz Mediana de Aragon, a knight from the Holy Order of Santiago. He is an expert with negotiation and politics, known tae us as the Conquistador. The man next tae him has a special place at Blackchurch. He returned with Lord Exmoor's sons from King Richard's crusade, and his father is a great Egyptian warlord who encouraged his son tae live amongst the English. His name is Aamir ibn Rashad, the warrior we call the North Star, because he is strong and constant. Last but not least, of course, is Ming Tang. He is a monk from far to the east and more than likely a better warrior than any of us. Treat him with the greatest respect, lass. He has earned it."

Apple was busy memorizing everyone's name. Payne had delivered a great deal of information in those introductions, and she was determined to remember it all. But there was one man left out, and she looked to him curiously.

"And your name, my lord?"

Payne snorted softly as Sinclair, across the table, spoke up. "That bold Scotsman is Payne Matheson," he said. "He is a former pirate turned noble warrior. He is called the Tempest, and there is no moniker more deserved. Everything about him is brutal, raw, and powerful, so do not cross the man. You will regret it."

Payne laughed softly, slapping Beti affectionately on the buttocks because she was leaning against him. "More wine, if ye please," he said. "My lads have had a hard day."

Beti darted off, taking Apple with her. As Payne returned to the rest of his meal, Tay spoke up.

"You forgot to mention Bowen," he said, chewing.

Bowen de Bermingham had been an assistant to Tay but was elevated to trainer about three years ago. Known as the Titan, he taught warrior responsibilities, etiquette, and discipline, something Payne didn't go in for and didn't agree with. There were no rules to fighting in his world, so Bowen and he had clashed from time to time—the veteran trainer and the new trainer who was highly educated and highly skilled. Bowen had chosen to remain at Blackchurch tonight, nursing a cough, and Payne had deliberately chosen not to mention him.

"I dinna forget," Payne said, dipping his bread into gravy.

Tay had a mouthful. "Do not be rude, Payne," he said.

"Bowen had more than proven himself."

"Says ye."

Tay shook his head, swallowing the bite in his mouth. "Is that a challenge?"

Payne wasn't stupid, merely stubborn. "It's between me and Bowen, Tay," he said. "I love ye like a brother, but dunna interfere."

Down the table, Kristian snorted. "Payne teaches the recruits to win by any method necessary," he said. "Bowen teaches men that they have a choice—to be honorable or dishonorable. Payne believes that is slandering him."

"It is," Payne insisted. "I tell my recruits that betraying a man tae win a battle achieves the objective."

"It does," Kristian agreed. "But Bowen teaches them that betrayal damages a man's honor in the end, and he must make the choice for himself because every situation is different."

Payne frowned at Kristian. "And the Viking speaks of honor?" he said. "Where is this honor when yer countrymen are burning down Scots villages and stealing our women?"

"Enough," Tay said, putting out a hand to stop the conversation from escalating. "Payne, you will apologize to Kristian, or I will tie you to a chair and let the women in this establishment have their way with you."

Payne grinned. "Ye'd have tae catch me first, laddie."

"Aamir can run twice as fast as you can," Tay pointed out. "Ming Tang can get in a kick to the head before you can get up from that chair, so I would think carefully if I were you."

The men at the table were chuckling into their food because Payne was the stubbornest Scotsman that Scotland had ever produced. He was right even when he wasn't. Kristian wasn't offended by his comment in the least, however. They had all worked and lived together for so long that little disagreements or arguments were never taken seriously.

But Payne was resistant to the end.

"I'm not sorry, and ye canna make me say it," he said, looking at Kristian. "If I offended ye, then cry about it. Ye'll not get another word from me."

Kristian burst into quiet laughter. "You have slandered my honor and must pay the price," he said. "I would watch your back if I were you. You may find yourself trussed up and lying on the deck of one of my ships before you realize it. I'll have the recruits make an example out of you."

"And I'll send my recruits tae burn yer ships!"

"My God," Tay said as he slammed his hand on the tabletop. "Can we not have a family meal where we are not lobbing threats at one another? Payne, shut your lips or I am going to write to your mother and tell her what a terrible son she raised."

That brought more laughter, even from Payne. "If ye do that, my mother will come down tae Devon and bring a stick with her," he said. "Ye'll be the first one she beats down."

Tay cocked an eyebrow. "As you have said, she'll have to catch me first."

More laughter and more insults were lobbed across the table, but it was all in good humor. Fox, who had remained largely silent throughout the meal because he simply wasn't in the mood for the usual banter, sat back in his chair to finish off his wine when he saw the entry door to the tavern open. It was directly in his line of sight, though several yards away, but he recognized the woman who had just entered.

He elbowed Tay.

"Tay," he said. "Your wife is here."

Tay's head snapped up and he caught sight of his wife, the

beautiful Athdara. Tall and lovely, and clearly pregnant, she entered the tavern, searching for her husband and his comrades. Tay was already on his feet, making his way to her, when she caught sight of him. He brought her back over to the table where he sat her down between him and Fox.

"What in the world are you doing here?" Tay demanded softly. "Did you travel here by yourself? In the dark?"

"Be at ease," she assured him. "I brought a couple of the soldiers from the south gatehouse with me. They are outside."

That made Tay feel a little better. "But why are you here?"

She sighed heavily. "Because I am tired of screaming children, too," she said. "You are not the only one who wishes to escape them from time to time."

"Who is tending the boys?"

"Marina," she said, referring to the woman who lived with them and helped with the children and the chores. "She offered to tend them while I came to The Black Cock, and I eagerly accepted. The thought of an hour or two away from screaming children makes me positively giddy."

Tay laughed softly, putting his arm around her shoulders and kissing her on the head. He didn't mind her coming, not in the least. In fact, he was a little ashamed he hadn't invited her himself. Tay had met Athdara when she had been a dreg, for Blackchurch would allow women recruits if they were strong enough. Marina was also a former recruit who had failed in her training, but she and Athdara had formed a bond. Tay had gone from an unmarried man with no family to a house full of women and children in the space of just a few years.

And he loved every minute of it.

"Eat something," he told her, waving over Beti to order food for her. "Enjoy yourself and cheer up Fox while you're at it. He could use some kindness tonight."

Fox heard him. He had been finishing off his wine, minding his own business, when Tay put Athdara's attention onto him. Fox liked Athdara a great deal, but he'd already bared his soul today. He wasn't going to do it again, because the more he let out his feelings, and his secrets, the more difficult it was to bottle them back up again.

"There is nothing the matter with me," he said as Athdara turned to him. "I simply did not sleep well last night, and your husband is making too much of it."

In spite of his denial, Athdara was looking at him with concern. "None of us slept well last night," she said. "Milo and Brendon were unhappy. Teeth are sprouting in both of them."

Fox smiled weakly. "I seem to remember hearing that giving them a chicken bone to chew on is helpful," he said. "Have you tried that?"

Athdara nodded. "I have," she said. "It works to a certain extent, but the best remedy is rubbing wine on their gums. It seems to give them some relief. I've been doing it quite a bit."

"Then I wish you well when they are both tipsy."

Athdara giggled. "It would be better than constant screaming."

"You may have just solved your own problem."

Athdara continued to giggle as her food and drink arrived. Fox was finished with his meal, but he remained at the table, nursing his wine and conversing with Athdara, who seemed to talk mostly about her children and her younger brother, Nicolai, who had come to Blackchurch to train. Athdara's father was the Duke of Toxandria, near Flanders, a man who had been murdered for his throne. Nicolai was the rightful duke, and those at Blackchurch were helping train the boy to someday regain his kingdom. It was the policy of the Blackchurch Guild never to take sides in any conflict because the guild only trained warriors and nothing more. They were staunchly neutral. But in Nicolai's case, St. Denis was making an exception. As long as none of the trainers pledged to fight for the lad and help him regain his kingdom, St. Denis was happy to train him.

It made for a bit of a complicated situation, but both Tay and Athdara were well respected in the Blackchurch community. Tay was more or less the unofficial leader of the trainers because he tended to speak for the group in certain situations. He, too, was committed to the integrity of Blackchurch's reputation, in all things.

Which was why it had surprised Fox that Tay had offered to ride to Canonsleigh when Fox had told him the entire story of Gisele and William Marshal. Tay was usually one of the first people to stress neutrality in any given situation—or at least he had been until he'd married Athdara and she was committed to helping her younger brother regain their hereditary home. Since then, he'd been a little more lenient about taking sides in conflicts. The neutrality was still there, but there was more heart and emotion behind it. Tay had come to realize that not everything was black and white.

Fox had realized that a long time ago.

The hour began to grow late, and Fox was quite exhausted from not having slept the night before, so he eventually excused himself to make the short walk back to the Blackchurch compound. It was really nothing more than walking up the street, for the southern gatehouse of Blackchurch was about a half-mile away. Certainly nothing long or exhausting. After bidding a good night to his fellow trainers, he headed out of the warm, stuffy tavern and out into the crisp night beyond.

Wearily, he began to head back toward the gatehouse, which he could see in the distance, lit up against the night with dozens of torches. Overhead, the night was clear, and he gazed up at the stars as he walked, wondering if Gisele was looking at the stars on this night also. He wondered that quite often, in truth. Perhaps they were looking at the moon at the same time, or perhaps even the sky or the clouds. The thought that they might be looking at the same things gave him comfort. It made him feel closer to her. As he lost himself in the memories, he heard someone call his name.

"Fox?"

Coming to a halt, he turned to see Athdara behind him. She was walking quickly to catch up to him, so he waited.

"Where is the horse you rode into town on?" he asked. "And where is this escort?"

She pursed her lips wryly. "I lied," she said. "Tay would have scolded me if I told him I'd walked alone."

"And where does he think you are now?"

"I told him that I was weary and was going to walk back with you."

Fox snorted and turned for the gatehouse. "Come on, then," he said. "Hurry back to your children, and I am going to hurry back to my bed. We have missed one another."

Athdara took up walking beside him, alternately watching her feet on the rocky avenue and looking at his profile as they traveled. It was clear there was something on her mind.

Perhaps her appearance had more of a purpose than simply going home.

"Fox?" she said after a moment. "I am going to tell you something, but you must promise me you will not become angry."

"How can I promise that if I do not know what it is?"

"You must promise," she insisted softly. "Please."

He nodded wearily. "Very well," he said. "I promise. What is it?"

"Tay told me about Gisele."

Fox came to a halt, grunting angrily but remembering he had promised not to rage. He put his hands on his hips as he stared at the ground, trying to calm his temper before replying.

"He promised me that he would not tell you," he said. "He swore this to me."

"I know," Athdara said gently, reaching out to put her hand on his arm in a soothing gesture. "But when he returned home this afternoon... He was so upset, Fox. I have never seen him so upset. He is deeply concerned for you, and given that he has a wife he adores, he understands your pain all too well. If you recall, he very nearly lost me those years ago. Do you remember?"

Fox did. Athdara had been injured in a fight, and there were a few days there that no one was sure she was going to survive. Tay had been mad with grief.

"I remember," he said. "But that still does not—"

"I swear to you that what he told me will never leave my lips," she interrupted him. "I would rather die than reveal what I know, Fox, but I wanted you to know that I know, and I am deeply sorry. You did not deserve what happened to you. But I have an idea."

Fox looked at her impatiently. "Athdara, I know you mean well, but there is nothing to be done," he said. "If Tay told you everything, then you know that I do not want to talk about this. It is agonizing to me, so I do not wish to speak of it. Ever."

Athdara was still gripping his arm. "I want to go to Canonsleigh," she said, ignoring his plea. "Please listen to me before you deny me, Fox, but I want to go to Canonsleigh and see if your lady is there. I can take a message to her from you. I can tell her that you are well. Don't you think she'd like to know how you are? Even if William Marshal has men watching the abbey, they will not think anything of a woman visiting, will they? I can come and go as often as I wish. Please... Let me go and see her on your behalf. Let me tell her that you still love her."

Fox very nearly yanked his arm away from her. His first instinct was to run away from her, to tell her to never speak of such things again, but he couldn't seem to manage it. His heart was beating against his ribs and his mouth was running dry. Her words were sheer torture. All he could do was grab her hand and squeeze.

"*Nay*," he finally breathed. "I am touched that you should want to do this for me, but nay. Please, do not speak of this again."

Athdara was heartbroken. "But I can—"

"Do *not* speak of it again," he said, more firmly. He looked her in the eye. "Does Tay know you have made this offer?"

"He suggested it."

Fox grunted unhappily again, hanging his head in sorrow. "Athdara," he said slowly. "I love you and Tay for wanting to do this for me. I do. But understand something—the wound where my heart used to be has a thin scab over it. It has taken me years to form that scab. What you are suggesting now threatens to rip the scab off, and I will surely bleed to death from the grief of it, so please... please do not suggest this again. Let things lie as they are. That is the only way I can survive. Do you understand?"

Athdara was in tears. "I'm sorry," she whispered tightly. "I thought I was helping. Tay and I so wanted to help you."

Fox pulled her into an embrace, squeezing her tightly and kissing her on the side of her head. He released her quickly, turned her for the gatehouse, and put his arm around her shoulder.

"I know," he said gently, walking her toward the gatehouse as she sniffled. "I appreciate it more than you know. And I would be lying if I said it was not tempting. But I have spent ten years coming to terms with this. Ten years of trying to function without the woman I love by my side, so your going to Canonsleigh… It would accomplish nothing. We still cannot be together. It would only be bringing back the agony of a love that can never be."

Athdara wiped at her eyes. "You are the bravest man I know, Fox," she said. "I do not know anyone who could withstand this with more resilience and courage than you."

He smiled without humor. "It has taken a long time for me to come to this point," he said. "Believe me, there have been times when I wanted to run to Canonsleigh and take my chances, but one thing has kept me from doing that."

She looked at him. "What?"

"The toll it would take on Gigi," he said. "I am a knight. I am used to warfare and conflict. But Gigi… My attempt to see her would put her in a position of peril. William Marshal threatened to take her away without a trace, to a place where I could never find her, and I am not willing to risk that. Right now, I know she is at Canonsleigh. She is less than a day's ride from me. Knowing she is there is more comforting than not knowing where she is. Does that make sense?"

Athdara nodded. "Perfectly."

"And we will simply let things be the way they are."

Athdara paused to look at him, forcing a smile as she wiped the last of her tears. "If that is what you want, we will support you," she said. "But if you ever change your mind, I will go to her the very same day."

He smiled weakly and patted her on the cheek. "You are brave beyond measure," he said. "To know I have such friends makes me grateful with every breath I take. You honor me."

There wasn't much more to say after that. Athdara had made a tremendous offer, but he had denied it. She understood his reasons, as sad as they were. In warm silence, they resumed their walk to the gatehouse of Blackchurch and into the quiet village beyond. Fox made sure she made it back to her cottage and went inside before he went to his. A cold, dark cottage that meant nothing to him other than a place to lay his head. No warmth, no comfort, no family... no Gisele.

But he was used to it.

When he finally slept that night, it was with dreams of teething toddlers, loud Scotsmen, and orange cats.

CHAPTER THIRTEEN

Pembroke Castle

"**M**Y LORD?" A soldier in a tunic bearing the scarlet lion shield of William Marshal was standing in the doorway. "Peter de Lohr has arrived. He says that he bears an important message for you."

Seated in the smaller hall in the keep of Pembroke Castle, William had been looking over a newer map he'd recently had commissioned. Drawn on a fine hide, it was the latest in cartography. His solar was cluttered and the light was better in the small hall, so he'd brought it in and spread it over the table. There were three lancet windows facing west that provided ample light in addition to an enormous chandelier overhead, which was nothing more than a wheel the wheelwright had fashioned set with several iron sconces meant for tapers. It was affixed to a chain that saw it lowered daily so the tapers could be lit, and then it was lifted back into position over the table.

Huddled over the map were two other senior soldiers who had been with the Marshal for many years, along with a knight who had served him for over twenty. Sir Blade Penden, son of the Steward of Rochester Castle and kin to the Earls of East

Anglia, was the garrison commander of Pembroke Castle. He never traveled with the Marshal as the man galivanted around the country, but rather stayed behind to ensure Pembroke remained solid and secure. He was powerful, sharp, and, above all, dutiful. His devotion to the Marshal was exemplary.

Blade was the one who answered the soldier before the Marshal could.

"Where is Peter?" he asked, stepping around the Marshal to face the man in the doorway. "Send him in immediately."

Commands from Blade were not meant to be disobeyed, but a voice behind the soldier assured him that his command had been heard.

"I am here," Peter said, marching purposefully into the chamber. "My lord, send the soldiers away. Send Blade away, too, if you do not wish for him to hear something quite critical."

So much for a polite greeting, which had the Marshal frowning. Peter wasn't normally one to throw demands around, so it was indicative of the importance of his message. He wasn't sure if he was irritated or concerned.

He settled for concerned.

"Go," he said to the soldiers. "Blade, you remain. I may have need of you."

There wasn't anything he kept from Blade, so he wasn't worried about that. The soldiers immediately quit the chamber, however, shutting the door behind them as Peter approached the table where the lovely new map was sitting. It was a depiction of the Bristol channel and the surrounding land. Peter heaved his saddlebags from his shoulder onto the table near the map, immediately going for the pitcher of wine that was at the end of the table. Taking the pitcher in hand, he drank straight from the neck.

"This must be serious," the Marshal said. "Shall I send for more wine?"

Peter downed most of the pitcher in three big gulps. Big, blond, and an elite knight as part of the prestigious de Lohr family, he shook his head as he swallowed. Removing the glove of his right hand, he wiped his mouth with the back of his hand.

"Later," he said. "I will stay the night and continue on to my father's home in the morning, but I had to come. I have a message from de Lara."

That information immediately set the tone, and now, the Marshal understood why Peter was so serious.

Nothing good ever came from de Lara.

Sean de Lara was his full name, and he was perhaps the greatest spy in the Marshal's stable. He'd been positioned next to King John for several years, pretending to be his bodyguard and acting the part when he was really spying on the king for William Marshal. It had been a terribly delicate balance for Sean, who went from a knight of great respect and prestige to perhaps the most feared man in the country at John's side. He even had a nickname—Lord of the Shadows.

He was the knight everyone in the kingdom dreaded.

But he was also the spy that provided the most important information on the king. Calmly, William sat on the tabletop next to his map.

"Proceed," he said steadily. "What does de Lara have to say?"

Peter took another drink from the pitcher, finishing it off, before continuing. "My lord, I am in possession of information related to something very few people know," he said. "You have evidently told de Lara, so he was aware when this issue arose with John. I happened to be in London for my father, and Sean sent me a missive to meet him, so I did."

The Marshal folded his arms across his chest. "I am listening."

Peter sat down on the bench across from him, weary from having ridden long and hard from London. It had taken him well over a week to go from London to Pembroke. Now that he was here, he realized that he'd nearly ridden himself into the ground. He was exhausted.

But he had news to deliver.

"Sean has been at John's side as he negotiated a marriage between a Plantagenet princess and Raymond of Toulouse," Peter said. "You may recall that Toulouse holds more lands in France than the royal family does, lands that were sacrificed by King Richard in order for his sister, Joan, to marry Raymond years ago. They were part of her dowry."

The Marshal nodded. "I recall," he said. "With Joan dead, Raymond still has the territory."

"Exactly," Peter said. "According to Sean, the king has been obsessed with regaining the lands, so he has brokered a marriage between Henry the Young King's daughter and Toulouse."

It took a moment for the news to sink in, and when it did, the Marshal's jaw went slack. Unwinding his arms, he stood up.

"Henry the Young King's *daughter*?" he said, horror in his eyes. "Do you mean Gisele of England?"

"That is exactly whom I mean," Peter said. "De Lara said you would want to know."

A hand flew to the Marshal's mouth, a reflexive action to prevent him from saying anything he hadn't carefully thought through first. He kept his hand against his mouth as he digested Peter's words, the news, and the situation at large.

Slowly, he removed his hand.

"The young woman is in a convent," he said, trying not to sound too shaken. "She cannot marry. Moreover, John does not know where she is."

Peter shook his head. "He does know," he said. "Evidently, one of his courtiers has a sister at the same nunnery. According to Sean, the brother is most ambitious, and the sister along with him. She told her brother about Gisele's presence, and the brother has used it to put himself in a good light with the king. That is what gave John the idea to marry the girl to Toulouse."

My God, William thought. *He knows where she is!*

Horrified, he turned away from Peter, pacing away as his mind worked furiously. He knew that Sean knew about his bastard daughter. He'd specifically told the man because of his proximity to John, in case the subject of Gisele of England ever came up.

It seemed that it had.

Peter's father, Christopher de Lohr, also knew of the Marshal's bastard. Christopher was the most powerful warlord on the Welsh marches and a close ally of William Marshal, but William wasn't certain that Peter knew. Or Blade, standing behind him. If they knew, it had been because someone else had told them. William wasn't in the habit of telling people that the girl believed to be Henry the Young King's daughter was, in fact, his child.

Deep down, he wondered if John knew and whether arranging the betrothal was his way of punishing William somehow. Their relationship had had its ups and downs, but at the moment, it was on an upswing. Was it possible that John thought he was doing William a great favor by marrying his daughter to Toulouse?

Nay... John wasn't that generous.

Therefore, William didn't think the man knew. He believed that Gisele was the daughter of Henry the Young King, which would make her a princess. But John did know that the Marshal had taken charge of the girl's welfare. He was the one who'd sent the girl to live in a convent.

Now, John knew where she was.

God help them.

"When is this marriage to take place, Peter?" he asked, turning to look at the man.

"As soon as Gisele of England can be brought to London," Peter said. "Sean told me that the king planned to send men to retrieve her, so it is possible they are on their way there as we speak. It is equally possible they have already taken her. In either case, Sean wanted you to know. He said to tell you that Lord Shillingford has been tasked with retrieving her."

That brought a reaction from William. He scowled as if he'd just been force-fed a spoonful of cod liver oil.

"That foolish bastard?" he said. "He's a parasite."

"Even so, he's been charged with the task."

William didn't like the sound of that. Shillingford was un-scrupulous at best. "He'll get nowhere with the lady if she's taken the veil," he said. "That was the intention. I suspect he'll not take it well if he arrives at the convent and realizes she's a nun."

"The lady will have the church on her side."

William sighed sharply. "That will not stop a man like Shil-lingford," he said. Then he looked between Peter and Blade. "I am going to tell you something that must never leave your lips. I must have your vow."

Both Peter and Blade nodded. "You have it, my lord," Blade

said.

William looked at the pair of them, trusted knights, before turning away again. He was about to make a confession, something he didn't like to do. He never liked to appear weak or fallible in front of his men.

In this case, it was necessary.

"Gisele of England is not Henry the Young King's daughter," he said quietly. "She is mine. Anyone who knows of her believes she is Henry's daughter, and I have allowed them to think that because to tell the truth would be to slander her mother, and I have no intention of allowing that. The issue is that John believes Gisele to be Henry's daughter, which is why he is trying to marry her off to Toulouse. Gisele is at Canonsleigh Abbey in Devon because that was her mother's dying wish, and Canonsleigh is where she is going to stay. If you were wondering why de Lara informed me of John's dealings with a minor princess, now you know."

Peter had already heard from his father that William Marshal had a bastard, so the revelation wasn't a surprise to him. But it was a great surprise to Blade, who was trying to conceal his shock.

"What will you do now, my lord?" Blade asked. "Is there anything to be done?"

William whirled to him. "There is," he said decisively. "I am going to Canonsleigh. I want as many men as we can mount and get onto the three cogs I have anchored at Milford Haven. How many men will one of those ships hold?"

Blade thought quickly. "At least seventy men and horses, my lord."

"Good," the Marshal said. "Then mount and heavily arm two hundred men with horses and move them to Milford

Haven. It would take too long to ride to Canonsleigh by land, so we are going to sail across Bristol Channel and dock near Minehead or Watchet. Canonsleigh is a couple of days' ride south of the Devon coast."

Blade was already on his way out of the hall, heading off to muster the troops. That left William with Peter, who was still sitting where he'd first planted himself, feeling his exhaustion more by the second.

"Do you want me to hurry on to Lioncross Abbey and rally my father's army to assist you?" he asked. "I do not know how many men John is sending to Canonsleigh, but you may need the help."

William shook his head. "Nay," he said. "But I thank you just the same. If I need more men, I'll send word to Dunster Castle. It's not far from where we'll be. That is the seat of Gart Forbes, you know."

Peter knew the legendary Gart Forbes, a veteran knight who was well respected. He'd married well, and his stepson was a powerful warlord, so the entire Forbes-de Moyon clan ruled the northern coastline of Devon.

"If a woman is involved, Gart will most certainly rise to your support," Peter said. "You know how he hates it when a woman is in peril."

The Marshal cracked a smile. "That is because he married a woman in peril," he said. "He also has several daughters, so I think he looks at every threatened female as he would if they were one of his daughters. If I need aid, he'll come, have no doubt."

"Is there anything more you would like me to do?"

William looked at Peter sitting pale and exhausted at the feasting table. After a moment, he shook his head.

"Nay, lad," he said quietly. "I suspect you have ridden hard and fast to bring me that news, so rest tonight. You have earned it."

Peter smiled weakly. "I intend to eat everything in your kitchens now."

William summoned a servant, who brought Peter more food and wine than he could hold. But as he was eating, William retired to his own solar to prepare for his journey across the channel. He could only pray that John's men hadn't reached Canonsleigh yet, because if they had, and Gisele had been wrested from the walls of the abbey, there was going to be hell to pay.

And John would be the one to pay it.

CHAPTER FOURTEEN

Weeks later
Canonsleigh Abbey

"Gisele?"

A soft voice came from the doorway of a room used for all methods of gardening, flowers and vegetables and anything else that would grow out of the ground. It was a bright room, with big windows facing a garden that had once been an area with nothing but dirt and weeds. Now, it was flourishing with flowers and other plants, all thanks to a young woman who had arrived at the abbey ten years ago and thrown herself into learning about growing things.

Someone close to her had requested it.

Gisele's head came up from where she was potting a small seedling.

"Sister Mary Perpetua," she greeted her visitor. "Come in and see what I am doing."

A small, older woman with pale eyes entered the room, smiling as she came over to the table where Gisele was working.

"And what is it?" she asked with great interest. "You grow so many wonderful things."

Gisele held up the pot she'd made from wood. There were many such pots all over the abbey—some rather crude from when she was just learning to make them, and others quite nice from when she'd gained practice. Each one was full of something green and growing.

"Do you remember the lemons Sister Mary Felice purchased last month?" she said. "They are such a rarity, but I saved all of the seeds. I am going to grow the trees in this room, and we shall always have a supply of lemons."

Sister Mary Perpetua looked in the direction Gisele was pointing, only to see neat rows of small pots with dirt in them. No trees yet, but the seeds were evidently buried in the dirt. A cat was curled up near them, in one small spot of sunlight coming through the window, while two kittens played among the pots. In fact, there were cats all over the garden room, which wasn't unusual when it came to Gisele.

The nun clapped her hands gleefully at the sight of the lemon pots.

"How wonderful," she said. "Do you really think they will grow?"

Gisele shrugged, taking the latest pot over to the rows and setting it down next to the others. "I hope so," she said, petting the sleeping cat nearby. "The fruit cannot survive our cold winters, so if I keep them inside with fresh air and warmth, I hope they will. I have been able to grow other things that way."

Sister Mary Perpetua smiled at her. "God has given you a gift," she said. "You are blessed with the ability to grow anything, and we are the better for it."

Gisele smiled modestly as she wiped her hands off on her dirty apron. She was clad in simple garments—undyed wool, simple in design, but sturdy. She didn't wear a wimple like many of the other women did, but simply braided her hair and pinned it to the back of her head. Even ten years later, she wasn't one of them.

She had never, and would never, take the veil.

"Mam!" A young lad of nine years of age came into the chamber, dragging a sack with him. "I have the dirt. Where should I put it?"

Gisele went to meet the dark-haired, blue-eyed lad who looked exactly like his father. Reaching down, she helped him lug the sack of earth over to her potting table.

"There," she said, brushing off her hands before patting him on the back. "Well done, Ren. Now, can you please water the new seeds under the window? They could use it."

Renard "Ren" Marshal de Salisbury nodded to his mother's request and immediately went to do her bidding. Gisele smiled at her boy, so like his father, so dutiful and kind and brilliant. He'd been the only thing keeping her sane and alive these past ten years. Since she couldn't have Fox, at least she could have his son. She'd even named him after his father.

Renard.

That meant Fox in French.

"He is a good lad," Sister Mary Perpetua said, beaming at the young boy who was carefully watering plants. "How proud his father would have been."

Gisele's smile faded. When she'd arrived at Canonsleigh, she'd been pregnant, only she hadn't known it until several weeks later. Up until that point, she'd not spoken of Fox or William Marshal or any other reason why she'd come. She'd been silent and withdrawn. Even the mother abbess couldn't get her to come out of her shell, but thankfully, they had been gentle with her. Everyone had left her alone.

Then the morning sickness started.

A child was coming.

Terrified, Gisele had no idea how the nuns were going to react if they knew she was unmarried and pregnant. Fox still hadn't returned for her, but one day, a man she'd never met before came to visit. His name was Keller de Poyer, he'd said, and he told her what happened when Fox had again asked William Marshal for her hand in marriage. Not only had Fox been denied, but the situation had turned ugly. Threats were made against Fox, enough so that he couldn't risk returning to Canonsleigh for his own protection and for hers. De Poyer assured her that it was grave, indeed.

Insurmountable, even.

Gisele had been devastated.

The only consolation de Poyer could give was that Fox was no longer serving the Marshal or Val de Nerra, but rather he was at the Blackchurch Guild, a training school for elite warriors, that was a half-day's ride to the south. He was close by. Should she ever need him, she could find him there, but de Poyer strongly urged her never to contact him unless it was a life-or-death situation. Fox would be punished, he told her, for any contact if the Marshal found out, so she would have to choose her moment wisely.

If at all.

And then de Poyer had left her.

Just like that, Gisele had gone from the hope that she would see Fox again to the knowledge he would be severely punished if he returned. She knew that it must have been a deadly threat for Fox to have surrendered to it, but still, the news had shattered her. This was not what she'd planned, nor was it what she wanted, but now she found herself committed to a convent with a child on the way.

The situation couldn't have been worse.

At that point, she did the only thing she could do—she lied to the mother abbess and told her that her husband had died and that she was pregnant. It was the only thing she could do so the child wouldn't be taken away from her. She invented a dead husband and became a beguine, which was a status within the church only allowed to widows. She wasn't a nun, but she was sheltered and fed and lived a life of chastity while making herself useful to the abbey.

That was what Fox had asked of her—*be useful.*

She was.

And so was Ren. He was educated at the abbey with other children from a few lesser noble families in the area, as often happened with younger children, but he was a tremendous help to his mother. He was very smart, and growing bigger, and Gisele lived in terror of the day when the nuns would tell her that he was too grown to live at the abbey any longer. Men simply didn't live at the abbey, not even the sons of beguines. When that day came, she had made the decision to send him to his father at the Blackchurch Guild.

A half-day's ride and a million miles away.

So close, yet so far.

Until then, she also lived in terror day in and day out that someone would arrive who knew her, and her situation, and her lies would unravel. So far, the only person she'd ever had visit her was Keller de Poyer. No one else had come in all those years, not even William Marshal. Not even any hint of him. But that didn't mean he wouldn't show up one day to see her and come face to face with Fox's son.

She could only imagine what he would do to Fox.

So… not all of her time at Canonsleigh was spent with contentment. There were horrors and fears she dealt with. But every time she saw Ren, how he watered plants or how he excelled in his studies, she was reminded anew of how God had taken one beloved man from her but given her another. Even if Ren had been born a bastard, he had been conceived in love.

So much love.

She hoped God took that into consideration on the day of her judgment.

Meanwhile, she was living a productive life, and one, frankly, that she was content with. As content as she could be, anyway. But there wasn't one day that passed that she didn't miss Fox down to her very bones.

It was an ache she lived with, every hour of every day.

"His father would indeed be proud of him," she murmured belatedly to Sister Mary Perpetua's comment. "They are very much alike, in fact. Sometimes I feel as if I am looking at his ghost."

Sister Mary Perpetua, having never been married, couldn't relate to a woman who longed for a dead husband, but she tried. She was a genuinely kind woman who had helped deliver Ren nine years ago. But she'd come to the plant room for a purpose, and she put her hand on Gisele's arm gently.

"I have some good news, I hope," she said. "A messenger has come for you. He is with the mother abbess. You must go to her."

Gisele was so startled by the news that she briefly lost her balance. She pretended that she'd stumbled simply to cover it up, but she had to grasp the table for support as she looked at the little nun. Her face was a mask of shock.

"A… a messenger?" she repeated. "Who is sending me a

message?"

"The king," Sister Perpetua said with some excitement. "There are royal soldiers outside of the gates. The messenger is from the king, Gisele! You must come quickly."

Terror filled Gisele. The last time she had contact with anything to do with a royal, it had been over ten years ago in the midst of an assassination attempt. Her breathing quickened and her body began to tremble, and her first thought was of her son. She'd spent so much time avoiding telling anyone who she was, and her true familial relations, that no one really knew her background. They had no idea she was, in a sense, hiding. But the royal messenger, clearly, had been told she was here.

They'd found her.

"Are… are you sure?" she asked unsteadily.

"I saw the royal standards myself."

The news was like a shot to Gisele's heart. She simply couldn't believe it. The hope of living the rest of her life in peace and anonymity had just been dashed. Horrifyingly dashed. But as the shock began to fade, her sense of self-preservation began to overwhelm her, because above it all, she had to survive. Her son had to survive. That was all that mattered. It took her a moment to recover, but when she finally lifted her head, she fixed the nun in the eye.

She knew what she had to do.

"Sister," she said, grasping the nun's little hands with her dusty ones. "I want you to listen to me carefully. Please."

Sister Mary Perpetua looked at her curiously. "Of course, child," she said. "What is it?"

Gisele took a deep breath, trying to remain calm. "What I am to tell you must not leave your lips," she said. "Will you promise me?"

"I will." The nun nodded hesitantly. "But why—"

Gisele cut her off, gently. "Years ago, Queen Isabella tried to have me killed," she said. "There is no time to explain more than that, but if the royals have found me, chances are it is not good. My son… If he has not already been mentioned, please do not speak of him. You know nothing of him. I want you to make sure he is hidden from them until it is safe. Please… will you protect him for me?"

Sister Mary Perpetua was confused but also concerned. "Surely they would not—"

Gisele cut her off again, tears in her eyes. "I cannot know that," she said. "I do not have time to tell you more, but you must trust me. They want me dead, but I will not let them have my son. Will you *please* hide Ren?"

She was starting to weep, and Sister Mary Perpetua nodded quickly, squeezing her hands. "Aye, I will," she said. "I will take him now. But you must go quickly in case they come to look for you."

"I'll go," Gisele said, quickly wiping at her tears. "But before I do, I must say something—if I do not return, you will send Ren to the Blackchurch Guild, to a man named Fox de Merest. Tell Fox… Tell him that Ren is my son. He will understand. He will protect him."

Sister Mary Perpetua was still confused, but she nodded. "Is he a relation?"

"He is."

The little nun accepted the request without asking more questions. She could see that news of the royal messenger had upset the lady deeply. Gisele had always been quiet and pleasant, a good worker and a kind soul, so her reaction to the news of the messenger was distressing. It made Sister Mary

Perpetua want to protect her and the boy, without question. She watched Gisele run over to Ren, who was still watering plants, and hug the child fiercely.

"I love you very much," she whispered to the boy. "We are going to play a game, and I need you to quickly hide. Hide from everyone and do not come out unless Sister Mary Perpetua tells you to. Please?"

Ren looked at his mother with the wide, guileless eyes of a child. "A game?" he said. "Why?"

Gisele was trying to smile because she didn't want to frighten her son. "It will be fun," she said. "I want you to hide where no one can find you. It must be a secret, and you must hide from everyone. Especially any strangers you may see. Can you do this?"

Being that he was a young boy and would rather play than work, Ren was delighted at this sudden game. "I know where to hide," he said. "I have a place where no one can find me, not even my friends."

"Go there," Gisele said, directing the child toward Sister Mary Perpetua. "Show the sister where it is, but no one else."

"I will."

He started to move, but she grabbed him by the arm, stopping him. "Wait," she said, pulling the child over to where Sister Mary Perpetua was standing. She addressed the nun. "There *is* something else you could do for me. Mayhap the most important thing of all."

With that, she began to fumble in the neckline of her dress. The well-washed woolen garment was over a softer shift, and she was fumbling with something on the top of the shift. When she finally pulled it forth, she extended her open palm to Sister Mary Perpetua.

"You must do something for me, sister," she said seriously. "I was told… I was told not to do this unless it was life or death, but I fear the appearance of the royal messenger means just that—my death. You must give this to a servant and have them take this to the Blackchurch Guild. Do you remember the man I just spoke of?"

Sister Mary Perpetua found herself looking at a silver brooch of a dragon's head with garnet eyes. Her brow furrowed in confusion. "The relative?"

"Fox de Merest."

"He is to have this?"

"Right away."

"But why? And where is this Blackchurch Guild?"

"Near Exebridge, half a day's ride to the north," Gisele said, putting the brooch into her hand. "You must send this to Blackchurch immediately, to the same man you will send Ren to if I do not come back. His name is *Fox*. Can you remember that?"

The little nun gazed at the brooch, nodding, but she was clearly bewildered. "Is this so important, Gigi?"

Gisele was fighting off tears again. "It is," she whispered. "Please, sister. Send the brooch now. The Stawley family has two older lads who could ride swiftly and be there in a few hours. You must do this for me right away."

The Stawley family were farmers not far from the abbey, with younger children who came a few days a week to learn their sums and the great passages of the Bible. The older boys would be more than happy to run an errand for the abbey, even to this mysterious place called Blackchurch, which sounded rather evil to Sister Mary Perpetua. But she could see by the look on Gisele's face that the only evil she perceived was the man dressed in royal colors who had arrived to speak to her.

Sister Mary Perpetua wanted to help.

"As you wish," she said. "I will do it immediately. Give me Ren, because you must go to the messenger now. They are waiting."

Gisele nodded, taking one last look at Ren before the boy took off running with Sister Mary Perpetua trying to keep up. Drying the last of her tears and taking a deep breath for courage, Gisele removed her apron and set out for the small chamber where the mother abbess conducted her business.

With every step, she prayed.

Please, God. Let Ren be safe.

And let Fox receive my message!

CHAPTER FIFTEEN

"LET ME SEE if I understand this correctly," the mother abbess said. "You received word that a royal daughter is living at Canonsleigh Abbey and you have come to speak with her? And this royal daughter, as you have named her, is Gisele of England?"

The messenger, clad in silk tunics and a mail coat upon his impeccably groomed frame, nodded patiently. "That is true, your grace," he said. "Did I tell you that my name was Lord Shillingford?"

"You did. How did you know she was here?"

Yarford Pickney, Lord Shillingford, was at the culmination of a long ride and wasn't feeling a good deal of patience, but he had what he'd come for. Confirmation that Gisele de Salisbury—or, more correctly, Gisele of England—was indeed at Canonsleigh Abbey. As an advisor to King John, although a minor one, he'd been sent on this mission on behalf of the king, and he'd brought twenty soldiers with him to ensure that an abbey full of nuns didn't stand in his way.

He'd come for a reason, and he didn't intend to leave without it.

"It is quite simple, really," he said. "One of the king's advisors, a Lord Willett, had a sister who served at Canonsleigh. She knew of Lady Gisele's presence and informed her brother."

The mother abbess wasn't happy to hear that she had a gossip in her midst. "Is that so?" she said. "Who was his sister?"

"Sister Mary Bernard."

The mother abbess looked at him in shock. Sister Mary Bernard had been close to her and knew all of the workings of the abbey as well as any secrets, feeble that they might be. Not that Lady Gisele's presence was feeble by any means, but she had made it clear that she didn't want anyone to know about her. She simply wanted to live a quiet life. The mother abbess knew that she was the daughter of Queen Margaret and Henry the Young King, as she'd known from the start, and Sister Mary Bernard had known also.

Now, the appearance of the royal messenger was starting to make some sense.

"Sister Mary Bernard died four years ago," she said. "Why come to speak to Gisele now?"

Lord Shillingford smiled thinly. He'd been running off at the mouth since his arrival and didn't seem to have any trouble telling her what she wanted to know and more besides, but he did it in a way that was meant to make her feel small and foolish. As if he had all the answers and she was nothing at all in the grand scheme of things.

"Your grace, I'm sure you understand the nature of politics," he said grandly. "Given that you are in charge of an abbey, you must understand or you would not be here. Even the church has its politics."

The mother abbess cocked an eyebrow at the snobbish courtier. "Mayhap I understand more than you do," she said.

"But you still have not answered my question."

Lord Shillingford's gaze drifted over her a moment; perhaps he was sizing her up. Was it possible this little nun knew more about politics than he did? Impossible! "Lord Willett has known for many years about the presence of Lady Gisele," he said. "Did you truly think you could keep her hidden?"

"We are an abbey. Being hidden from the world is in our nature."

That was true, but Lord Shillingford wouldn't acknowledge it. "Be that as it may, Lord Willett was a wise man," he said. "He realized that he knew what the king did not, and recently, he fell out of favor. Then he shared the information, which saw him regain favor in the king's eyes."

The mother abbess wasn't stupid. She could see this for what it was—an ambitious courtier out of favor using the information of Gisele's whereabouts to put himself back in the king's good graces, helped along by his sister. When William Marshal had sent men to secure the girl's future at the abbey those years ago, they'd made no mention of concealing her identity—that had come from Gisele herself when she arrived. She didn't want anyone to know. Now, the mother abbess was starting to see why. As the daughter of a former king and queen, Gisele could be a valuable royal commodity.

Especially to an unpredictable uncle.

Aye... Things were starting to come clear. The mistake the mother abbess had made was in confiding to Sister Mary Bernard about Gisele's identity. She'd relayed the information to her brother, who used it to help him gain favor with the king when the time was right. Feeling stupid that she'd been betrayed by a woman she had trusted, the mother abbess tried to maintain her composure.

"I see," she said after a moment. "He bargained with the information for his own benefit."

Lord Shillingford shrugged. "We have all done it," he said. "I am sure you have, as well."

The mother abbess looked at him, her eyes taking on something of a hard countenance. "Be careful, my lord," she said, surprisingly threatening. "You forget to whom you are speaking. Unless you want a sour relationship with the church, as your king has, I would be more respectful if I were you."

That seemed to take Shillingford down a little. "I did not mean to offend you, your grace," he said. "You asked how the king came about such information, and I was simply telling you how. Now, the king wishes to communicate with his niece, who has been tragically hidden from him."

The mother abbess was fairly certain Gisele wouldn't categorize her relationship with the king in that fashion, but she didn't comment on it. Instead, she turned in the direction of her table.

"You may speak to Lady de Salisbury, but not alone," she said. "I will be here when you deliver your message."

Now it was Lord Shillingford's turn to look surprised. "*Lady* de Salisbury?" he said. "Is she not known as Gisele of England?"

"She has presented herself as Lady de Salisbury."

"Is she married?"

"She is widowed."

Lord Shillingford thought that was rather odd, but he didn't say so. He knew the woman to be Gisele of England, daughter of Henry the Young King and his wife, Margaret. He hadn't heard of a marriage, and nor had that been mentioned in any of the information he'd received from the king himself.

A puzzling situation, indeed.

Resigned to an impatient wait, he looked around the modest chamber in disdain, going to sit on a chair but running a finger over it to see if it was dirty. He evidently didn't like what he saw because he refused to sit. The mother abbess didn't care.

She simply kept watching him.

Like a hawk.

It wasn't until some time later that Gisele finally showed herself. There was a nun guarding the door in the hallway, and the woman opened the heavy wooden panel, admitting Gisele into the chamber. Lord Shillingford, who had been looking from the window at an unimpressive view, quickly turned to face her. His face lit up with glee at the sight.

"My lady," he said before the mother abbess could speak. "My name is Lord Shillingford. It is an honor to meet you."

The mother abbess put herself between Gisele and the over-eager messenger. She frowned at the man.

"This is a nunnery, Lord Shillingford, not the great hall of Windsor Castle," she said sternly. "You will not speak to any of my charges unless you are introduced first. Is this clear?"

Lord Shillingford was properly rebuked, showing some humility for the first time since entering the chamber. "Forgive me, your grace," he said. "I spoke out of turn."

"You did," the mother abbess said, eyeing him for a moment before turning her attention to Gisele. Her features softened and she forced a smile. "Lord Shillingford has come from London, my child. He has come with a message from the king, your uncle."

Gisele wasn't happy in the least. In fact, she looked quite fearful. Her gaze moved from the mother abbess to the overdressed messenger, who seemed like an eager puppy to her. The entire energy of the chamber was brittle, unsettled.

Already, she didn't like him.

"How did you know I was here?" she asked him.

Lord Shillingford glanced at the mother abbess before responding. "I was telling—"

"You were betrayed, I'm afraid," the mother abbess said, interrupting him. "I realize you wanted to live a quiet life, but you were betrayed by one of us who know who you were. I am afraid she told her brother, who is a courtier, and he told the king. I am sorry, Gisele."

Gisele looked at the woman, stricken. "*Who* betrayed me?"

The mother abbess shook her head. "It does not matter," she said. "She is dead, and we shall not speak ill of those who have passed on. What matters now is that Lord Shillingford has come bearing a message. I will stay with you while he delivers it."

She was leading Gisele over to a chair near her table. Gisele was moving stiffly, her gaze never leaving Shillingford and his stupid clothing dyed to match his stupid hair. The man's hair was crimson, and so was his royal tunic. Everything about him was stupid.

Her hostility began to build.

"Lord Shillingford, before you begin, know that I have no interest in what you have to say," she said. "I do not care to have any association with the king or anyone else at court. I have lived at Canonsleigh peacefully for many years now, and this is where I will remain."

Shillingford seemed puzzled by her reaction. "But it is a great honor I bring you, my lady," he said. "The king has instructed me to tell you that you are to be married to one of the richest men in France. You will be a very powerful lady and forge an alliance between the royal family of England and the

Count of Toulouse, the largest property holder in all of France. The king has long coveted an alliance with Raymond of Toulouse because the county was lost when Raymond married the king's sister, Joan, many years ago. Now, there is the opportunity to reclaim it through marriage."

That was not the message Gisele had been expecting. She didn't know what she had anticipated coming out of the man's mouth, but a marriage hadn't been it. Frankly, it had been the furthest thing from her mind. Shillingford seemed quite excited about the offer and presented it in grand fashion, but the mere mention of her assuming her place in the royal family, as a pawn of marriage, no less, had her bolting out of the chair in outrage.

"Are you quite mad?" she said. "I am not a thing to be toyed with at the king's whim. He has ignored me his entire life, except when his wife tried to kill me. Do you truly believe I would accept something like this? From people who tried to have me assassinated? The king must be mad himself to suggest something like this. You can return to him and tell him that I soundly refuse all offers of marriage!"

It had never occurred to Shillingford that such an offer would be rejected. Shocked, he found himself facing a very angry woman.

"But... my lady," he said, scrambling for words. "The king means this only as the greatest honor. Next to the Queen of France, you will quite possibly be the most powerful lady in the entire country."

"And bound to obey John when he commands me."

"He is your uncle."

Gisele's anger cooled a little, but not much. She laughed, completely without humor, as she wagged a finger at Shillingford.

"I understand completely," she said. "I am to be the king's pawn in Toulouse and bound, by family loyalty, to do whatever he says. It is not enough that I will have a husband. I am to obey John even over him. Am I correct in this assumption?"

Shillingford was still at a loss as to why she should be so upset. "It will be a strong alliance," he said. "This marriage will make you rich and powerful."

"And I am to thank the king by spying on my new husband?"

Now, Shillingford was coming to see what had her upset. "Spying is a harsh word," he said. "Of course, your loyalty should be to your king. The man who made you very rich with an advantageous marriage."

Gisele stared at the man for a moment. He was just the messenger, so it would do no good to argue with him. He didn't make the decisions. But she needed to make her position clear.

"I entered Canonsleigh ten years ago," she said, trying to keep calm. "I am a beguine. I have accepted a life of religious contemplation, and unless you wish to provoke the ire of the church, you will leave me in peace."

Shillingford looked at her as if she'd gone mad. "My lady," he said slowly. "Do you not understand? The king is offering you a wealthy life as the wife of a great man. Your marriage will be very important."

"To whom? The king?" Gisele shook her head. "I am sorry you have come all this way, but I am content with my life as it is. The king will have to find someone else to marry Toulouse, for it will not be me."

Shillingford went from patient and considerate to stiff and unhappy in the blink of an eye. "You misunderstand, my lady," he said. "The decision has been made. I am to escort you back to London, where you will meet your king and discuss the marriage."

Gisele had a feeling that was going to be his position. Certainly, John never asked a woman for permission a day in his life. He was telling her. He wasn't asking her.

But Gisele wasn't going to make it easy for him.

"Nay, *you* misunderstand," she said. "I am not meant for the Count of Toulouse, and I am not meant for the king to use as something to bargain with. You will return to London and tell him so, and if he has issue with that, he can speak to the pope."

"He is your king."

"The pope is my king."

Technically, that was true. The pope was the only person in England who could compete with John on that level—loyalty and obedience. At that point, the mother abbess moved between them, looking at Shillingford with some disdain in her expression.

"I believe enough has been said today," she said quietly. "I will not allow you to continue to harass the lady. She has made her position clear. You will do her the courtesy of respecting her decision."

Shillingford was close to having a tantrum at this point. He very nearly stamped his foot in reply. "She does not seem to understand," he said, pointing at her. "The king is ordering her to do her duty. He is not asking. She cannot disobey a command from the king."

The mother abbess faced him. "The king has no power here," she said. "Leave now and I will not write to my superior and tell him of your disrespect. I suspect John does not need any further trouble from the church because he has trouble enough, so do not create a problem for him. I am certain he will not appreciate it."

That caused Shillingford to back down. John did indeed have a difficult relationship with the Catholic Church, so the last thing Shillingford wanted to do was rock the boat further. Nay, John would not appreciate that. But he'd been sent to collect Gisele of England, and he wasn't leaving without her.

He would be back another day.

"Forgive me, your grace," he said to the mother abbess. "If I have upset your charge, I apologize. Mayhap I did not explain myself well enough. May I take this opportunity to make things clear?"

The mother abbess shook her head. "Not today," she said. "This discussion is over."

"May I return, then?"

The mother abbess turned to look at Gisele, who was pale and angry. But even Gisele knew that when dealing with the king, one must be careful. John knew where she was now. If he really wanted her, he could send his army to take her and deal with the consequences later. This was not some simple lord trying to force her into doing something she didn't want to do. The man before her was a messenger from the King of England. She was dealing with a much higher power now.

And she was terrified.

"In a few days," Gisele said, looking between the mother abbess and Shillingford. "You must give me time to think on this. I am sure you would rather have my cooperation, wouldn't you?"

Shillingford nodded. "We would not wish for you to be unhappy, of course."

Gisele almost laughed. If he did not wish for her to be unhappy, he wouldn't be asking to return so he could coerce her into submission. That was all he wanted to do, and she knew it. But she needed time.

Time for Fox to receive her summons, if he was still at Blackchurch.

She needed him, now more than she ever had in her life.

"Come back in a few days," she said, turning for the door. "I will be in a better frame of mind then, and we may speak rationally."

Shillingford watched her move to the door. "As you wish, my lady," he said. "I will…"

She went through the door and shut it before he could finish his sentence. Insulted and trying not to show it, he looked to the mother abbess.

"It would be in her best interest to accept this gift from the king," he said in a tone that bordered on threatening. "I will return and we will speak again."

The mother abbess nodded. "You may return," she said. "Your men may not. We do not permit men with weapons on the grounds."

"They will remain outside the gate, as they are now," Shillingford said. "May we camp outside the walls?"

The mother abbess shook her head. "Nay," she said. "We have women and children here, and your men would be too much of a threat so close to the abbey. The village of Wellington is up the road, about a mile. They have lodgings. You may stay there, but no closer."

Frustrated, Shillingford bowed abruptly to her and quit the chamber, storming out of the abbey as the nun who had been guarding the door scurried after him. He slammed the entry

door as he left, leaving the nun to do something unprecedented—she threw the bolt to keep him out. When she turned to tell
her superior what she had done, the mother abbess was already
standing there. She had seen what the nun had done.

And she approved.

Within the hour, the rest of the abbey was locked up and
the gates to the courtyard were closed and locked. That wasn't
something they usually did, but something told the mother
abbess that Lord Shillingford wasn't going to take Gisele's
refusal lying down.

It was just a feeling she had.

CHAPTER SIXTEEN

Blackchurch Guild

"**I**F YOU HOLD your hand out in that manner when a man is coming at you with a dagger, he is going to stab you in the hand," Fox said to a recruit who thought he could use brute strength to block a dagger strike. "Look at the trajectory—he's going to stab you straight through the palm and your hand will be useless. In a situation like this, you must come from underneath him and grab the wrist if you can. If you cannot do that, then kicking the dagger from his hand is perfectly acceptable. Or kick him in the ballocks. Either way, you will disarm him."

The recruits laughed at the vulgar defense suggestion as Fox grinned. A light rain was falling around them—storm clouds had moved in during the night and the rain began that morning—but the recruits and dregs at Blackchurch trained rain or shine. Axton put himself between the two recruits to show them how to effectively disable a man with a dagger and ended up getting cut on his arm when he slipped because of the rain. Fox watched the man to see if he was going to lose his temper, which he'd been known to do, but he managed to keep himself under control.

That was a good sign.

Perhaps Axton was finally settling down a little.

Fox stood back to supervise as the man wiped the blood on his arm, bellowing to the men to pair off and pick up a weapon. They were about to run through some exercises defense exercises when Aamir appeared, coming up the rise as the rain grew heavier. Fox saw him coming, and instructed Axton to start the drill as he went to meet the man.

Aamir was more than a trainer at Blackchurch. Because of his background as a Muslim warrior, and the fact that his father was a great warlord in Damascus who commanded thousands upon thousands of men, he had a special place here. Although he did teach recruits, he was the last trainer they had. Men would make it through everyone else, and if they survived—for men who fell out of a class due to failure or injury were not allowed to return—then they would be taught by Aamir. He taught military techniques from armies across the known world. He spoke several languages, among his many talents, and was an advisor to St. Denis. If Blackchurch had a chancellor, Aamir would be it.

He was well respected by all.

"What brings you out in this terrible weather?" Fox asked as he blew the rain off his lips. "You would do well to stay inside today."

Aamir looked up at the sky. "This is what I love most about this country," he said. "In my land, rain is rare."

"That is because it all comes here."

Aamir chuckled. "True," he said. "But days like this are a blessing. You should be grateful."

Fox lifted an eyebrow. "Not if you were born into this," he

said. "I will take sun over rain any day. I've heard your land is full of sun and sand. I would like to see it someday."

"You did not go on Richard's crusade," Aamir said. "Why not?"

Fox shrugged. "My father wasn't keen on what Richard was doing," he said. "In fact, he did not like Richard. The man barely spent any time in England, and my father felt he only used England to fill his coffers. He did not love England as a true Englishman would. I was nineteen years of age when Richard called for arms, but my father refused to let me go. He would not pay for my horse or equipment or anything else if I went, so I did not."

Aamir understood. "It is difficult for some to support a king who shows no love for the land he has claim over," he said. "My father draws strength from the very earth he walks on, so he understands the love of the land."

"Do you ever think to return home?"

Aamir grinned. "Will you go with me if I do?"

"Why not?" Fox said. "If Denis would allow it. It would be an adventure."

"True," Aamir said. "Speaking of Denis, he has summoned you. Come with me, you weak Englishman, and I will take you to the warm chamber and fire you have been crying for."

Fox chuckled, but he was already walking. "I have spent all morning in the rain," he said. "The thought of warmth makes me feel as giddy as a bridegroom on his wedding night."

Aamir laughed softly, walking with Fox down the slope and heading for Exmoor Castle, where St. Denis was located. They passed through Payne's field, where he had his recruits ambushing one another and was teaching them how to turn the tides of such a thing, before continuing past the old cloisters where the more advanced recruits slept.

Exmoor Castle was directly ahead.

Exmoor was really just a keep with a wall around it, but it was a big keep and a big wall. Quite big. There was a solar on the entry level that took up most of the floor, and that was where they were headed. It was the heart of Blackchurch, where business was conducted for the guild and had been for several generations. Fox and Aamir headed up the wooden steps and into the entry, where Fox took a moment to shake off the water that was literally dripping off him. He was soaked to the skin.

Aamir continued on into the enormous solar that had seen two centuries' worth of men pacing the floors. Great accomplishments had happened within those walls, as well as great sorrows. Fox followed him into the chamber, which was quite warm, and noted that Ming Tang was there. He acknowledged his friend as he headed straight to the hearth to dry out. He got close enough to the flame that steam was already rising off his body as an older man, seated behind an enormous, carved table, glanced up from the vellum he was reading.

"The weather is bad today, Fox," St. Denis de Bottreaux said, stating the obvious as he laid down the vellum in his hand and picked up another. "Why not take your recruits into one of the barns? It would provide some shelter."

Fox was wringing out the bottom of his tunic. "Because men will fight in bad weather as well as in good," he said. "The harsher the conditions, the more they suffer. And the more they learn."

"You sound like Tay."

Fox grinned, now trying to wring out his sleeves. "He has a point," he said. "Axton is out there as we speak, making sure the men are learning."

"And what do we think about Axton, anyway?" A younger man who looked a good deal like St. Denis was back against a wall, seated, inspecting several weapons spread out in front of him on a small table. St. Sebastian de Bottreaux was the heir to the empire, a likable man with a good head on his shoulders. He was looking at Fox seriously. "It seems to me that Axton will do whatever he needs to do in order to take your position, Fox. The man is very ambitious."

Fox shook his head. "He may be ambitious, but he is not obvious," he said. "He knows that if he does something that displeases me, I will toss him out on his head. He cannot best me in a fight, so do not worry. He's good, but he is not *that* good."

St. Sebastian wasn't convinced. "Is that the epitaph I am to put on your gravestone?"

Fox chuckled. "You worry like a woman, Sebo," he said, addressing the man informally because he was a friend. "Axton will make a fine trainer someday, but not yet. He has some learning to do himself."

"I hope you are right," St. Sebastian said. "While were are on the subject of new trainers, Papa has been talking about expanding the education we provide into history, mathematics, and philosophy. So our recruits will have more education along with their training. What do you think?"

Fox shook out his wet hair. "As long as I do not have to teach it, I think it is an excellent idea," he said. "I was terrible with mathematics, unfortunately."

"We would bring a tutor from the University of Paris," St. Denis said, reading something that was lying on his table. "I have sent word to several universities, and I am getting responses already. This particular man wants to teach the mathematics of the Bible. Is there even such a thing?"

Ming Tang, who had been helping St. Denis look through the letters from men interested in teaching at Blackchurch, nodded his head. "In your Bible, Noah speaks of the size of the ark he is to build," he said. "That is mathematics."

St. Denis frowned. "So the man teaches them how to build an ark?" he said. "That seems extreme. Mayhap he can build one, and Kristian and his recruits can try to sink it."

That brought laughter from the men in the room. Kristian's entire course was on water, and Lake Cocytus had two, fully fledged longships where the recruits were taught water warfare. Sometimes, he did water landings on the shores of the lake, and his recruits would storm the dreg field and take prisoners. It was all great fun, and good practice, until Tay and Payne teamed up against Kristian and his recruits and a mild war ensued. St. Denis had sent Aamir and Fox and Sinclair to break it up, but it was fun while it lasted.

"I would like to see that," Fox said. "Applicable mathematics could be helpful to the recruits."

St. Denis snorted. "By building an ark?" he said. "I think it is madness. Ah, that reminds me, I did summon you for a reason, Fox. Something arrived for you this morning."

Fox shook off more water as he headed over to the table where St. Denis was holding something up for him. It was wrapped in a piece of cloth, and he took it, unwrapping it as he headed back over to the hearth. He had no idea what it was, or what it could be, and was unconcerned as he peeled back the damp cloth.

But what he saw in his hand stopped him in his tracks.

For a moment, he simply stood there, unable to breathe. He was unable to think. For a brief and terrible moment, Fox's mind was a void because he couldn't adequately process what he was seeing.

But then it hit him.

He drew in his breath in a great, sucking gasp.

Everyone in the room heard him. Ming Tang, Aamir, and St. Sebastian looked over at him to see why he'd let out such a strange sound, but all they saw was a man who had just seen a ghost. He was looking at something in his hand with the expression one had when beholding the dead.

"Fox?" Ming Tang said, puzzled. "What is it?"

Fox couldn't even speak. He shook his head, still staring at what was in his hand, and Ming Tang went over to him, wondering what had the man so stunned. But the moment he looked in Fox's hand and saw the dragon's head brooch with the garnet eye, he knew.

Instantly, he knew.

"Fox," he gasped softly. "It is from *her!*"

Fox was struggling to speak. Finding his voice, he looked at St. Denis. "Who brought this?" he asked hoarsely. "Is he still here?"

St. Denis was looking at Fox with some concern because everyone else was. "Nay," he said. "It was a young man who rode in here earlier today and told the gatehouse guards that this was meant for you. They brought it to me about a half-hour ago. Why? What is it?"

Fox didn't know how to tell him. He didn't know *what* to tell him. All he could do was stare at that brooch, knowing Gisele would have sent it only if it was a matter of life or death.

"Fox?" St. Denis said again, puzzled and concerned. "What is the matter? *What* is it?"

Ming Tang was standing next to him, looking at Fox with

great sympathy, waiting for him to speak, but Fox couldn't seem to do it. He put his hand on Fox's arm.

"Fox," he whispered. "Shall I tell him? Or will you?"

Fox tore his gaze away from the brooch, looking at Ming Tang's expression. The man was his friend. He would never suggest something that wasn't in Fox's best interest. In this case, Fox was being summoned by a force more powerful than anything on earth—the power of love. That moment he had dreaded had become real.

"She sent it," he whispered. "After all these years, she has sent it."

Ming Tang nodded. "I know, my friend," he said. "She needs you."

Fox's breathing was starting to quicken with emotion. "Those dreams," he muttered. "Those dreams were a harbinger. Something is wrong with her."

"And she has called to you," Ming Tang agreed. "But if you wish to go to her, you must tell Denis. He must know."

Fox knew that. As difficult as it was, he knew he had to tell the man something. With effort, he cleared his throat and turned to St. Denis.

"Because telling the entire story behind this brooch is too painful, I will tell you what it represents," he said. "We all have those moments in our lives that are too difficult to recall or too difficult to speak of, and this is mine."

St. Denis was on his feet, as was St. Sebastian. In fact, St. Sebastian went to Fox and put his hand on the man's shoulder in a comforting gesture.

"Tell us what you can, old man," St. Sebastian said softly. "What does that amulet mean? Who has sent it?"

Fox had to take a deep breath. "I know I've not spoken of

my past since I've been here," he said. "But this is from my past. It is the reason why I came to Blackchurch. My lord, you are friends with Keller de Poyer. He was the one who brought me here."

He was addressing St. Denis, who nodded. "Keller and I are old friends," he said. "I accepted your fealty without question based on his recommendation. It was one of the best things I've ever done."

"Thank you, my lord," Fox said, smiling weakly. "It was one of the best things *I've* ever done. But the truth was that when I came to Blackchurch, I was running away."

"From what?"

"William Marshal's wrath."

St. Denis couldn't help the surprise in his expression. "Why?" he said. "What did you do?"

Fox took another deep breath and looked at the brooch in his hand. "I loved his daughter, and she loved me," he said softly. "His daughter, however, was a bastard. Her mother was the wife of Henry the Young King. I wanted to marry her, but the Marshal had already made arrangements for her to take the veil when she came of age. Nothing I could say would change his mind. We fought, and the decision was made that I would no longer serve him. In fact, he threatened me should I ever try to see her again. The woman I love is at Canonsleigh Abbey, about ten miles to the south of Blackchurch. Before I left her, I told her that, if she ever needed me, to send me this brooch. She would only send it in a life-threatening situation, and now she has. I must go to her, my lord. She needs me."

St. Denis' expression of surprise turned to one of grief. "Oh… Fox," he said softly, with great sorrow. "I'm so sorry, lad. But are you sure she sent this? If the Marshal threatened you, could this be a trap of some kind?"

Fox shook his head. "The Marshal didn't know about the brooch," he said. "The only people who knew about it were me, my lady, and de Poyer, and I doubt de Poyer would have told Pembroke anything."

"You must go to her, Fox," St. Sebastian insisted. "She is in trouble, and you must go."

"If Denis allows it, I shall go with you," Ming Tang said. "If for no other reason than to watch your back. If you've not spoken to her in all this time, and the Marshal threatened you if you were to see her again, then it would not hurt to have help at the ready."

"And me," Aamir said. "I will go with you. Please, Fox. I would like to come."

St. Denis was watching his trainers pile on to Fox's cause, and he knew it would be a battle to try to stop them. He didn't want to appear ungenerous in a clearly gut-wrenching situation like the one Fox was facing. He didn't know the full story, but with William Marshal involved, he could only imagine how difficult—and possibly dangerous—it could be. But more than anything, he could see the anguish on Fox's face.

He had the look of a tortured man.

"I do not know William Marshal well," he said after a moment. "Of course, we have met from time to time, and some of his men and women have trained here. For not being friends or even allies, we have shared a sort of reciprocal alliance because of what Blackchurch does and what he does. I know he is a man of conviction and truth. I have never known him to be unjust, Fox, so I do not know why you were not permitted to marry his daughter, but he must have had his reasons."

Fox nodded, but it was with great regret. "De Poyer told me

that it was because he promised the woman's mother, Queen Margaret, that their daughter would take the veil," he said. "Evidently, he loved Margaret. He wanted to please her. That promise is what has prevented Gisele and I from marrying. An old promise made to a dead woman who should never have... Forgive me. I should not speak ill of her."

He looked away, struggling with his composure, as St. Denis considered the situation. But more than that, he considered the man. Fox was as true and noble as they came. He was an excellent trainer and had never caused any trouble. He was also as loyal as the day was long—they didn't come any more faithful than Fox de Merest. To hear the man's backstory— though he knew he had one, because Keller had alluded to it— was genuinely distressing.

But he had to make a decision.

There was only one he could make.

"If the lady is sending you the brooch to ask for your help, then clearly, she must be in peril," he said, turning back for his table. "At Blackchurch, we remain neutral in all conflicts. That is how we have survived so long. I will not break that rule by going against William Marshal's wishes. That would be devastating for Blackchurch and for the Marshal, quite frankly. I know you understand that, Fox."

Fox was looking at him with great sorrow. "I do," he said quietly, lowering his gaze. "I thought that might be your answer. If that is the case, then I will resign my position immediately. Gisele needs me, and I must go to her, with or without your permission."

St. Denis paused and held up a hand. "I realize that," he said. "You must allow me to finish what I was going to say. Although we do not take sides in any given conflict, I do not see this as a conflict. It is not a war. It is a family situation, and, like it or not, we are family at Blackchurch. All of those trainers out in the rain are your brothers, Fox. Even now, Aamir and Ming Tang and even Sebo stand at your side, ready to help you. Brothers help brothers, and I know that when word spreads of your trouble, every trainer here will flock to you. There will be a mass exodus to follow you to Canonsleigh, and I cannot stop them. More than that, I will not try. In fact, I want them to go with you. If your lady is in danger, there is no telling what that danger is. You may need their help."

When Fox realized what the man was saying, he nearly collapsed with relief. "Thank you, my lord," he said sincerely. "It does not seem adequate to say those words, but I will say them just the same. Know that I am deeply grateful."

St. Denis smiled weakly. "As if I could stop you," he said. "As if I could stop all of you. Now, you will go and tell Axton to continue your class for the day, and possibly the next several days, or at least until you return. You should tell the man you are going and do not know when you will be back, but assure him that you *will* be back. I do not want him getting any ideas about becoming your permanent replacement."

Fox nodded quickly. "I will, my lord."

St. Denis looked to Aamir and Ming Tang. "You will go to each trainer and tell them that Fox is in trouble," he said. "Rally them to gather their weapons and anything else they may need and then gather in the stables. Fox, gather whatever you may need and meet them there. You will leave as soon as everyone has gathered. But whatever you find at Canonsleigh, settle the business and get back here as quickly as you can. There is no need to linger, but if you need the backing of Blackchurch soldiers, send word to me. I will bring them myself."

Blackchurch, in spite of being a neutral entity, had over a thousand soldiers spread out among the grounds, mostly to protect the perimeters or to police the recruits. But it was still a big army, by any standards. Aamir and Ming Tang started to move, leaving St. Sebastian standing by himself.

"What about me?" he said. "Can't I go, too?"

St. Denis looked at his son, clearly undecided. "The last time your brother went to help in a situation not dissimilar to this one, he was killed," he said. "I could not stand to lose you, Sebo. Will you stay here?"

St. Sebastian wasn't happy about that. "Papa, you cannot build a wall around me," he said. "I am a knight, and a damn fine one, but the opportunity to prove that is rare. I would like to help Fox. Please?"

St. Denis didn't want to let him go. He'd lost his eldest, St. Gerard, a few years ago in a tragic mistake, and he simply couldn't stomach losing his last surviving son. But St. Sebastian was right—it wasn't as if St. Denis could build a wall around his Kenilworth-trained son. It was the gold standard of all knights, to be trained at Kenilworth, so St. Sebastian was more than qualified. St. Denis knew it would create a problem if he denied him. More than that, St. Sebastian would lead Blackchurch one day, and these men, so a sense of loyalty to each other was paramount. Everyone wanted a leader they could respect.

Reluctantly, he nodded.

"Very well," he said. "Go if you must. But if you die, I will marry a young woman, have a dozen sons, and tell them all how stupid their brother Sebo was. That is how you will be remembered if something happens to you, so take heed."

St. Sebastian snorted and put his arms around his father, obnoxiously kissing him before he fled from the chamber after

Aamir, Ming Tang, and finally Fox. When all four of them had gone, leaving St. Denis alone with a snapping fire and a heart full of concern, the mood of the chamber seemed to grow strangely still. St. Denis could feel it. He sat behind his table again, thinking of what Fox was about to face and praying that, in the end, all of his trainers returned whole and unharmed. When entering into the realm of the unknown, particularly when it pertained to William Marshal, there was no telling what could happen. Even for Blackchurch knights.

St. Denis could only hope he'd made the right decision.

CHAPTER SEVENTEEN

Canonsleigh Abbey

T HEY HADN'T LEFT.

Although Lord Shillingford had promised he would take his army to the village of Wellington and await Gisele's willingness to discuss the subject of a royal marriage again, they had not gone to the village, nor had they maintained the proper distance that the mother abbess had requested.

In fact, children who were coming for their lessons reported a soldier's encampment less than half a mile away. When questioned by the nuns, the children described the crimson tunics with the yellow lions on them, which was indicative of the royal standard. Infuriated, the mother abbess made the unprecedented decision to walk to the encampment and demand Lord Shillingford move his men back to Wellington.

She'd been met with resistance.

Lord Shillingford, being devious, insisted that his men were no threat and were quite enjoying the lovely spot they had chosen for their encampment. It was next to a small lake, and his men could fish for their supper. After about an hour of arguing without any results, the mother abbess returned to

Canonsleigh in defeat. Not trusting Shillingford or his men, she ordered everything locked up.

The children who had come to the abbey for their lessons were sent home and told not to return until the soldiers had left. The nuns were told not to wander outside of the walls, which was uncommon for Canonsleigh. The nuns as well as the people who attended mass were unused to any kind of restrictions, and it had been that way for many years, but now they were being told that there was a threat. That was something that terrified the local farmers, who didn't want their children threatened by a nearby encampment, so the entire area was nestled under a blanket of suspicion and fear.

And Gisele couldn't have felt worse about it.

Not only did she have to deal with Lord Shillingford nearby, but she felt guilty because the people who had always come and gone so freely from the abbey were now prevented from doing so. The abbey was fairly self-sufficient when it came to food, but there were supplies that they needed to purchase from Wellington or from any number of the farmers in the area. That commerce was now suspended, so the mother abbess sat down with Gisele and several of the other nuns to discuss how they would have to live until the royal troops decided to leave.

All of this, of course, was accomplished within the first couple of days, when they realized the royal army had set up camp on their doorstep. So far, there hadn't been any hardship, but it was still early. Things could change rapidly if Gisele refused the king's marriage offer again.

And she would.

Then there was Fox.

Gisele had sent the brooch to Blackchurch, and the farmer's son told her that morning that it had been delivered to the gatehouse. It made it there, but the truth was that Gisele didn't even know if Fox had received it. Perhaps he was no longer there. Perhaps one of the gatehouse guards stole it. Perhaps Fox had somehow passed away in the past ten years, a thought that brought her to tears, but one she had considered from time to time. Having had no contact with him for all of those years, she didn't know if he was even still alive, and that was a terrifying thought. Perhaps the Fox she knew was only in her memory.

And then there was the worst thought of all.

What if he had married?

That would have crushed Gisele most of all, even though she knew it was foolish. He'd promised to wait for her, no matter how long it took, but she had no idea what William Marshal's threats were against him, so perhaps he'd decided that it was futile to love a woman he could never have. She wouldn't blame him for that. Perhaps he'd met a young woman he'd fallen in love with and married her. If that was the case, she truly hoped he'd found happiness, but she wished with all her heart that she could have been that young woman. As long as he was happy, however, that was all that mattered to her.

She truly did wish the best for him.

Her thoughts were lingering heavily on Fox on a bright morning following a day and a night of rain, as she tended to an apricot tree that was growing from a seed planted in one of those wooden pots she'd made. She was on her knees, trimming some dead leaves off the little tree and giving them to the cats to play with, when Ren came into the garden room. Catching sight of her son, Gisele lifted her head and smiled.

"Why are you not with Sister Mary Ruth?" she asked. "It is time for your lessons."

Ren frowned, kicking at the dirt as he wandered in then

plopped down by a cat. "Not today," he said, stroking the orange feline. "None of the other children can come today, so there are no lessons."

Gisele's smile faded. "I see," she said, pushing herself up to a standing position. "Then you must find something to do."

He leaned against a table that held seedlings and a few empty pots. "But what can I do?" he said. "I have nothing to do and no friends to play with."

He was bored, and fidgety, so she grasped him by the shoulder and pulled him over to a small cabinet that contained everything she needed for her gardening. Opening the cabinet doors, she rummaged around inside until she found what she was looking for.

"Here," she said, handing him a small handsaw. "Take your saw. You know the old ash tree near the chapel?"

He took the saw from her carefully, as it was one of his prized possessions and she only let him use it with her permission. "The one with the dead branches?" he asked.

"That one," she said. "But not all of them are dead, and some are low to the ground. Go and cut as many as you can for me."

He frowned. "And then what do I do?"

She turned him for the door that let out into the garden. "Then you will strip the leaves off them and put them in a basket," she said. "You can find one outside near the outbuilding that contains things to help the garden grow. Fill the basket with the leaves and then bring the branches back here. We will make more pots."

He didn't think that sounded very exciting. "Mam…"

"*Go,*" she said, lightly swatting his behind. "Be careful with the saw and do not come back here until you have completed your task. And under no circumstances are you to go outside the walls. Do you understand?"

He nodded solemnly. "Aye," he said. "What are we having for the nooning meal?"

He was hungry. But, then again, Ren was always hungry. "I do not know," she said. "But if you are very good and do as I say, I will see if the cook has any fresh bread for you to eat when you are finished."

He hung his head, unhappy that he had to wait for something to eat, but just as he trudged off with all of the enthusiasm of a prisoner going into a mine, his mother called him back and gave him a big green apple. It was tart and juicy, and he bit into it happily as he ran off with the saw, listening to his mother call after him, telling him to be careful.

He was always careful.

At least, that was what he told her.

The garden of the abbey that his mother tended was open on one side. That was why the abbey's cats wandered in so freely. Three sides were bordered by the chapel, his mother's garden room, and the cloister, but the fourth side opened into the bailey with the wall beyond. He was headed toward the old ash tree on the eastern side of the chapel, and as he walked, he found other sticks lying on the ground, blown there by the rainstorm the night before, so he picked them up and tried to cut them with the handsaw. They were too wet, however, and only wanted to bend or fray, so he tossed them aside as he headed toward the old tree. Once he cleared the chapel, the courtyard was open all the way to the big gates, which were to his right. They had rarely been locked shut, and he was intrigued. He thought that, perhaps, if he looked through the iron bars that constituted some of the gate, he might be able to see the royal soldiers he'd heard tale of.

Curiosity lured him.

He was eager to see the army. He'd been run off the day before by his mother, told to hide, and he'd heard nuns whispering about the soldiers, so he thought that was why his mother wanted him to hide. Soldiers carried big swords and shields and other weapons, and he was quite intrigued with them. He didn't want to live at an abbey his entire life. He wanted to be a soldier, too, someday. Or maybe a farmer. He wasn't sure yet.

But he knew he was interested in men with weapons.

As he was trying to see the army up the road, the thunder of horses caught his attention, startling him. He turned to see a group of men on horseback approaching from the west. The road that led to Canonsleigh curved around the perimeter of the walls and continued on to the east, so the men had come from the north as they swung around the western side of the abbey on their way to the gates. At least, Ren thought they were coming to the abbey because they were heading right for him. He took a few steps back, startled by so many big men on very big horses. The biggest and most fearsome horses he had ever seen. More than that, the men riding them were armed to the teeth for battle.

Knights.

Ren was both terrified and fascinated.

The group of knights came to a halt, and the man riding in the lead dismounted. He was wearing mail from head to toe and an enormous great helm. Over his mail, he wore a white tunic with a big black cross on it, only the vertical part of the cross was actually a sword. Ren could tell because there was a hilt on the top of it. The man wearing it was the biggest human he'd ever seen, and he backed up as the knight came near the gate.

"Little man," he said in a deep, smooth voice. "Is this Canonsleigh Abbey?"

Ren nodded unsteadily. "Aye," he said. "Are... are you a knight?"

"I am," the man said. "Will you please tell the mother abbess that I wish to see her?"

Ren crept closer to the gate, looking at the man's weapons through the iron bars. "Can I see your sword?"

The knight unsheathed it without hesitation, holding it up for the boy to see. Ren gasped in appreciation. "It's big!" he said.

"And it weighs as much as you do," the knight said, resheathing it. "Will you please tell the mother abbess I wish to see her?"

Ren eyed him. "Are you with the soldiers?"

"What soldiers?"

"The soldiers that came," he said, pointing. "The are camped down the road, and we're not allowed to open the gates."

The man paused a moment before turning to look up the road as if to see what the boy was indicating, but all he saw was dirt and trees.

"Who are the soldiers?" he finally asked. "Why are they here?"

"I don't know," Ren said. "But they came yesterday. My mam made me hide from them."

"You live here?"

Ren nodded. "With my mam."

"I see," the knight said. Then he paused a moment, clearly contemplating something. When he spoke again, his voice was quiet. "Do you know of a lady named Gisele de Salisbury? Does she still live here?"

"That's my mam."

After a moment, the man removed his helm, looking at Ren with flushed cheeks and wide eyes. "Your *mam*?" he repeated, sounding startled. As he spoke, a couple of the knights behind him dismounted and came to his side, but the knight only had eyes for Ren. "Your *mother* is Gisele de Salisbury?"

"Aye."

"How... how old are you?"

"I have seen nine years," Ren said. "How old are you?"

The man looked as if he was about to cry. "Nine years...?" he muttered. "And your mam... Gisele... is here?"

Ren pointed back toward the abbey. "In the garden."

"What is your name, lad?"

"Ren de Salisbury."

After that, the man didn't seem to be able to speak. Ren came nearer to the gate as two of his friends spoke softly to him. One man put a hand on his shoulder. He seemed overcome about... something. Ren didn't know what. But, then again, he didn't understand grownups.

"Do you want me to get the mother abbess?" he asked, trying to figure out why the man seemed to be weeping.

The man, his face turned away from the gate, shook his head as one of the men next to him, quite enormous and bearing the same white and black tunic, approached the gate.

"Go and get your mother, lad," he told him calmly. "Tell her that Fox has come."

"Why?"

"Run swiftly to tell her, and I will give you a coin."

Ren's eyes widened. "Money?"

"Money."

"Do you promise?"

The man dug into the purse on his belt and held up a silver coin to prove it.

Ren didn't ask any more questions, taking off at a dead run around the side of the chapel and into the garden his mother had planted. He bolted through that, knocking into a lavender bush, as he darted inside his mother's garden room.

She was still there, bent over a tree.

"Mam!" he yelled. "You must come!"

Gisele looked up from the branches. "Why are you shouting?" she said. "Why must I come?"

Ren was jumping up and down, pointing. "At the gate," he said. "The knight said he'd give me a coin if I told you!"

"Told me what?"

"That Fox is here!"

Gisele didn't even remember running from the garden room. Suddenly, she was racing into the courtyard, around the chapel, and the main gate was in front of her. She didn't even know how she got there. Her next conscious realization was that she was about halfway to the gate, seeing a collection of knights standing outside of it, and she suddenly slowed. She didn't even know why she did that, either. All she could see or think about or hear were the knights on the opposite side of the gate. Someone was tugging on her hand, urging her toward the gate, and she realized that it was Ren. He was pulling her toward the oak and iron panels.

Fox is here.

Oh, God... Was it true?

Was it really true?

Overwhelmed and dazed, she somehow managed to walk

the last few feet to the gate only to see Fox on the opposite side. He looked just as she remembered, hardly changed at all except for some silver hair around his temples. But he didn't look old or haggard or even irritated that he'd been summoned.

He looked beautiful.

Her hands flew to her mouth.

"Fox?" she whispered tightly. "My God… Is it really you?"

Fox heard her voice, and the tears began to fall. "It is really me," he said hoarsely. "I received your message. I came as soon as I could."

Gisele couldn't speak. The words wouldn't come. Suddenly, she was flying at the gate, throwing the big bolts on the top as Ren removed the ones from the bottom. Ren wanted the money; she wanted Fox. When the boy had thrown the last bolt, he yanked the gate open and toppled over as it crashed into him. Embarrassed, he picked himself up as his mother faced the knight known as Fox.

It was a moment of sheer joy that even the angels would remember.

"Sweet Mary," Gisele finally murmured, drinking in the man's face. "I have imagined this moment a million times in my dreams, and now that it is here, I hardly know what to say."

Fox was in much the same position. Beside him, Ming Tang and Tay had moved back to the horses to give them some privacy, but Ren was standing next to his mother, gazing up at the knight as if he was part of this conversation.

"Are you well?" Fox asked. "Just tell me you are not hurt or ill."

Gisele shook her head, the tears flowing as quickly as she could wipe them away. "I am not injured or ill," she said. "And you? Have you been well?"

"I am perfect," Fox said, taking a step toward her. He lifted his trembling hands. "May I take you in my arms? May I please do that?"

Gisele was cognizant of Ren by her side, so she shook her head. "It is with the greatest sorrow that I must deny you," she murmured. "I wish we could, but... we cannot. Not now. But it is enough that you are here, Fox. I did not know if you would come."

Fox suspected the boy, and the abbey itself, had something to do with her not rushing into his arms, and he wasn't troubled by it. Disappointed a little, but not troubled. He understood.

"I told you I would come if you sent the brooch," he said. "I will always keep my word to you. I know that de Poyer came to you those years ago. He told you what happened with the Marshal."

Gisele nodded quickly. "Aye," she said. "He told me. The Marshal must have said something terrible to you for you not to have returned, Fox. I was never angry with you for it. I want you to know that."

The shock of seeing her was starting to wear off, and all of the emotion he ever felt for her was beginning to swamp him. His palms were sweating, his knees were weak, and he could hardly breathe because of it. But in his periphery, he caught sight of Ren gazing up at him with interest. He felt tears stinging his eyes anew.

"The boy," he whispered. "Is he...?"

Gisele nodded before he even finished. "He is," she said, not too loudly because she was going to have to explain a few things to Ren after this reunion. "He was born about nine months after you brought me here."

Fox looked down at the boy. Even he could see how much

the child looked like him, and his features threatened to crumble. "Dear God," he breathed. "Why didn't you tell me?"

She could see how overcome he was. "Would it have done any good?" she asked. "We could not be together. Knowing about him would have made you mad. I do not know what the Marshal said to you to make you stay away, but I did not want you to get yourself killed trying to take me from the abbey. It was better not to tell you. But his name is Renard—it means 'fox' in French. He was named for his father."

Fox was laboring with everything he had not to lose his composure, but as he listened to Gisele, one thing was clear to him—the woman he knew had grown up. Somehow, someway, she had matured into a reasonable person, one who put the needs and wants of others over her own. He remembered one of the last times they ever made love, how she'd locked her feet behind his buttocks when he tried to withdraw from her body so he was forced to climax inside of her. He'd accused her of trying to get pregnant to force him into marriage.

And that was the irony of the situation.

She *had* gotten pregnant.

Fox's seed had found its mark. But in order to protect Fox, she hadn't sent him word about the child because she knew what that would mean. She knew he would break his neck trying to get to her, so she'd made the decision to keep the birth of his son from him. A selfish woman would not have had such restraint. Although he understood completely and respected the fact that she hadn't tried to make a difficult situation even more difficult, he was still crushed that he hadn't known.

Ren.

"Is this why you sent me the brooch?" he finally asked. "To tell me about the boy because so much time has passed?"

Gisele shook her head. "Nay," she said. "There is something much more sinister to deal with. I am in trouble, Fox. I need your counsel and, if possible, your help."

"Does it have anything to do with the soldiers Ren mentioned?"

"It has everything to do with them," she said, turning to her son. "Ren, open the gates. Let the knights in."

Ren threw back the gate that had tossed him to the ground and ran to push the other one open as Gisele stood back, with Fox following her, as the knights who had accompanied him entered the courtyard. There were ten of them, to be exact, all heavily armed. Gisele had been around knights her entire life, and she'd never seen such a group of big, frightening men, all of them wearing the white tunic with the black cross on it. As Ren ran out to tell the knights where to put their horses, Fox watched the child, his heart nearly bursting.

"He is very helpful," Gisele said, standing next to him. "He reminds me so much of you in that regard. He also has your devilish sense of humor."

Fox turned to look at her, reacquainting himself with her face. He was calmer now that their initial shock was over, but the warmth in his eyes was still there. If anything, it had grown stronger.

"I am overwhelmed, Gigi," he said. "I would be lying if I said I had not prayed for something like this, but I never imagined... I did not know when such a thing would be possible. It has been ten years since we last saw one another."

Gisele wanted to ask him so many questions, but she wasn't sure how receptive he would be. "Is it appropriate to tell you that I still love you as I always have?" she murmured. "That has never changed, Fox. But I understand if you cannot say the same. Ten years is a long time to be separated."

He put up a hand to silence her before she even finished speaking. "I told you once, and I will tell you again," he said. "I will wait for you. It has been ten years, and still, I have waited for you. There is no other woman for me, Gisele. There never has been and there never will be."

"Then... then you did not marry?"

He looked at her as if she'd lost her mind. "Of course not."

"I would have understood."

"How can I marry one woman when I love another?"

That was all Gisele needed to hear. Fox had stayed true to her, as she had stayed true to him. The hesitation, the uncertainty, fled.

He was still hers.

She put her hands over her heart, looking at him with an expression that suggested she was deeply touched. But that soundless gesture also conveyed her love for him, something that had only deepened over the years.

"That is why I have never taken the veil," she whispered. "Somehow, it did not seem right to. I knew you would come for me, someday. I knew we belonged together. But I will tell you that the nuns believe I am widowed. Had I not told them that, I am afraid of what they would have done with Ren. They might have sent him away. This way, I am a beguine, a respectable widow, and they allow him to remain. For now, anyway."

He grunted softly. "I understand," he said. "Ren told me that his family name is de Salisbury."

"I kept the name. I hope you do not mind."

He shook his head. "I do not," he said. "You had no choice. When I delivered you to the mother abbess those years ago, I introduced myself by my full name, so she would have known something was odd if you called yourself Lady de Merest and had the boy carry my name."

"Exactly," she said. Her gaze moved out over the knights, who were settling the horses while Ren seemed to be following the biggest of them around. "Lord de Poyer said you were at Blackchurch. Are these men you serve with?"

Fox nodded. "They are my friends and my brothers," he said. "When you summoned me, they would not let me go alone in case danger awaited."

"Do you serve the lord of Blackchurch, then?"

He shook his head. "We will speak of that in a moment," he said. "I want to be clear, Gigi. I did not come here only to find out why you sent the brooch. I came here to take you with me. I made that decision the moment I received the brooch, and seeing Ren has only confirmed it. You are coming with me, and to hell with the Marshal. I've not seen the man in ten years, and if he tries to punish me now... There are ten knights and about a thousand men who will stand with me against him. I want you to know that."

Gisele was deeply touched. She was also thrilled. "Oh... Fox," she whispered, tears pooling in her eyes again. "Is it true?"

"Of course it's true," he said. "I told you I would return for you. Here I am."

He said the last three words with a glimmer of mirth in his eye, and she smiled, her heart so full she thought that it would surely burst.

"What took you so long?" she teased gently.

He grinned, looking so much like the man she'd first fallen in love with. "I had some difficulty with my horse," he teased in return. "Lazy beast, you know. Moreover, all the women in Devon are after me, and I had to fight them all off. They tried to block my way back to you."

Gisele could see he hadn't changed at all. "How terrible for you," she said. "I would say that all of the men in Devon were after me, but the fact that I live in an abbey pokes holes in that story."

His eyes were twinkling at her, and a smile was on his lips. "Still, I would believe it," he said. "What man wouldn't want you? You are more beautiful than I remember."

"I had hoped you would say that."

"I want to kiss you so badly right now that my hands are fairly aching to touch you," he said. "But I'm afraid that Ren might not take it well. I do not want to upset the lad."

They both looked over at the boy, who was speaking to the tallest man Gisele had ever seen. "I do not think the nuns would take it well, either," she said. "Though I would dearly love for you to. But I am certain the mother abbess has caught sight of you, so we should go inside to speak with her. Your men must wait out here."

"I am at your service, my lady."

Gisele couldn't help it. She reached out to gently touch his hand, dying to touch the man, however innocently after all these years, but Fox grabbed her hand and lifted it to his lips for a discreet kiss. He dropped it quickly, but the first kiss after ten years apart meant something. It was a stolen kiss, one of great promise and pleasure and hope. They were together again, and that was all that mattered.

Nothing else had ever been, or would ever be, more important.

As Gisele and Fox turned for the entry to the chapel, they caught sight of the mother abbess emerging.

Things were about to get interesting.

CHAPTER EIGHTEEN

"W HO IS THIS lowly woman who refuses the king? How dare she disobey the king's summons!"

It was afternoon, the second day after Lord Shillingford's arrival at Canonsleigh Abbey. Two days of frustration and drinking, of hunting in the local forests and stealing a cow from a local farmer. The smell of roasting beef was heavy in the air, along with the smell of smoke, as Shillingford sat around a fire with the soldiers he'd brought with him. Twenty royal soldiers who would ensure his directive was successfully completed.

"You should have never let her walk away," said the soldier next to him, a man who had been in the royal ranks for twenty years and went by the name of Ham. "You should have demanded she come with you immediately. You have given her time to think, and now the abbey is locked. We will have to break the gates down to get to her."

Shillingford didn't like being lectured by a mere soldier. Never mind that his father had been one. He didn't like to acknowledge his humble beginnings. He'd come into the king's household as a servant because of his father's service to the Crown, but he'd managed to sleep, borrow, and beg his way into a position of mild power. He was willing to do anything for the king, and everyone knew it, including anything nasty, lascivious, or degrading. He'd proven that time and time again.

And now he was here.

"A willing lady is much more pleasing to everyone than a combative one," he said. "I was hoping the mother abbess would convince her that she cannot refuse. I am not willing to wait days or weeks or months for her to come to her senses. Nay, I will not wait, and nor should the king. Raymond of Toulouse is awaiting a royal bride, and I am charged with bringing her. And I shall!"

Ham eyed the other soldiers, who thought Shillingford was a ridiculous twit. He was a man who craved power, and he queened it over the soldiers, who were all mostly seasoned warriors and didn't take a man like Shillingford seriously. But in this case, with escorting a royal relation from the abbey she'd been confined to for the past several years, they were simply anxious to get it over with and get home to London. However, being seasoned men, and ultimately commanded by a king with no moral compass, they didn't see the walls of a nunnery being much of a barrier to their final objective.

"Will you take a bit of advice, m'lord?" Ham said, chewing on a rib bone. "I'm sure you're thinking the same thing as we are, but I'd like to make it clear."

Shillingford was still frowning, thinking about the stubborn woman at the abbey who was going to ruin his relationship with the king, but Ham's words caught his attention. "Of course I'm thinking the same thing you are," he snapped. "But… What are you thinking?"

Ham tossed the rib bone to the dirt. "You're a smart man, m'lord," he said, pointing to his head. "You know that in the wilds like this, anything can happen. That abbey is small, and it's not important. It could burn to the ground, with no survivors, and no one would know what had happened."

Shillingford wasn't following him. "Burn to the...?" he repeated, trying to pretend he knew what Ham was talking about. "Of course it could. Fires happen all the time."

"They do," Ham agreed. "If we were to go over the walls before dawn and break into the nunnery tonight when everyone was asleep, we could find the lady and take her away. Anyone who saw us would be caught in the fire and burned. No witnesses, m'lord. That's what you were thinking, wasn't it?"

Now, Shillingford understood. "I was," he said quickly. "But the lady would know. She would tell."

"She wouldn't know if she didn't see it," Ham said. "We'd render her unconscious and take her away, burning the abbey once she's clear of it. What she didn't see, she can't speak to. And the dead can't tell anyone what they saw."

Shillingford was warming to that plan. "That is exactly what I was thinking," he insisted. "That is what we shall do. Tonight, when everyone is asleep, we will climb the walls, capture Gisele of England, and burn the abbey behind us."

Ham slapped his thigh. "An excellent plan, m'lord," he said, looking to the men over his shoulder and giving them an exaggerated wink. "You're a brilliant man."

Shillingford sat straight, feeding off their praise. "I am," he agreed. "You shall all be greatly rewarded for your assistance. If you find anything in the abbey of value, take it."

"Does that include women?" someone asked.

There was laughter around the campfire as Shillingford shrugged. "If she's pretty enough, why not?" he said. "But let me be clear—Gisele of England is to be untouched. She is going to the Count of Toulouse, and if the man is given damaged goods, it will come back on us. Do you understand?"

Everyone did. It wasn't as if some of them hadn't done something similar to this at one time or another. They were soldiers. They knew how to get the job done.

And if anything went wrong, they'd pin it right on Shillingford's pointed head.

Breaking up the group around the campfire, they went about preparing for the evening's assault.

CHAPTER NINETEEN

Canonsleigh Abbey

"I WOULD BE lying if I said I was surprised to hear this," Fox said. "John has been known to use his family like pawns, all of them, so this is not surprising. A marriage to Raymond of Toulouse for the daughter of Henry the Young King? That is quite prestigious. And quite terrible."

Gisele, Fox, and nine of Fox's comrades were sitting with the mother abbess in the very room Lord Shillingford had come to discuss the king's unsavory offer. When the mother abbess recognized Fox as the same man who had brought Gisele to them ten years ago, she permitted him and his associates into the abbey. Usually, she would have made them all wait outside, but these were sworn and solemn knights, and a couple of men who were not knights at all—but she trusted her gut. They seemed honorable, and Gisele trusted them.

So, the mother abbess let them in.

"It was my sense that he was returning sooner rather than later to try to coerce Gisele into accepting the offer," she said. "Although I did not know Gisele had sent for you, I must admit that I feel much better to see you here. Lord Shillingford is a courtier, and he was clearly unused to being denied. Men like that will often do anything for the favor of the king, including violating the sanctity of the abbey."

"Is that why it was locked when we arrived?" Tay asked, standing back by the door. "And the boy seemed frightened when he saw us."

"When Lord Shillingford arrived yesterday, I told him to hide," Gisele answered him. "Once Shillingford had left, I told him of the soldiers for his own safety. Ren is quite curious and would have walked right into their midst had he not known better."

"You were right to tell him," Fox said, his gaze soft on her. "The last thing you need is the boy putting himself in peril, but the fact remains that Shillingford and his men are camped a half-mile from us. How many men are there?"

The mother abbess shrugged. "At least thirty or so," she said. "I do not know, frankly. I did not count them. But enough to damage the abbey should they try."

Fox looked over at Creston and Cruz. The two traveled in a pair and were the closest of friends, but they were also the spies and killers out of the group. Creston in particular taught things like interrogation and torture to Blackchurch recruits, so the man was well acquainted with the dark underbelly of their profession.

Shillingford, as devious as he was, had nothing on Creston de Royans.

But the man looked like a choirboy. No one would suspect the killer's heart underneath. Like everyone else, he and Cruz had leapt to Fox's aid, and they'd just listened to the story of a slimy courtier from John who had come to take Gisele to her new husband, an inarguably powerful man. But it was a horrible situation for Gisele, and a terrible offer for any woman, who would be expected to spy on Toulouse for the king. Nay, it wasn't a good circumstance, and when they saw Fox turn in their direction, they perked up.

"What do you need, Fox?" Creston asked.

"Scout the army," Fox replied. "You and Cruz will find the army and see how many there really are and how well armed they are. If they make a move against the abbey, especially while we are here, we must know their strength."

The pair was already on the move, taking Aamir with them as they went. Aamir, who knew every tactic from nearly every army in the world, would be of great help. With those three out of the chamber, Fox looked to Payne and Kristian.

"Can you two evaluate the defenses of this place, such as they are?" he said. "Something tells me that we may need to know."

Payne nodded, pushing himself off the wall. "The damnable *sassenach*," he muttered. "I'd like tae set a few traps for them that they'd never forget."

Fox had to fight off a grin at Payne. He hated the English, but loved his Blackchurch brethren, and he relished any real-world opportunity to go against an English army.

"Mayhap later," Fox told him. "Just check the defenses for now. See to any weakness. Kristian, do not let him build any pits for an army to fall into. If the army doesn't come, we'll have nuns and children falling into those pits and breaking necks. And take Bowen with you."

Bowen de Bermingham, the last and newest Blackchurch trainer, had come along on this mission because he wanted to help. But he also came because it was a bonding opportunity and, as the newest member of the group, it was important that he participate. But he would be bonding with Kristian and his archnemesis, Payne, in this case, so Payne merely rolled his eyes as he headed out of the chamber. Kristian laughed at him, slapping a hand on Payne's back as the man walked past him, toward the door, and giving him a shove. He followed him out of the chamber with Bowen, quiet and steady and very much the water to Payne's oil, bringing up the rear.

With those three gone, that left Ming Tang, Tay, Fox, Sinclair, and St. Sebastian remaining in the chamber. When Payne and Kristian cleared out, St. Sebastian spoke.

"Did this Lord Shillingford give you any reason to think he was going to attack the abbey, your grace?" he asked the mother abbess. "It would be a foolish man, indeed, to threaten a church."

The mother abbess shrugged. "He is a man used to having his own way," she said. "I do believe he'll return. I do believe that if Gisele refuses him again, he will bring his army. Why else bring soldiers if he does not intend to use them?"

She had a point. St. Sebastian looked at Fox. "Then we need to clear out the entire abbey," he said. "If they come and no one is here, then no one can get hurt. But if we take Lady Gisele and leave everyone behind…"

Fox understood the implication. "They might interrogate the nuns to find out where she's gone," he said. He looked at Gisele, who was gazing back fearfully, before returning his focus to the mother abbess. "Your grace, these men serve John, who has a very unsteady relationship with the church. Surely you know this."

"I do, my lord."

"Then you know that one more murdered nun or desecrated abbey will not make any difference to the king," he said.

"You have heard what Sebastian has said. He's right, I'm afraid. You must consider evacuating the abbey, at least until the army has gone, for your own safety."

The mother abbess lowered her gaze. She was sitting at her table, neatly lined with things necessary to administer her small abbey, pondering the situation. After a moment, she stood up, wringing her hands as she went to stand next to the very window Lord Shillingford had gazed from when he had come. The window overlooked the stone courtyard and the gate beyond.

Her beautiful, bucolic abbey was under threat.

It was unfathomable.

"These walls have stood since the days before the Normans," she finally said. "They used to be wooden, but about a hundred years ago, everything was rebuilt with stone. It was built to withstand anything. Even a selfish king."

"I do not dispute that, my lady," Fox said. "But the walls are not tall enough to prevent men from simply climbing over them, and once they are inside, it will be a matter of time before they gain access to the abbey. They will not care if you are a nun or not. If you do not give them what they want, they will punish you."

The mother abbess' expression was one of peace. "That is why God has sent you," she said. "You are to be our archangels, defending the righteous. I have prayed on this, but God has already had a hand in this by telling Gisele to send for you."

Fox could see that although she understood the situation, she was putting her faith in prayer. "If that is true, then God would wish for you to listen to us to protect the abbey and the occupants," he said. The problem was that Fox had never been particularly pious, and he wouldn't be so arrogant as to debate the mother abbess on her own ground. He looked to Ming Tang standing back in the shadows. "Would you not agree?"

Ming Tang could see that Fox needed a little help with the mother abbess, so as a man of philosophy, he came forth. "Indeed," he said. "It is said that God helps those who help themselves. He has brought you ten heavily armed men, your grace. He would be pleased if you let us do what we are trained for. That includes listening to our experienced advice."

The mother abbess' gaze drifted over him—he wore traditional robes of the Shaolin, but also leather breeches and pieces of leather protection on his arms and wrists. It was a strange mix.

He, in fact, seemed a little strange.

"You are not from England," she said. "Where were you born?"

"Far away, your grace," Ming Tang said. "A place called Henan."

"You are a knight?"

"He is a Shaolin monk." Sinclair, who had thus far remained silent since arriving at the abbey, went to stand next to Ming Tang. All of the Blackchurch trainers were fiercely protective of him. "He was committed to a religious order when he was quite young and learned to fight through rigorous training. He can outfight any man here with his hands, feet, and a staff. He is quite skilled."

"Religious order?" the mother abbess repeated. "What religious order is this?"

"Shaolin *is* the religion, your grace," Ming Tang said. "It is a way of life, a way to serve our deity, known as Buddha. We believe in discipline and mindfulness. That this life is a transition to a higher way of living. That is the simplest way to put it, but we believe what you believe—that peace is the way of God."

The mother abbess nodded faintly. "And you have committed yourself to this order?"

"I have, your grace."

"Yet you fight with knights."

Ming Tang shrugged. "Monks have been fighting for centuries," he said. "We do not advocate aggression, but we will fight when called upon to defend the right and the just."

The mother abbess pondered that for a moment before nodding. "I would like to know more of this peaceful order," she said. "I wish I had time now, but alas, we must accept the fact that we are facing a dire situation. Understanding different philosophies will have to wait."

"I would say so," Fox said. "May I beg your pardon for a moment, your grace? We were unaware of the situation with John's army when we arrived, so I would like to speak with my comrades for a moment, if I may."

"Please," the mother abbess said as she rose from her chair. As she passed Gisele, who was perched on a wooden chair, she motioned to her. "Come with me, my lady. Let the men have their time alone."

Gisele stood up, looking at Fox somewhat anxiously, but he smiled and winked at her, telling her silently that everything was going to be fine. She smiled in return, though it was forced, and followed the mother abbess from the chamber. Once they were gone, Tay let out a hiss.

"God's Bones," he muttered, dragging his hands wearily over his face. "John's army a half-mile away? Christ, Fox, they're going to take her by force and burn this place down."

Fox sighed heavily. "I'm surprised they have not done it by

now," he said. Then he looked to St. Sebastian. "We must evacuate these people to Blackchurch. Surely your father would not mind giving safe haven to these women to save them from John's destruction?"

St. Sebastian shook his head. "Nay, he would not," he said. "You know his stance on getting involved in another man's war, but this is not taking sides. This would be protecting helpless women from the king's men. He would agree."

"She will not come," Ming Tang said quietly. Everyone turned to look at the man as he shook his head sadly. "The mother abbess, I mean. She will not come. This is her home, her sanctuary, and her responsibility. She will not leave it. Would you?"

Over near the door, Sinclair nodded. "I most certainly would," he said. "If she believes John's men will not breach these walls, then she is a fool."

"She is no fool."

"Then she must come with us if she is to survive," Sinclair said, pointing in the general direction of the bailey. "More than that, her people must survive. Surely she would not prevent that by standing on ceremony and declaring God will save her."

"God sent us, remember?" Ming Tang looked at him, his dark eyes twinkling. "Even if you do not believe in fate, we are certainly where we need to be at the moment. We are trainers of men, that is true, but more than that, we are warriors. We were born warriors. This is the greatest cause I can think of."

"We need to get everyone out," Fox said quietly. "That is what we ultimately must do. I'm all for a fight, especially with John's men, but we have women and children to think about in this case. We must prepare them immediately."

"What of Lady Gisele?" Sinclair said. "I do not know the

entire story, Fox, and I'm not asking you to tell me. Tay told us enough when he told us you were in trouble back at Blackchurch. But it is clear that you are not leaving without the lady, regardless of what the mother abbess says."

Fox shook his head. "I am not," he said, looking to the men in the chamber. "And I'm sure you are wondering who the boy is. You all saw him. Tay spoke with him. I will tell you now, without shame, that he is my son. When I left Gisele at Canonsleigh ten years ago, she was pregnant, though I did not know it. She said that she did not want to tell me about the child because the Marshal had threatened me if I ever contacted her again. She was afraid for me. But now… If the Marshal were to burst through that door at this moment, I would fight him to the death if he tried to stop me from taking the woman I love and our son to safety."

Over near the window, Tay was smiling at him. "He is a fine lad, Fox," he said. "He will make a great playmate for my sons."

Fox smiled weakly. "From what I've seen of Ren, he might wear your boys out."

"I would welcome that."

Fox laughed softly, but quickly sobered. "I cannot imagine the Marshal would take issue with my saving Gisele from John's scheme," he said. "In spite of our troubles, William Marshal is a decent man in his heart. He would not want Gisele to have anything to do with John or a political marriage. But there is one flaw in that theory I cannot seem to get out of my mind."

"What is that?" Tay asked.

Fox looked at him. "William Marshal is an advisor to King John," he said. "Didn't he know about this marriage proposal between Gisele and Raymond of Toulouse? Worse still, did he sanction it?"

"You served the man, Fox," Sinclair said. "Only you can answer that question. What does your heart tell you?"

"That John did not tell the Marshal about it," Fox said, rubbing his eyes wearily. "You must remember that John, and nearly everyone else, believes that Gisele is the daughter of Henry the Young King. Very few know the truth, that she is the Marshal's bastard. John believes he is conducting family business, so why would he tell him?"

It was a logical conclusion in a situation that was rife with speculation. "Then I would think the Marshal would thank you for removing Gisele from John's grip," Sinclair said. "No decent man wants their wife or daughter involved with that man."

Fox stood up. "The Marshal and the king have a contentious relationship at best," he said. "The more I think on it, the more I cannot believe the Marshal had anything to do with this marriage proposal. If he did, he'd probably be here right now. But that has me thinking… Sebo, you must ride to Blackchurch and tell your father we need some men. Depending on how many royal soldiers Creston and Cruz think there are, we can ask your father for a comparable amount. It would make the fight fairer and give a better chance for us to triumph."

St. Sebastian nodded, but in the same movement, he frowned. "Why should I go?" he said. "Send Ming Tang. He does not hold a sword, and a sword is what will be needed when John's men attack."

Ming Tang fought off a grin as Tay put himself in front of St. Sebastian. "You do not think Ming Tang can take on a man with a sword?" he said. "*Any* sword? You know better than that. And you're the logical choice to return to Blackchurch. You will be in command one day, so it is up to you to tell your father what we are facing rather than face it yourself like a common knight. Commanders are leaders, Sebastian. They are not part of the group."

St. Sebastian knew that, in theory, but he didn't like it when he couldn't be part of the excitement. "Oh, very well," he said snappishly. "I'll go when Creston and Cruz and Aamir return. But don't think I like it!"

Tay shrugged, but he turned his back to St. Sebastian, grinning at Fox because he, more than any of the Blackchurch trainers, liked to harass St. Sebastian from time to time. Most of them had known him a long time because when they'd come to Blackchurch, St. Sebastian had still been the obnoxious little brother to St. Gerard.

To some of them, he would always be that obnoxious little brother.

With nothing more to speak of until Creston and Cruz returned, Fox left the chamber in search of Gisele. But he was more in search of Ren. As thrilled as he was to see Gisele, that little boy who looked just like him had his attention for the moment.

His son.

He could still hardly believe it.

Emerging from the front of the abbey, it didn't take him long to find the lad. Payne, Bowen, and Kristian had picked up a tail, and the tail's name was Ren. The two trainers were standing near the gate, talking, and as Fox approached, he could see Ren speaking to them because they both looked down at the child. Payne, who was usually the most volatile of all the trainers, seemed to be showing the child an inordinate amount of patience. He was even looking at something Ren was showing him—which, as Fox drew nearer, he noted was a saw.

Payne caught sight of Fox.

"Well?" he said. "Do ye want our assessment? Because it willna take long, lad."

Fox came to stand next to Ren. "I'm afraid to ask," he said.

Payne snorted. "Ye should be," he said. "Any army will have no trouble breaching these walls. And the gate could be kicked down by my mother."

"The same mother who will beat me with a stick if I insult her boy?"

"My mother is more knight than some knights."

Fox chuckled. "I would believe it," he said, looking at the wall, which was no more than eight feet in height. His smile faded. "Who thought it would be safe to build a wall this short?"

"Fools," Kristian said grimly. "Fools who believe that God will divinely protect them from an encroaching army. There is simply no time to reinforce it or make it taller. Everyone at this abbey is vulnerable, Fox."

Fox looked down at Ren, who was gazing up at the knights, listening to every word they said. Even at nine years of age, he had a sharp little mind, but he wasn't showing fear.

"I will cut their legs off with this saw," he said when he realized the men were looking at him. "I can do it. As soon as they try to come in, I will be there with the saw and cut them down."

Fox had to admit that the boy's bravery made him proud. "I believe you would," he said, but his attention returned to Payne and Bowen and Kristian. "We must wait until Creston and Cruz and Aamir return. We need to know how many men to expect, so until then, I would suggest you figure out how we can escape with everyone if the army is upon us. There has to be a postern gate."

Payne nodded. "There is," he said. "We'll go see how clear

the way is should we need tae use it."

The men headed off, heading toward the walled kitchen yard, leaving Fox and Ren standing side by side. Fox looked down at the boy again and smiled.

"Is that your saw?" he asked.

Ren nodded. Then he shook his head. "It belongs to Mam," he said. "She wanted me to cut branches off the ash tree. Would you like to see me do it?"

Fox's smile broadened. "I would be honored."

Ren grabbed him by the hand and began pulling him across the courtyard, toward the area between the chapel and the wall. Fox could see a big, shaggy tree up ahead, but he was mostly enamored with the touch of his son for the first time. His big fingers clutched by that little hand. Ren wasn't afraid of strangers, that was for certain, and Fox was utterly fascinated by the boy, noting how much he looked like his own father. He even had some mannerisms of Fox's brother, Felix, which Fox found strange, but the family lines were strong in young Ren.

He was a de Merest to the bone.

They reached the old ash tree, and Ren let go of his hand, grabbing one of the low-hanging branches and holding up the saw.

"I'm going to cut this," he declared. "My mam needs it."

Fox touched the branches that were within his reach, feeling that they were soft from the night's rain. "Why does your mam need it?"

Ren was trying to get the branch at a good angle so he could start cutting. "She makes pots," he said. "She grows things in them. She grows flowers and trees. She makes a lot of things grow."

"Oh?" Fox said with interest. "What about you? What do

you do here?"

"I help my mam," he said. "I learn my lessons, and she lets me play with my friends."

"You have lessons here?"

He nodded, still struggling with the branch. "I learn to read and write and do sums," he said. "But I want to learn to be a soldier."

"You do?"

"Or a farmer. So I can make things grow, too."

"That is admirable."

He stopped grabbing at the branch and looked at Fox with an expression quite reminiscent of Fox's father. "I heard that if I'm a pirate, I can be rich!"

Fox chuckled at the boy's dreams. "Pirates are not very nice," he said. "Well, most of them, anyway."

"Why not?"

"Do you know any?"

Ren frowned. "Nay," he said. "Do you?"

"I do."

"Do they have names like Red Beard and ride sea serpents?"

Fox snorted, trying to keep a straight face. "They do not," he said. "The ones I know have big ships and are led by a man named Abelard. They call themselves Triton's Hellions."

Ren's dark eyebrows shot up. "Are they rich?"

"Aye," Fox said. "But do you know *how* they get rich?"

"Because they are pirates!"

"True, but they have to do something to get rich," Fox explained. "I regret to inform you that pirates do many things to get rich. Sometimes, they steal from people. That is dishonest."

"It is *terribly* dishonest," Gisele said, walking up behind them. She had been back in her garden when she caught sight of them over by the ash tree. She'd watched for a few moments before deciding to join them, and was now looking specifically at her son as she spoke. "I thought I told you that you could *not* be a pirate."

Ren frowned. "But if I am rich, we can live in a fine house," he said. "I can buy you everything you want."

Gisele's gaze moved to Fox. "I have everything I want," she said, looking into his eyes. "Finally. I have everything I could ever want."

The romantic comment was completely missed by Ren, who went back to trying to cut the branch. "I will buy you gold rings," he said. "And fine dresses. You can have servants and tell them what to do."

Gisele grinned at her son. "I think I will have those things anyway," she said. "Someday."

"Why?"

"Because I will marry well, and my husband will give them to me."

"He certainly will," Fox muttered so the boy couldn't hear him. "Mayhap you will be married sooner than you think."

Gisele forgot all about her conversation with Ren, and was now looking seriously at Fox. "Why do you say that?"

He lifted an eyebrow. "I told you I wasn't leaving without you," he said. "We will be married when we reach Black-church."

That statement seemed to suck all of the air out of her, and her dreamy eyes grew moist. "Truly?" she said softly. "We will?"

He nodded, gazing deeply into her eyes. "Do you think I would waste one more moment without you?" he said. "We have a family, Gigi. I swear I will make a very good husband and an excellent... you know..."

He was dipping his head in the direction of Ren, not wanting to say too much until Gisele was ready. She understood, but she was overwhelmed with his statement that they would be married immediately.

It was a dream come true.

"Oh, Fox," she whispered softly. "Promise me. Promise me that this time, it is true."

"It was always true. It just had to be the right time."

"And the time is now?"

"It is now."

"But what of the Marshal?"

Fox shrugged. "When he is told about Ren, he will not protest, I am sure," he said. "It is the right thing to do, by any man's standard. Moreover, if you are already married, the king cannot marry you to Toulouse. You will be safe and you will be my wife, and that is all that matters."

"At Blackchurch?"

"That is where I serve."

"De Poyer said it was a training school for soldiers?"

He cocked his head. "Aye," he said. "Did he not tell you anything more?"

She shook her head. "I had never heard of it until de Poyer came to tell me that you served there," she said. "He did not tell me much more than that."

He shook his head. "It is a training guild for the most elite warriors in the world," he said. "I have been training men for ten years, Gigi. And the men who came with me to Canonsleigh are trainers, as well. The finest, most skilled men in the whole of the world. Together, we shape the men who shape nations."

Gisele smiled, intrigued and delighted with what he was telling her. "And we will live there?"

Fox nodded. "Safe from the world, safe from the king, and safe from William Marshal," he said. "It is my world, Gigi. I want it to be yours, too."

Tears glistened in her eyes. "I can hardly believe it," she said. "I have dreamed of this day for so long, and now, it is here."

"It is."

"When will we leave?"

"Before dawn. I am taking you and Ren away from here, and we will never look back."

The tree next to them suddenly shuddered, and they turned to see that Ren had sawn off a small branch. He was quite proud of it. He handed it to his mother, slapping her with the leaves as she dodged them hitting her in the face. But she grabbed him from getting away as he tried to rush back to cut another.

"Wait," she told him. "Lower the saw. That's a good lad. Ren, I need to talk to you because things are going to happen quickly, and I want you to be prepared."

He looked at his mother curiously. "What will happen?"

Gisele glanced at Fox, a smile playing on her lips. "May I?" she whispered.

He appeared quite emotional at the question, knowing she meant to tell the boy the truth about them, and he nodded. "If you think it best," he murmured.

"He should know," she said. "If you're serious about everything you've said, then I must tell him so he is not confused."

"I am serious. Tell him."

Gisele refocused on Ren. "It seems that we are going away," she said. "We are leaving the abbey."

Ren's brow furrowed. "We are?" he said. "But why?"

"Do you remember the soldiers who came yesterday?"

"Aye."

"They want to take me away so you will never see me again."

Ren's eyes widened. "They can't!" he nearly shouted. "I will not let them!"

Gisele shushed him because he was starting to tear up. Ren was very protective of his mother, and she was cognizant of that. "Do not worry," she assured him. "You saw all of the knights who came today. They are going to protect me so the soldiers cannot get to me, I promise. Do you remember how you told me that you want to learn to be a soldier?"

Ren was wiping his eyes rapidly, embarrassed by the tears. "Aye," he sniffled. "Or a farmer."

"We are going to live at a place where warriors are trained," she said. "We are going to live with your father."

That stopped his tears quickly, and he was back to looking puzzled. "My father lives there?"

Gisele nodded. "What have I told you about your father?"

"That he died."

"Nay," she corrected him. "I told you that he went away."

"The other children said that you meant he died."

"They were wrong," Gisele said. "He did not die. I know I have never spoken much of your father except to say he was a great knight. Do you remember?"

Ren nodded. "That is why I want to be a soldier," he said. "But... but my father isn't dead?"

"Nay."

"Then why has he not come to see me?" the boy said, greatly puzzled. "I have asked you about him, but you would not tell me."

Gisele could hear the pain in her son's voice, and it was

cutting. "I never spoke of him because it was painful for me to do so," she said. "I am sorry if that left you wondering about him, Ren, truly. It was better not to speak of him."

"But what happened to him?" Ren persisted. "Doesn't he want to know me?"

"He wants to know you very much, Ren," Fox said. He couldn't help himself. "He could not come to see you because in order to keep you safe, he had to stay away. Bad men threatened to hurt your mother if he came to see her. Do you understand that?"

Ren had to think about that before he finally nodded. "Aye," he said. "I think so. He didn't come so we would be safe?"

"Aye."

"But... what now?" he said. "We are going to live with him now?"

"Aye," Fox said. "He loves you very much."

"He knows about me?"

"I do now."

Ren stared at him a moment, processing the last few bits of the conversation and coming to realize that the big knight had said something strange. He wasn't quite sure he understood, but he thought he might. He peered at Fox suspiciously.

"You know about me?" he said. "Will you tell him?"

"I am your father, Ren," Fox said softly. "My name is Sir Fox de Merest, and you are my son."

Ren's eyes widened. His reaction was one of shock or fear or both. It was difficult to tell. His gaze darted between Fox and his mother in disbelief before he turned on his heel and ran off, dropping the saw as he went. Gisele called after him, but Fox stopped her.

"Nay," he said. "Leave him."

Gisele was looking at her son in concern as he rounded a corner and disappeared from view. "He should not have run like that," she said. "That is not like him. I must find him and…"

Fox had her by the arm, tugging on her gently. "Leave him, Mother," he said. "He has just heard some life-changing information. He must reconcile it in his own mind now. Let him be."

She looked at him, worried. "He really is a good lad, Fox," she said. "He is polite. I am sure he did not mean to insult you by running off."

Fox was smiling. They were over by the tree, in the shade, and quite alone. Reaching up, he cupped her face between his two big hands, and his pale eyes soaked in her lovely face.

"He did not insult me," he whispered. "I have a bright, handsome son, and soon I will have a wife I have loved for as long I can remember. Nothing has ever changed between us, Gigi. You were my love sixteen years ago, and you are still my love now. It's as if those ten years of separation never happened."

Gisele forgot all about her caution when it came to kissing Fox in public. He was here, he was touching her, and her resistance was smashed. Her mouth fused to his, her arms went around his neck, and Fox took her into his powerful embrace, kissing away ten long years of agony and sorrow. In the history of kisses, it was one of the most powerful ever displayed, and in this case, it was well deserved by both of them.

They were together again.

And their love had only deepened.

When Payne, Bowen, and Kristian came around the corner

and saw Fox and Gisele in an amorous embrace, they quickly changed direction and went the other way. Their report on the postern gate could wait a few minutes longer.

"Give them a moment, lads," Payne said. "We'll make ourselves useful elsewhere."

Bowen, who had nearly been stepped on when Payne abruptly turned around, eyed the Scotsman. "I am proud of you for showing such understanding," he said. "I did not know you had it in you."

Payne's eyes narrowed as he looked at the young, and very capable, trainer. "There are a lot of things ye dunna know about me, laddie," he said. "I hope ye live long enough tae find out."

"I hope you live long enough to show me."

Payne was still scowling, but Bowen was fighting off a grin. Such was the relationship between the pair. But they agreed on one thing—leaving Fox and Gisele a few minutes alone.

God only knew that Fox and Gisele had earned it.

With what was to come, they might never get another chance.

CHAPTER TWENTY

IT WAS DARK and damp, a perfect night for sleeping, but no one was really sleeping at all.

They were waiting.

All of Canonsleigh was alert and preparing. Creston, Cruz, and Aamir had returned from their reconnaissance of the royal soldiers to the east with news that there were about twenty men. There was no great army hidden by the trees, just a paltry handful.

But that paltry handful was preparing for battle.

Creston, Cruz, and Aamir had watched the army douse their cooking fires, clearly in preparation for departing. Since night was on the approach, it was unusual for an army to douse all of their fires and pack up their gear, but the royal soldiers had done just that. No tents or shelters or bedrolls were left out. That led the Blackchurch men to believe that the army was preparing to move.

Hidden in the bushes, Creston and Cruz and Aamir had observed the soldiers sharpening their swords, coiling up sections of rope, and any number of things that led the Blackchurch knights to believe an attack was coming. Since the soldiers seemed to be ready for travel, that told them the attack would be soon. Probably at dawn.

In stealth, the Blackchurch men raced back to the abbey.

Fox and the others were informed of the twenty-man army preparing for a raid, and the word spread amongst the rest of the abbey. They would be prepared. The abbey itself only had about twenty nuns, not including Gisele or the mother abbess, and Fox had suggested the women be moved out immediately through the postern gate. Surprisingly, the nuns refused and, in fact, ran from the knights who were trying to help them. They ran back into their dormitory, or into the kitchen, and began searching for weapons—anything to hold off an attacking army—which surprised the Blackchurch knights.

Though, given the tenacity of the mother abbess, perhaps not so surprising.

The nuns were prepared to fight.

When the Blackchurch men returned and spoke of the small army preparing for attack, Gisele had taken Ren into the chamber they shared to pack up their belongings. She pulled out the old satchel, the one she'd brought with her to Canonsleigh, and between her and Ren, they managed to stuff the thing.

Clothing, an extra pair of shoes for Gisele, plus soaps and combs and the pillow that Ren used because he didn't want to leave it behind. Gisele was trying to move quickly with a child who wanted to know why he could not bring the cats with them. Gisele tried to explain it to him in a way he would understand, how the cats belonged to the abbey and they would want to stay there, so he gave up asking. But then he wanted to know if he could bring his saw, which Gisele tried to talk him out of. She was standing in the open door of their chamber, which faced toward her garden room, when she heard footsteps behind her.

Fox was approaching.

He was bearing a torch against the darkness, but Ren couldn't see him from where he was standing. The last time he'd had contact with the boy, Ren had run off, so Fox didn't want to upset the child. But he was compelled to see Gisele and Ren. When he made eye contact with Gisele, she smiled.

"We're nearly ready," she said. "We are sorting through the last of Ren's possessions, of which there are few, unless you count the rocks and leaves he likes to collect. This is an order that takes a vow of poverty, but the mother abbess has been generous with Ren and me. She has allowed us a few things."

Fox nodded. "That was kind of her," he said. "But as soon as you are ready, we must depart."

Gisele's smile faded. "Tonight?"

"Aye."

"Do you really believe they are coming at dawn?"

Fox shrugged. "That would be the educated guess from all of the Blackchurch men," he said. "It makes the most sense, tactically speaking."

"What about the rest of the abbey?" Gisele said. "Did you convince the nuns to leave?"

He shook his head. "Nay," he said. "They refuse. The mother abbess has refused. They are determined to protect their abbey, and we will not force them to leave, so Tay and Sin and the others are helping them secure windows and make weapons with whatever they can find. We will try to keep them from getting into the abbey, but if they do, then the nuns will need to protect themselves."

"We?" she asked quietly. "You mean you are staying and I

am leaving?"

"Nay," he said. "When I say 'we,' I meant Blackchurch as a whole. Sebo has already departed to ask his father for soldiers, but I am taking you and Ren out as soon as you are ready."

Gisele looked into the room, watching her son as he tried to jam a few of his small wooden soldiers into the satchel, little toys that one of the local farmers had carved for him last year.

"Give him a few minutes," she said quietly. "It is difficult to decide what to take from a place you have lived your entire life."

"Has he said anything about me?"

She shook her head. "Nay," she said. "But stay there a moment. Do not move. I will talk to him, and you can listen."

"Do not push. If he does not wish to accept me, he does not have to."

"Aye, he does," Gisele said firmly. "You are his father, Fox, whether or not he likes it. He simply must become used to the idea, so we are not doing him any good by pretending you will go away. You are here to stay, and he must accept that."

Fox didn't say anything. She was the boy's mother, and he would trust her to know best. As he stood against the wall, next to the open door, Gisele stepped into the chamber.

"Would you like me to help you with the soldiers?" she asked Ren.

"Nay," the boy said, ramming in the last one. "They will fit."

Gisele went down on her knees next to the satchel to tie it up. "They will have many new adventures at Blackchurch," she said. "So will you. Although I know you have grown up here, we are going to a new place with new people. And lots of knights. We will be happy there."

Ren stood there, watching his mother tie up the satchel. It was a few moments before he answered. "What if I want to stay here?"

Gisele looked at him. "Why?"

"Because this is my home."

Gisele shook her head. "Ren, have you noticed that only women live here?" she said. "You are a boy, and you are growing up. You could not stay here much longer."

"Why not?"

"Because a nunnery is only meant for women," she said. "If you want to become a knight, then we must go to Blackchurch."

"Because... him... the knight lives there?"

It took Gisele a moment to realize what he meant. "Aye," she said. "*Fox* lives there. You can say his name. In fact, you should apologize to him. It was very rude of you to run off earlier."

Ren sighed heavily and looked at his feet. "Mam?" he said.

"What is it?"

"Do I need a father?"

He was hesitant and fearful. Not that she blamed him, because things were happening very quickly in his young life. Gisele understood that, but it was time for Ren to understand that life was a changeable thing, and one had to adapt. Better he learn that now while he was still young.

She reached out and grasped his hand.

"I want to tell you a little about Fox," she said. "You do not have to love him if you don't want to. I will not force you to. But you should know that Fox is a very kind and thoughtful man. He only wants the best for you. I know it is shocking to know your father is alive, especially when you believed that he was dead. My father—a man I've never spoken of to you— threatened Fox and told him to stay away from me. He would punish him if he did not obey. I want you to understand that

Fox did not stay away from us because he wanted to, but because he had to. Do you need a father? You do not. But it would be nice if you could at least be friendly to him. He does not deserve your rudeness. Can you at least do that, please?"

Ren shrugged. Then he nodded, but it was barely a nod. Gisele kissed his hand and picked up the satchel.

"Good," she said. "Thank you for being nice to Fox. Now, you must put on your cloak and your hood. We will be leaving soon."

"Can I bring my saw?"

She wasn't sure about that. "I'm afraid you might hurt yourself."

"But I may need to use it," he insisted. "If the king's men try to get us."

She nodded, but it was with great reluctance. As Ren went to find his cloak, Gisele stepped out into the corridor where Fox was still standing. Handing him the satchel, she smiled timidly.

"He will accept you at some point," she said softly. "He simply needs to become accustomed to you."

Fox was trying not to show the sadness he felt. "He has never had a man around, much less a father," he said. "Of course he is confused. Frankly, I've never had a son or a young boy around either, so this is confusing for me, too. But I'm confident that there will be a peace between us at some point."

Gisele's smile turned genuine, and she patted him on the cheek. "Of course there will," she said. "As I said, he is very much like you. You will come to see that as the days go by. In fact, I—"

She was cut off by a shout toward the entrance to the abbey. The corridor they were standing in went straight into the entry and the mother abbess' chamber beyond. Both Fox and Gisele turned to see Sinclair standing there, sword in hand.

"The army is here, Fox," he said with calm urgency. "If you are going to take the lady and the boy out, do it now. We will cover you."

Fox was shocked. He started running toward Sinclair with Gisele on his heels. "They're coming *now*?" he said. "In the dead of night?"

Sinclair nodded. "We can see them far down the road, bearing torches," he said. "They do not know we are here. They think they are breaching an abbey filled with women, so they are not concealing themselves in the least."

Fox nodded quickly, realizing Gisele was next to him. He turned to her. "Get Ren," he said. "Hurry, now. Get back to the kitchens, and I will meet you there."

Gisele, her face full of fear, began to run. Fox didn't even watch her go—he was more concerned with getting to his equipment, which was out in the bailey with the horses. There were nuns moving about now because the Blackchurch trainers had been informed by those watching the road that the royal army was coming. They could no longer help the nuns find weapons. But Tay was telling the nuns to get into the abbey and lock everything, having to push a couple of them back into the abbey when they wanted to follow him outside, while Fox and Sinclair ran out into the courtyard with the gates beyond.

There was a sense of urgency in the air.

The unexpected had happened.

Payne, Ming Tang, and Aamir were at the gates, trying to stay out of the line of sight of anyone on the approach, but they were watching the road. Fox grabbed his broadsword and shield off his horse as Bowen and Kristian collected all of the horses and led them into the back, where the kitchens and the stables were. Broadsword strapped on and shield slung over his left shoulder, Fox crept over to the gates where the others were.

Watching.

Waiting.

"How far out are they?" he whispered loudly.

Ming Tang always had the innate ability to see in the dark where others couldn't. He pointed toward the northeast. "There," he said. "See the dots of light?"

Fox had to strain his eyes, but finally, he saw it. "Aye," he said. "If they are approaching the abbey, thinking they will meet with no resistance, then we should be clever about this."

Ming Tang looked at him. "Do you have something in mind?"

Fox nodded. "Aye," he said. "Unlock the gates."

Everyone looked at him in surprise. "Why?" Ming Tang said incredulously.

"Think about it," Fox said. "If we unlock the gates, they have one point of entry. If they are forced to scale the walls, they will come in all over. That will be more difficult to cover. We will hide in the shadows around here, concealing ourselves. When they enter the gates and head for the entry, we will ambush them."

"Creston has a crossbow," Payne said. "I wish I had one myself."

"Where is Creston?" Fox asked.

"The last I saw, he was telling the nuns to lock up the kitchen yard," Payne said, pointing to the west. "Back there."

Fox slapped Payne on the shoulder. "I'll tell him and anyone else I see to get to the gates," he said. "Sin, with Sebo gone, you'll have to command the ambush. Get everyone into position."

Sinclair, the trainer known as the Swordsman because he taught hand-to-hand combat and offensive warfare, among other things, was the man best suited for the job. He had a natural air of command about him. He began to direct the men at the gates while Ming Tang went to unlock the panels. Meanwhile, Fox raced down the courtyard to the kitchen yard, where the horses were gathered. Tay, Creston, Cruz, Bowen, and Kristian were there, making sure the animals were secure, but Fox caught their attention.

"Get up to the gatehouse," he told them. "Sin is in command. We're going to open the gates for one point of entry, rather than the army jumping over the wall in various places, and ambush them as they enter. Cres, get your crossbow. You'll have your pick of targets."

In the darkness, Tay grinned. "I like that," he declared. "Come along, lads. We'll hold the line to give Fox and his family time to leave through the postern gate."

As they headed off toward the gates, with Creston grabbing his crossbow off the back of his saddle, Fox watched them go with somewhat of a euphoric feeling.

Fox and his family.

That was the first time he'd ever heard it spoken aloud. *His* family. The woman he loved, his son… They were indeed his family. For a man who had spent the past ten years without the woman to whom he'd given his heart, resigned to the lonely days and nights, the realization that he now had a family—with her—was something to celebrate. It lit him up like nothing he could have ever imagined.

But the truth was that any celebrations of joy would have to wait.

If they didn't leave now, they might not be able to leave at all.

He was about to head back toward the chamber Gisele shared with Ren when he saw them both running in his direction. He motioned them over to Merlin as he strapped on the satchel, which he'd still been carrying. After pulling his steed away from the others, he lifted Gisele up by the waist onto the saddle before moving to lift Ren, who pulled back and insisted he could mount the horse himself. Fox didn't want to dispute the lad, but they had no time for foolery. Frustrated, Gisele extended a hand to her son, and he took it, and she was able to pull him up partway. Fox had to help the rest of the way, and soon, both of them were mounted. Fox quickly headed for the postern gate.

Moving through the gate, there was nothing but darkened trees beyond. He wasn't able to lock the gate from the outside, so he took the hilt of his sword and bent the iron latch, essentially jamming it. Once that was done, he turned to Gisele and Ren.

"I'm not familiar with this area, so you must help me," he whispered. "I must make my way to the road north, but I do not want us to be seen right now. Which way should I go?"

Ren, in front of his mother, pointed straight ahead. "That way," he said. "There's a brook and then a field with frogs in it. Once you get through the frogs, there are more trees and the road is on the other side."

Fox nodded shortly. "Thank you, Ren," he said. "I will do that."

"*Stop!*"

An abrupt shout came from off to the left, over toward the perimeter wall. It was a startling sound. Suddenly, a man was running toward them in the darkness, and Fox could see his sword glinting in the moonlight.

From that point forward, the fight was on.

CHAPTER TWENTY-ONE

S HILLINGFORD MAY HAVE wanted to have the glory of leading an army—even twenty men—but he didn't actually want to be in the fight.

The truth was that because his father was a soldier, and not part of the nobility, he hadn't actually fostered and learned to fight. He'd only, and always, been a servant who had worked his way up. Shillingford, whose name before the lordship was granted had been Bevis Rye, led his men down the road toward Canonsleigh, declaring they would be victorious within the hour but reiterating that Gisele of England was not to be harmed. He thought he was rallying troops to triumph, when the truth was that they were all laughing at him. He was a little man with a little brain and even less experience, but he was good where it mattered—in the bedchamber. He'd married the right woman and had himself declared her father's heir as the man lay dying.

The Lord Shillingford title was his.

But he didn't know a hilt from a blade when it came to warfare, even though he had an exquisite sword that had belonged to his late father-in-law. He shouted speeches that he'd heard others spout because he wasn't clever enough to come up with any of his own. His men slowed as they reached the abbey, which was completely dark at this hour. Most of his men dismounted and a few of them went to peer inside the gate, which was, surprisingly, unlocked.

No one seemed to think it strange.

They thought it was more of a blessing.

As his men pushed the gates open and timidly entered the dark courtyard, Shillingford decided to stay out of the way. He didn't want to be involved in the slaughter of nuns because the sight of blood made him ill in spite of his telling the men otherwise, so he slipped down the side of the northern wall, shadowed by the ash trees that few on that side of the abbey, and continued toward the end of the wall.

Then he saw it.

A horse was coming through the postern gate, led by someone he couldn't quite see. All he could see was a figure. Upon the horse were two more figures, including a woman. He could see her flowing cloak. The horse moved into a gap in the shadows, with moonlight illuminating it, and Shillingford could see that it was the very lady he was looking for.

He jumped away from the wall.

"Stop!"

He was shouting in the darkness, not even noticing who was actually leading the horse because he'd only had eyes for the woman on horseback. He had his sword pointed at her, running for her, and he shouted again.

"*Stop in the name of the king!*"

Unfortunately for Shillingford, his lack of training as a knight meant he wasn't watching his surroundings. He wasn't watching who was leading the horse. He only had his eye on the prize. That meant that when Fox stepped forward, deftly swinging his shield onto his left forearm while bringing his sword in an upward movement, Shillingford was completely unprepared. He'd just assumed the horse and the lady would stop and whoever was with her would bow down to him because he expected it.

He never expected a sword to slice into his gut and nearly cut him in half.

With a scream, Shillingford went down, face-first into the earth. He was bleeding out, unable to speak, but his shouts had caught the attention of his men. At nearly the same time, all hell broke loose in the courtyard of Canonsleigh. The sounds of sword against sword and men grunting and fighting filled the air. The Blackchurch trainers attacked, and Shillingford's royal soldiers were caught off guard.

It was a massacre from the start.

Fox could hear the fighting. With Shillingford dead at his feet, he quickly turned to Gisele and Ren.

"We must run for it," he said. "If they find—"

He was cut off when the sound of a flying arrow filled the air. There was nothing like that familiar, high-pitched scream to indicate that death was near. As he turned and lifted his shield to protect himself and Gisele and Ren as much as he was able, the arrow ricocheted off the metal edge of his shield and flew right into Gisele's left arm. The sheer force of it toppled her off the horse as Ren cried out and leapt off after her. Horrified, Fox tried to move around his horse to get to her, but the shadows and the movement had spooked the animal, so Merlin bucked and took off running.

Now, Gisele was on the ground with an arrow in her arm. Fox could see movement coming his way as men ran in his direction. Not knowing if they were friend or foe at this point, he had to assume foe. Gisele wasn't unconscious, but she was dazed from the fall. He bent over her, saw that the arrow had hit her in the meaty part of the arm, and quickly ripped it out.

"God!" Gisele grunted in pain, slapping a hand over the wound. But she knew they were in trouble, so she had to be brave. "I'm well, Fox. I can still ride. We must go!"

Fox ripped off the hem of her dress, which happened to be the same traveling dress she'd worn when he brought her to Canonsleigh those years ago. The sturdy fabric was about to do double duty as a wound dressing.

"I know you are well," he said steadily, wrapping the torn fabric around her arm as tightly as he could. "But we have no horse, and the enemy is approaching. Ren, can you take your mother to hide in the trees?"

Ren was absolutely petrified but not incoherent. "Aye," he said breathlessly. "Mam, get up! Come!"

Fox pulled her to her feet, making sure to put her right hand over the bandaged wound. Quickly, he kissed her. "I love you, my darling," he told her with as much calmness as he could muster. "Now, press hard on the wound and the bleeding will stop. Ren, get your mother to safety. *Go!*"

Ren didn't hesitate. He grabbed his mother by her bad arm and pulled, running with her into the trees to the west of the abbey. Fox didn't even have time to see them go before men were descending on him.

It was a brutal fight from that point forward.

One of the men wanted to follow Ren and Gisele, but that was the first man Fox cut down. Because it was dark, he couldn't see how many men were truly upon him, and as it ended up, there were only three. With one cut down, he disabled the second man before stabbing the third. Removing a dagger from his belt, he used it on the second man to cut his windpipe before using his sword to disembowel the third man as he tried to get to his feet.

The fight was over almost as quickly as it began. Then, and only then, did he turn to see where Gisele and Ren had gone, but it was impossible. The trees were dark and there wasn't any noise that he could hear, like people running through the brush. It was oddly silent. But he knew they were safe for the moment, so he raced back to the entry gates only to find a bloody battle going on.

The Blackchurch trainers were winning.

Fox wasn't even sure he was needed at all. He could see Tay—taller than any man around—slicing through a couple of opponents while Payne and Bowen, the mortal enemies, made short work of a pair of fools who tried to storm the entry doors. Creston and Cruz had at least four men between them, but Creston had one of them in a headlock while Cruz was simply snapping necks. There were no weapons involved with those two.

Only skill.

Off to his right, he could see Aamir making short work of his opponent while Ming Tang was using hands, feet, and a branch he'd found on the ground to disable a couple of men. There were probably more who had fallen victim to Ming Tang's flying feet because there were several men on the ground, none of them Blackchurch men.

And then Fox saw Sinclair.

He wasn't known as the Swordsman for nothing. He could fight with one sword or two, using the blades in tandem like some macabre dance, but in this case he was only using one sword and expertly defeating anyone who came in his direction. There couldn't have been more than five or six royal soldiers still on their feet at this point when the entry doors to the abbey abruptly flew open and about a dozen nuns poured out into the courtyard.

Chaos ensued.

The nuns had iron pots and clubs in their hands, and they were using them with eager furor. They banged on heads and clubbed men in the knees, and the remaining soldiers began dropping like stones. Fox heard snorting over to his right, and he turned to see Tay standing there, a little bloodied, laughing his head off at the antics of the nuns. Even the mother abbess was getting in on the carnage, and they watched her strike man after man on the skull with an iron pot, even if the man was already down, and then crossing herself afterward every time.

Hit, cross. Hit, cross.

Fox burst out laughing when he saw that.

The Blackchurch men backed off a little when they realized the nuns wanted their piece of flesh, even if the men were already down and beaten. In Fox's opinion, the women had earned it. They were the ones who had been under threat, the ones who would have suffered under the hands of the royal soldiers who were more than happy to violate the sanctity of an abbey. In fact, all of the Blackchurch trainers started to laugh at the nuns beating down the soldiers who had come to the wrong abbey. Payne was even yelling encouragement to them, telling them when a man was moving on the ground so they could knock him still. It was absolutely hilarious.

Until Fox began to hear the sounds of distant thunder.

Horses were coming down the road.

Tay heard it, too, and he began shouting at the Blackchurch

trainers to form a line at the gate. The horses were traveling too fast for them to shut the gates in time. Ming Tang tried to convince the nuns to go inside the abbey and shut the door, but they wouldn't. This was their home, and they intended to defend it. They, too, formed a line.

If anyone else wanted to get into their abbey, they would have to go through the nuns.

The horses were drawing closer, and by the sounds of them, it was a much bigger army than the one so recently defeated. But the Blackchurch trainers stood fast and without fear, bravely facing the army on the approach. The moon was shining on the road, in between the trees, so they could see movement. The torches that had been brought by the royal army were still burning all over the courtyard, and the mother abbess and a couple of other nuns picked up several, moving to stand with the Blackchurch trainers, lighting the night against the coming army.

And they waited.

Very quickly, the army came into full view, a line of heavily armed men and horses. Tay didn't see any royal tunics, which was a relief, but he seriously wondered if he was about to make his last stand.

But then he saw it.

The scarlet lion.

William Marshal!

In fact, William on his big gray horse was the first person Fox saw. He didn't know if he felt better or worse by that realization, but he took a few steps forward, torch in hand, and held up his sword.

"Stop!" he boomed. "Come no further. This place is under the protection of Blackchurch!"

The army came to a halt. The Marshal leaned forward in his saddle, trying to get a look at who was at the gate, when he suddenly flipped up his visor.

"Fox?" he said in disbelief. "Is that you?"

"It is, my lord."

"My God... *What* are you doing here?"

Fox gestured to the pile of bodies in the courtyard behind him. "Protecting Gisele."

That was enough to get the Marshal off his horse and heading in Fox's direction. "You *what*?" he gasped. "What is going on here?"

Fox didn't move. He wasn't going to go out to meet the man, and he wasn't getting out of the way. Tensed, he held his ground as the Marshal approached.

"John sent men to take Gisele to London," Fox said. "It seems that the king made a marriage contract between her and Raymond of Toulouse."

"I know," the Marshal said, still reeling with disbelief. "I know all about it. I was coming as quickly as I could to fend them off, but you... you were already here."

"I was, my lord."

"But how?"

"I serve at Blackchurch these days," Fox said. "Gisele knew this, and she sent me a request for help. I brought my Blackchurch brethren with me, and we made short work of John's men."

It was a succinct explanation. The Marshal moved around Fox, heading back into the courtyard, through the line of Blackchurch men and Canonsleigh nuns, to survey the damage. He was absolutely astonished. After looking over the mess, he turned back to Fox and the men and women surrounding him.

When he realized the women were nuns, he snorted in disbelief.

"I see you had help," he said, pointing to the bloody pots. "And thank God you did. I did not know if I would be in time."

Fox was trying to read the man. Was he angry that he had found him here? Or was he genuinely thankful? Fox had learned to be on his guard with the Marshal, but that didn't mean he couldn't be civil.

"They arrived two days ago," he said. "A man named Shillingford delivered the news to Gisele, who naturally refused. She—"

"Gisele?" the Marshal cut him off. "Where is she?"

"I am here."

They all turned to see Gisele standing at the edge of the gate, holding the bloodied rag to her arm. Ren stood next to her, his eyes wide at the destruction and death, but Gisele's gaze was riveted to the Marshal. For a moment, neither of them spoke. They simply gazed at each other until Gisele broke the spell.

"Do you remember me?" she asked. "You used to come to Selborne Castle when I was younger."

Something in the Marshal seemed to change. His yellowed gaze fixed on her, and he moved in her direction as if she and Ren were the only two people in the world. As if they didn't have an entire audience watching them, including Fox, who was coiled now that the Marshal was moving in Gisele's direction.

But the Marshal wasn't paying any attention.

He only had eyes for his daughter.

"I would have known you anywhere," he said quietly. "You look a great deal like your mother. You have her eyes."

Gisele thought she was being quite strong, but the softness in his voice unsteadied her. "I would have liked to have known her."

The Marshal smiled faintly. "I am certain she would have liked to have known you, too," he said. But his gaze inevitably drifted to her arm. "What happened?"

Gisele took her bloodied hand away from the bandage. "An arrow hit me," she said. "Fox wrapped my arm and sent me into the trees with Ren to hide, but we could see what was happening. We saw you arrive."

The Marshal looked around. "It seems that I was not needed," he said. "You have Blackchurch at your disposal. I cannot do better than that."

"Are you going to punish Fox now that he has had contact with me?"

The Marshal looked at her sharply, realizing that she was referring to his threat from years ago. That horrible, nasty threat that damaged his relationship with a knight he'd truly been fond of. Inhaling deeply, he hung his head for a moment, deliberating her question.

"Is this the only time you've seen him since you came to Canonsleigh?" he asked.

"Aye," she answered. "I've not seen him in ten years until today."

"Then I will not punish him."

Gisele studied the man who had given her life. He wasn't her father, but he'd given her life. Then something occurred to her—years ago, Fox wouldn't let her plead their case to the Marshal. The Marshal could very well send Fox away now and tell her she could never see him again, and a massive battle would be set up, perhaps one that would be truly damaging, but she wasn't going to let that happen. For once, she was going to take a stand against this man who seemed to control the entire world.

This was her time.

"William," she said, a boldly informal address. "I want you to meet your grandson."

She had her hand on Ren's shoulder, and when William realized what she was saying, his eyes widened. He wasn't one to show his astonishment, but in this case, she had caught him off guard. His jaw went slack as he looked at the boy with the small saw in his hand.

"I… I don't understand," William said. "You have a *son*?"

Gisele nodded. "I do," she said. "You see, his father and I loved each other deeply. We still do. We love each other so much that he will never marry unless he can marry me, but I have been committed to a convent by a man who has only seen me a handful of times in my life to fulfill a promise to a mother I've never met. Because of your decision, my son is a bastard. William Marshal's grandson is a bastard, just like his mother. Now, if you had just one ounce of feeling for my mother, if you've ever felt love in your life, then you know how painful this is for those of us whose lives you control. I have never asked you for anything in my life, but I am going to ask you for your permission to marry Fox. We are a family, William. We love one another. I have spent ten years in Canonsleigh. Don't you think you think that is long enough to fulfill your promise to my mother? She has been gone for many years. Surely you have fulfilled her wish by now."

William's jaw was tense, his brow furrowed. He was looking at the boy, who was gazing back at him with the innocence all children had. William had four sons, four grown men who had married well, but none of them had any children, and from his married daughters, all he had were granddaughters. Lots of them. But here before him was a treasured, precious grandson, something he wanted very badly.

Of course he didn't want the child to be a bastard, but he had been caught very much off guard by the situation. He wanted to rage, to deny Gisele her request, but gazing at that little boy... he couldn't seem to do it.

Would a little child actually change his mind about Fox and Gisele?

Was that what it would take?

"Lad," he said, crooking a finger at Ren. "Come here."

Ren didn't hesitate. He went over to the Marshal, gazing up at him. William could see him a little better now, seeing how much he looked like Fox. But, he thought, the child might look a little like him, too.

He could dream, anyway.

"What is your name?" he asked.

"Renard," the child said. "Renard Marshal de Salisbury, but Mam calls me Ren. Would you like to see my saw?"

William closed his eyes tightly, briefly, and with great emotion when he heard the child's full name. After that, it was a struggle to keep his composure.

"Aye," he said hoarsely. "Let me see your saw. What do you use it for?"

Ren peered behind the Marshal at the bodies in the courtyard. "Well," he said slowly, looking around. "I was going to use it on the soldiers. I was going to saw their legs off so they could not fight."

That had the Marshal bursting into soft laughter as he handed the saw back. "My God," he breathed. "You *are* a Marshal."

"He is a de Merest," Fox said, coming to stand beside Gisele.

"He has the finest blood in all of England in his veins. He will make us proud, my lord. But he deserves parents who are married."

William stared at the boy a moment. What could he say to that? "He does," he finally said. "But I am certain you were planning on marrying Gisele with or without my blessing. That is why you are here, isn't it?"

"I came because she was in trouble," Fox said. "But I did not know about the boy. Now that I do... Aye, I will be marrying her with or without your blessing. But I should like it to be with your approval. We were friends, once, you and me. You trusted me more than you trusted anyone else when you sent me to guard your daughter. I took very good care of her, my lord, but I also fell in love with her. How could I not? She is a Marshal. She is strong beyond measure, and I worship her. And the boy... He is every man's dream, my lord. Surely you understand that."

The Marshal was watching Ren as he fussed with his saw. There was much more he could say to all of this, but as he opened his mouth, Ren spoke.

"I want to be a soldier," he said, looking up at the Marshal. But he pointed to Fox. "Mam says he's a knight. Him... He said he's my father, but I've never had a father before. I live here, with women and no men. I need my father to teach me how to be a soldier. I don't want to be a farmer any longer."

The Marshal's eyebrows lifted. "You wanted to be a farmer?"

"To make things grow," Ren said. "But now I want to pro-tect people, like my father does. Like you do. Will you show me your sword?"

The Marshal's features grew soft at the request of a child.

Unsheathing his sword, he extended it hilt-first to the boy, who took it eagerly.

"This will be yours someday," he said quietly. "Be careful. Do not hurt yourself."

Ren was entranced with a sword that was nearly as tall as he was. As William watched the lad's face, he knew that he had been defeated. How could he deny a child who wanted to have a father? But it was more than that. He'd been denied happiness, once, too. When it came to Gisele, he was standing on old promises and useless dreams.

Perhaps it was time to right things once and for all.

"When I came here, it was with the intention of protecting Gisele from John, but I see that I was not needed," he said, sounding resigned. "Furthermore, I suspect if you do not marry her, John will simply find another husband for her, so your marriage will protect her. I cannot think of a better man to do it, Fox. You have my permission."

It felt as if Fox had waited to hear those words all of his life. He looked at Gisele, unable to keep the smile off his face. She looked at him in return, breaking into a wide grin, as Fox threw caution to the wind and pulled her into his arms, kissing her deeply. Meanwhile, Ren held up his saw to the Marshal again and asked him if he wanted to see him use the tool. As Fox and Gisele lost themselves in a kiss of epic proportions, they could hear the Marshal laugh as he told Ren that, most certainly, he would like to see that.

The Marshal ended up over at the old ash tree as the sun began to rise in the east, watching a little boy saw on some branches while his men moved in to help the Blackchurch trainers remove the bodies of John's army. The nuns lent a hand, and the bodies were moved back to the kitchen yard for a proper burial. Already, Payne and Kristian and Bowen were grabbing shovels and beginning to dig.

They'd done what they'd come to do.

Canonsleigh was saved.

As for Fox and Gisele, they were married that morning at a small church in Wellington by the same priest who came to Canonsleigh twice a week to say mass. Witnessed by the Blackchurch trainers and William Marshal, it was the moment they'd both been waiting for, the culmination of dreams that had finally come to fruition.

As Fox had told Gisele the day he'd left her at Canonsleigh, he would remain tender and true, only to her, forever.

It was a promise he'd kept.

And so had she.

EPILOGUE

Year of Our Lord 1218
Blackchurch Guild

"HE HAS ARRIVED, Fox."

The words came from Axton, who had just come from the southern gatehouse of Blackchurch. It was a bright day, with puffy cotton clouds scattered across the sky, as Fox heard those fateful words. Part of him was happy, but the larger part of him was quite sad.

Ren would be leaving them.

His son would be moving on to higher education.

"Does my wife know?" he asked.

Axton nodded. "I sent a soldier to your cottage to tell her," he said. "Ren is still over with Sin."

Fox nodded in resignation. "I will go to him," he said. "You can finish the class."

Axton stepped into Fox's shoes, as he was so eager to do, bellowing to the men who were working in pairs on a hand-to-hand defense exercise. That gave Fox the break he needed to head to the top of the rise, where Sinclair and his recruits were working on swordplay.

Ren was with them.

As Fox reached the top, he immediately saw Sinclair and his class, also working in pairs as they learned the finer art of broadsword battle. He strolled across the green grass, his focus on a particularly young recruit with dark hair, long limbs, and, already, a big voice. Sinclair saw him approach, smiling at Fox as he joined him.

"Do you see him?" he asked.

Fox nodded, watching Ren practice against a much older opponent. "He has a natural way about him, doesn't he?"

Sinclair nodded. "Very much so."

"I was knighted at seventeen years, you know."

"He is well on the same path, I would say."

Fox watched the lad, who had his mother's bright smile, laugh when he bested his opponent. There was so much of Gisele in that laugh. His dark hair was cut short in the back and on the sides, but the front of it flopped over his eyes. He kept having to toss his head to keep his hair out of his face, but he wouldn't cut it off no matter how Gisele and Fox begged, scolded, or tried to bribe him. Even at thirteen years of age, Ren knew what he wanted.

Fox was going to miss that youthful arrogance.

"The Marshal is here," he finally said.

Sinclair looked at him. "I thought he wasn't coming until next month?"

Fox grunted. "You know how he cannot stay away from Ren," he said. "He sees the future of the Marshal empire in him, as his only grandson. I've told him that Ren is the future of the de Merest empire, but he doesn't seem to think that matters."

Sinclair chuckled. "God help Ren with a grandfather like William Marshal," he said. "Still, he can do a lot for the lad and your other children. He is a good family relation to have."

"I suppose," Fox said, uninterested. "But he tries to bully me into letting him take the younger children back to Pembroke. As if I'm going to let a three-year-old and a toddler go with him. To learn what? How to go into battle at five years of age?"

"Fox!"

Both Fox and Sinclair turned to the shouting that was coming from the south to see Gisele approaching. A small, dark-haired boy was running toward Fox, while Gisele held a toddler in her arms. She was waving at Fox with her free arm, and he waved back just as William Marshal de Merest, who went by Marshal, reached his father and his Uncle Sin. Fox's children, as well as Tay's, had many uncles at Blackchurch, as all of the trainers were known as such. Marshal ran past his father and straight to Sinclair.

"I want a sword!" he demanded. "A sword! A sword, please!"

Marshal was a little over three years of age, but a very verbal and bright child. He also wanted to do everything his eldest brother did, which meant swordplay. Sinclair had been forbidden, by Gisele, to give the younger children actual swords, so he was forced to deny the boy.

"I have nothing for you, lad," he said. "I am sorry. You must ask your mother."

That wasn't good enough for Marshal, who spied Ren and darted onto the practice field. That had Fox and Sinclair bellowing at the men to stop practice, because a child was on the field, as Marshal ran straight to Ren, who saw his little brother coming. Taking his sword with him, Ren went to meet Marshal. Swinging the child up in his arms, he came off the practice field.

"Here, Papa," he said, handing his sword over to his father as his brother squirmed in his arms. "Come, Marshy. We will play!"

Marshal was torn between the lure of the swords and playing with his eldest brother, whom he dearly loved. Ren put the lad to his feet and encouraged him to follow several feet away from the training field, where the summer grass was warm and about ankle-high. Ren fell down to his knees and finally rolled in the grass as Marshal jumped on him gleefully.

That brought the baby.

Canon de Merest was, as some of the Blackchurch trainers termed him, a beast of a baby. He had been the largest baby born to Gisele and Fox so far, an enormous child that had taken nearly three days to be born during some of the most terrifying hours of Fox's life. Canon was big and solid at fourteen months of age, and he moved very well for just having learned to walk a couple of months prior. With his curly, dark blond hair and his father's blue eyes, he squealed when he saw his brothers rolling around and darted off to join them. As Gisele came to stand with her husband and Sinclair, the three of them watched the boys playing in the grass.

"William is here," Gisele told Fox.

"I know," Fox said.

"Does Ren know?" she asked.

Fox shook his head. "I have not told him, but I'm sure he has heard," he said. Then he sighed wistfully. "I am going to miss these days with Ren and the younger boys. They shall never come again now that Ren will be leaving us."

He heard sniffling and turned to see his wife in tears. Smiling sympathetically, he put his arm around her shoulders and kissed her temple, trying to give her some comfort.

"He is going to go on to do great things," he assured her softly. "He is going to train at Pembroke Castle and also at Lioncross Abbey Castle. Those are two of the biggest castles in England, and certainly among the most prestigious. They are going to teach him to be a great knight, Gigi. He will be in good hands."

Gisele knew that, but it didn't take away from the fact that she was going to lose her eldest son to his education. "But we've had so little time with him," she sniffed. "He is only thirteen."

"And he should have been gone years ago," Fox said. "Most boys start their training at nine or ten years of age. But we kept him with us longer than we should have. I kept him with me longer than I should have because I was making up for the time I did not spend with him when he was younger. It is my fault. But now, he must go."

Someone let out a squeal, and they looked over to see Ren being tackled by Canon, who threw his whole body into Ren's torso. Ren grunted as the wind was knocked out of him by a bull of a baby, and Marshal, taking advantage, wrapped his arms around Ren's neck. They all went down in the grass. Standing next to Gisele and Fox, Sinclair chuckled.

"Canon is going to be a force to be reckoned with," he said. "I am terrified of him already. He is utterly fearless."

Gisele smiled, still wiping her tears. "He has grown up around men who encourage such things," she said. Then she caught movement over Sinclair's shoulder and noted that her dear friend, Athdara, was bringing her children up the rise. Milo, Brendon, and Anton Munro came bolting up the hill, heading for their good and close friends Ren, Marshal, and Canon. When the Munro lads came into contact with the de Merest boys, it was joyful chaos.

And that was what it became now.

It was Ren against the five little boys who were all trying to dogpile on him. Gisele smiled at Athdara as the woman came to stand next to them, watching her children pummel Ren.

It was glorious.

"We heard that the Marshal has come to take Ren," Athdara said. "I've had the kitchen servants set up some tables in the village so we can feast together and give Ren a wonderful send-off. It will be something for him to remember fondly in the years to come."

Gisele was trying very hard to be brave, but that comment had her dissolving in tears as Athdara and Fox tried to comfort her.

"I cannot believe my Ren is going away to become a knight," she said, sniffling. "It does not seem possible that he is old enough."

"He will make a fine knight," Athdara said. "Nicolai says so."

Gisele wiped at her eyes, looking at Athdara with a smile on her lips. "He says that he wishes to go with your brother when he returns to Toxandria to regain his dukedom," she said. "I am so thankful for Nicolai. He welcomed Ren those years ago when I married Fox and we came to live at Blackchurch. I do not know what Ren would have done without another boy his age to be his friend. He loves Nicolai dearly."

Athdara's smile faded. "The feeling is mutual," she said. "Truthfully, that is why Nicolai is not here. He knows the Marshal has come to take Ren, and he is heartbroken. He will miss his friend."

"The Marshal offered to take Nicolai with him, too."

Athdara's smile returned, though sadly. "Nicolai has a different path than Ren," she said. "He is training here, with Tay and Fox and the others, to learn enough to fight for what was taken from him. To regain what my uncle stole from him when he killed my father. But I know that Ren and Nicolai will always be close friends. When Ren is finished with his training, mayhap he will, indeed, join Nicolai in his quest to regain his dukedom."

Gisele smiled in return, hoping that her son and Athdara's younger brother did indeed remain faithful friends. Nicolai was a young man with the weight of a dukedom on his shoulders, one that had been stolen from him, as Athdara had described. Nicolai's one wish was to return to Toxandria and regain what was rightfully his, someday.

But that was a story for another time.

The sounds of horses caught the attention of the adults, and they turned to see William Marshal making his way up the road that divided some of the training grounds. He had Tay with him, on foot, as well as a few of the other trainers who had grown close to Ren during his stay at Blackchurch. They all knew that the Marshal would be coming for Ren when he grew older, taking him back to Pembroke to train him as a knight. It was a prestigious destiny for the son of Fox and the grandson of William Marshal, but they'd all grown fond of the lad. He was eager and hardworking and talented.

They wanted to give him a fine farewell.

"Greetings!" Gisele said, moving away from Fox and Athdara, waving at the Marshal as he came to a halt. "It is a fine day for travel."

The Marshal dismounted his big gray horse, moving stiffly because he was an old man and extensive travel, for him, was becoming increasingly difficult. In fact, his health in general had been in a steady decline, but like most men, he refused to acknowledge it. He lifted his hand in greeting to Gisele.

"It is," he said. "How are my grandsons?"

Gisele grinned. "You might ask how their mother is first," she said. Then she laid her hand on her slightly rounded tummy. "We are doing well. I suspect this is another grandson, so you may as well include him in your question."

The Marshal smiled with delight. "Undoubtedly," he said. "You have given me three of the brightest, worthiest lads I could imagine. I am grateful."

Gisele chuckled as she stood on tiptoe and greeted the man with a kiss to the cheek. Over the past few years, they'd become fond of one another, and although she still didn't call him "Father," they shared a pleasant and familial relationship. William had even begun to acknowledge that she was his daughter publicly, because he had to in order to acknowledge Ren as his grandson. Truthfully, the marriage of Henry and Margaret had been so fraught with drama, because of a young king who didn't want to be married, that no one really gave a second thought to Gisele being William Marshal's bastard from Henry's queen.

To them, she was simply his daughter.

And he was proud of it.

But his acknowledgement of Gisele also had another effect—any enemies of Henry the Young King, or any jealous Plantagenet queens seeking to seek favor with their husbands, no longer had a reason to harass her. Given that she lived at Blackchurch, they had a snowflake's chance in hell of getting inside in any case, which gave both Gisele and Fox a great deal of comfort. She was safe from that kind of madness, forever.

The public knowledge that she was William Marshal's

daughter had its advantages.

"You are welcome for your grandsons," Gisele said. "But you should know that Val and Vesper were here to visit about three months ago. They claim them, too."

The Marshal frowned. "I will fight that man if he says so," he said, pointing a finger at her. "Make sure he knows that."

Gisele had to laugh at a man so protective over his grand-children. "He said the same thing about you," she said. "I will stay out of it. But I do want you to know that I am quite upset."

"Why?"

"Because you are here to take my eldest away."

The Marshal lifted an eyebrow, catching sight of Fox behind his wife. He could see the smirk on Fox's face because they'd both had to deal with Gisele's reluctance to let go of her son. In this case, he and Fox were definitely on the same side, so he took the gentle approach with the pregnant mother. All jesting aside with the claim of Val de Nerra and his grandsons, his mood sobered.

"It is time, Gisele," William said softly. "He is talented, but my men and I are going to teach him to be the greatest knight in England. That is what men call me, you know—England's greatest knight. What a legacy Ren will have to carry on. This is a good thing for him, I promise."

Gisele sighed heavily. "I know," she said. "But I am allowed to be sad. I will miss him."

There wasn't much more the Marshal could say to that. He'd developed a bit of a soft spot over the years where Gisele and his grandsons were concerned, so he showed her a little more sympathy than most.

Besides... she'd given him grandsons.

In a rare gesture, he put his arm around her shoulders and

began to walk with her back toward the village. As he moved, he whistled between his teeth, motioning to his grandsons when they looked up from their roughhousing. Tay's boys took hold of Marshal and Canon and began to follow, because they knew the Marshal, the grandfather of their friends, had been known to give out coins on occasion, and no one wanted to miss out on that. Athdara followed, but Tay remained behind with Fox, Sinclair, Payne, Creston, and Cruz. They were all waiting for Ren, who was picking himself up out of the grass after being smashed into it by eager little boys.

He joined his father and the others, picking grass out of his hair.

"Come along," Fox said, helping Ren by picking out a blade of grass or two. "We must gather your things so you can say farewell to your mother."

Ren brushed his arms and chest of grass. "Isn't William staying the night?" he asked.

He called his grandfather William because his mother did, and the Marshal had never corrected him. Fox shook his head to the question.

"Probably," he said. "But I believe he wants to get back as quickly as possible. I suspect he took one of his ships across the channel and anchored in Minehead again. He's a busy man, Ren. You are going to find out just how busy, but these will be glorious days for you, I promise."

Ren knew that. He was quite tall these days, much taller than his mother and nearly as tall as his father, but he hadn't filled out. He still had the skinny, rather gangly body that would soon shape up with the rigorous training the Marshal was going to put him through.

"I still do not understand why I cannot stay here and train

with you and the uncles," he said as they began to head over to the road. "You can train me to be a knight as well as anything William can do."

"The Marshal can do for you what we cannot," Fox said, answering for the group. "He will introduce you into the heart of the English nobility. You will learn the people and the politics. You will make friends and alliances that you could not possibly make here. As the grandson of William Marshal, you will take your place of prestige beside him."

Ren knew that. He'd been told that, but much like his mother, he was already missing his family and friends. He didn't want to be separated from them.

But it was time.

"I can come home if I want to, can't I?" he asked.

Fox nodded. "After you have finished your training, I am certain St. Denis would be most agreeable for you to return."

"He has been a good teacher," Ren said. "He has taught me mathematics and reading and writing. I have learned a great deal from him."

"He's a better teacher than the nuns at Canonsleigh?"

"*Much* better."

Since the birth of Tay and Fox's children, St. Denis had taken to tutoring the young boys, something he quite enjoyed, leaving the management of Blackchurch to St. Sebastian for the most part. It was a transitional time for father and son, much as it was a transitional time for Blackchurch in general. Trainers were marrying, children were born, and the Blackchurch legacy was growing.

Times were changing, indeed.

"I know he has enjoyed it," Fox said. "In fact, we've all enjoyed training you as much as we were able without running you into the ground like we do the other recruits. We hoped to give you a foundation to begin your formal training with the Marshal."

"Ye've got a good mind, lad," Payne said, strolling slightly behind him. "I've seen ye size up situations faster than yer father can, so keep tae it. Ye'll do well."

Ren glanced at the fiery Scot. "You've been a good teacher, Payne," he said. "I will miss you."

"Shut yer lips or ye'll have me blubbering like my mother."

"The same mother who can best men in a fight?"

"I'll have tae introduce ye to her someday."

"I would like that."

Ren and the others chuckled. Payne's mother was legendary at Blackchurch, although none of them had ever met her. The group came to a bend in the road that would take them into the village where there were tables set up in the village center. People milled around, preparing for the coming feast. The smell of roasting meat and bread was heavy in the air, and as the trainers continued on to the village, Fox pulled his son to a halt so they could have a moment alone.

There was something he wanted to give him.

"I do not think we'll have another opportunity to be alone," Fox said, his gaze drifting over his handsome son, on the cusp of becoming a man. "I hope I have been a good father to you, Ren. I know we have only spent the past four years together, but I hope I've done well for you. I've tried."

Ren smiled. "I love you, Papa," he said. "I cannot remember when you haven't been with me."

"Unfortunately, there were those years when you were at the nunnery."

"I don't even remember that. All I remember is you."

That touched Fox's heart deeply. "Thank you," he whispered, putting his hand on his son's cheek. "Because you have made my life complete. You and your mother and your brothers. I was only half a man before you came to me. Now, I am whole. And there is no father alive who has been prouder of his son than I am of you. Always remember that."

Ren was both touched and embarrassed. "Thank you, Papa," he said. "I promise to remember everything you've taught me. I hope I continue to make you proud."

"You will," Fox said. Then he dug into a pocket in his tunic, pulling forth a small pouch. Opening it, he lifted Ren's hand and shook out the contents. "In fact, I want you to have this. It is a family heirloom I want you to take with you."

The dragon head brooch appeared. Ren scrutinized it for a moment, tipping it so he could read the inscription on the top.

"*Tenera et vera*," he said.

Fox nodded. "That means tender and true," he said. "As you know, my father was the Earl of Keddington, and my mother's father was the Earl of Morton. Scots. You have proud blood in your veins, lad. This brooch is the family motto for the Earls of Morton, and my grandfather gave this to my mother on her wedding day. I gave it to your mother, but she wants you to have it. Rightfully, it belongs to you. It is the most important thing we own, and it is a mark of greatness. It will bring you luck as you continue your training. As long as you remember the motto—tender and true—and use that as your guide, you will always do good things. You will become the knight you were born to be."

Tender and true.

Ren studied the brooch a moment longer before looking to his father, a smile of hope on his face. Hope for the future, hope for everything he wanted it to be.

Hope that his parents had for him.

"Thank you, Papa," he said, throwing his arms around the man and embracing him. "I will remember."

With that, he released Fox and ran off toward the village, seeing his friend Nicolai and shouting to him, excited to show him what his father had given him. Gisele was there, as were his younger brothers, and they swarmed around him, admiring the brooch, soaking up the last moments with him before he went away.

Fox stood there a moment, watching the activity, reflecting back on the life he'd had. There had been so much good along with the bad, but there was nothing in his life that he regretted.

Not one bloody thing.

For the man known as the Protector, he had the best life he could imagine in the wilds of Devon, with the only woman he had ever loved and a family he adored. As he'd told Ren—*use the motto as your guide and you will do great things.* Fox had followed his own advice, long ago.

Tender and true.

They were words to live by.

He and Gisele would, forever.

❧ THE END ☙

Children of Fox and Gisele:
Renard "Ren"
Marshal
Canon
Wells
Reece
Lenora
Daniella
Madelaina
And a dozen cats

KATHRYN LE VEQUE NOVELS

Medieval Romance:

De Wolfe Pack Series:
Warwolfe
The Wolfe
Nighthawk
ShadowWolfe
DarkWolfe
A Joyous de Wolfe Christmas
BlackWolfe
Serpent
A Wolfe Among Dragons
Scorpion
StormWolfe
Dark Destroyer
The Lion of the North
Walls of Babylon
The Best Is Yet To Be
BattleWolfe
Castle of Bones

De Wolfe Pack Generations:
WolfeHeart
WolfeStrike
WolfeSword
WolfeBlade
WolfeLord
WolfeShield
Nevermore
WolfeAx
WolfeBorn

The Executioner Knights:

By the Unholy Hand
The Mountain Dark
Starless
A Time of End
Winter of Solace
Lord of the Sky
The Splendid Hour
The Whispering Night
Netherworld
Lord of the Shadows
Of Mortal Fury
'Twas the Executioner Knight
Before Christmas
Crimson Shield

The de Russe Legacy:
The Falls of Erith
Lord of War: Black Angel
The Iron Knight
Beast
The Dark One: Dark Knight
The White Lord of Wellesbourne
Dark Moon
Dark Steel
A de Russe Christmas Miracle
Dark Warrior

The de Lohr Dynasty:
While Angels Slept
Rise of the Defender
Steelheart
Shadowmoor
Silversword
Spectre of the Sword

The Gorgon

The House of De Nerra:
The Promise
The Falls of Erith
Vestiges of Valor
Realm of Angels

Highland Warriors of Munro:
The Red Lion
Deep Into Darkness

The House of de Garr:
Lord of Light
Realm of Angels

Saxon Lords of Hage:
The Crusader
Kingdom Come

High Warriors of Rohan:
High Warrior
High King

The House of Ashbourne:
Upon a Midnight Dream

The House of D'Aurilliac:
Valiant Chaos

The House of De Dere:
Of Love and Legend

St. John and de Gare Clans:
The Warrior Poet

The House of de Bretagne:
The Questing

The House of Summerlin:
The Legend

The Kingdom of Hendocia:
Kingdom by the Sea

The BlackChurch Guild: Shadow Knights:
The Leviathan
The Protector

Regency Historical Romance:
Sin Like Flynn: A Regency
Historical Romance Duet
The Sin Commandments
Georgina and the Red Charger

Gothic Regency Romance:
Emma

Contemporary Romance:

Kathlyn Trent/Marcus Burton Series:
Valley of the Shadow
The Eden Factor
Canyon of the Sphinx

The American Heroes Anthology Series:
The Lucius Robe
Fires of Autumn
Evenshade
Sea of Dreams
Purgatory

Other non-connected Contemporary Romance:
Lady of Heaven
Darkling, I Listen
In the Dreaming Hour
River's End
The Fountain

Sons of Poseidon:
The Immortal Sea

Pirates of Britannia Series (with Eliza Knight):

Savage of the Sea by Eliza Knight
Leader of Titans by Kathryn Le Veque
The Sea Devil by Eliza Knight
Sea Wolfe by Kathryn Le Veque

Note: All Kathryn's novels are designed to be read as stand-alones, although many have cross-over characters or cross-over family groups. Novels that are grouped together have related characters or family groups. You will notice that some series have the same books; that is because they are cross-overs. A hero in one book may be the secondary character in another.

There is NO reading order except by chronology, but even in that case, you can still read the books as stand-alones. No novel is connected to another by a cliff hanger, and every book has an HEA.

Series are clearly marked. All series contain the same characters or family groups except the American Heroes Series, which is an anthology with unrelated characters.

For more information, find it in **A Reader's Guide to the Medieval World of Le Veque**.

ABOUT KATHRYN LE VEQUE

Bringing the Medieval to Romance

KATHRYN LE VEQUE is a critically acclaimed, multiple USA TODAY Bestselling author, an Indie Reader bestseller, a charter Amazon All-Star author, and a #1 bestselling, award-winning, multi-published author in Medieval Historical Romance with over 100 published novels.

Kathryn is a multiple award nominee and winner, including the winner of Uncaged Book Reviews Magazine 2017 and 2018 "Raven Award" for Favorite Medieval Romance. Kathryn is also a multiple RONE nominee (InD'Tale Magazine), holding a record for the number of nominations. In 2018, her novel WARWOLFE was the winner in the Romance category of the Book Excellence Award and in 2019, her novel A WOLFE AMONG DRAGONS won the prestigious RONE award for best pre-16th century romance.

Kathryn is considered one of the top Indie authors in the world with over 2M copies in circulation, and her novels have been translated into several languages. Kathryn recently signed with Sourcebooks Casablanca for a Medieval Fight Club series, first published in 2020.

In addition to her own published works, Kathryn is also the President/CEO of Dragonblade Publishing, a boutique publishing house specializing in Historical Romance. Dragonblade's success has seen it rise in the ranks to become Amazon's #1 e-book publisher of Historical Romance (K-Lytics report July 2020).

Kathryn loves to hear from her readers. Please find Kathryn on Facebook at Kathryn Le Veque, Author, or join her on Twitter @kathrynleveque. Sign up for Kathryn's blog at www.kathrynleveque.com for the latest news and sales.